DATE DUE

WORKING
GOD'S MISCHIEF

Tor Books by Glen Cook

THE INSTRUMENTALITIES OF THE NIGHT

The Tyranny of the Night
Lord of the Silent Kingdom
Surrender to the Will of the Night
Working God's Mischief

An Ill Fate Marshalling
Reap the East Wind
The Swordbearer
The Tower of Fear

THE BLACK COMPANY

The Black Company (The First Chronicle)

Shadows Linger (The Second Chronicle)

The White Rose (The Third Chronicle)

Shadow Games (The First Book of the South)

Dreams of Steel (The Second Book of the South)

Chronicles of the Black Company
(comprising *The Black Company, Shadows Linger,* and *The White Rose*)

The Books of the South
(comprising *Shadow Games, Dreams of Steel,* and *The Silver Spike*)

Return of the Black Company
(comprising *Bleak Seasons* and *She Is the Darkness*)

The Silver Spike

Bleak Seasons (Book One of Glittering Stone)

She Is the Darkness (Book Two of Glittering Stone)

Water Sleeps (Book Three of Glittering Stone)

Soldiers Live (Book Four of Glittering Stone)

WORKING
GOD'S MISCHIEF

BOOK FOUR
OF THE INSTRUMENTALITIES OF THE NIGHT

GLEN COOK

TOR®

A Tom Doherty Associates Book
New York

WORKING GOD'S MISCHIEF

Copyright © 2014 by Glen Cook

A Tor Book
Published by Tom Doherty Associates, LLC
175 Fifth Avenue
New York, NY 10010

www.tor-forge.com

Tor® is a registered trademark of Tom Doherty Associates, LLC.

Library of Congress Cataloging-in-Publication Data

Cook, Glen.
   Working God's mischief / Glen Cook.—First Edition.
       p. cm.—(Instrumentalities of the night ; 4)
   "A Tom Doherty Associates book."
   ISBN 978-0-7653-3420-6 (hardcover)
   ISBN 978-1-4668-0907-9 (e-book)
   1. Imaginary wars and battles—Fiction.   2. Brothers and sisters—Fiction.   3. Good and evil—
Fiction.   4. Fantasy fiction, American.   I. Title.
   PS3553.O5536I57 2014
   813'.54—dc23

                                                                         2013028356

Tor books may be purchased for educational, business, or promotional use. For information on bulk purchases, please contact Macmillan Corporate and Premium Sales Department at 1-800-221-7945, extension 5442, or write specialmarkets@macmillan.com.

First Edition: March 2014

Printed in the United States of America

0 9 8 7 6 5 4 3 2 1

For the granddaughter clowder:
Elie Belle, Katie Cat,
Hannah Beans, Josie,
and lonesome Josh, "the Boy"

Working God's Mischief

Arnhand, Castauriga, and Navaya lost their kings. The Grail Empire lost its empress. The Church lost its Patriarch, though he lives on as a fugitive. The Night lost Kharoulke the Windwalker, an emperor amongst the most primal and terrible gods. The Night goes on, in dread. The world goes on, in dread. The ice builds and slides southward.

New kings come. A new empress will rule. Another rump polishes the Patriarchal Throne.

There is no new Windwalker, nor ever will be.

The shock reverberates across the world and the Night. The oldest and fiercest of Instrumentalities has been destroyed—by a mortal!

The world, battered by savage change, limps toward its destiny. And the ice is coming.

1. Antieux: The Stress of Peace

Brother Candle settled at the breakfast table, still sleep-groggy. "Look at him being smug. All fruit and berries, there."

A dozen people shared the table, Count Raymone Garete's intimates. His spouse, the Countess Socia, had made the disparaging remark.

Count Raymone's cousin Bernardin said, "Don't mind her, Master. She's looking for a fight again. Or still. Calm down, girl. Peace has broken out. Enjoy it."

Brother Candle nodded. He agreed.

Socia knew it could not last.

The world would pull itself together and get back to the horrors soon.

Following a bite of melon, the old man observed, "The world has rolled over complete when Bernardin Amberchelle is the voice of reason." To the Countess, so like a daughter after all they had suffered, he said, "Control your emotions. For the sake of the child."

Socia was gravid in the extreme. That exacerbated her naturally abrasive character. The baby was overdue. It would be her first. She was plagued by all the first-time terrors. She refused to follow the custom of her station and go into seclusion.

Socia Garete was no ornament to her husband. She was a working partner, even a managing partner. She did not want to miss anything.

The Count, the Maysalean Perfect Brother Candle, and everyone else for whom she cared, and who cared for her, had abandoned hope of getting her to behave as a proper noblewoman.

Hell, she spent half her time with an equally injudicious commoner refugee heretic from Khaurene, Kedle Richeut. She idolized Kedle. Kedle Richeut had made a difference. Kedle had killed a king.

Brother Candle had known Socia since she was a bloody-minded teen living with three brothers in a small stronghold on the Connec's northeast frontier. Never had she shown the least inclination to be a good girl, focused on embroidery and producing children.

As always, Count Raymone showed only amused indulgence. He loved Socia with the passion and depth sung by the Connec's jongleurs, unusual in a time of negotiated marriages. But Raymone Garete had come into his patrimony young. Those who would have strapped him into a loveless political alliance had passed on before he could be fitted to harness.

Count Raymone had chosen Socia on brief exposure because he had recognized her instantly as a soul perfectly complementary to himself.

Count Raymone said, "At this point, my love, you should listen attentively when the Master speaks."

Startled, Socia shut her mouth.

Raymone continued, "I understand. I have my own problems adjusting to an absence of enemies. The fact is, we aren't likely to have any till Anselin gets home or Serenity makes a startling comeback."

Bernardin said, "Anselin shouldn't be a problem. He won't let his mother bully him. I'll bet a shilling now that he stuffs her into a convent."

Socia made snarling noises to remind everyone that she was in a foul humor. Still.

Raymone ignored her. "I can't even fritter time chasing Society brothers. The survivors are hidden so deep they've forgotten which way to swim to find the light."

Brother Candle grumbled, "If they cared about the Light they wouldn't be in the Society for the Suppression of Sacrilege and Heresy in the first place."

Bernardin chuckled through a mouthful of salt pork. He professed the Maysalean creed but refused to observe its dietary whims. "Been a few weeks since I've nabbed one. But the rest aren't buried as deep as they hope. The new bishop isn't as clever as he thinks."

"LaVelle?" Brother Candle asked.

"The very one. The latest. Dumber than a keg of rocks but the first honest one since way back before Serifs. I'm going to make sure he survives."

For a decade Episcopal Chaldarean bishops had shown a remarkable inability to stay healthy in a bishopric the Church was determined to scourge and flense for tolerating heresy.

"Honest?" Brother Candle asked.

Bernardin offered a wobbling hand gesture. "Comparatively. He did bring along a clutch of deadbeat relatives. But he's no holy bandit like Meryl Ponté or Mathe Richenau."

Count Raymone interjected, "Darling, when was your last visit to Mistress Alecsinac?" Alecsinac was her senior attendant midwife.

Clever, in Brother Candle's thinking. Stopping Bernardin from admitting he had an agent close to the new bishop, in case LaVelle or the Society had an agent close to the Count.

There was a point to Raymone's question beyond that.

Socia did not deliver a definitive response.

"I thought so. Master. Once you finish, see my lady Socia to the midwife. Making no side trips and accepting no delays or excuses."

"As you will." Brother Candle allowed himself a satisfied smile.

Count Raymone seldom invoked a husband's prerogative. When he did, he meant it. There was no appeal.

Brother Candle asked, "Does LaVelle have any support from Brothe?"

Amberchelle replied, "We're trying to figure that out. Serenity appointed him, but only two days before they ran him off. Serenity didn't know him. He was put up by one of Anne of Menand's tame Principatés, Gorman Sleight. Sleight doesn't know LaVelle, either. He nominated LaVelle on behalf of Valmur Joss, one of the Society chiefs in exile in Salpeno. Joss is Connecten. But even he doesn't actually know LaVelle, whose name originally got dropped into the process by a cousin, Laci Lindop, another Connecten Society exile. LaVelle has no prior Church connection, except as a worshipper. So nobody knows what we're getting."

The Perfect stared. Bernardin Amberchelle was a short, wide, dusky, rumpled man who looked like a dimwit thug. And he played that role on Raymone's behalf. In private, though, he betrayed surprising depth.

Amberchelle winked.

Refusing to be left out, Socia asked, "Do we know where Serenity went when he ran away from the Captain-General?"

"That would be the Commander of the Righteous, dear one. Piper Hecht. He used to be Captain-General, before Serenity. Pinkus Ghort is Captain-General now. Serenity's man, bought and paid for."

"Not so much anymore," Bernardin said. "Ghort gets on fine with the man Hecht installed in Serenity's place."

"But where is Serenity?" Socia demanded. "And how big a pain is he likely to be?"

"Right now he's on Little Pinoché in the Pinoché Islands, off the Firaldian coast two-thirds of the way up between the mouth of the Teragi and the mouth of the Sawn. He'd be a major pain if he could but he can't communicate very well. Sonsa and Platadura are blockading him. Queen Isabeth intends to keep him fixed till she makes him pay for what happened to Peter."

He meant Isabeth of Khaurene, sister of Duke Tormond IV, wife and queen of Peter of Navaya. After an outstanding career taming the enemies of the Church, Peter had fallen defending his wife's home city from Arnhanders who had invaded with the blessing of the Church.

Serenity had an obsessive hatred of the Connec. He had suffered terribly when he was Patriarchal legate in Antieux. Before becoming Patriarch he had participated in several campaigns against Antieux.

"He'll find ways to communicate," Socia muttered. "There'll be a reason he fled to those islands."

"Yeah." Bernardin laughed. "There is. That's where the storm put him down." He explained. Serenity's convoy, hugging the coast, had been caught in a squall and driven off shore. Serenity's vessel had gone aground on rocks off Little Pinoché. The deposed Patriarch was among the few survivors. "He was headed for Arnhand. Anne of Menand would have taken him in." But ships from Navaya's allies had set a blockade almost before Serenity had gotten himself dried out.

Brother Candle pushed back from the table. "I've begun to suffer an intellectual malaise. I've become too comfortable here."

Bernardin observed, "Here he goes, fishing for compliments."

Socia snapped, "Bernardin, you're too cynical. He's a Perfect. They're never happy unless they're barefoot in the snow, starving, and being hunted by people who want to burn them."

"This one squeals like a pig whenever we ask him to do something where he might get his tootsies wet."

Pressed, Brother Candle would have admitted as much. But he was sixty-eight years old. That slowed a man. It left him inclined to ease the strain on his bones. "I'll be back on the road soon enough to beat the first snow." Snow arrived earlier every winter.

All conversation died. All eyes turned to the Perfect.

"What?"

"Why on earth would you . . . ?"

"At your age?"

"My age? My age wasn't a factor when somebody wanted me hustling messages and tokens back and forth between Antieux and Khaurene."

Socia said, "It's a factor because you mean so much to us. We don't want you to leave."

The Count agreed. "That's as plain as it can be said, Master."

Socia added, "You keep up this nonsense, I'll get Kedle to break your leg."

"That seems harsh."

"Tough love, old man. Tough love."

"I'll keep that in mind. It is an intimidating journey and these old bones do have too many miles on them already. Meantime, though, I have to deliver you to the mercies of Mistress Alecsinac."

"I was hoping you'd forget."

"Get going, Socia," Raymone snapped.

"An' it please Your Lordship." Socia rose, offered a mock bow. It was none too deep. Her stomach got in the way. Leaving the room a step behind the Perfect, she said, "Mistress Alecsinac may know how to convince this beast that it's time to leave."

2. Realm of the Gods: Great Sky Fortress

A small world. Just a harbor town with a mountain behind. Suddenly, sharp as a hammer strike, all color vanished.

The small world went on, but in tones of gray.

"The Aelen Kofer are gone. The Realm is closed."

Nothing and no one could escape.

The spike of a mountain reared into ill-defined clouds of a darker gray. A determined eye might discern a ghost of a rainbow outside the structure that crowned the mountain, the Great Sky Fortress of the Old Ones, the gods who once ruled the northern middle world.

Light leaked from one trio of windows high on the face of the fortress. The Aelen Kofer, the wondrous dwarves who had created the Great Sky Fortress and its rainbow bridge, had abandoned the Realm of the Gods to folk from the middle world, the world of men.

THE ROOM BEHIND THOSE WINDOWS WAS LARGE BUT CROWDED BY nine people, including sorcerers, soldiers, women, children, and two men deeply tainted by the Night. Of artifacts most notable were four falcons loaded with shot capable of slaying the very gods and four huge bottles dwarf-blown from silver alloyed glass, teardrop shaped, with stems that narrowed to the diameter of a finger after a right-angle turn into the wall opposite the windows. Tables groaned under an abundance of materials and instruments both mundane and magical.

The sorcerers and Night-touched were up amongst the silver glass alembics, preparing. The others waited at the falcons with smoldering slow matches in hand. The woman in the forward group turned. "Everyone ready? Vali? Lila?" Those two girls stood behind the falcons farthest left and right. They nodded nervously. "Piper? Anna?" The man and woman at the center pair of falcons nodded. "Pella? Set to jump in where you're needed?" The surly boy behind everyone else also nodded.

"All right, then. Let's conjure some gods."

She was Heris, elder sister of the soldier, Piper Hecht, playing the role of sorceress here though she had no talent in that area. The men forward with her were Cloven Februaren, Ferris Renfrow, called the Bastard, and Asgrimmur Grimmsson. Februaren might be the great sorcerer of the age. Renfrow was the get of a human hero and minor goddess. Grimmsson carried shards of the souls of that goddess and her divine father within him.

Heris turned slowly, considering the hundred lanterns and scores of mirrors that would make certain there were no shadows in which a supernatural entity could hide.

"Well?" the Bastard demanded, though in a whisper, as he scratched at a bandage on his left wrist.

The woman raised a beaker containing an ounce of his blood. Only the blood of a descendent of the Old Ones had the power to complete the ritual of opening. It had taken a year to gather everything else.

Heris emptied the beaker into a tulip-shaped piece of glass on the end of a long glass stem. The blood was still warm.

A scarlet bar an eighth of an inch in diameter descended the hollow stem.

Tension mounted.

Heris blurted, "Shit! I think I overlooked . . ."

The chamber shuddered. Glass rattled. Sputtering slow matches moved nearer the touch holes of falcons.

One of the silver glass alembics rattled. Both the Bastard and the ascendant, Grimmsson, talked to the wall, neither in a modern language. The Bastard spoke a tongue he had used as a boy, centuries ago. The ascendant spoke both Andorayan of centuries past and a language garnered from the fragmentary souls inside him. Both men counseled patience and caution. Anything less would be rewarded with instant oblivion at the hands of mortals who had discovered the art of killing gods.

The Night knew the soldier, Piper Hecht, as the Godslayer. He had found the means. His sister Heris had ruthlessly extinguished Kharoulke the Windwalker, the most wicked of the deities who first plagued the middle world.

The mission here was to release gods of the generation that had overthrown Kharoulke and his kin. Gods who had been tricked into imprisonment by the ascendant.

Some doubted the need for a release effort. Kharoulke was no longer a threat to make himself supreme god of a world buried under ice. Heris had ended that threat with help from the Aelen Kofer.

Heris wanted divine allies. One evil had fallen but Kharoulke had kin who were growing stronger, too.

The Bastard and the ascendant talked fast and loud. The Old Ones had to understand that there had been changes. If they behaved with customary divine arrogance they would be exterminated before they could collect their wits.

Piper Hecht said, "Stay calm, ladies," from behind his falcon, to his companion, Anna Mozilla, and their adopted daughters. "The jars will hold them long enough for them to grasp their situation."

Heris said, "As long as we don't get a really nasty one first." The rattling alembic filled with sudden smoke.

"Well, shit!" Renfrow swore.

The ascendant rumbled, "You had to say it, woman! That's Red Hammer."

"Of course," Hecht muttered. The ever-impulsive and never-bright god of thunder always handled a situation by smashing things.

The ascendant roared in the tongue of the gods, face inches from the rattling big bottle—avoiding getting into lines of fire.

The other alembics filled, less quickly.

The emotions of the escaping gods were potent. Hecht felt them clearly. They were not pleased.

A second Instrumentality now shared the alembic first filled by Red Hammer. Ghost faces glared through the silver glass. Hecht did not recall the god's name but did sense his role in the pantheon of the Old Ones.

He was War. The thinker. The most dangerous in the long run.

That Instrumentality had a fierce hold on Red Hammer. War saw that the mortals were confident. War recognized the scent of god killers.

Other Instrumentalities bled into other silver glass vessels, most afraid to be hopeful. After an initial burst, they became calm and calculating. But they had been sealed into an inescapable pocket universe, with their dislikes for one another, for subjective ages.

They ought to be raving mad.

Heris said something to the Bastard. Renfrow eased over to the bottle farthest left. Meanwhile, the ascendant murmured what sounded like a roll call.

Each bottle contained multiple Instrumentalities. The pantheon of the Old Ones included numerous lesser deities, some of whom had been swept into Asgrimmur's trap in his time of madness, following his unexpected ascension.

Heris said, "We're short one. Where is the Trickster?"

Renfrow said, "He won't come out. He thinks he'll be blamed for everything."

"That would be the history, wouldn't it?" Whenever anything went wrong for this clutch of Instrumentalities, the Trickster was at the disaster's root. "But he's bullshitting this time. What's he really up to?"

Asgrimmur opined, "He's waiting for us to make a mistake. He'll only need a second to get away."

"Close the petcocks, Double Great."

Chuckling, Cloven Februaren stepped to the farthest right bottle. He turned the handle of a silver valve in the tube connecting the alembic to the wall. He then wrapped the tube from the valve to the wall in silver foil. "One down."

The Bastard and ascendant did the same to the alembics on the left while Februaren sealed off the bottle containing Red Hammer and War. Dark fog flooded the tube to that one an instant after Februaren shut the petcock. "He wants to play, now. Should I let him through?"

Asgrimmur rumbled, "Make him wait. The others will be more pliable if we keep him out of the way."

Hecht volunteered, "That sounds good," though he had no real say. This was his sister's project, one hundred percent.

Heris said, "And that's how we'll proceed. Stay alert. This has gone the way it should, so far. Let's not assume that it will keep on."

Despite the admonition Hecht did relax. The time of highest risk had passed. The Old Ones had chosen to listen. Hard to stay intensely alert when there was no obvious threat.

No obvious threat? When these beings were what they were? And the plan was to compel them to serve, as though they were sprites or ifrits?

Hecht stared at Asgrimmur's back, wondering. The man was the most alien of his experience, because of what he carried inside him. Yet amongst the personalities gathered here Grimmsson was only slightly outside normal.

Asgrimmur stepped to the leftmost alembic, flashed a smile at Vali, who kept getting more nervous as everything went well. "These are the gentle ones." Sweet young female faces formed on the inside of the glass, drifted, distorting. "Eavijne is, anyway. Hourli, so-so. Not so much, Fastthal and Sprenghul." He set his left hand on the glass. The only hand he had. He had lost the other to a fat old lord of the Grail Empire during an ill-conceived attack back in the time of his madness. Streaks of color, like a network of veins, spread through the nearby glass.

Hecht called across, "Asgrimmur, get out of Vali's line of fire." He hoped Vali would fire regardless. He was not sure she had what that would take. He had no doubts about Lila, though. Lila was hard. Lila would do what needed doing.

"No call to concern yourself, Commander. These four grasp the situation. They accept our terms."

"Just like that?"

"Just like that. They are of the Night. They make decisions without agonizing." A shot at the Commander of the Righteous of the Grail Empire. Hecht sent men into dire peril all the time but never without soul-searching beforehand and agonizing afterward.

Heris said, "Can it, Piper. My operation. Be quiet. Do your job."

Hecht exchanged looks with his mistress. Anna could not restrain a grin. She enjoyed seeing him be one of the spear-carriers. Or match men.

Heris asked, "Can we trust them, Asgrimmur?"

"Yes."

"You understand that your ass is on the line here, too?"

"I do, sweetheart. I'll be the first to feel the pain if I'm wrong. But something down deep tells me the Trickster is the only one whose word can be suspect."

"Then release them when you have their oaths. Once you're absolutely sure. Understand?"

"I do."

Piper Hecht stared at Heris. Was there more going on than just the business of the moment? He squinted at the ascendant.

"Piper, for heaven's sake. Pay attention." Anna, with a gentle reprimand because he was not watching his targeted alembic.

"Huh? Oh. Right." Just the right time to get distracted by something stupid.

Trying to save face, he grumbled, "Asgrimmur, comfortable or not, you need to stay out of the lines of fire."

The ascendant eased to the side of the silver glass teardrop. He disconnected it from its petcock, then spun the bottle so its stem pointed between Vali and Anna.

A puff of dense smoke shot out. It stretched into a vertical bar. The bar dispersed into a bipedal shape, translucent, gained color and solidity, became a well-preserved graying blonde in her forties, five feet tall and naked, who stepped to the side of the alembic opposite Asgrimmur.

Another puff. This was an Instrumentality with a sense of humor. The puff emerged as a smoke ring, then followed the precedent already set, producing a similar naked form, but darker. Hecht thought she must be aspected to night. He felt creepy, looking at her.

The first out acquired clothing in a style centuries out of date.

Third to arrive was a woman with hair a washed-out ginger.

The second out was fashion-conscious. The clothing she assumed mimicked Vali's.

Last out was a tall, thin blonde who seemed terribly worried. Her aspect was younger than the others.

None of the four projected any strong sense of the supernatural. Dressed appropriately none would have turned heads on a Brothen street. None seemed driven to cloak in a glamour. The last was the most attractive, but in a nonthreatening way.

The ascendant made introductions. "Fastthal. Sprenghul. Hourli. And Eavijne."

The tall woman said, "Eavijne, who must tend her orchard immediately or your work here will have been wasted."

Eavijne spoke a dead language but the Commander of the Righteous understood. Meaning reached his mind without troubling his ears.

Her pantheon depended on her golden apples. They had been away from the fruit for an age.

Her orchard was in a state so sad it might never produce again.

Hecht eyed the ascendant. What was his opinion? Heris did the same, and asked, "Asgrimmur?"

"It's unavoidable. And we have her word. Release her. Though I can't imagine where she'll find the magic she needs."

Heris decided. "Go, Eavijne. The rest of you, get out of the way. Back where the floor is painted green."

Eavijne left. The Old Ones, tight of lip, moved to the green. Hecht suspected they had tasted the world and had found it unable to deliver any magic. They had no choice but to abide by their word.

The connection to the alembic in front of Hecht rattled. The silver foil wrapping curled back slightly, revealing a tube gone dark as night. The Trickster's panic could be felt, faintly.

Hecht's son Pella joined his sister Vali. They shifted the aim of her falcon to the rattling bottle.

The Instrumentality settled down. It could not break the tubing.

Heris asked, "Asgrimmur, who's next?" The ascendant was helping the Bastard watch Cloven Februaren reconnect the first bottle to its feed.

"Hammer and Zyr."

"Sounds risky. Why?"

"Red Hammer *is* risky. He's emotionally juvenile. But War is the opposite. He's the most thoughtful Shining One. The others respect his wisdom. He's the one most likely to adapt."

"Double Great, you done with that? Good. Asgrimmur, make it happen."

Cloven Februaren joined the ascendant. He disconnected the bottle from its petcock while Asgrimmur laid hand on and talked fast.

Voice choking, Anna said, "Asgrimmur, get out of my line of fire!"

The ascendant stepped aside. "There isn't a problem that . . ."

Anna's face went white. She stabbed her slow match into the touch hole of her falcon.

A shadow burst out of the silver glass bottle's opening.

Enriched godshot shredded the Instrumentality called Red Hammer. It shattered the bottle and the entity still inside it, too, along with everything else between Anna and the wall. It ripped the clay pad there. The blast shifted tables and broke small glassware. The roar deafened everyone.

It stunned or rendered unconscious those who had been in front of the falcon's mouth.

Seeing no one else fit, Hecht took charge. By means of signs he got his family to drag the others back behind the falcons. Some hearing returned by the time they finished. Hecht told Pella, "Help your mother reload and shift her aim. I'll take care of these folks."

There was little he could do now. Time would bring them back.

His own hearing returned quickly. First voice he heard was Anna wanting to know if she had done the right thing.

"Absolutely, darling. The demon meant to attack Asgrimmur."

"But . . ."

"You did the right thing." That was what she needed to hear.

The lesson was not lost on the watching goddesses. They looked stricken.

Massaging his ears, the ascendant stood. "They've just fully realized that they're in the presence of the Godslayer. Ironically, their fear of him triggered the cascade of events that brought them to this."

"Godslayers," Hecht mumbled. Grimmsson looked like a man with a biting ulcer. "What's the matter?"

"There isn't much Gray Walker left but what remains is distraught. Red Hammer was his son. Zyr was his only real friend."

Hecht eyed the ascendant's stump. That lost god-friend, Zyr, had been a one-hander, too. "What about Arlensul?"

"I get nothing."

"Wasn't Red Hammer her brother?"

"Half brother. Like most of the early gods, the Walker got around."

"Didn't call him All-Father for nothing, eh?"

"No. Also, Arlensul didn't like Red Hammer."

"Where do we stand now?"

"Heris will now get all the cooperation she wants. Extinction means more to immortals with no expectation of an afterlife. Mortals arrive in the world under sentence of death. We know it, we don't like it, but we accept the fact that we can't do anything about it."

"Let's hope she does get what she wants." He was not sure what that was, though.

She did, for sure, have her entire self wrapped up in it, though.

FOUR HOURS FLED BEFORE EVERYONE RECOVERED ENOUGH TO CONtinue. Some ate. Old soldier Piper Hecht napped.

Ferris Renfrow tried communicating with the freed goddesses. They were not gracious. Had they not been at a disadvantage they would have had nothing to do with Arlensul's half-breed get.

When awake Hecht kept an eye on Cloven Februaren. The old boy's mad, adolescent sense of humor might cause him to do something absurd.

Heris and the ascendant cleared the mess left by the falcon blast. They tossed the wreckage out the windows.

Pella helped. Though afraid of heights he liked watching stuff fall.

Hecht came out of his nap to find the Old Ones gone. He started to demand an explanation, stifled himself. He was not used to not being in charge. Nor did it matter where they had gone. They could not leave the Realm of the Gods.

"How are you holding up?" he asked Anna.

"I'm all right. I napped some, too. Not as enthusiastically as the Snore King, though."

This was good. She could joke. "How about . . . ?"

"I worked it out. I had no choice. And Vali would have taken the shot if I hadn't, anyway."

Hecht glanced at Vali. She nodded.

Heris said, "Stop fussing, little brother. She's good. We're all good. We can hear again. No harm done, and nobody is hungry. Let's get to work."

"All right. But I'm wondering where we're going, Heris. You killed the Windwalker. He was the reason this all got started."

"Kharoulke had a family. Vrislakis. Zambakli Souleater. Djordjevice the Foul."

"And?"

"And they are all spawn of the primal Night, freed by the ice and going unchallenged because Asgrimmur imprisoned the Old Ones. They're starting to recover," said Heris.

"Kharoulke couldn't fight you off."

"He was alone. I wasn't. And other old evils are wakening, too, Instrumentalities who think in millennial terms. They can wait for help from wicked people."

"Huh?"

"Rudenes Schneidel? People doing what we are but with bloody evil intent?"

Hecht gaped, startled by her passion.

"You know er-Rashal al-Dhulquarnen, Piper. How many resurrections has he been tied to? He won't stop till he succeeds. You thwarted him in the Connec and at Arn Bedu but he'll be up to some other villainy by now."

Hecht stared. Heris said, "You know where destiny is taking you. You'll need all the help you can get on the way." She gestured at the remaining alembics. "If our clumsiness hasn't turned them against us."

"I suspect clumsiness doesn't account for much."

Heris nodded. Her expression turned grim. Then she winked. "Onward, little brother. To the next step."

"Did anybody check for blast damage to the connector tubes?"

"Double Great did. They're sound at the wall. He rigged the bowl for the soul egg feed to the one that connected to the bottle Anna shot."

"But that one didn't have the double petcock."

"No. The one in front of you did. The tube had a bigger diameter and bent down behind, to the second petcock, but it got cut by shrapnel."

Hecht eyed the head-high bowl Februaren had rigged. "That's too precarious. You put weight in there, it'll tip over. Why not wait and see what you can do with the right feed once we let those things out?"

Heris restrained her stubborn determination to be in charge. "Double Great. What do you think?"

"That this time Piper's head is working right. We need the double valve to manage the Trickster."

"All right. Let's do that."

THE NEXT RELEASE BROUGHT FORTH THREE OLD ONES, ALL FEMALE. Of those Hecht already knew one, Wife. That was a name, not a title, though Wife was the spouse of the Gray Walker.

Hecht watched them swear oaths that bound them to good behavior.

Asgrimmur leaned closer as the second goddess swore. "Sheaf. Aspected to grain and crop fertility." As though that ought to mean something. "She'll need watching. She was Red Hammer's number-one wife. And these Instrumentalities can be big on revenge. And the pretty one is Aldi."

Cloven Februaren joined them. "One more bottle. And one unhappy Trickster still in storage."

The ascendant missed his tone. He nodded. "The last two. One god, one goddess. But she's Red Hammer's mother."

Februaren said, "I'm thinking we have more trouble than you've let on, friend Asgrimmur."

"What do you mean?"

"That this can't be on the up-and-up. You supposedly trapped all of the Old Gods here, except Ordnan and Arlensul. Right?"

Silence overran the chamber, the Great Sky Fortress, the Realm of the Gods. Cloven Februaren had used a name never to be spoken by mortal men.

Asgrimmur started shaking. "Aaron's Balls, old man! Have a care!"

"Why? He's gone. Less than the whisper of a ghost. Right?"

"Names have vast power."

"A root theorem of magic. So. How about you share some names that we might not find on the roster of Instrumentalities we're bringing back here," said Februaren.

"I don't understand."

"I doubt that. This old man didn't spend all his time with Iron Eyes swapping tall tales and seeing who could drink the most dwarf beer."

Heris was behind Asgrimmur now, and distinctly unhappy. "What's the story, Double Great?"

"An old one, maybe. But I'm not quite ready to say we've been hornswoggled."

"Double Great!"

"All right! There are problems with our situation. Anomalies."

"Such as?" Heris asked.

"I got Iron Eyes to tell me what he could about the Old Ones. Now I'm raising questions. There are whole platoons of gods and goddesses who didn't get stuck inside Asgrimmur's pocket reality. Assuming twelve really is how many were trapped here. Which is what the Aelen Kofer claim."

Asgrimmur slumped. "It's true. I should've seen it. But it's also true that these twelve are all who were here when I locked them up. I'm thinking now, maybe, thanks to Korban's father. He was here, I think. My memories aren't very clear."

Februaren said, "I've studied this mythology, Asgrimmur. There are problems with your story."

"There are inconsistencies in every faith, old man. We blind ourselves willfully. What's your particular problem?" The ascendant grew more disturbed as the old sorcerer prodded.

"The Trickster."

"Uh . . . and?"

"The tale of the Old Ones is a long one. It's convoluted and filled with the aforementioned inconsistencies. They defeated the primal Instrumentalities, Kharoulke, Vrislakis, and their kin. But the Gray Walker wasn't top Shining One back then. He had a father and a grandfather. He had some brothers. It took them all to make the middle world and create people. Zyr was around before most of the Old Ones. He may have been a friend of Ordnan's grandfather. The dwarves say he was a more important god, way back.

"Then there was the War Between the Gods. The Old Gods against the Raneul. The Shining Ones won but the Raneul weren't destroyed. Some moved in here and became Shining Ones themselves. The rest are around somewhere. Likewise, a whole raft of missing original Old Ones. And, after that, there's still the Trickster matter."

Asgrimmur drew a long, deep breath, released it in a long, loud sigh.

"Knowing all that, then, you no doubt know that the missing Instrumentalities are to be found in Eucereme."

"I don't know that name. It isn't one Iron Eyes ever used."

"We talk about the Nine Worlds but the only ones we've dealt with are this one, the middle world, and that of the Aelen Kofer. Your missing gods and goddesses are probably hiding in the world of the Raneul, where they won't have to deal with Godslayers."

That was an answer, of a sort, but not one that satisfied, there being a normal human inclination to expect secret meanings, motives, and movers.

Heris said, "Double Great, this is all interesting as hell but how about we finish the job we've got?"

"Good idea. But first let's make sure it doesn't finish us. Asgrimmur. About the Trickster."

"What about him?"

"He is in there, right?"

"Yes."

"How does that work? I thought he'd been thrown out of the Realm of the Gods because of tricks he played on the other Old Ones."

"I don't know. He probably talked his way back in once the All-Father went down."

"Double Great. However he got here, he's here. Deal with that."

"I'm trying. I think it might be useful to know why he came back."

"He came back because he thought he could score with the Gray Walker out of the way. You want to poke and pry and figure things out, see if the Trickster didn't set Ordnan up somehow. But do it on your own time."

Cloven Februaren looked at Hecht. "I think the success with Kharoulke has gone to her head."

Hecht did not smile. He was tired and worried and wanted out of this suburb of the Pit. "Let's finish up so we can get out and go home."

"You, too? All right. I blame it on Grade Drocker, her father. But don't worry about outside. Time goes slower out there. They aren't missing you, yet."

So now the old man was poking him with a stick.

Hecht refused to play.

Still arguing, Heris and Februaren, with Ferris Renfrow behind, made another round of everything up front, looking for possible problems.

"Asgrimmur?" Heris called. "You ready?"

"Sorry. Woolgathering, I guess."

He had gone thoughtful the moment Heris suggested that the Trickster might have had something to do with the Gray Walker's misfortunes.

Hecht watched closely as the ascendant established a dialog with the last two Old Ones. He wished there were a way to gauge how potent the ghosts within the man really were.

3. Lucidia: Tel Moussa

For a month frenetic preparations alternated with boredom at the watch fortress atop Tel Moussa. The Mountain, General Nassim Alizarin, had grown thoroughly frustrated. God Himself must be testing him.

His patience was gone. His faith had grown weak.

Alizarin spent his days in the parapet of the highest tower, enduring the hot winds off the Idiam. His men had installed a canopy to provide shade while their old general wrestled his ghosts and conscience.

Nassim Alizarin had been a great champion and commander of the Sha-lug, the mighty slave soldiers of Dreanger. None had stood higher save the Marshall, Gordimer the Lion. Then, for no reason ever made clear, Gordimer had permitted the murder of Nassim's son Hagid. Nassim rebelled. So he was here, now, a tool of Dreanger's enemies.

Alizarin now understood that the Marshall's part in the murder had consisted of omission and indifference. Lost in the distractions that came with power, Gordimer had become an unwitting puppet of the sorcerer er-Rashal al-Dhulquarnen.

The Rascal had ordered Hagid killed. That debt had yet to be repaid.

Meantime, the Mountain served the kaifs of Qasr al-Zed. He had hoped to gather other disgruntled Sha-lug to oust Gordimer and er-Rashal.

As an ally of Qasr al-Zed, Alizarin had been effective; as an agent for change in Dreanger, not so much.

His current task was to control traffic between Lucidia and the Holy Lands so the crusaders would gain no clear picture of what was developing in the Realm of Peace.

Indala al-Sul Halaladin, with most of the might of Qasr al-Zed, had launched the Grand Campaign into Dreanger, to unite the kaifate of al-Minphet with that of Qasr al-Zed so he could turn their combined strength against the infidel in the Holy Lands.

Indala had suffered severe losses while achieving dramatic successes. He had captured al-Qarn. He had taken possession of Kaif Kaseem al-Bakr. He controlled most of the shrines of al-Minphet. But he had not yet humbled Gordimer the Lion, nor had he eliminated er-Rashal al-Dhulquarnen. The Marshall was maneuvering west of the River Shirne, trying to initiate an encounter that would honor his particular advantages.

That dance had been on for weeks. Indala would not be drawn. He meant to temporize till Gordimer's forces melted away, an eventuality, Nassim suspected, that might hamstring Indala first. His followers were farther from home.

Whoever else abandoned him, Gordimer would retain the finely honed professional Sha-lug.

Nassim never stopped wrestling his conscience. He feared that he was in the wrong, now. Worse, he suspected that Indala wanted to make him a puppet Marshall.

Why could not the kaifates join forces against the infidel without savaging one another first?

"What is it, Mohkam?" Nassim did not turn to see who had joined him. The night was afire with stars.

"You saw the rider arrive, General?"

"I did."

"He brought news from our friends in Vantrad. Black Rogert is moving."

"Finally. What do we have to look forward to?"

"His party numbers more than four hundred."

"All armed men?"

"Twenty-four knights, mostly Brotherhood of War. Their squires, their serjents, their servants, and so forth. The rest are mercenary foot recruited from pilgrims who came to see Unbeliever holy sites. There are some wives and children, too," said Mohkam.

"Where would Rogert find money to hire mercenaries? They'd want their pay up front because he's cheated hired swords and Gisela Frakier before. The Brotherhood of War wouldn't finance him. They're probably along to keep him in check, not to help him."

Gisela Frakier were Praman tribesmen allied with the Arnhander invaders, usually because their traditional tribal enemies were not.

"The money flows from the same spring as the nomination to return to Gherig. Queen Clothilde."

Clothilde, queen of Vantrad, related to Black Rogert and, possibly, his lover, was a woman as foul as he.

King Beresmond of Vantrad was fourteen years younger than Clothilde, who held him in complete contempt. He suffered from several afflictions, not the least of which was his spouse. He was not a strong personality.

Beresmond was nominal sovereign of the Crusader States. Very nominal, of late. Several counts and princes had taken advantage of his weakness even as du Tancret played the viper in his nest.

Nassim considered the boy king's great weaknesses his niceness and trusting nature.

Any man less nice and trusting would have had some throats cut.

"Why did I ask? Who else would give him money? Dare I hope that she is coming with him?"

"Her moral decline hasn't reached that depth. But don't be surprised to hear that the Queen will make a progress through the Crusader States, with a stop at Gherig."

"Do we know Rogert's itinerary?"

"No," Mohkam admitted. "But the road will define the way."

Before Nassim stopped trade countless caravans had moved between Lucidia and Dreanger, some so huge they required a thousand guards. Every year thousands of pilgrims took to the roads, and not just the Faithful. The Holy Lands had been Chaldarean, Devedian, and Dainshaukin before the Praman Conquest.

When last he was lord of Gherig, Rogert du Tancret had shown no reluctance to attack the caravans. He had slain thousands, including diplomats and fellow Chaldareans. He took their goods and treasure and saved only those who could be ransomed or would fetch a good price on the slave block.

On one occasion he had captured and mistreated females from Indala's own household.

Rogert bragged about having masterminded an expedition into the Peqaa wastes to profane the holiest holies associated with the Founding Family. He brayed that he would do so again and next time would expunge everything having to do with the origins of the Faith.

Rogert du Tancret was, to most Pramans, the Adversary incarnate.

Nassim asked, "Again, anything useful concerning his itinerary?"

"As I said. He has to follow the roads, from water to water."

FEW SECRETS SURVIVED LONG IN THE HOLY LANDS. WHATEVER ANY-one did, it would be seen and talked about by people who had nothing invested. Most natives saw not only the crusaders but the Faithful as invaders, adventurers, and oppressors. They helped when compelled, or paid, but opted out of the struggles otherwise.

News of Black Rogert's return spread faster than the plague. Du Tancret was an object of universal loathing.

No one passed the word when small bands of Lucidians slipped through the wilderness, leading heavily laden camels. Not to the crusaders or Brotherhood of War.

ROGERT DU TANCRET BELIEVED HIMSELF SAFE IN THE SHADE OF THE protective umbrella of the Crusader States. His party constituted a small army. He had riders out front and trailing. That was necessary even in peacetime. But his flankers were not out as far as they ought to have been.

Du Tancret had a remarkable sense for personal danger. He had been accused of having one foot inside the Night, on its darkest side.

He had been uneasy for hours.

Two hundred screaming Lucidians swarmed from amongst tumbled boulders, following arrows and long lances. Once the lances broke, sabers came out. But these attackers were not interested in a stand-up fight. They wanted to do all the damage they could, quickly, especially among the knights. Then they would flee.

Their pursuers chased them into a defile where they turned and fought but fell back under pressure from du Tancret's followers.

Then Nassim Alizarin's falcons ripped swaths through the invaders.

Black Rogert reined his people in. His enemies would try to lead him into further traps. He would not fall for that again. He abandoned his dead and some of his wounded and resumed travel.

Nassim asked, "Did anyone even get close?"

Several men claimed to have seen their arrows strike Black Rogert's shield. None had gotten near enough to ply lance or saber. Mohkam said, "And it wasn't like anybody made an effort to protect him."

Al-Azer er-Selim grumbled, "They love him no more than we do. He is truly beloved of the Night."

Nassim asked al-Azer, his Master of Ghosts, "What did you try?"

"I concentrated on his horse. It didn't respond."

Old Bone snarled, "He's the Adversary's little brother."

Not a new proposal. Du Tancret obviously enjoyed unnatural luck.

Mohkam said, "The men report killing seventeen and wounding thirty. After factoring for exaggeration. The truth could be more optimistic."

Nassim growled, "Not as good as I'd hoped."

"They didn't panic."

"And I was expecting that." Had the Crusaders taken to their heels there would have been a grand slaughter.

Nassim said, "Send a patrol back. Tell them to look for a casualty in good enough shape to be questioned."

Al-Azer observed, "Let's count ourselves lucky that Black Rogert doesn't waste time burying his dead."

"Which will win him more enemies."

Nassim paced the crusaders, right or left, wherever he could raise the most dust. He launched nuisance attacks. He resisted calls to poison the wells along the way. He did not want the enmity of locals who depended on those same sources of water.

The crusaders reached Gherig having suffered fewer losses than the Mountain had hoped to gift them.

*   *   *

NASSIM RETURNED TO TEL MOUSSA. THERE HAD BEEN NEWS FROM Dreanger. A huge battle had been shaping up in the desert west of the Shirne, near a village called Patel.

That news was a week old. Nothing further had been heard.

4. Alten Weinberg: Empress Apparent

Helspeth Ege, Empress Apparent of the New Brothen Empire, placed herself in front of a full-length mirror. She wore nothing but smallclothes. "Hilda. Am I homely?" She knew she was not plump enough but, otherwise, could not judge what she saw before her.

"That's hardly a fair question."

"Why?"

"There's no way the Empress can count on my answer being truthful."

Helspeth scowled. Hilda Daedel had been her principal lady-in-waiting for ages. They had become friends, as much as they dared. Hilda was familiar with Helspeth's insecurities and obsessions. Lack of confidence in her looks was high on the list.

"Don't go all philosophical on me. I just need an honest answer."

"But when I tell you you're drop-dead gorgeous, instead of believing me you'll accuse me of telling you what I think you want to hear. If I say you're plain you'll accuse me of—"

"Hilda! Why must you be exasperating?"

"I? Hilda Daedel? Of Averange? Exasperating? Maybe because . . ."

"Let's stop this."

"Right behind you, Helspeth."

"Hilda, I'm terrified. When the news breaks . . ."

"You'll have Captain Drear and the Braunsknechts behind you. All of the Braunsknechts. They're yours, now. You'll have the Commander of the Righteous when he gets here. Not to mention Ferris Renfrow. And, if the old men do try to brush you aside, the only legitimate successor they could put up is your crazy old Aunt Aneis. She doesn't know what century it is."

"They might think that's good."

"Enough. Your problem isn't vulnerability. You have too much time on your hands. You use it to fuss, worry, and obsess."

Helspeth would not see what the mirror reflected. She was not a great beauty but she was a slim young brunette more attractive than most women her age.

"I don't want to be Empress, Hilda."

"The last Ege who asked for the job was your father. And, from what my father says, he didn't develop a taste for it till he'd had the job ten years."

"Why are undergarments always so heavy and rough?"

Lady Hilda was accustomed to Helspeth's darting attention. "Because they need washing more often. If you saw what the washerwomen do to keep them clean you'd understand. You'd probably wonder why they aren't made of iron."

"Must you always be literal and reasonable?"

"Someone has to bring balance . . ."

"Damn you! I need . . ."

"No. You don't. Still, I could develop a fierce case of emotional dependence and go home to plague my husband."

"Hilda?"

"I'm thinking about having another child."

"Stop it."

"Lady va Kelgerberg could take over. She knows the ins and outs."

"Damn it, stop!"

Lady Hilda shifted approach but did not stop. She meant to conquer Helspeth's mood. "What will you do about the Commander of the Righteous once you're officially Empress? He'll be yours to do with as you please."

"You go too far."

"The Commander. The Righteous. Katrin's crusade. You need to think about them."

"I will. I have been."

"And?"

"Hilda, I'm a virgin. I'm going to die a virgin."

"You're talking crazier than ever, now. Your value on the marriage market is about to soar."

That was true. She knew it. But she meant what she said. The pressure to wed would be relentless. The old men would want to see an heir.

"Where are they, Hilda?"

This time Lady Hilda lost the intellectual trail. "They? They who, Helspeth?"

"Renfrow. The Commander of the Righteous. Why aren't they here to help me?"

"They'll be here. But right now they're in Firaldia, dealing with the consequences of a huge Imperial triumph."

Helspeth continued to worry and fuss.

She was suffering imposter insecurity. Helspeth Ege could not possibly deserve the position that God, fate, or the Instrumentalities of the Night were putting into her hands.

"I'm terrified, Hilda. It's easy to be a great emperor when you only have to do it in your head. But now it's going to be real."

Where were they?

She felt more exposed, more vulnerable, than even she had when her sister had driven her into internal exile, hoping she would do the convenient thing and die.

5. The Connec: Antieux

Count Raymone Garete was an able war leader and a deft administrator, and he had a gift for convincing others of his righteousness. He had been excommunicated several times by several Patriarchs. Excommunication was a potent threat. It terrified Episcopal Chaldareans. Count Raymone, though, made light of such tribulations. Those excommunications had come from Patriarchs considered illegitimate by Connectens so why should they carry any weight?

His latest, however, had been issued by Serenity, legitimately Patriarch via massive bribery. As a man, Bronte Doneto, Serenity bore the Connec and Antieux that abiding grudge. The sole weakness to Serenity's writ was that he had been run out of office.

Even so, the exiled Serenity had influence and friends. Anne of Menand was especially supportive. The armed might of Arnhand stood behind Anne.

"For the moment," Raymone told Socia as they lay together. "We need but bide our time. There will be changes when Anselin gets home."

"And how do you—ouch! This is a boy for sure. He's trying to kick his way out."

"How do I what?"

"How do you know Anselin will change anything? Do you know him?"

"I do not. But know his situation. My spies in Salpeno have investigated him thoroughly."

"Meaning?"

"Meaning the new king in Arnhand could become one of our best friends because his mother hates us." Raymone Garete knew something about the troubles a son could have with his mother.

"Oh! The waiting is almost over! Your little bastard is going to hit the ground running." She made mock of the Brothen Episcopal Church, saying that. Their marriage had not been sanctioned by the Patriarch. But Raymone did not smile. Socia said, "You need to make your meaning more clear." She wanted to nudge his thoughts toward something else that annoyed him.

He said, "Anne always treated Anselin badly, blatantly favoring Regard. Some say because Charlve the Dim wasn't his real father. But Regard is dead. Anne's own machinations make Anselin the only heir."

Raymone rested a hand on Socia's belly. The skin there had stretched till it glistened. Her navel had become a strange little knot that looked like it was about to pop off. His touch was featherlight.

"So Anselin will reverse Anne's policies just because they're hers?"

"Some. Maybe most. But he'll still have to deal with people who aren't his mother. They won't let him do whatever he wants." Half a minute passed while Raymone contemplated Socia's stomach. "Anne of Menand may find herself locked up in a cloistered nunnery before they finish cleaning up the coronation mess."

"She's slippery, though." Socia could not concentrate on politics. The baby was clog dancing. "So you think we've won."

Raymone Garete thought nothing of the sort. "I haven't looked at it that way. You could be right. We'll have a respite, at least."

"So why so disappointed?"

"It means a huge change in our lives if, suddenly, nobody is trying to kill us and steal everything."

"I need something to drink. No! Good God! Not wine. Water. Or small beer. No. Better. The water the Master blessed." And, once Raymone delivered that, "It's time for Mistress Alecsinac." She groaned. "The pains are real, now. Yah!" She suppressed a scream. "Now, love! Get the midwives. And the Master." She had no idea what use the old man could be but he had been there for all the landmarks of her life since she was fifteen. He needed to be there for this—especially if something went wrong.

Terrified, suddenly, she needed Brother Candle desperately.

"Wait! One thing. Who will you marry if I don't survive?"

Raymone Garete was no genius where women were concerned but he did slip this snare. "No one, heart of my heart. I will go on only to rear my son, in your memory."

Even that was only marginally acceptable. He should have tried for reassuring.

"What a bullshitter. Go on. Get the midwives."

* * *

WHEN BROTHER CANDLE MET THE INFANT LUMIERE HE WAS SUR-
rounded by women, some unfamiliar. Those he did know included
Kedle Richeut, Mistress Alecsinac, and the ladies of Count Raymone's
diminutive court. Those he did not know included a wet nurse and
Raymone's fiercely disapproving mother. Sister Claire had spent her
last twelve years cloistered. She had come to see her first grandson at
Count Raymone's insistence.

Raymone's mother said nothing in his hearing but she was unhappy about the presence of heretics and witches. Nor did she approve of her son's choice of wife. The border brat was little better than
a peasant.

Brother Candle was gracious toward the cross old nun but somewhat boggled. Not once had Raymone ever mentioned his mother.
It was obvious he had little love for the woman. So why was she
here?

Count Raymone Garete operated by a complex code of his own
device. He could not articulate it fully even to himself.

The Perfect would learn later, from Bernardin, that the Count believed his mother had been involved in the death of his father when
Raymone was a small boy. There might have been cuckoldry involved.
A Connecten romantic love may have gone wrong. Or religion might
have been involved. Bernardin would not explore the matter.

Socia was sitting up. Two women were trying to make her more
presentable. A touch of vanity not evident before?

"Master. I'm delighted. Come here. Shove those crows out of the
way."

Brother Candle did no shoving. He moved carefully. It was clear
which women were Seekers and which were Chaldarean. It was harder
to tell which of those honored Brothe and which clung to the lost
Viscesment Patriarchy. The Episcopals were offended by his presence.
He was a man, and a heretic.

Socia inspired further indignation by patting her bed. "Sit. Look at
him. What do you think?"

He said what he thought. "He ought to be in the arms of his mother,
suckling his mother's milk."

Silence conquered the room. Every woman stared, amazed. Nor
was Socia best pleased.

"You're his mother, Socia. Be his mother. Don't put vanity between
you. Or whatever it is that moves you. Sister Claire. You didn't nurse
Raymone, did you?" Point hammered home, Brother Candle said, "He's

a beautiful boy, Socia. Perfect in every way. Properly raised, he should be a worthy heir to Count Raymone."

Irked, Socia nodded. She had heard Brother Candle's opinions about why so many noble sons turned wicked or were just plain incompetent.

It was hard to deny that the greatest, most successful, and best loved lords often gave way to bad sons.

Socia said, "Riann. Hand me the child, please." She took him from the wet nurse. "He'll be called Lumiere, Master."

"Excellent. May the Good God grant that he lives up to his name."

Count Raymone's mother ground her teeth and muttered but did not expose herself to censure. She must have been warned.

Brother Candle sighed. This religious contention was mad. When outsiders let it alone the Connec ran as smoothly and painlessly as it had in the shelter of the Old Empire.

Socia said, "You will, of course, be his godfather."

"Is that wise? I don't have many years left."

"Wise? I don't know. It's what I want. It's right. Do you want to hold him?" The baby was asleep, nuzzling her chest.

"I'd end up dropping him on his head. Or something."

"You would not and you know it. You manage fine with Kedle's imps."

"If I fumble one of her devils I won't have a fire-breathing count jumping on me before the brat stops bouncing. Speaking of fire-breathers, where is he?"

"I don't know. I saw him after the delivery. He said he was taking a patrol out. Something is happening on the Dechear, up near Viscesment. Maybe Anne and Serenity aren't being as quiet as they should."

Brother Candle scowled. On the day his son was born? Bernardin could have handled that.

Count Raymone had to learn to delegate.

Socia became animated. She forgot Lumiere when she got into politics, which this would be if Anne or the Patriarch were involved.

The old man took one of Socia's hands. He held on while he considered the other women.

He saw little to encourage him about Lumiere's upbringing.

The boy would follow his father's path, getting close to no women but his wet nurse and nanny. He would be taught to belittle them or hold them in quiet contempt. That attitude would, in time, come to include everyone not of his own class.

A failing that Count Raymone had, miraculously, avoided.

"Socia, you know me. The eternal pessimist. Don't take too much to heart my gloomy assessment of Lumiere's future."

He had made a decision. For the infant's sake he would not return to Sant Peyre de Mileage.

Maybe he could get the boy's feet on the ground before the Good God called.

"Eternal pessimist? You might be a little too positive about your bleak seasons, old man. We could surprise you. So. Get it into your head right now. You stay till you see Lumiere grow into a man."

"It may take that long to rediscover the Perfection I've lost since I met you."

"Always with the clever words. Always with the jokes. Come on. Take him. I insist."

There was an edge to Socia's voice the Perfect found troubling.

He took the infant. One blue eye opened momentarily, unfocused, but Brother Candle imagined himself being cataloged in the mind behind.

Babies did seem like supernatural beings at the beginning.

6. Realm of the Gods: The Tyranny of the Night

The Old Gods all took human form. Even Asgrimmur could not say if that was compelled by the presence of humans or if it was just convenient. Some had trouble keeping the shape. They all shimmered occasionally. Which might explain why, in their prime, they had been called the Shining Ones.

"There's no power!" one beauty complained. "The magic is gone."

Most of the revenants had gone out into their world. A few had stayed to watch the mortals. Piper Hecht remained dreadfully uncomfortable, for reasons of offended faith and of concern for his family—though Asgrimmur continued to assure him that there would be no trouble.

"They know they've just moved into a bigger prison. They know they're dead if this world stays closed. They need magic to survive here. There is none. They know bad behavior means no way out. This world will dwindle till, in time, it becomes smaller than a pinprick."

"All part of the Aelen Kofer design, eh? Those sneaky bastards."

"This one is the gods' fault. It's their design. The Aelen Kofer just built the furniture."

Hecht backed away from the discussion. However confusing, all things were true inside the Night.

The woman called Sheaf came in. She was eating what looked like an overgrown, deformed crabapple. "Eavijne's first crop. They're not good but there are enough to go around. Get one." She ambled around, looking over shoulders, curious.

Hecht was curious himself. How had she become fluent in modern Firaldian? Those must be potent apples.

The Bastard, Cloven Februaren, and Heris finished readying their first dump of Instrumentality soul eggs. More than a hundred pounds lay in the glass hopper, set to go.

The ascendant was not much use just now. The suggestion that the All-Father's fall might have been engineered had hit him hard. Had he been manipulated himself? How had he, newly ascended and quite insane, been able to create a pocket world into which he had herded twelve gods?

Asgrimmur kept trying to discuss it with Heris. Heris was busy.

She finally grumbled, "Will you quit stressing about what happened back when? We have problems now. The Trickster ended up in there because what's inside you spent what was left of him to make it happen. Now help me with the hammer mill."

Some of the soul eggs were too large for the injection tube. Heris meant to break those up. The eggs would shatter when hit hard.

Anna and the children had been making themselves useful by moving equipment and materials no longer needed out of the chamber. The divinities were not pleased by their indifference.

Two sizable, still-warm soul eggs had been set aside, on a table all their own. Two falcons not so subtly pointed their way. Heris talked about trying to reverse their misfortune.

Hecht would as soon see them all destroyed. To the last and least these entities mocked the religion of his youth *and* the religion he had adopted since coming west.

His mind might know that all things were true inside the Night but his heart desperately wanted that not to be so. There is no God but God!

"Piper?" Heris asked.

"Huh?"

"You're daydreaming. Again."

"Have to. It never gets dark here." He glanced toward the doorway. The green area boasted a half-dozen Old Gods who looked like ordinary people with anachronistic senses of style. They included one of Red Hammer's mothers—different myths assigned the honor to dif-

ferent goddesses—and his wife and that wife's daughter by an unknown father.

They made Hecht nervous.

Cultures that had worshipped the Old Ones had had strange notions of justice.

"In a world of an eye for an eye the last man standing has got the
world by the balls."

Heris said, "Piper?"

"Nothing. Something Pinkus Ghort said." He checked his family.

They were spent emotionally. Pella had begun spelling them at the
falcons. The boy could be a surprise when he set the attitude aside.
"How much longer do you want the falcons manned? Asgrimmur says
we don't need them anymore. But I'm more suspicious than him. I
can't help thinking how honorable I'd be if the Old Ones had the upper hand."

Cloven Februaren said, "You're the product of thousands of years
of the Instrumentalities having had the upper hand. You'd need to live
that long with them to grasp their thinking. The simple fact that death
is something that only happens to somebody else makes a huge difference."

Hecht said, "That should be changing."

"The change started centuries ago. But they got it wrong, which is
why we are where we are today."

"Why did you come over here interrupting, Double Great?"

"I wanted to tell you to get on with your work and stop worrying
about the numb-nuts hangers-on."

"I missed your point. Assuming you had one."

"Stop worrying about the gods. They can't interfere. That would
be suicidal. You got them by the short hairs. Yank or squeeze, as appropriate, when the mood takes you."

That did not reassure Hecht till he recalled that the Old Ones were
inside their Paradise already, specially constructed by the Aelen Kofer.
Suicide would not take them onward to any wondrous eternity.

The Adversary's cunning termites of doubt kept gnawing at the
foundations of his faith.

"If I understand Double Great right, Piper, it's all right if Anna and
the kids take off. All we have left is to dump the trash through the
midden hole." Heris waved. "Let's do the drop, Renfrow."

"As you wish." The Bastard fiddled with petcocks. A thousand am-
ber beads, from pinhead size to an inch in diameter, rolled down through
silver glass tubing. A silver ball followed so nothing of the Night could
head in the other direction.

The Bastard closed and opened petcocks again. Beads and ball disappeared into Asgrimmur's pocket universe.

"There's one load gone," Heris said. "Let's get crushing and grinding. We'll have this done in another hour. In two we'll be sucking down Aelen Kofer ale."

Hecht checked his family again. "You're sure you don't need fire support?"

"You stay. Pick a falcon." Heris stepped past him. "You gods get a sudden notion to knock boots with a mortal girl, just remember that their mother, father, and aunt already wrote the last verse for four major Instrumentalities."

It was more than four but Hecht was not about to start threatening gods. Heris ought to have better sense, too. She should have noticed, as well, that only one of these gods was male.

Hecht was distracted by the novelty of her concern for Lila and Vali.

Some of the divinities did have reputations. Old northern myth and culture valued virginity, chastity, and fidelity much less than did the followers of Aaron of Chaldar. And Chaldareans were less obsessive than Pramans, who stoned somebody if they even thought about sexual congress with anyone but young boys or the renewable virgin houris of Paradise.

Anna and the children left. Hecht leaned on his falcon and brooded about the quirks of religion.

The Founding Family had been crystal clear and bloody fierce in matters sexual. There was no room in the Faith for buggery. But, as people generally do, the Faithful overlooked rules they found inconvenient. Nor did useful pre-Revelation gods vanish in the light of the god who was God. They put on disguises and went to work as ifrits and other spirits, now supposedly in thrall to the Adversary. And the thing about boys . . .

That had confused and appalled Piper Hecht even when he was young Else Tage.

He thought of Osa Stile, ensorcelled so he would remain a pleasure boy all his life. Osa was still out there, nearing forty, looking a small twelve, still unconvinced that those who had warped him did not deserve his loyalty.

The hammer mill cycled. It shook the chamber. The smash and rattle startled Hecht out of his dark reverie.

Heris joined him. "This is going all right but it's taking longer than I expected."

"Everything does."

"Why? The individual steps aren't causing complications."

"My staff call it friction. Natural drag that just slows things down even when there aren't any problems. Titus Consent has an equation he uses to guess how much friction we can expect in an operation. And, guess what?"

"It doesn't help?"

"It does. But the attempt to calculate friction causes friction of its own. I suspect an undiscovered law of the universe."

"And that doesn't drive you nuts?"

"Of course it does. But if you accept it, don't fight it, and take it into account, things go fairly well. Most leaders can't handle friction. They make things worse by screaming, yelling, threatening and punishing. People slow down when they're afraid to make mistakes."

"More philosophy. More intellectualization. More friction."

"You could be right. They're ready to run another load."

Februaren had sieved the material processed in the hammer mill. The finer stuff went into the tube for delivery into the void. Big chunks would take another pass through the hammer mill. "If we mixed this with water it would go through faster."

"Or oil," the Bastard suggested.

"Oil would create a viscous slurry." A vigorous debate commenced.

Hecht wrestled his temper. These men, participating in the industrialized destruction of the Instrumentalities of the Night, were bickering over the easiest way to make an end of the last relics of entities who might have existed for millennia.

Did longevity qualify them for special empathy? Their long lives had provided them untold opportunities to rain down misery on mortals.

"Piper, do you know where you want to point that thing?" Cloven Februaren asked.

"What?"

"Your loudmouth toy. You leaning on it has got the business end pointing at the floor."

"I was going to skip the shot off the deck."

"A creative approach. But it might do more damage to the good guys."

"Upon reflection, I agree. How much longer?"

"Depends on your sister. She wants to wrap everything this one trip. I could use a few hours down in the tavern, though. And a good long nap."

"Must be a trying life, being a bitter old man."

"Damned straight it is."

Heris was right there to hear herself discussed, and to see the ascendant and Bastard nod. She ignored them all.

The hammer mill made the place shake.

PELLA DASHED IN, PUSHING HIS WAY PAST INDIGNANT DIVINITIES. "Dad . . . The bridge . . ."

"Get some air inside. Then tell it like it's old news."

The boy drew several breaths. "The bridge. That goddess with the apples. She's stealing the magic from the rainbow."

"Asgrimmur?"

"Damn! The bridge is the only magic left. But who would think that any of these dimwits could unravel Aelen Kofer work?"

Hecht said, "We could drag one of these boomers down the hall, tilt it out a window, and take a shot."

"Not necessary. Let me talk to Eavijne. Heris?"

"Go. I'll stay and figure out how to fly down."

Hecht's companions were more cautious once Asgrimmur left. No one turned a back on the divinities. But the Instrumentalities had their own problem. The eldest female gestured. The youngest took off after Asgrimmur. Hecht intuited that she had orders to support the ascendant.

No point escaping prison if you just ended up in a bigger cell.

The senior goddess said something.

The Bastard said, "That's classical Andorayan. The Old Gods still had a rural following when I was young. I might be able to talk to her."

Heris said, "Chances are, she's following everything we're saying. She wanted to talk to you without the god killers understanding."

Hecht said, "A leopard is a leopard and a lion is a lion, Renfrow."

"Folksy, but what does it mean?"

Heris knew from her middle-eastern days. "That you're deluding yourself if you think a lion or a leopard can be turned into anything but a lion or a leopard. A major Instrumentality, even with his balls in a vise, will go right on thinking like a god."

"Understood. And understood." Renfrow faced the goddess. Who seethed, clearly.

Hecht expected nothing more. He thought Heris was trying to domesticate leopards.

Heris picked up the two soul eggs still nearly too warm to touch. "They aren't gone permanently." The hammer mill cycled. "But we won't try to restore them while any of us feel uncomfortable about any of you."

Ferris Renfrow asked, "We're taking hostages?"

The goddess responded, "Save the bluster. I'm not Red Hammer. An offense to my dignity won't shatter my reason. I know we're dependent on your good will. That's galling but even the gods themselves bend the knee to needs must."

"No knee bending required," Heris said. "Just cooperation. Tit for tat. We aren't asking for anything beyond our lifetimes."

"The situation is clear in all its aspects, Godslayer Heris. Go ahead with your work." She turned.

The lone male deity appeared. He carried maybe fifteen feet of rope.

"Where was that hidden?" Heris grumbled.

"I'll be damned!" Renfrow said, in pure awe.

"What?" Hecht demanded while Februaren nodded as though he understood, too.

"Geistrier, Commander."

"Bless you. What's happening?"

"Geistrier is a rope that's always as long as it needs to be and so strong the giant Blognor couldn't break it when it was used to tie him up."

A beautiful, shining girl turned up carrying a spear. It looked perfectly ordinary, an infantry spear, made for thrusting, not throwing. Shaft eight feet long, blade adding another foot and two inches wide at its hips, its edges sharpened. The spearhead glowed with the opposite of light.

"Heartsplitter," Renfrow said, clearly in awe.

Soon afterward someone turned up with a horn, then a hammer, ragged silk slippers, and a flute. None of the relics looked like much.

The Bastard muttered, "It'll be scary as hell getting out if the bridge is gone. But we can do it with their help."

"I'm still wondering what I'm doing here. I have a big war in the east that I should be getting ready for."

Pella had not lingered after delivering his shaker. Now Vali rushed in. "Heris, Asgrimmur says to tell you the situation isn't as bad as he thought. The rainbow is still solid. It's just not wide enough for carts anymore."

"I'll strangle Iron Eyes next time I see him. That stubby prick saw this coming."

Most mortals had to ride goat carts across because they were not psychologically fit to walk on air. The Aelen Kofer had taken the goats along when they scurried out of the Realm of the Gods. There would be no escapes from the Realm, however inept the overconfident middle-worlder mortal rescuers were.

Whatever happened, no one, mortal or Instrumentality, would depart the Great Sky Fortress without walking the rainbow bridge.

It was there for anyone with the nerve to walk it.

THE HAMMER MILL CYCLED FOR THE LAST TIME. THE GREAT SKY FORtress creaked and shook. Heris made sure every crumb of cracked egg, every recoverable speck of dust, preceded a silver ball into the hidden universe. "All right. Time for a beer. Or three. Or ten. And then a week of sleep. I'll decide what next when I wake up."

Nobody asked questions. Nobody wanted Heris thinking of something else that needed doing. Excepting the Trickster.

Even the least sensitive, like Piper Hecht, felt the desperation building as the trapped Instrumentality finally understood that he would not be released.

His peers were indifferent. He had exhausted their patience and friendship.

Hecht watched Heris pack the soul eggs of Zyr and Red Hammer, admiring her detailed and meticulous work, even in circumstances that encouraged haste and sloppiness.

Heris asked, "What should we do about the falcons? We can't take them with us."

"Damn! Give me a second to think like Kait Rhuk or Drago Prosek." The observing Instrumentalities seemed intrigued.

"I'll fix them so they can only be unfixed by one of my experts." A challenge to the gods. "Iron Eyes will come back someday. After he gets over the beating I'm going to give him. He can rebuild the rainbow bridge, then haul the falcons out on his goat carts."

"Make sure they can't be used against us later, then let's go drink some beer."

"Where's that keg of firepowder? All right. I see it. Go ahead and take off." He wondered about her thirst as he pounded a sliver of iron into the touch hole of a falcon. Heris was not a drinker, unless she had developed a taste since coming to the Realm of the Gods.

The room shivered. Hecht felt a hint of rage from the trapped Instrumentality. He reflected momentarily. "Better do it. Just in case." He collected the firepowder keg.

"Dad? You going to futz around all day?"

"Vali. How come you're back up here?"

Glassware fell, crashed. They both jumped.

"Anna sent me to find out why you didn't come down when Heris did."

"Work to do here." He fiddled with a spring. "I'm almost done."

"They've started crossing the bridge."

"I didn't realize I was taking too much time."

"She's just worried. You know she worries."

"Uhm." He surveyed the falcons. All spiked. Firepowder keg, set to go.

"I mean really worries, Dad. When you're away."

"Let's go."

The room shivered again. Hecht thought this tremor was weaker. The prisoner had spent his strength and fury.

CLEVER GODS HAD MADE CROSSING THE BRIDGE EASY. ONE TOOK AN end of Geistrier across and tied it to a boulder. Heartsplitter, thrust into the fabric of the bridge, supported the rope midway. The near end was tied to an old, green brass post of memorial significance. Nobody remembered of what. Asgrimmur said, "It may have a part in the Twilight War. I'm not sure. You changed everything. A destiny that has been fixed since the beginning just isn't anymore."

"I wish I *was* that important to history. But Anna and Heris are bigger god killers than me."

"Not true. You forget Seska and the ancients you put down in the Connec. But why worry about that? We have a bridge to cross."

Hecht had been trying to tame his dread. There were heights and heights. This was the kind where you could not see a place to stop falling.

Nothing in his training had prepared him for this. Such a challenge could not arise because a situation like this could not exist. This was a fever dream of savages not yet blest with the Word of God.

Asgrimmur said, "Just step up to the post, take hold of the rope, close your eyes, and head out. I'll be right behind you."

Hecht took a quick look round. Most everyone was across. Lila was halfway over, striding confidently, fingers lightly dragging along the rope. A goddess walked in front of her. Another moved behind. Neither was close enough to help if the girl lost her footing.

Anna was over and waiting. If she could manage, he could.

Vali raced past as he moved toward the head of the bridge, ran out onto the span like it was a mile wide and built of granite. The youngest Shining One, Aldi, was close behind. Her courage flagged when she came to the bridge. Vali ran till she overtook the slow mover behind Lila.

"Say nothing," the ascendant cautioned softly. "Don't distract her."

"No. But I'm not so sanguine about the one chasing her."

"She's safe. But I'll remind her not to irritate the god-killing folk."

"Good. And the god-killing folk will have a come-to-Aaron meeting with their daughter, in case she did something stupid."

"There you go." Asgrimmur sounded like he was having trouble not laughing. "They're just young people having fun."

That was plain enough from the body language Vali and Aldi showed.

Hecht ground his teeth, shut his eyes, groped for the rope, grabbed hold, and started walking.

Anna swarmed him when he reached the other side. "You made it."

"Of course I did. It's like crossing a creek on a fallen tree."

"Only it takes you longer to get wet after you slip. Piper, we need to talk to the girls."

Vali and Lila were just a few feet away, the former striving mightily to look like butter would not melt in her mouth. Meaning it was certain that she had started whatever it was that he had witnessed. "Yes. Where is Pella?"

"He's still over there. With that Eavijne."

"Really?"

"It's a crush that won't go anywhere. She's taken."

"Good. I don't want any of us getting friendly with these devils."

"Jealous?"

"Worried about our souls."

Pella approached the nether end of the bridge. Asgrimmur went back to help.

Hecht asked about that.

"He's helping everybody."

"So. I guess that's a good thing."

"Better than any of the gods. They won't even help each other."

True. Those who were over already were headed down the mountain, indifferent to anything happening behind them.

"Just like real people."

"More so. They're much too sure of themselves."

Ferris Renfrow and Cloven Februaren were on the path downward, too. They had no interest in what was going on behind them.

Pella was deathly pale when he arrived. "Dad, I hope we don't ever do anything like that again. I'm not good with heights."

"You and me both. Asgrimmur, who's still over there?"

"Just Eavijne, trying to nurture her orchard."

Pella said, "She doesn't want to believe things turned out the way they did. It's like she hopes that if she just wishes hard enough the world will be what she wants it to be."

Hecht said, "Some mortals think the same way."

Anna opined, "That's how it is for gods, though, isn't it? They wish for stuff and that's what happens."

"Here she comes," Asgrimmur said.

Eavijne trudged onto the bridge. She carried a red sack. "Apples," Pella explained. "Sick apples, all weird and shriveled."

"Where'd she get the sack?" Hecht asked. "More wishful thinking?"

Heris said, "The dwarves left it. It was used to haul ammunition."

Eavijne had just grasped the spear Heartsplitter when an explosion ripped a dozen square yards out of the face of the Great Sky Fortress.

7. Tel Moussa: Specter of Tomorrow

The Mountain and his henchmen hungered for news from Dreanger. The longer it was delayed the more likely it was to be bad. Rumor had the disaster so great, no one had lived to tell the tale.

No veteran believed that. There were survivors, always.

Nassim Alizarin spent most of his time in the parapet, watching, unsure for what. His soldiers indulged him.

Mohkam came. "A messenger is coming." Which Nassim could see for himself.

Feeling half as old as time and burned clean of emotion, Nassim said, "This rider comes not from the south. This could be about something trivial." His gut disagreed. This would be the news they had been awaiting. And it would spark no joy.

Alizarin sighed, said, "Let's go offer the man a civilized welcome."

The great room of the fortress was the common space where the garrison took meals and did the day's handwork. General announcements occurred there and battle plans were rehearsed. It began to fill.

The messenger arrived barely able to remain upright. He radiated exhaustion. He wore clothing common to Indala's bodyguard. Nassim did not consider that a good omen.

The general had food and drink brought. He had men eager to ask questions pushed back and silenced. It cost nothing to wait a few minutes more.

The messenger nibbled some, drank some, recuperated visibly. "All right. I'm set. There was a chain of engagements. Some went Indala's way, some went Gordimer's. Days when Gordimer took the honors saw us lose more deserters than casualties. The Marshall had the same trouble. His Arianist Chaldarean troops left the field just before his Maxtreans took money to change sides."

"Then Indala was victorious?" Nassim asked.

"Barely. The fighting hasn't stopped. The Sha-lug refuse to give up. Er-Rashal unleashed great evils. Indala was badly injured. His brother took command. Then Gordimer died leading a Sha-lug charge that almost reversed our fortunes."

"So. The prophecy came to pass. Gordimer was brought low by an army out of the north. It just wasn't the army he expected."

"So they say."

"So Dreanger is taken. Now what?"

"Indala will regain his health. His champions will silence the die-hards and unify the kaifates so we can cleanse the Holy Lands before the new crusaders arrive."

That had been the plan from the beginning. Nassim observed, "There may be a hitch. Tsistimed the Golden. He could attack Lucidia before the Commander of the Righteous reaches the Holy Lands."

The messenger managed a grunt of interest.

"Tsistimed has been having trouble managing his sons. Despite his losses in the war with the ice country savages, he's sending armies into the Ghargarlicean Empire again, smaller forces commanded by his sons. If they reclaim territories lost when Tsistimed was preoccupied with the Chosen, he'll send them against the kaifate next, to keep the boys too busy to revolt."

"Not my concern, General. I've delivered my news. Now I need to lie down for a week. On my belly."

Nassim chuckled. He had been there. "I understand. A place has been prepared. Mohkam will show you."

Levering his stiffened body upright, the messenger said, "One more thing, from Azim al-Adil. Er-Rashal may flee this way instead of into the Hills of the Dead. Prisoners say he planned that after we captured al-Qarn."

Al-Qarn lay between the fighting and the wilds of Upper Dreanger, where a hundred generations of the dead of antiquity lay buried. Er-Rashal had gone into hiding there whenever he was unwelcome in al-Qarn.

The Mountain had a sinking feeling. "Why come this way?"

"Andesqueluz, apparently. He's more comfortable with the dead."

"Marvelous. Mohkam. Show him his bed. The rest of you. Officers. My old companions. To the parapet."

*   *   *

NASSIM ASKED, "AZ? A QUESTION?"

"Just a thought. That was grim news. Indala will have a hard time holding on to Dreanger. The Sha-lug will battle on."

A troop captain, from Indala's own tribe, said, "Your great enemy is no longer Marshall. What will that mean, here?"

"Joy and sorrow. Joy that he is no more. Sorrow that it was not my doing. But that isn't the answer you want. You want to know if Gordimer's demise changes our relationship."

"Correct, sir."

"I have an agreement with Indala. A contract. I will honor it. Further, Gordimer wasn't nearly the great enemy that er-Rashal was. Is. If he is headed our way he won't resist the impulse to do us harm."

Bone said, "Was I him, I'd hook up with Black Rogert. If I really wanted to have at us."

Could er-Rashal be wicked enough to turn on his own people?

Yes. Nor would it be the first time. Hell, he had turned on God Himself.

"He'll think about it. But his main interest will be Andesqueluz. Az? Am I right?"

"Probably. We brought him those mummies, back when. Nobody knew why. It looks like they didn't matter because he never did anything with them. It makes sense that he'd head for the Haunted City if he couldn't reach his usual hideout. There's something important to him there."

Nassim mused, "We don't know that he didn't get what he wanted from those mummies. He wouldn't tell anybody."

"He would have, in his own way. He would have used it."

"Probably so. Let's forget it. Let's look at tomorrow. What can we do to make him miserable if he does turn up?"

"Why are you looking at me?"

"Because you're the only Master of Ghosts within a hundred miles."

"But useless as a racing saddle on a pig in a face-off with er-Rashal."

"I don't want you to face off. I might ask you to be a Judas goat. And not that if we can lure him some other way."

Silence descended. After a time, one of the Mountain's old followers said, "The Lion has been laid low." He used a wondering tone suggesting that the point not be overlooked.

Bone said, "He's right, General. And Gordimer, being Gordimer, never made no arrangement for who should take over next. But, damn! I wanted it to be us who took him down."

Nassim said, "God has His Plan."

More silence. Alizarin's old companions retained little fervor for the Almighty's mysterious design.

Nassim added, "But God's Will is best executed by those who prepare most carefully. What could we do if we did lure er-Rashal into a trap?"

"You need to back up," the Master of Ghosts said.

"Az?"

"Before you go worry about that you need trustworthy intelligence on where the Rascal is, where's he's headed, and what he means to do once he gets there."

"Of course I do," the Mountain said. "But how will I get it? Send you out to ask him?"

Bone suggested, "You can't go wrong starting with his character. Who he is will determine what he does and the way he does it."

That precipitated a vigorous exchange. Anyone who knew anything about er-Rashal tossed it in.

In time, Nassim said, "I'm worn out. Let's sleep on this. The key points are: the Rascal's inflated opinion of himself, his contempt for the intelligence of others, and his hatred for us. That's where we'll find our leverage."

Alizarin went to his pallet wondering if he did not think too much of himself, too. Would the world's most powerful sorcerer, however petty, bother with the nagging fleas of Tel Moussa?

He should worry about Rogert du Tancret. Black Rogert meant to rid himself of the nuisance wasps' nest called Tel Moussa. That was common knowledge. The Mountain's Lucidian youths, who mixed with locals, heard it every day.

Of course, what they heard might be what Black Rogert wanted them to hear. The man was a cunning villain.

Nassim had plans for Black Rogert, built upon du Tancret's character.

Alizarin fell asleep wondering if his enemies studied him.

8. Antieux, in the Connec: Sorrow Wakens

Brother Candle watched two young girls care for Lumiere. Even without Kedle Richeut's cousin Escamerole supervising they would have treated the baby like a new little god. For all their savagery and bad temper, Count Raymone and Countess Socia were venerated in Antieux.

Bernardin Amberchelle found him. "Master?" He beckoned.

Stepping out, the Perfect remarked, "You're back. And you look excited."

"I am. A messenger came from Khaurene. The Queen says it's time for Raymone to take over as Duke. She wants to get back to Navaya."

"She's had a change of heart?"

"Sort of. She's decided she needs Connecten support to offset the Navayan nobility. Raymone is the only Duke most Connectens will accept."

"I thought she got along with her nobility."

"You know the class. There are always villains looking for a chance."

The way of mankind, Brother Candle reflected. A breed never satisfied and often willing to indulge in the ugliest behavior to snatch up any gossamer strand of power. "All right. But there's more, right?"

"Yes. We didn't find what we were after. But that was because the ship sent to get Serenity off his island ran into a Plataduran galley." Bernardin had friends in remarkable places. "But here's the hot stuff. Next time Serenity tries he may have Anselin with him. Anselin has disappeared. Those who went to the Holy Lands with him don't know what became of him."

"You mean to head them off on the river?"

"We'll go back out as soon as we refit."

"And you want me to tag along to bear witness to your wonder work."

"Not at all. We want you to stay here and make Socia act like she's somebody's mother."

The Perfect's mouth opened and shut but he had nothing to say.

"Raymone isn't blind. He sees Socia making a bad start. We both suffered through bad mothers. He hoped Sister Claire would make his point. But Socia is Socia. That was far too subtle." Which explained Sister Claire, using Raymone's logic. "Raymone wants Socia to be a better mother than his was. But he doesn't know how to get her to do it."

"And I do?" Why not just shove Socia up against a wall and tell her? The girl understood plain speech, directly delivered.

"Socia worships you. Maybe because she never knew her father."

"I understand that."

"She does listen to you."

"On rare occasions. When I trick her into thinking she came up with the idea herself, then challenge it, so she gets stubborn and defends it."

"There you go. You've found a way the rest of us couldn't." Bernardin continued, "We won't stay long. We want to be gone before the bishop's spies figure out what we're doing. So Raymone says. But I think he wants to go before Socia decides she's healthy enough to tag along."

"I agree. Socia does need to understand that her obligations as a mother didn't end with the delivery."

"Excellent. I'll tell Raymone he can count on you."

"About Khaurene . . ."

"Use that to distract Socia. Let her organize the expedition while she learns how to care for Lumiere. Raymone means to head west as soon as we handle this. Maybe dragging some high-profile prisoners." Bernardin chuckled. "Wouldn't Isabeth love to lay hands on Serenity?"

"I wouldn't want to be in his boots. Or even Anselin's. Though she'd probably ransom Anselin. He hasn't done anything."

"Tell Socia not to make you walk. You deserve a sedan."

"Now you're trying to bribe me."

"Maybe. Take care. We shouldn't be gone more than two weeks."

SOCIA WAS ON A RANT. SHE STAMPED AROUND, ARMS FLAILING. SHE used disreputable language and made no sense. Brother Candle had to suffer her wrath because Raymone was beyond reach. He paid little attention.

"You're not even listening to me!"

"What's that? I wasn't listening."

"Pay attention!"

"Not necessary. I won't hear anything new."

"You're up to something, old man. What the hell is it?"

"What's your child's name?"

"What?" Taken off guard. "Lumiere. Why ask me a dumb question like that?"

"Who is Lumiere's mother?"

"I am. What are you doing, Master?"

"What did you think of Sister Claire? Raymone's mother?"

That stoked her fire. The only people she thought less of were people she had not met: Anne of Menand, Serenity, and, maybe, the Captain-General of the Patriarchal forces. Maybe.

Brother Candle asked, "Did Raymone tell you about having that woman for a mother?"

"Yes." Another rant, but shorter and tremulous. She knew she was being set up.

"Where is Lumiere?" The trap began to shut.

Frowning, "I'm not sure. With his nurses."

"No doubt. No doubt. But here is the question I need you to answer. The important one. Give it some thought. Don't just blurt something."

"Shoot."

"Why isn't Lumiere with his mother? Why doesn't his mother know where he is?" And, as she was about to explode, "Why does Raymone dislike his mother so much?"

BROTHER CANDLE DID NOT EXPECT TO WORK MIRACLES. SOCIA'S CHARacter had been under construction for years. A fresh recollection of Sister Claire only provided a small hammer.

Because he was who he was and his opinion mattered, Socia made an effort. But, even with the best intentions, she could not make herself into the perfect mother for the next Count of Antieux.

She shone much brighter at organizing the convoy for the journey to Khaurene.

Socia snarled, "I'll never thank you for telling me I'm like Raymone's mother. It makes me feel awful."

"I understand, girl. You are what you are. But you have to make the effort. For Lumiere's sake."

"Master, if there was any way . . ."

"Maybe if you'd had a father and mother yourself . . ."

"Stop. I can't be a traditional mother. I hurt because I have that lack. But I will do my best."

"That's all I ask. Raymone's mother never tried."

Socia indulged in a rant against her own failings.

"Really, girl, all you need to do is show the child that he means enough for you to make an effort. Whatever your feelings, remember that you're not alone. Raymone is there. Have him remind you that though there are good men who had bad mothers there aren't many bad men who had good mothers."

"There you go again. No matter what I do, I can't win."

"Aren't you getting more fanciful by the minute."

BERNARDIN AMBERCHELLE RETURNED TO ANTIEUX SIXTEEN DAYS after his last conversation with Brother Candle. Three injured men carried him. He was the worst injured of the four.

Brother Candle heard it first as a rumor. Something dire had happened. He hastened to the Garete family citadel.

Furtive villains with a Society look were sneaking and lurking already.

*   *   *

"THERE YOU ARE!" SOCIA GROWLED WHEN, IN ACCORDANCE WITH IN-structions, Brother Candle joined her in Count Raymone's audience chamber. He found the mix there curious. In addition to those func-tionaries to be expected in a crisis there were representatives from the religious minorities and the magnates of trade. And, close by the Count-ess, an especially grim Kedle Richeut, who beckoned Brother Candle.

Socia finished saying something to Alfeas Machin, the region's pre-mier vintner, and turned to Brother Candle. "Raymone came out on the short end."

"It was a trap?"

"No. But the effect was the same. The big dummy forgot that Se-renity was the bull sorcerer of the Collegium before he bought the Patriarchal Throne. He tried to capture the man instead of just killing him. A serious advantage for Serenity, who had no reason to hold back."

The old man could think of no response.

"Bernardin says Serenity's gang was wiped out. Serenity was hurt but escaped. Our survivors weren't in any shape to chase him."

"And Anselin?"

"He wasn't there. Oh, fun!"

Bishop LaVelle had arrived. He was dressed in state and attended by lesser priests. He headed for the Countess, pushing people out of his way. He showed no deference to the Countess, no doubt consider-ing her "just" a woman.

On the other hand, Brother Candle did not see the all-consuming arrogance characteristic of LaVelle's predecessors.

The bishop commenced some sort of declaration.

Socia said, "Kedle, it is time."

Kedle smacked the bishop in the back of the head with an axe handle. His companions found themselves facing swords, spears, and crossbows. Socia said, "Put them into the cells. I'll deal with them later. Round up any Society vermin who come out of the woodwork."

Kedle said, "I'm on my way." She prodded the groggy bishop with her axe handle.

Many of Count Raymone's retainers went along when Kedle left.

Brother Candle started to speak.

"In a minute." Socia stood. She had been sitting in the seat that belonged to the Countess of Antieux. "The situation is in hand, people. Go back to your lives. Report unacceptable behavior when you see it. Raymone may be gone but that changes nothing. Antieux will be what Count Raymone Garete made it."

Socia drove her point home by moving to her husband's high seat.

The crowd buzzed while leaving. Socia leaned toward Brother Candle. "I'll need you more than ever, now."

"Really?"

"I'll need you close to rein in my wrath. Terrible things are cooking inside me."

"We can deal with that if you're honest with me. Right now you need to focus on keeping the peace." Outrages and atrocities were afoot already, he was sure.

"This isn't a good day to be a known Episcopal. Or, worse, a member of the Society." Slight smile.

Brother Candle had a sinking feeling.

She meant to let the mob exhaust itself on the Brothen Church, guilt or innocence irrelevant.

"Or to be Devedian or Dainshau?" Those minorities always suffered when civil order lapsed.

"No. I won't tolerate that."

A curious, violent child, Socia Rault. How would she enforce the safety of the traditional scapegoats?

Brother Candle prayed to the Good God that Raymone Garete was just lost. Or up to something deeply secret, and not truly dead. Otherwise, there would be no restraining Socia's darker side.

He knew the hope was vain while hoping it.

9. Realm of the Gods: Twilight of the World

Gray smoke boiled out of the face of the Great Sky Fortress. A fierce rumble descended upon Piper Hecht and his companions, followed by a hailstorm of debris. Two smaller explosions followed that.

"What the hell?" Heris demanded. "What was that?"

"Somebody tripped my booby trap," Hecht replied.

"Who could?" Anna asked. "Everybody is out."

Debris kept falling. The stench of burnt firepowder arrived.

Hecht watched Eavijne. The explosion had so startled her that she had lost her hold on Heartsplitter, then her footing. She snatched at Geistrier but snagged it with just one finger. She lost her sack of apples, then her grip when she tried to save the fruit.

She commenced the long fall. Knife-edged basalt awaited two thousand feet below.

The ascendant changed shape, violently and painfully. He screamed as he plunged after Eavijne, a giant eagle driving itself downward faster than the goddess fell.

That was drama enough to halt all progress down the road to the harbor.

Heris asked, "Did you include godshot in your booby trap, Piper?"

"I did. Everything I could find, including two falcons. Whoever set it off has to be one of the devils."

"That's probably good thinking."

The eagle caught the falling goddess. The pair passed out of sight.

Heris said, "How about we get on down, too? Before somebody gets into mischief down there."

Hecht grunted. He was watching the rent in the Great Sky Fortress.

Heris suggested, "We might cobble up a couple more infernal devices." She helped Hecht stare.

The breeze dispersed the smoke.

Hecht said, "Didn't do damage enough."

A black stain like heavy treacle flowed out of the breach and down the face of the fortress. Its boundaries were defined. It left no trail.

"The Trickster," Hecht said. "He broke out."

"The violent vibrations of the hammer mill must have weakened some of the seals. We didn't notice."

"That would explain why we felt his emotions toward the end. We should have been suspicious."

"Stuff happens when you get in a hurry. The bucket is turned over now. Let's get down there. I have the tools to deal with this."

Hecht was amazed. Heris remained unconcerned. The escape of a seriously wicked Instrumentality was just a piece of business to be handled.

While the old folks fussed the girls ran to the edge of the gap to see what happened to Asgrimmur and Eavijne. Lila said, "Can't see them. But they'll be the first ones down."

The girls considered the creeping stain on the face of the fortress. They considered the bridge, then the gap beneath. They whispered. Then Vali darted across the bridge.

Hecht bit down on a potentially distracting bellow. Asgrimmur was not there to catch another falling girl.

Anna held her tongue, too.

Pella said, "I love her, but that girl is a freak."

Hard to argue, watching her fearless dash across colorful air.

Vali whipped Geistrier off the brass post and headed back, coiling as she came. She plucked Heartsplitter out of the fabric of the bridge, then managed it and the rope both as she came on.

Anna said, "You'd almost think she was one of them."

"Yes." For the first time in a long time Hecht wondered about Vali Dumaine.

She came straight to him, handed him the spear. "Can you believe it's that light?"

Hecht exchanged looks with Anna while the others watched Geistrier shorten to its original length.

Vali tied the coil to her belt. "Where did that hammer end up? I bet we could break the bridge with it."

The creeping treacle had vanished behind the curtain wall surrounding the Great Sky Fortress.

Hecht responded, "That could be. But it's not here. Girl, we need to talk about you taking risks." From the corner of his eye he caught Lila pulling a face at Vali, then smirking.

Heris said, "Save the lecture, Piper. We're going to be last down the mountain as it is."

"Let's get hiking."

Anna quipped, "This should be easier than coming up."

"Kids. No running."

THE BLACK STAIN FLOWED INTO EAVIJNE'S GARDEN. IT POSSESSED JUST enough energy to keep moving. Saturated with silver dust, it suffered abiding agony. Already diminished by its struggle to break through compromised seals, it had not been alert enough to smell the silver powder trap.

It lived, but with little power or strength, little ability to reason, and little sense of identity. Instinct took it to the orchard where it found just one overlooked, shriveled green apple that did little to restore it.

It did what no rational god would have done. It engulfed the only living tree. It understood the enormity of its action only after it finished.

That was the last tree. There might be no more golden fruit. Starved for life and restored immortality, the Trickster might have written the deaths of all the Old Ones.

Hatred and rage so possessed him that he did not care for long.

He took the shape of a slim youth of middle height, his hair a mixture of streaks and shades of ginger that made it look like his head was on fire. He had a hatchet face, flushed because of his emotional state.

He stepped through the broken orchard wall, headed for the rainbow bridge. He thought he was moving brisk and businesslike. An observer might have suspected intoxication or mental defect.

He started across.

Once again hunger trumped reason.

He swallowed some of the magic holding the bridge together. It was Aelen Kofer magic. He did not gain much from it. He would need massive draughts to benefit, like a man surviving by eating grass and river mud.

The rainbow unraveled.

He cried out once, startled, as he began his fall.

He had stolen just enough magic to change into a generic-looking gliding thing that, nevertheless, could do no more than slow its descent enough to choose a place to smack down.

The harbor extended a siren call but it was in the open. He would be seen.

He did not want his escape to be known. There was revenge to pursue.

He passed over the Aelen Kofer town, toward the scrubby wilderness beyond. One wing tip brushed a stunted treetop. He spun. He hit the ground hard. Pain became his universe.

Even gods, if incautious or inattentive, must suffer the laws of physics.

GODS, GODDESSES, AND MIDDLE-WORLD FOLK CROWDED THE AELEN Kofer tavern. Vast quantities of ale disappeared. The dwarves had been kind enough to leave many barrels.

Ferris Renfrow and Cloven Februaren dragged themselves well under the weather. Asgrimmur tried but no longer had the knack. He was trapped in eagle form. Eavijne was not there to celebrate with or for him. The instant she set her feet on solid ground she rushed off to recover her dropped nubbins. Anna became tipsy. The children became incensed because they were allowed neither to celebrate nor to wander out of sight. Pella, especially, thought he could be helping Eavijne.

Hecht whispered to Heris, "I thought you were hot to get down here and suck up some of Iron Eyes's finest."

"I was. I am. But I can't let my hair down till I have everything tied up. I don't."

"Uhm?"

"You saw what came off the mountain behind us."

"The Trickster, I presume."

"No one else. So what I'm going to do is get some sleep, then I'll get out there and do something about him."

Hecht had questions. He let them slide. What Heris hoped to accomplish remained an enigma. It did seem obvious that the Trickster had to be eliminated from the process.

"I'll go with you."

"Piper . . ."

"Knock it off, Heris. You know . . ."

"By Aaron's Hairy Balls, Piper! Are we two of a kind, or what?"

"Or what, as Pinkus would say. You're right. Neither of us can help thinking we know better than the whole damned rest of the world. Lucky for me, I'm right."

"The folk of Santerin have a word for what's coming out of your mouth. That word, rendered in my finest Church Brothen, is bullshit!"

A snicker interrupted them.

Cloven Februaren had appeared, quietly. "You kids want to do some god-hunting, you'd better round up all the allies you can. The Trickster is a first-ranker. He won't go quietly."

Hecht admitted, "He's got a point."

Heris nodded. "He does. You volunteering, Double Great?"

"After I sleep it off. Though I'd say volunteerism isn't relevant. The Trickster has to be dealt with if the rest of us want to get out of here. So, tame him or kill him. Soon. Because we're locked up till Iron Eyes knows that letting us out won't be a disaster for the Nine Worlds."

"Right," Heris admitted. "So get your sleep. We'll start early."

"Where are you going?" Hecht asked.

"To the smithy. To find out what tools and options the Aelen Kofer left. Then I'll put me away for the night, too."

FEBRUAREN ASKED, "HOW MANY FRIENDS DOES LUCKE HAVE AMONGST our Old Ones?"

"Luck?" Hecht asked, looking past the old man at the Instrumentalities joining the hunt.

"The Trickster. He's like Ordnan. His name is seldom spoken. It has a lot of regional variants. Luke. Lucke. Luche. Luck. And others."

"Oh. Right. Where's Heris?"

"Here," from behind him.

Februaren said, "He's out there. He's badly hurt. On the surface it looks like he has no friends and no way of regaining any strength. Eavijne got her fruit back—with Pella's devoted assistance."

Ferris Renfrow, ragged and hung over, arrived. He grumbled, "So let's do this. So I can go back to bed."

Hecht exchanged glances with Heris. They had been killing gods long enough to know that the Trickster still had options, especially if he was up for a little divine cannibalism.

The myths did not define his limits or boundaries.

Heris asked, "Double Great, do you or your cronies have any idea where he is? Or how strong he is?"

"He's weak as a baby. As gods go. Weaker than Kharoulke was. And getting weaker because there is no magic to tap. I can't tell you where he is. I do know the right direction."

"Thank you." Heris exchanged looks with Hecht.

Hecht asked, "What resources do we have now that we didn't have on top of the mountain?" He had seen the gap in the rainbow bridge.

"Lots of iron. Aelen Kofer love iron. And some silver. That surprised me. I thought for sure they'd take every grain. And there's a partial keg of firepowder but nothing to use it in except a couple of old hand-helds."

"We won't need to shoot him if he isn't agile. We can scatter coins and iron filings on him and watch him melt."

Heris said, "There aren't any coins. The dwarves took those. Unless you have some in your pocket."

"A few pennies. I'll ask Anna and the kids. They'll have a few in their shoes or up their sleeves."

HECHT, HERIS, FEBRUAREN, THE BASTARD, AND THE ASCENDANT formed the advance party. Asgrimmur flapped around overhead, scouting. He was hard to understand when he shouted down. A half-dozen Old Ones followed at a distance.

The Trickster was not hard to find. He was a straight walk out through uncomfortable terrain, still where he had fallen, two miles from the Aelen Kofer town.

He was a disappointment. A once major Instrumentality had become a semitransparent blob pulsating slowly amongst the rocks and debris of the woodland floor. That blob inspired neither fear, nor awe, nor dread. Dirt and broken leaves covered it. It leaked. In the middle world it would have been the focus of a storm of insects.

Hecht said, "Let's kill it and go." He pointed his hand-held at a purple-brown kidney shape inside the blob.

Which began a feeble flow into the shadow under a rock overhang. Before Hecht fired, Februaren asked, "Why not try to make contact? We could have the cleverest god ever managing our dirty tricks for us."

Asgrimmur waddled close. He tried biting the blob. Hecht suspected the ghosts he harbored wanted some vengeance of their own.

Heris said, "Or we can kill him and never have to watch our backs."

She and Hecht fired their hand-helds. Hecht followed up with silver coins. Heris scattered iron filings from the smithy.

A divine psychic shriek followed, freighted with despair and disbelief, the death cry of an entity long convinced that its end was a mystic impossibility.

The blob began to liquefy and melt into the soil.

Heris observed, "I'd say this is anticlimactic."

"But useful in the extreme." Hecht nodded toward the posse of gods watching. "Look at them. Appalled. Crushed. The shiftiest one of all got rubbed out by a couple of middle-world mortals. Let's hope they keep that in mind."

Renfrow, Februaren, and Asgrimmur all made noises of indeterminate meaning. Renfrow added, "And the Gray Walker did nothing to keep that from happening."

Asgrimmur croaked, "Patience ran out."

In myth Ordnan had tolerated mischief, wickedness, and outright betrayal. In myth Lucke was supposed to bring on the fall of the Old Ones. His children would be great monsters on the plain of final combat, fighting against the Old Ones.

Hecht said, "This kind of changes all that, doesn't it?"

Februaren said, "All that changed at al-Khazen."

Renfrow said, "Or al-Khazen could have been the Twilight struggle beginning. The myths could just be an interpretation."

Hecht did not want to hear that hypothesis.

The last of the liquefied Instrumentality sank into the earth.

Heris said, "Suggestions? Anyone? Let him be? Dig all this up and burn it? Scatter it? Mix in poison, like iron ore that will kill him if he tries to pull himself back together?"

Renfrow said, "How about all of the above? Heating this earth in a smelter with the iron ore." He showed a thin smirk.

Heris eyed him suspiciously.

He said, "When you've been around as long as me it gets easy to infer plans from actions. You've been especially interested in the smithy."

Februaren asked, "Where's the egg? There ought to be a big one. Right?"

Heris said, "So Renfrow sees what I've been thinking. We'll need every able body, though. Renfrow. One last time. Would anyone here try to help the Trickster get through this?"

"No." But, then, "Not on the surface. Secretly, maybe. The motives of the Night . . ."

"Mysterious ways. Asgrimmur, flap back there and tell those folks what we're going to do."

The eagle gave a raptor shriek, clumsily took to the air.

Watching his short flight, Hecht said, "I think he likes the eagle shape."

Februaren responded, "He'd better. He'll be stuck in it if we don't get out of here."

Asgrimmur returned, settled heavily onto a boulder. He spoke slowly and carefully. "We do not have much time. The world is dying. What used to be . . . the distance is all fog and gray." He flew away again.

"Isn't that special news?" Heris said.

Februaren said, "Worth keeping in mind."

Rattled, Renfrow asked, "You do have a plan for getting out, don't you?"

Heris growled, "We would've been gone already if this asswipe hadn't gotten loose." She kicked the ground.

People and divinities brought tools and buckets. Heris took a shovel, turned over some earth, told them, "I need all the dirt that looks like it's soaked with oil. Haul it back to the smithy."

She filled two buckets and headed out.

HERIS HAD PAID ATTENTION WHEN KHOR-BEN JARNEYN HAD WAXED eloquent about dwarfish industrial techniques.

"The girl is like that," Cloven Februaren grumbled. "Iron Eyes bored the socks off the rest of us. The more excited he got, the more boring he was. But Heris ate it up. You want to talk dirty to that girl, talk the metallurgy of the Night."

"You're in a fine mood, Double Great," Heris said, breaking dirt up and feeding it to the smithy furnace, burning just warm enough to cook the moisture out and hot enough to kill anything living in the soil that the Trickster could use as a condensation point. That done, she increased the heat, created several hundred pounds of grossly impure glass. The liquid went into ceramic molds once used to cast ingots. It cooled. And at the center of one lay a glowing soul egg that looked like it contained living fire.

"Look at this, Piper! Am I a genius, or what?"

"When it comes to doing nasty unto the Night, you are the queen."

Heris sweet-talked the one male god into showing off by demon-strating how far out into the harbor he could chuck the glass ingots. But the one containing the fiery egg she took to the tavern, where it went on display.

Asking Ferris Renfrow, Cloven Februaren, and Asgrimmur to be attentive to potential reservations and possible loopholes, Heris treated the Old Ones to a fresh round of oath bindings. She then told Hecht, "Finally! I can settle down and have a beer." And, then, "If I get too drunk don't any of you bastards take advantage of me." Then she broached her own small keg of dark ale.

PIPER HECHT HAD A HANGOVER, HIS FIRST EVER. HE DID NOT ENJOY it. Nor did the fact that so many others suffered equally improve his mood. Anna and the children had avoided the curse by going to bed before the celebration got rowdy.

"I didn't do anything but take a few sips," Hecht complained to Asgrimmur. He got no sympathy. The ascendant had been unable to do the kind of drinking he would have liked. Drinking had been a manly art in the culture of his youth.

Hecht had nursed one mug all evening, shaking his head at the Old Ones. They, like their original worshippers, thought a good time was to get stinking drunk and start a fight.

They had done some serious damage to the tavern.

Anna brought Hecht a breakfast of ham slices and cheese chunks. Both were old and smoked and required determined chewing. "Piper, tell Heris we really need to get out of here. The Instrumentalities are devouring everything. We'll be down to nothing but beer tomorrow."

Hecht grunted. He rubbed the heels of his hands against his tem-ples. That did not help. "Are we out of bread?"

"Yes. And most of the ingredients for baking it. We have a little cured meat and hard cheese. Even the dried fruit is gone."

Vali materialized. "I found some onions, Dad. Must be two hun-dred pounds."

Onions sounded better than desiccated ham.

"None of us will mind onions before long. Now what?" The Old Ones had just jumped as though collectively goosed. They began mur-muring.

"Get Heris." Hecht produced his handheld firepowder weapon. It clunked against the tabletop.

He had no match handy but doubted that would matter. The Old Ones did not understand the weapons. They had trouble with most things mechanical. That was Aelen Kofer stuff.

He chewed tough meat and watched. Heris joined him. She chewed tough meat, watched, and said nothing, either.

Cloven Februaren arrived. Ferris Renfrow followed. Both were suffering.

Februaren moaned, "In a sane world an accomplished sorcerer could banish a hangover in seconds."

Renfrow grunted and growled, "In a world with color and magic."

There was no color in the tavern whatsoever, which Hecht took to indicate a total lack of magic.

He felt his left wrist. His amulet was there.

Februaren noted the movement. Weakly, he said, "No magic at all."

Two Old Ones left their crowd. Male and female, they looked like healthy humans about forty years of age. Hourlr and Hourli. They were twins. And not originally Shining Ones. They were Raneul, gods the Old Ones had defeated in the War of the Gods. Some of the defeated had left their world for the Realm of the Gods after that war's end.

The curious character inside Piper Hecht wanted to ask questions until he ferreted out details of that conflict.

The twins faced him. Their manner was respectful. The female said, "It is plain that you do not trust us, despite the oaths and assurances you have extracted."

"Talk to Heris." He indicated his sister. "She decides here." A nod. "As you wish." Hourli nodded.

The male god spoke to her. "You judge us all by the example of Lucke. You believe that his behavior is what can be expected of us all. That is not the way it will be."

Hecht was inclined to observe that only one rogue Instrumentality was needed to bring on the pain. He kept silent.

Heris said, "Most knowledge of you has vanished from the middle world. You live on only in the folk stories of peasants and Asgrimmur's recollections from the Great Sky Fortress. And in the Bastard's mind. None of those sources offer any reason to trust the Shining Ones."

"Perhaps. The mortal perspective must, of necessity, be different. However, mortality is being taken into account. We are investing in our own survival. We must immigrate to the middle world for the power. While we are there, during your time, we will cleave to our promises. Without trickery. Without treachery. Without legalistic mumbo jumbo being used to evade understood obligations. We face extinction. That is no sweet prospect."

The female divinity continued, speaking to Hecht. "It used to be

thought best for us to be seen as clever and tricky—though that reputation came more from muddled, delusional mortal thinking than
from deliberate divine mischief."

Hecht was not sure he understood, but that sounded good.

KORBAN IRON EYES BURST INTO THE TAVERN, STUMBLED, NEARLY FELL.
Audacious but inauspicious. A dozen short, wide, hairy, ferocious-
looking dwarves followed. All wore armor and an arsenal of sharps.

The Aelen Kofer.

Every dwarf had a slow match sputtering atop his or her helmet.
Every dwarf's personal weaponry included at least two handheld falcons.

Hecht muttered to Heris, "I didn't think it would be long before
they started playing with firepowder toys."

"Good news, them turning up, though."

The return of the dwarves meant a way out of the Realm of the
Gods. If Iron Eyes decided to let them go.

None of the Old Ones bullied the Aelen Kofer. Wise, considering
survival was at stake.

The crown prince of the dwarves strutted around, eyeballing each
Old One and middle-worlder. He got the cold eye from Piper Hecht,
then a snicker.

"Something amusing you?"

"Your hair is on fire."

"Yikes!" Smoldering because of a rogue slow match, Khor-ben Jarneyn was less intimidating than he hoped.

Jarneyn's son dumped water on his father's head. The indignity
wrung the tension out of the moment.

Iron Eyes pretended amusement. "Heris. Girl. You've exceeded my
expectations. You winkled them out and you tamed them. What were
the odds?"

Copper said, "I knew you'd do it."

"Are you flirting with me?"

Nothing of the sort had been in the younger dwarf's mind. He
sputtered like the match atop his helmet.

"Just messing with you. Iron Eyes, stop pretending to be some serious badass and help us get out of this dump before we starve."

"Living on onions and beer? Sounds like paradise to me."

"You've been listening at keyholes."

Hecht was startled. That was daring. Iron Eyes had a real capacity
to make her miserable. "Heris."

"I know. I'll stop, now."

Iron Eyes said, "I apologize. I really didn't think you'd get it under control."

"We're all set. Agreements are in place. In exchange for freedom the Shining Ones will help Piper. And, once they have their strength back, they'll help with Kharoulke's extended family. So. Talk to me about how to get home."

"It's pretty basic, my love. Same as when we opened the way for your elderly relative, before. Pack your bags and strap on your sea legs."

"All right." Heris started to rise.

"Let me look around first. Just to make sure everything is what it seems."

"You're the judge. You get to do whatever you want. That was our deal."

"Such a mixture of temptation. Letting everything just fade away is huge. The Aelen Kofer would feel that some balance had been achieved. But we did make promises. Though we reserved the right to be flexible concerning our own survival."

"But not so worried that somebody might recognize you as major bullshitters. Come on, Iron Eyes! I've seen you in action. I know what you're up to."

"You are a marvel, Heris. I do wish you had been born Aelen Kofer. I'd add you to my harem."

"Pity, that." As one of the squat and hairies delivered a solid punch to the crown prince's left bicep. "But I'd insist on exclusive rights. So, we're going sailing."

"Rowing. It's the only way."

"A half truth but why cavil about paths through the world of the Aelen Kofer? I want to go home. Though I do have something to do before we go." She left briskly. Iron Eyes exchanged interrogatory glances with the men around the table, then shrugged.

Heris came back with the soul eggs of the Trickster, Red Hammer, and Zyr. She fumbled them onto a table facing the Shining Ones, indicated which was which. "It's possible I could restore these three. I'm the only one who can. I'll hear arguments, for and against. I'll keep in mind the characters of the individuals." Not so subtly saying she was disinclined to hear support for the Trickster.

The gods had opinions. They expressed those, loudly.

"Stop!" Heris barked. "I don't want a debate. We'll vote. And I claim a vote for myself. First, Lucke. I vote for no mercy. The son of a bitch stays here."

Six Old Ones agreed. Sprenghul and Fastthal dithered, then reluctantly agreed with the others.

Little patience was accorded them. They were the least of the rescued Instrumentalities.

"All right. Excellent. The Trickster stays." She indicated the soul egg of the war god. "I have no opinion. I know nothing about him. I'll vote only if there's a tie."

A tiebreaker was not needed. The quiet, no longer well-known Zyr was universally respected. His peers seemed to think he should take over as top deity. He was the eldest and wisest.

"Which leaves Red Hammer, no thinker or planner, which is why he ended up this way. I've heard the arguments about him. They don't make me think that he won't do something else deadly stupid if I restore him."

The Old Ones voted. Three were in favor of restoration. Two were against it. Hourli and Hourlr abstained, as did Red Hammer's stepdaughter, Aldi.

The rest did not care, one way or another.

Heris said, "I'll stand with the nays. For now. Meaning we have a three way tie. Iron Eyes. Take care of Lucke and Red Hammer. Lucke to be left here. Red Hammer can go home with you and be preserved. And why do I see a gleam in your beady little eyes, all of a sudden?"

"Lucke at the mercy of the Aelen Kofer? When he has done so much evil to us? Priceless."

"You can't take revenge on him, Iron Eyes."

"But . . ."

"To do that you'd need to restore him. That can't happen. Avoiding any chance of a comeback is why I want to leave him here. If he leaves this world, sooner or later he'll come into contact with people like those in the Connec who wanted to resurrect those Old Ones there."

Iron Eyes gave these Old Ones an ugly look. "So you'll lay it all off on me?"

"For now. One day when Red Hammer isn't a danger anymore I'll bring him back."

Sheaf protested.

Heris told her, "Not for a while. I don't want him coming out swinging again. Understand?"

Piper Hecht caught Februaren's eye. His ancestor seemed astounded by the modern Heris, too.

*   *   *

A SHIP LAY AGAINST THE QUAY IN THE HARBOR. THE DERELICT WAS A permanent fixture. It barely remained afloat. When the magic was strong, though, it became the golden barge of the gods.

Dwarf oarsmen drove the barge across the harbor till it encountered an invisible barrier. From the quay the view to seaward ended in fog. At the barrier, though, a good hard squint let a viewer see the middle world beyond: choppy, dark gray, frigid waters scattered with random chunks of ice calved not far to the north. This corner of the middle world had forsaken summer.

Iron Eyes told the Old Ones, "Brace yourselves. The middle-world magic isn't strong anymore but what remains will bite sharper than anything you've tasted in years. Don't lose yourselves when it hits you."

Asgrimmur had assumed a solitary station aft. Hecht asked Heris, "Is he sulking?"

"He's scared. He doesn't want to walk the Construct again. Last time he nearly didn't make it out the other end."

"I know that terror." His experiences had been soul-crushing. "Though it wasn't so bad doing it in a big family glob. Tell him to fly. He's got wings."

"Good idea. Though he'd really like to get his human shape back."

Iron Eyes and his crew worked on the gate to the middle world. Everyone recognized the instant the first gap opened.

The gods gasped. Several shrieked. Faint though it was, the magic tasted delicious.

"Easy!" Iron Eyes bellowed. "Don't make me knock heads!"

The gods became restless but rationality survived. Iron Eyes went around reminding them that only patience would assure survival. The way had to be opened so the barge could pass through.

Threads of color raced through the harbor water. Golden light sparked on decomposing wood.

"And here we go," Iron Eyes soon said. "Discipline couldn't last."

Several Old Ones abandoned human form to become gray mists that tangled and struggled to get to the magic.

"They'll spread some terror round the islands where the mer live," Februaren said.

The hunger overpowered several more. Heris said, "Let's hope they remember their obligations."

The opening of the way continued. Iron Eyes proceeded cautiously. Hecht asked, "You expecting trouble?"

"After what Heris did to Kharoulke? With the obvious assistance of the Aelen Kofer? Why would I be careful sliding into his world? His ilk will want to make sure that never happens to them."

"Can't stop it now. The knowledge is loose. Not even God Himself can make it go away."

Blasphemy! God could do anything. There were no limits on Him. Hecht wanted to believe that. He could not. Not anymore.

"That truth won't keep the primal Instrumentalities from trying, Commander of the Righteous."

No doubt.

Asgrimmur came up to check the size of the opening as the last two Old Ones surrendered to their hunger. He raised a wing some, let it relax. "Almost time. Heris. Be careful making your transition." He hopped onto the rail, balanced precariously, flung himself forward. He came within inches of ending up wet. He did dip each wing tip once before gaining altitude.

Hecht asked Heris, "There something going on between you two?"

"Not yet."

"Heris!"

"I didn't mean that the way you're thinking. Though it wouldn't be any of your damned business if I did."

"Heris!" He tried out his boss male voice.

"Butt out, little brother. Or look forward to a long walk home. Shouldn't take you more than three months if you survive the swim to Friesland."

Februaren and Renfrow were amused but kept quiet.

Heris grumbled, "For thirty-eight years men told me what I could and couldn't do. And I was miserable. That's done. I'll make my own misery, now, thank you very much."

Februaren made a small gesture, out of her sight, suggesting that Hecht shut the hell up.

"As you will," Hecht said, conceding her personal sovereignty, but confused by her desire.

Each time he thought he had adapted his new world smacked him with something else.

Iron Eyes shouted in the Aelen Kofer tongue. The oars backed water. The barge rotated, then surged through the gateway.

Even Piper Hecht felt the difference when the barge crossed over.

Renfrow was gone in seconds, by whatever means he used. That left only Piper Hecht and his hodgepodge family.

Heris asked, "Double Great, are you going with the rest of us? Or are you up to something of your own?"

Februaren's answer seemed more calculated than it should have been. So Hecht thought.

"I have my own chores to attend. I'll see you at the townhouse." He vanished with an audible pop.

Heris told the others, "Get in here close, around Piper. Anna, you and Pella need to be in the middle, too. Lila and Vali, same as before. Piper, hang on to this." She handed him the soul egg of Zyr, wrapped in Aelen Kofer cheesecloth.

He was startled by the weight. It was as heavy as iron. "What?"

"Just hang on to it. Going through. I'll need my hands free. You drop it in transit, we'll all end up sorry. Maybe. I can't say for sure. I just know that I can't take you home and mess with that at the same time. Pella. Come."

The boy was admiring the cold Andorayan Sea and cliffs of ice to the north. His aunt had destroyed the Windwalker up there just a way.

Hecht shoved the egg inside his shirt, adjusting it securely.

Korban Iron Eyes shouted at his rowers to turn the barge. He meant to head right back into the Realm of the Gods.

The family Hecht clumped up. Iron Eyes said, "In a few hours there'll be no more Nine Worlds. We'll seal the Realm and let it die. Heris. Caution your ancestor against jumping in there again. He'll die. There will be nothing left but the Trickster's soul egg."

"I'll tell him, though I can't imagine him wanting to go back."

"It's been a joy knowing you, Heris. Recall the Aelen Kofer well, with an occasional much of ale, if you can."

Hecht grasped what Heris did not. Iron Eyes was saying goodbye forever. He meant to have no congress with the middle world henceforth. For him this was a chapter writ complete.

Hecht felt the soul egg. It now felt as heavy as a dozen bricks, and warm, but it was secure. He wrapped arms around Anna and Pella, who did the same to him. Heris and the girls squished in hard against the core threesome, holding onto one another as well.

The light went out for Piper Hecht.

10. Alten Weinberg: Fearful of Tomorrow

Empress Apparent Helspeth was depressed. She did not foresee a time when she might feel normal again. News of Katrin's demise had not yet officially reached Alten Weinberg. Even so, the Empress-to-be felt the crushing weight of Empire. How much worse would that become once every greedy Elector and noble started bullying her?

Where were Ferris Renfrow and the Commander of the Righteous? Especially Piper Hecht? Algres Drear was fierce and tough but he was not enough.

"Hilda, why do I obsess about a man older than me and already taken?" Helspeth had confessed her uncontrollable interest in the Commander of the Righteous. Lady Hilda had not been surprised.

"Hardly uncontrollable, if painfully more obvious than you think," Lady Hilda had told her. Now she said, "Maybe because you miss your father."

"My father was still alive when I caught this fever."

"Yes. I know. Plemenza." Lady Hilda had heard it over and over once Helspeth opened up. "Why ask questions if you won't listen to answers?" Lady Hilda returned to her needlework, almost sullenly, till, suddenly, she giggled.

"What?"

"You've had how many chances to make your fantasies come true since Katrin brought him here? But you're still a virgin."

"I'm not just me, Hilda. I'm a symbol. And a commodity."

"I've heard it all. What the hell is she doing here?"

Hilda meant Lady Delta va Kelgerberg, whom she detested. The feeling was mutual. Va Kelgerberg had been one of Helspeth's ladies, once upon a time, but had weaseled her way into Empress Katrin's court.

"Whatever, she's sure to be as unpleasant as possible." Helspeth gloated secretly. In just a few days va Kelgerberg's life would turn very difficult indeed. In just a few days her harvest would begin to come in.

Helspeth had no immediate opportunity to find out why Lady Delta had appeared. Algres Drear intervened. "Your Majesty."

"Captain?" Drear needed schooling on etiquette, especially in front of her women. A half dozen of those sat around the big room, every one a spy for her husband or lover. Or for both.

"Ferris Renfrow begs an audience. I know you like to hear his reports as soon as possible."

"Since he's seldom seen these days I should seize the opportunity. Hilda, see to Lady Delta, in the annex, then post yourself at a distance so I can see Renfrow privately without my reputation being sullied."

Muttering, "I'll take care of va Kelgerberg!" Lady Hilda did as asked. She had chaperoned Helspeth's meetings before. The Princess Apparent's enemies tried to make something of those but the charges only elicited mockery and disdain. Alten Weinberg knew Helspeth Ege too well.

Renfrow came in as Lady Hilda herded the other women out. Lady Delta was furious because Renfrow had been given precedence. Drear posted himself just inside the door. He, too, would stand witness to Helspeth's prudent behavior.

Helspeth told the chief Imperial spy, "Yet again you arrive looking like you're fresh from work on a hog farm. I cannot imagine how it would harm you to indulge in the occasional bath."

"I'll keep that in mind, Your Grace. But I'm here, now. Can we retire to a quiet room?"

"No. The only one handy is being rebuilt. I took your advice, had them inspected. They all leaked. I've ordered them rehabilitated. If they still leak afterward I'll have some necks stretched."

"Good, if inconvenient now." Renfrow produced a doeskin sack, shook out its contents. Black beads scattered, opened up like sow bugs. Many-legged black things scooted around, looking for invisible eavesdroppers. "When your workmen tell you they're done, I'll do the follow-up examination."

"I'll mention that. For now, your bugs should hold the Night at bay. So. What's so important this time?"

"Not as big a wow as you becoming Empress, but you should know. Remember the rules. No interruptions. But I will answer questions once I'm done. If they're pertinent."

"When have I ever been impertinent?" She considered Captain Drear and Lady Hilda, by the door. And wondered if Hilda had added Drear to her list of conquests.

"You have a point." Renfrow considered the chaperoning pair, too. His thoughts were not obvious.

Renfrow told the tale of his adventure into another world, where he had met gods the Church insisted did not exist along with creatures from fairy tales: dwarves and the mer, who lived in the sea.

Helspeth was fascinated by the mer Philleas Pescatore, who had had so obvious an impact on Renfrow's libido. "She was a virgin every time she took human form so she could leave the water?" How handy a skill would that be?

"Yes. Questions after." He went on.

Helspeth noted the filthy bandage on his left wrist.

"The Commander of the Righteous has a sister?" She zeroed in on the personal part of the story.

"If I pulled the evidence together correctly, he does. And their father was a Brotherhood general named Grade Drocker. Who, in turn, was the illegitimate son of Principaté Muniero Delari, one of the most powerful members of the Collegium."

"I met him when we were in Brothe."

"I expect you did. Principaté Delari, in turn, appears to be the grandson of Cloven Februaren, known as the Ninth Unknown. Februaren was there for everything. A remarkable character. And a sorcerer of considerable stature who hides it well."

"I know someone else like that."

"You do. Though it does get more difficult to do every day. The woman, Heris, called him Double Great, apparently because he's the grandfather of her grandfather. She and the Commander's adopted daughters have developed remarkable talents. Hecht and the boy, Pella, remain ciphers, however."

Helspeth was not happy about the Commander of the Righteous having daughters, adopted or not, though he had not concealed that. Renfrow's story made the girls more real.

She refused to ask even one question about that Anna Whoever.

Renfrow did nothing to help her relax.

"You talk like you were gone a long time. It's been two days."

"Time moves differently there. There's no fixed ratio but, right now, it's at least ten days to one."

"Is he coming? Are they coming here?"

Though she kept her voice neutral, she knew she was not fooling Renfrow. But she was not thinking of the spymaster. Someone might be eavesdropping.

"Those people didn't worry about keeping Ferris Renfrow informed. They know too much about me. But life produces patterns that we can interpret. The Commander of the Righteous will rejoin his troops on the road. He may bring the boy, Pella, because the lad has become too much for his mother to handle. The rest mean to stay in Brothe. The girls are being educated in one of the Church's more exclusive academies."

"So everything will go back to where it was before Jaime got killed and Katrin went crazy."

"Except that we'll have a new Empress. And, now, I believe I'll go have that bath you wished on me."

"And then off on another adventure? Or dare I hope you'll become a little more accessible?"

"Possibly. I'll be here throughout the transition, after the news about Katrin gets here. I saw the Graf fon Rhejm a while ago. See him if you can. He and his brothers would be valuable friends."

The Graf and his four brothers were the brothers of Hildegrun Machen, Katrin's mother, who had died when Katrin was an infant. The uncles had been Katrin's guardian angels. Overall, Helspeth had gotten on with them better than she had with her half sister.

She watched Ferris Renfrow leave. What had he told her that could not have waited another hour? Or even another day? She noted that he had not recovered his mystic sow bugs. Perhaps there were none left to recover.

THE LITTLE MAN WHO CAME OUT OF NOWHERE BY TURNING SIDEWAYS did so as Lady Hilda started to bring Lady Delta and the other ladies into the sewing chamber. Lady Delta had been given coffee. The implied honor had brightened her mood.

An instant before the sorcerer appeared time stopped for everyone but Helspeth and the little man himself. He sniffed the air. "He's been here. The Bastard. He's quick. I should've kept a better eye on him, back when."

"What do you want?"

"I meant to bring you up to date on the Commander's adventures. But the Bastard seems to have brought the news already."

"If by that you mean Ferris Renfrow, yes. He just left. From what he said, you must be Cloven Februaren, the so-called Ninth Unknown."

"That'll save a lot of palaver. Outline what he told you. I'll fill in what he left out."

Would Renfrow keep her in the dark? Yes. Almost certainly. Even close allies were not honest all the time. She hit the highlights. And understood by the old man's amusement that there had been points ignored or passed over lightly. "So what did he leave out?"

"Not much that you really need to know. Just little things, like the fact that he worked for me a long time ago. And just how successful we were in a world that our religious leaders promise us doesn't exist."

"So how successful were you?"

"Extremely. Though the whole truth remains to be seen. I'll reserve some facts myself. Ignorance could save you a lot of grief someday. In any event, we don't want you distracted when the news about your sister gets here. But take heart. Piper Hecht and the Righteous won't be far behind."

He turned sideways.

Time resumed.

"Captain Drear. I want to see the Graf fon Rhejm or one of his brothers. Go." She turned to Lady va Kelgerberg. The sooner dealt with the sooner that misery would end.

CAPTAIN DREAR FOUND THREE OF KATRIN'S UNCLES. ALL THREE responded to the Princess Apparent. Helspeth told them, "Thank you for coming so quickly. I barely dared hope that any of you would."

The Graf fon Rhejm inclined his head slightly. "The fact of the request made it clear that it was important."

Albert fon Rhejm reminded Helspeth of her father. He was not a big man, unlike the other two, who were built in the long, lean, blond mode of their niece, Katrin.

"I apologize because I have no quiet room. I picked a bad time to find out that they were all compromised. But what I have to tell you will be common knowledge soon enough." The youngest brother, Friedl, must have come twenty years after Hildegrun. He had a touch of that same appeal that drew her to the Commander of the Righteous. He also had a wife and was faithful.

"And that would be?"

"I'll preface by saying this comes from Ferris Renfrow. He recommended that I let you know immediately. He has unusual means of acquiring information."

"So rumor would suggest. So?"

"It's hard to just throw out. He says Katrin is dead. For reasons no one understands she went galloping along the bank of the Teragi, in Brothe, fell in, and drowned. And that's all he told me."

Katrin's uncles said nothing. The younger two eventually turned to the Graf fon Rhejm, who choked out, "God has a black sense of humor indeed, to take the daughter that way after what He let happen to her mother. You have no other details?"

"No. But she must have been upset about something if she was out galloping. That was one of the ways she coped."

"It was. She must have been. Though agitation had become her natural state. She had begun to suffer bouts of insanity. There's a congenital inclination in the family." He bowed his head as though to pray. Helspeth did not interrupt.

After some moments the Graf looked up. "Her end could be a blessing for the Empire. For some of us the disease persists for decades. The damage she could have done is inestimable."

Helspeth noted moisture on one of the Graf's cheeks. His brothers were doing their best to remain hard and silent. She said, "We'll get the full story when the Righteous arrive. Several witnessed the actual event, I understand. And several drowned trying to get Katrin out of the river."

"Helspeth, I'm grateful that you took time to tell us all this. Katrin wouldn't have done anything of the sort."

The middle brother, Rodolf, who had said nothing yet, mumbled, "This explains why the Braunsknects are all stirred up."

Helspeth admitted, "It does. They don't know why, yet. They'll find out when everyone else does. But they will have key points already secured."

The Graf fon Rhejm thanked her again. He and his brothers departed, the Graf pausing at the door. He considered her enigmatically.

She hoped she had done the right thing.

It would not do to make enemies of those men.

11. Antieux: Deathwives

Two days after Bernardin's return to Antieux a troop of forty lances left the city with orders to travel fast, far, and light. Still, with equerries, serjents, and servants, and with every man sharing the workload, the party really consisted of a hundred souls and three hundred animals.

Everyone had to ride. Everyone had to bring food, tents, and equipment. Warhorses, usually asked to do no more than amble along till fighting time, ended up carrying supplies.

Brother Candle watched from above the city gate. He marveled at what these fighting men considered light. Nothing like the horse soldiers of the east, though he had heard that those riders often had vast trains of camels in trail.

The Perfect was troubled. Those men were in dire awe of their captain. Even the animals might be a little intimidated.

Countess Socia had given Kedle Richeut command, then had disdained all dissenting arguments. Nor had she been reluctant to be heavy-handed with anyone who tried to thwart her.

There had been surprisingly few attempts at that.

KEDLE'S REPUTATION HAD GROWN SINCE EVENTS IN KHAURENE. AND Socia had been around Antieux long enough to have made an abiding impression. No one forgot her massacre of those men at Suralert Ford, all privileged by birth or status in the Church.

Most folk of Antieux had been satisfied with Count Raymone's rule. The Countess promised more of the same, possibly more intensely.

But . . . ! A woman commanding warriors? However fierce a woman? That was legendary stuff. It did not happen in modern times.

Against that argument Socia named Queen Isabeth herself, Anne of Menand, and Empress Katrin and her sister Helspeth. Both daughters of Johannes Blackboots had seen combat during the Calziran Crusade, when they were younger than Kedle Richeut. Then there was the Countess of Antieux herself. Socia Rault had been handling weapons against armed foes since she was sixteen. And she was sending Kedle Richeut out only because she could not yet sit a saddle herself.

The Countess was who she was and Count Raymone's judgment was trusted. Socia's wishes were accepted by the nobles and magnates.

Antieux would ignore the unnatural arrangement as long as Socia and Kedle produced results.

Brother Candle watched the riders head into the dewy sunrise and blamed the moisture on his cheeks on the morning damp. He was sad. Kedle was walking away from her life to do this thing.

Kedle meant almost as much to him as Socia did. He had known her since she was in diapers. She was the only surviving child of two good friends. He had brought Raulet and Madam Archimbault to the Good God before Kedle was born.

Raulet and his wife were distraught. They had not been able to bring themselves to watch Kedle ride away, armed, surrounded by a hundred crude men. Her hunger for bloody action pained them deeply.

Pacifism was ingrained in the Maysalean Heresy. Although the Good God insisted that evil be resisted by all means, including use of arms, most Seekers would not fight. Brother Candle himself never raised a hand in anger. Kedle not only embraced violence, she abandoned her children to follow its call.

The time between Bernardin's return and the departure of Kedle's expedition was full for Brother Candle. He spent a lot of time with Raulet and his wife, reminding them to remain strong for the sake of the grandchildren. He had to endure, in silence, Socia's robust pogrom against all things Brothen Episcopal, including public execution of eleven members of the Society for the Suppression of Sacrilege and Heresy. She imprisoned forty-three suspected agents of the Brothen Church, then ordered the expulsion of Episcopal priests known to have been honestly active before Count Raymone's misadventure.

The priests got to go only due to Brother Candle's appeals. Socia wanted to herd them together and burn them the way the Society did with Seekers.

Brother Candle left the wall for the house Socia had provided for Kedle and her fellow refugees. Scarre the baker and his wife had set up on the street level. They were developing a clientele for Khaurenese soft breads. The Archimbaults, with Guillemette and

Escamerole, and grandchildren, all crowded in there. Guillemette and Escamerole took care of the children and worked in the citadel, mostly caring for the Countess and Lumiere. The Archimbaults had not yet found full employment. Raulet was a tanner. Antieux's tanning industry was depressed. So was the butcher trade. Invasions, attacks, and sieges had eliminated the livestock once common in the countryside.

Leatherworkers, too, were having a bleak season.

Twice during his walk to the refugee home Brother Candle witnessed purported friends of Count Raymone rounding up the Count's supposed enemies. The old man was sure Bernardin had someone inside the Society. He knew who they were. He knew their fellow travelers. A settlement of old scores had begun.

Brother Candle dared not poke his nose in. The Maysalean creed was strong in Antieux but many Seekers had been rendered harsh by the wars and sieges. They had no forgiveness left and no tolerance for him who preached it.

Raulet Archimbault observed, "The wolves are loose. That's why we didn't see Kedle off."

Not true, but the Perfect offered no challenge. Raulet had his right to disapprove of his daughter. "I came by to see how you're doing. I can't stay long. The Countess keeps me busy."

She did. She had a big political problem: what to do about the ducal throne to which Raymone was supposed to ascend. With Raymone gone that was lost unless, implausibly, Isabeth let the dukedom devolve on Lumiere.

Brother Candle had to handle the correspondence because he knew Isabeth. There had been no answers, so far. But it could not be long before the disappointments began to arrive.

Brother Candle's visit let the Archimbaults follow Kedle's progress without them having to set aside their disapproval.

A Maysalean family could generate as much drama as any other.

Brother Candle visited the grandchildren, finished chatting with the Archimbaults, then headed downstairs to see Scarre and his wife. His knees ached from the up and down. He promised to see everyone at weekly services, then headed for the citadel armed with a fat loaf of Scarre's best. Socia had developed a taste for soft bread while she was hiding with the Perfect, at the Scarre bakery, in Khaurene. Brother Candle delivered the loaf to the Countess three hours after Kedle led her hundred off to war.

Socia expected a lecture. She had a guilty air. She was behaving badly according to her religion. Brother Candle failed her expectation. He saw no point. He could no more control her than he could convince a storm to withhold its fury.

Socia's rage had to run its course.

She asked, "They got off all right, then?"

He pretended his news would be the first she had heard. "They did. They moved out briskly, like well-motivated men." He tried to appear content. He did not want to argue. He was too old to keep on fighting the stubborn fight.

And, maybe, the girl would *think* if she was not focused on defending herself.

He was sure that Kedle had permission to go beyond recovering the fallen. That would be done, surely, but the fiercest riders would hurry onward, hoping to overtake the injured Patriarch.

Serenity, as Bronte Doneto, had survived several collisions with Antieux, all at his own instigation. Kedle would try to end his run.

Privately, Brother Candle implored the Good God's intercession. He did not want the stain of what would follow Serenity's capture besmirching the souls of Socia Rault and Kedle Richeut.

Eight days after Kedle's departure a ragged gaggle of peasants and carts appeared at Antieux's gate. Kedle had hired them to transport the fallen, all in an advanced state of putrefaction. The corpses included all the local fallen—Count Raymone, too—and those of Serenity's companions whose relicts might be ransomed.

The peasants, all of whom claimed to worship Count Raymone, brought some live bodies as well: two men who had ridden out with Kedle, now wounded, plus a dozen Society brothers, several Episcopal priests, and six Arnhander prisoners.

Kedle had run into an Arnhander force three hundred strong, also looking for Serenity. They were inexperienced and led by Society vermin associated with Anne of Menand. Kedle launched a massacre. Her force suffered one dead and the two walking wounded.

Two hundred enemy had fallen, supposedly.

Kedle was headed north. Her soldiers had fallen in love with her. Socia was jealous.

Later, in the privacy of his cell, Brother Candle muttered, "The Adversary moves in strange and mysterious ways."

12. Brothe: Brief Homecoming

Piper Hecht and his family arrived inside Principaté Muniero De-lari's Brothen townhouse. The place had been damaged badly during the fighting when the Righteous occupied the Mother City.

Hecht and his sister each began bleating about how the other should have remembered that the townhouse was not habitable.

Pella said, "Dad, I'll check on Anna's house. We can't stay here." He took off before he could be pelted with unwanted instructions.

Pella's estimation proved to be inaccurate. Delari's staff—Turking, Felske, and Mrs. Creedon—remained in place, in charge, and adequately housed.

Heris told Hecht, "Keep a low profile, little brother. You don't have an army behind you now."

He had begun to brood on that already.

Years ago, when he was another man, er-Rashal al-Dhulquarnen had armed him with a wrist amulet that warned him against danger from the Night. The Ninth Unknown had replaced that with another that er-Rashal could not track.

In times of no threat he forgot the amulet. He had done so in the Realm of the Gods, though Februaren did say that it would not work there. But now Hecht was back in a world where the charm was efficacious.

He felt a continuous, low-grade, maddening itch around his left wrist.

"And where is my egg?" Heris demanded.

"Right here." Inside his shirt. But it felt different. It was cold, and lighter. "Here."

"What happened? It's dead. Or something. What did you do?"

"I didn't do anything. You were there. You know."

Mrs. Creedon, Principaté Delari's cook, intruded upon their attention. "Don't argue where the workmen can hear. Come with me. Turking will inform the master that you have returned."

"Good point," Hecht said. "Let's go. And that was the easiest transition yet. I hardly felt it."

"I'll save your butt from the local villains by jumping it back out before word gets around."

"It'll take all of you." He was not prepared to transition with Heris alone. "What about the egg?"

"I don't know. I expected something like, it would go away if Zyr connected with his other soul. Maybe the old old man can figure it out. I'll be damned. This part of the dump held up pretty good. Looks like hell from outside, though."

The cook had taken them into the kitchen, pantries, and servants' quarters. "The cellars are fine. We can put you down there."

Anna appeared glum. She would be on her own again, soon. And the children had had a taste of adventure. The girls in particular were sure to get into mischief. And Pella wanted to get back into the field with his father. He insisted that the education Hecht wanted him to get he could pick up from Titus Consent, Drago Prosek, Kait Rhuk, and others. And that was hard to deny. They all indulged the boy.

Hecht said, "Remind me to see Noë and the kids before I go. If I can get away with it."

Felske made them as comfortable as she could while Mrs. Creedon fed them.

Anna said, "I'm surprised looters haven't torn this place apart."

Mrs. Creedon said, "Some had the notion. The master anticipated them. Someone comes in that the house doesn't know, it tears them apart."

Osa Stile strolled in, made a startled sound, locked gazes with Hecht. The catamite did not look an hour older than when they had run into one another during the first siege of Antieux. He wanted to demand an explanation of Stile's presence, then recalled that Osa had been rescued from the same cellar where Cloven Februaren had found Pella imprisoned. "Armand. You're looking well."

"As are you, Commander. I wonder, sir. Will the new Empress have the Righteous go on building a Holy Lands expedition?"

"Remains to be determined. Why?"

"Time spent in a lightless cell, without hope, has a way of turning one's thoughts inward. I found a spiritual side I didn't know I had. I would like to make the pilgrimage. I have a debt to repay a certain rascal."

Hecht inclined his head just enough to let Stile know he understood.

"I can be useful, Commander. And I've overstayed my welcome here, playing to the Principaté's residual affection."

"Can you get to Alten Weinberg? And can you behave yourself?" Hecht could not state it explicitly but found Stile's sexual proclivities repulsive.

"Yes to the first. To the second, honestly, I can say only probably. I have no desires at the moment but that could change."

The catamite, shaped by sorcery to remain a boy indefinitely, had suffered bad times and bad people in order to spy for er-Rashal and Ferris Renfrow. He soldiered on.

Turking reappeared, having made remarkable time. He said Principaté Delari would arrive soon.

Pella turned up not long afterward. "Anna's house is in good shape but three men are living there. They say Paludan Bruglioni sent them because the senate made Pinkus Ghort stop using constabularii to guard the place."

Hecht said, "I should see Pinkus. It's been a long time."

"You'd do better to give up wishful thinking," Heris said. "You might be friends with Ghort and Saluda and even Paludan Bruglioni but that doesn't change the political environment. It doesn't change the fact that you're suddenly the hero of the Grail Empire, what's been the Patriarchy's dearest enemy for two hundred years."

"This is what happens when you engage the world at more than a tactical level."

"I won't even pretend I understand what you just said. Turking, we aren't ignoring you. We just have too much fun bickering. Did you have something besides the fact that Grandfather is on his way?"

"No. Nothing more than that, Lady."

"Ha! You heard that, Piper. Everybody heard it. I've got one man so bamboozled he thinks I'm a lady."

"I'm sorry to hear that."

"Enough of that, children."

Muniero Delari had arrived. Quietly. Evidently, little that he saw pleased him. He held his thoughts, joined the cook. "That looks delicious, Mrs. Creedon. I hadn't yet eaten when Turking came. Can you stretch that to include me?"

Mrs. Creedon grunted. His question required no answer. Of course she could. He paid her wages.

The Principaté eyeballed his descendents again and was no more pleased. "Anna, your adventures have put some red into your cheeks."

Flattery Hecht heard with no sense of threat. The old man preferred nubile boys—though he had shown little interest there since he parted with Osa Stile.

Heris growled, mood darkening by the moment. Hecht thought she might want to be told what a good job she had done with the Old Ones.

Whatever he said now would sound contrived.

Lila sensed it, too. And it was not too late for her. "You should have seen Heris, Opah. She was amazing. There were all these old-time gods and she wrapped them around her fingers. Except for the ones Anna blasted. You should've seen."

Opah? That was a way of saying Grandpa, up north.

Delari did not object. This was not a first offense.

You missed the changes when you were away in the field. On the other hand, you did notice them.

Delari said, "Do tell. Heris, you amaze me. You've grown dramatically since Grade brought you here. Mrs. Creedon, are you ready? Yes? Let's sit. The lamb pie smells wonderful. Lila, go on. Tell the whole story." He eyed the other children suspiciously. They were unnaturally quiet. "Armand, you are not to repeat any of this."

"You won't believe me, but I never have."

Stile had it right. Hecht believed little that he heard from the catamite. He scratched his wrist. He had not realized how all-pervasive the power was in this world.

Lila was full of surprises, lately. Her ability to tell a story was another. Vali acted as chorus, chiming in with interesting details at intervals separate enough that her interruptions were not obnoxious.

"Interesting," Delari said when Lila finished, by which time everyone but she had filled up on lamb pie. "Quite an adventure. I envy you, Heris. I've never had an adventure."

Hecht and the catamite both stared.

Osa, Turking, Felske, and Mrs. Creedon congratulated Lila on a tall tale convincingly told. It could not be true, of course. Those devil gods could not possibly exist. And she had best not tell her story where priests could hear her. The Church was a tad more tolerant now, thanks to the Commander, but the small minds of the Society had long memories.

Hecht's amulet itched so badly that he said, "Principaté, you need to check this thing Februaren put on me. It's driving me crazy. Oh. Never mind, then."

Pillars of sparkle formed in the small bit of open space left in the crowded kitchen. They became Hourli and Hourlr.

Pella cracked, "Lila really can bring a story to life, can't she?"

There could be no doubt that these were Instrumentalities of the Night.

The male twin faced Heris. "There you are. It has been difficult, tracing you. We're feeling better, now, thank you. The magic is thin but it does still exist. A wallow in a well of power would be divine."

Hourli faced Hecht. "Your world has grown strange, Godslayer. We are nearly forgotten."

No one seized the moment to take a fundamentalist stand.

No one seemed to know what to say, either.

Mrs. Creedon asked, "Would you like some lamb pie?"

Hourlr replied, "If we take a mortal shape our bodies require mortal sustenance. So, yes, dear lady, I would love some lamb pie."

Mrs. Creedon blushed.

Hourli nodded. She was willing, too.

Heris asked, "Where are the others?"

Hourlr replied. "Running free. Basking in what power there is. Seeing the changes in the world. Wondering what you did that has never been done before."

Hecht studied the reactions of Muniero Delari's staff. Delari himself was taking it all in stride, despite his place as a Prince of the Church.

Some religious insiders did admit that all things were possible within the Night—so long as someone believed. They strove to control that by managing the belief.

Principaté Delari mused, "Piper is entertaining heretical thoughts." He chuckled. "Yes, Piper, some of us do understand that the Night is bigger than our one God. Most of us do. And most of us can square that with our faith. In Old Andoray they followed one family from the generation of deities known generically as the Old Gods. Only a few people believe in their existence anymore, but the Old Ones still believe in themselves, which is more important today. Overall, the Church, rather than deny what anyone with eyes can see, has reassigned the Old Ones to servitude in the house of the Adversary. As demons they can continue to exist without stealing glory from God in the Highest."

"Or you can make saints out of them if they are especially beloved." Hourli and Hourlr sneered.

They sensed the drift of his thoughts. Hourli said, "They can't change our nature through dogma, Godslayer. Things are not what mortals think they are but only because mortals observe with mortal eyes and with mortal hearts shaped by mortal experience. But that is of no consequence. We have a contract. It will be observed on our side. By this assemblage of Old Ones. The Shining Ones. Other revenants, and the Primal Gods, won't be bound by our agreements."

Heris would not be distracted. "You're running free? How can that be? Back when you were trying to murder my brother, even the All-Father could barely touch the Grimmssons here. Once they moved south of Brothe only the Exile could stick with them."

"Arlensul *was* the Exile, operating independent of the Realm," Hourlr said. "You changed everything for the rest of us. You let us out of the Realm. You opened this whole world to us, though there are still severe limits to our range. We will explore it as much as we are able."

Hecht demanded, "What did she do for the first time?"

"She brought the Shining Ones back free from the old constraints of belief. She believes we exist. Your eyes agree. There are fewer restrictions on us today. Freedom gained at the cost of power."

Hecht looked at Heris. She looked back. They frowned. They had enjoyed religious upbringings, each in a dramatically different belief system. Neither understood this, here, now. It could not be hammered and filed to fit what they had been taught.

Heris asked, "You can summon the others if I need them?"

Hourlr said, "Yes, but not quickly. However, if we open the way to Raneul we can then manage to do everything at the speed of lightning."

Accepting a second portion of lamb pie, Principaté Delari mused, "No doubt also releasing a horde of supernatural miscreants not bound by oaths sworn to my grandchildren."

Hecht mused. The twins needed mortal help reaching their native realm?

"We have sworn," Hourli snapped, irritated, plainly irked by the continued distrust. "We will fulfill."

"Do you have any sense of where the others are?" Heris asked.

"Not precisely," Hourlr conceded.

"Where is Zyr?"

Hourlr's eyes narrowed. His gaze darted. He seemed both puzzled and inclined toward evasion.

"Well?" Hecht snapped.

Hourli blurted, as though compelled, "Here. But I can't see him."

Heris asked, "Hourlr?"

"I feel him. He's watching. And he's immensely displeased with us for revealing that fact. But I can't see him."

Heris looked like she was about to turn nasty. "The trickery has started already, then?"

Hecht caught her arm, squeezed, shook his head. "He hasn't broken the rules. Remember, Instrumentalities are all about sound and fury and loopholes."

Heris produced a hand-held. "I've got two ounces of silver bead loophole filler right here."

She was close to losing control. Hecht said, "Us mortals ought to get some rest. We had to deal with a lot today."

The twins shrugged. Hourli said, "This is a city of immense wickedness. We'll explore it."

"Go. Have fun. We'll see you later."

The twins vanished almost the same as Lila, Heris, and Cloven Februaren could.

Heris was in a mood to squabble.

"Heris, you're too anxious. Don't get all worked up and break the contract from our end."

Clearly, she had not considered that. "Oh! I was on my way there, wasn't I? They were provoking me."

"No. They weren't. They do mean to execute their bargain, letter and spirit, for the rest of your life. They honestly see that as advantageous."

"How can you know that?"

Hecht shrugged. "Think. It's the rational thing to do."

"I don't see it."

"You're looking through a lens of prejudice. Look. You got them out of Asgrimmur's trap, then you got them out of the Realm of the Gods. Now they're seeing that the middle world is just another, bigger prison. Mortality is the rule, here."

"Whoa, little brother. You're going all spooky on me."

"They're going to need believers. Right now all they have is us. And we don't worship."

"I thought them believing in each other was what freed them to go where they want."

"Sure. Sort of. They can get to places they couldn't go before. They might even be able to visit the Wells of Ihrian. But they still have two souls to feed."

Everyone stared at Hecht like he had sprouted green hair.

"I'll take your word, brother. It applies, how?"

"They're not saying so but they need more than one kind of nourishment. The magic isn't enough. Us accepting their existence isn't, either. We aren't true believers. They need worshippers to hang on to their immortality."

His audience just stared. He continued, "Real worshippers. It's what they want to find during one ephemeral generation as our allies, as gods who actually can be seen doing something, regularly. If they fail, their own divine mortality will overtake them. They'll fade into the Night."

The air stirred. Cloven Februaren rotated into being. "Excellent analysis, Piper. But I do wonder how you managed it. You're a clever lad but you only use that to find new ways to whack on people who don't want to do what you tell them."

"I didn't give it any special thought. It seemed obvious. And I still think we all need rest. We have to be fresh to cope. And I need to get back to my army, which, I'm sure, Sedlakova and the rest have let go to hell."

HECHT SLEPT EIGHTEEN HOURS. HE WAKENED TWICE TO URINATE BUT stumbled right back to his cot. He still felt unready to rise when Anna poked him awake.

"Piper, you have to get up. There's going to be trouble."

He shook the cobwebs out. "Trouble?"

"Word is out that we're here. Delari figures the place was watched by Night thing spies. There will be trouble. Addam Hauf will take me and the kids into the Castella again. We'll be safe while Pinkus deals with the unrest."

Hecht shook his head again. "We should have expected this."

"The old men did. Which is why arrangements are in place with Hauf, Pinkus, and the Patriarch. Who really should pick a reign name if he wants the mob to take him serious."

"Gervase doesn't take himself serious yet. What's the plan?"

"You eat, then Heris and Lila will take you to the Righteous. The rest of us hole up till the excitement blows over."

"There were things I wanted to do while I was here. There were people I wanted to see."

"There are people who want to see you, too. And they're not your friends."

True. He would be a tempting target while he was without the Righteous behind him. "All right. I'm up."

"I'll tell Mrs. Creedon."

Hecht found Heris and Lila hovering in the kitchen while Mrs. Creedon delivered a platter to her one sound table. Mostly pork, of course. "Are you all anxious to be shut of me?"

Heris confessed, "We are. There's ugly talk out there. Ghort doesn't have the manpower to save you. The Brotherhood can't help you, legally. And some people who do like you won't lift a finger if it looks like that would help a Patriarch they aren't so sure about."

"I see. Pella, this means I can't take you with me. How about you go grab my stuff? We'll fix up something later."

Anna caught his eye. She mouthed, "Thank you," assuming he had found an excuse to leave the boy in safety.

Surly, Pella made the same assumption.

Cloven Februaren rotated into existence an instant after Lila rotated out. She and Heris were taking turns observing events. Februaren muttered at Heris, who nodded. Lila came back. "There's a mob gathering in the Madhur Plaza. The ringleaders sound like Society types."

"That's pretty far off," Heris said. "We have a while. But let's don't waste time. We don't want them finding anything but booby traps when they get here. Lila, get your father out, then shift the others to the Castella."

"Not inside," Lila said. "Just close by. The Brotherhood would have fits if we turned up without them having to let us in."

"Yeah. You ready, Piper?"

"Me? No." He nearly panicked, recalling the unpleasantness of solo transitions with Heris.

She and Lila enveloped him in a hug. Lila nodded over his shoulder.

Twist.

Darkness, haunted by terrible things, none of which thought him worthy of notice. Then morning sunshine and cool air. He was in the foothills of the Jagos, outside the mouth of the Remayne Pass.

Heris asked, "That wasn't bad, was it?"

"No. Maybe I'm getting used to it."

"But you sound suspicious."

"I am suspicious. The attitude of the Night toward me can't have improved."

"We need to put that runt Armand in a fool suit and have him follow you around telling you that you aren't nearly as important as you think."

"You miss picking on me when we were little, don't you?"

"Could be."

"My point is, the Night doesn't think I'm important anymore. After all that trouble trying to kill me."

"So the Night finally understands that the genie can't be shoved back into the bottle."

"That would be one interpretation. Giving the Night too much credit."

"Your theory is?"

"The Night forgot me because it found you."

"I don't think so. Asgrimmur would've warned me. Lila and I need to get back. Just sit. The Righteous will be along later."

"You plopped me down ahead of them? How am I supposed to explain that?" He tossed a look of appeal at Lila but the girl was infatuated with the view. The air was crystalline. The Jagos were dressed in magnificent grays and purples, wearing capes of pristine white. The breeze from the high slopes was cooler than the coolest morning air in Brothe. Hecht shivered.

Heris said, "You'll come up with something. You're so clever. Hell. Blame it on sorcery. Or divine intervention. It'd all be true."

"And no one would believe me."

"So much the better, eh? Lila! Time to go."

"You go ahead. I'll catch up. I want to look at the mountains."

Heris shrugged. "Don't be too long." She turned sideways.

Lila waited half a minute to say, "Promise you'll be careful." She stepped close, hugged him, squeezed his right bicep and his left wrist as though disguising a check to make sure his amulet was still there. It was. And it still itched. "You're the closest thing to a father I ever had." Said like it was torture to get out.

Lila turned sideways, so close he felt the breeze when she vanished.

He took a deep breath, shivered some, decided to warm up by walking. He headed downhill. The road into the pass had to be close by.

He found the road. He perched on a boulder to wait. There was no traffic, which was not a good sign. Could it be because soldiers were coming?

LILA ARRIVED IN BROTHE TO FIND HERIS AND CLOVEN FEBRUAREN already heads together scheming to move her, Vali, and Muniero Delari into the hidden Chiaro Palace basement where the Construct lay hidden. Anna and Pella had been transitioned to the vicinity of the Castella already. They could cross a bridge and approach a gate, get inside, and prepare quarters where the girls could join them.

Mrs. Creedon, with Turking and Felske, had been sent to Principaté Delari's apartment in the Chiaro Palace. There could be no safer place for them.

As Heris explained, the Ninth Unknown, laughing, turned sideways with the Eleventh, who entered the nothing squawking.

Vali joined Lila and Heris. All three rotated into the bright lights and bustle of the secret world of the Construct—though not where their arrival would be witnessed by the career priests and nuns perfecting what looked like a vast and intimately detailed relief map of the known world. Brothe was its pivot. It revealed ever less exact detail as the eye tracked toward its edge.

The environs of Brothe and central Firaldia were defined so minutely that an observer with a sharp eye and determined focus could discern minuscule dots moving along the roads and streets. A ghost of a haze drifted toward the sea west of the Firaldian peninsula.

A Patriarch and a Collegium centuries past had ordered the Construct developed as a means of seeing and understanding the expanding Chaldarean world. It had been, from its inception, an undertaking that beggared any cathedral project. It had been secret from the start and of such little popular interest that no one had bothered spying. In time it became lost even to Church insiders. The only recent Patriarch aware of the project—a definite anomaly—had been Hugo Mongoz, sitting the Patriarchal Throne as Boniface VII.

The project would continue. Cloven Februaren and Muniero Delari, the Ninth and Eleventh Unknowns, hoped to polish Heris into the Twelfth.

They wanted to keep the magic in the family.

Heris was not yet fully aware of their ambitions.

She growled and snapped and pulled her companions into a huddle away from the project staff. "There's something wrong with Piper."

The others awaited specifics. Nobody asked. She could not deliver her punch line. That irked her.

The whole damned family was that way.

Cloven Februaren yielded enough to observe, "He did develop some quirks after he died and we brought him back. But I thought he'd worked through those."

"He learned how to hide them, you mean."

A shrug. "Could be."

"He even hid from himself. I think his transitions were rough because they reopened him to influences from the Night."

"The answer is in the question."

That confused Heris. "Excuse me?"

"Make him walk if transitions cause him distress."

"It's not that simple. I wish he'd made transitions before he died. We'd have something to compare."

"Did he suffer much today?"

"Not this time. He might be getting used to it. Though I don't actually believe that. There was something weird about him."

Februaren asked, "What do you think, Lila?"

"I think he's worried about us. And he has a hard time because his world keeps changing. Remember where he came from."

"Is that it, Heris? Is he turning into a lost soul because everything he ever believed has turned to smoke?"

Heris hated to admit that that might be what she sensed. But she had her own moments on slippery footing and she never had believed in anything, truly. But that was not all of it. Not even the majority of it. "So let's just keep an eye on him, look out for him, and get in the way if he starts heading in a bad direction."

She would figure it out. Piper was her brother. Family. That was what family did.

Heris had not had a family before. Not one to which she belonged by blood and emotion.

HECHT WAS SOUND ASLEEP ON THE GROUND WHEN VEDETTES FROM the Righteous discovered him. It was two hours after noon. Those advance riders were some of the more superstitious of the Righteous. One stood nervous guard while the other galloped off to report.

Two hours passed before someone senior arrived. By then fifty soldiers had surrounded the snoring Commander.

Titus Consent and Clej Sedlakova arrived together, the chief of intelligence and master of the horse of the Righteous, respectively. Consent and the Commander had a friendship that went back to when Piper Hecht had been a hired sword working for the Bruglioni, one of the Five Families of Brothe. Even now Consent was just in his middle twenties, though gray flecked his dark hair already. He slid down off his bay, waited to see if Colonel Sedlakova needed assistance dismounting.

Clej Sedlakova, onetime associate of the Brotherhood of War—and still reporting back, probably—had only one arm. But he managed, even in a fight. He had no trouble dismounting. He had become accustomed to his situation.

Consent asked, "Who found him?"

The scouts responsible raised their hands.

"You didn't try to waken him?"

"No, sir. Sir, if he wasn't breathing we would of thought he was dead. He ain't moved since we found him."

Hecht lay curled on his right side, hands bunched in front of his mouth. "Sleeping like a baby," Sedlakova observed. Sedlakova had a thin oval face and clover honey hair thinning all over. There was no fat on his lean frame. Excepting the absent arm he looked the perfect example of what he was: a career soldier. He was one of those men who remained clean and neat even in the roughest circumstances.

Titus Consent, on the other hand, remained permanently just over the line toward rumpled. He was lean, too. The Righteous were all lean. Even in garrison they lived an active, austere life.

All the fault of that man sleeping there in the cold.

Consent considered the gathered soldiers. Hecht had to be way out not to hear all their racket. He walked round his friend, saw no hint of anything remarkable—other than the man's inexplicable presence.

Sedlakova said, "He isn't dressed for this weather."

"No. You're right." Hecht wore what he usually did in the field, nondescript clothing you could find on any workman. There were no layers. He had come from somewhere warm. "Good eye. I didn't notice that." Consent knelt, shook Hecht's left shoulder.

It took more than a minute to get a response, and that was not the expected startle reaction. It was bleary-eyed confusion, then disbelief, then a baffled, "Where am I? How did I get here?"

"I was hoping you could tell us. We're in the approaches to the Remayne Pass, just south of where they ambushed us before. How you got here is something you'll have to explain."

"I don't know, Titus. I was in Brothe, at Principaté Delari's townhouse. I had strange dreams about old-time gods. Not nightmares. Just dreams, like memories of things that never were. Then you shook me. And here I am, freezing." He was sitting now, but looking like he would need help getting to his feet.

Titus Consent was not as skeptical as a good Chaldarean ought to be, nor even as skeptical as the Devedian he had been before his conversion. But he had spent a year in the Connec hunting and extinguishing revenant devils from antiquity. "We put them all down. Rook was the last one. You were there when we got him."

"Different Old Ones, Titus. The northern ones."

"Donner? Ordnan? Due? That crew?"

"I know the middle one. Remember that big explosion outside al-Khazen? That was him getting a taste of what we gave Rook, Hilt, Kint, and that lot later."

"They have a bunch of different names, depending on where they were worshipped. Some even overlapped the bunch we cleaned up. The ancient Endonensins liked the northern war god. Their warriors hoped to be claimed by the Choosers of the Slain."

"All right."

"Due was the war god. He had more different names than anybody, including just plain War. Donner was Ordnan's son. He was big and dumb and famous for a magic hammer that was so heavy nobody else could lift it. Thunder—which is what Donner meant—happened when Donner was playing with his hammer. Or, more likely, when he dropped it."

"Red Hammer."

"Uhm."

The Righteous got their Commander upright and gave him a dead man's coat. Everyone passing got as close as possible, to see if the rumors were true. Regimental field cooks brought food. The Commander ate heartily.

He seemed bemused. Or, better said, preoccupied.

Hecht's staff eventually gathered round. They did not say much. Though good men and old friends, they were troubled. This latest mystery left them more uncomfortable than they had been since that assassin took the Commander down and dead—just before he got up and walked again.

His very title sheltered him from darker suspicions: Commander of the Righteous. Anointed captain of God's Own Army, destined to cleanse the Holy Lands of an infidel infestation. The Commander of the Righteous would have no congress with devils, demons, or darkness. Would he?

Still, Hecht's staff and captains worried.

THE RIGHTEOUS WERE SHORT ON MOUNTS AND DRAYAGE. THE COMmander ended up riding a mule. He refused to commandeer a mount. The mule's name was Pig Iron. Hecht had known him and his human traveling companion, Just Plain Joe, from the beginning of his career in the west. Just Plain Joe liked animals better than people. Because of Joe that side of the Righteous functioned better than it did in most armed forces. Joe had had the same impact wherever Hecht commanded, all the way back. Just Plain Joe had no ambition greater than to ease life for his four-legged friends. By doing so he improved life for the two-leggers as well.

The officer corps of the Righteous stipulated Joe's good work but disdained their Commander's friendship toward, indulgence of, and adamant support for a dullard peasant.

It was simple. Just Plain Joe had set a sentimental hook. Hecht could explain, "There are only four of us left from the band that went to the Connec to punish Antieux for defying the Patriarch and Joe is the only one still with me. We have a bond."

The other survivors were Pinkus Ghort and Bo Biogna. Ghort had become Captain-General of Patriarchal forces, a post little more than that of head policeman in Brothe, now. Biogna had gone missing. When last seen he had been an undercover agent for Ghort, or Bronte Doneto, or the Church. Or maybe all three. Biogna and Just Plain Joe were close. If Biogna was alive he would contact Joe eventually.

The Righteous moved on into the chill of the high Jagos. Their Commander spent most of his time brooding. He did not notice the cautious attitudes of his companions. He did recall that there were other survivors of that first murderous campaign against Antieux, but none who had been with him doing the grunt work. Bronte Doneto had been there. The deposed Patriarch still nurtured a fierce hatred for the Connec. Osa Stile had been there, as the plaything of the Brothen Episcopal bishop of Antieux, Serifs, and as a spy for the Empire.

Did any of that mean anything anymore? Other than emotionally? Probably not.

Once the Righteous began the descent of the north slope of the Jagos, Hecht's brooding shifted from the past to the future. There was no evidence that the new Empress would not want him to go on preparing for a crusade. And next spring was no longer far away.

Too, he had to prepare his people for the changes that would follow once the special assistance commenced.

The Old Ones, surely, would be smart enough to take on disguises. But how could they help giving themselves away?

Humility was not in their characters.

In which case they might not have to wait long to find out what Red Hammer had discovered already.

13. Tel Moussa: Two Devils Dancing

Black Rogert's character did, indeed, prove to be a weapon that could be used against him, but not in the way Nassim Alizarin planned, and not nearly as soon as he hoped.

Every fault du Tancret had discovered and honed during his first tour as castellan of Gherig came back with him, exaggerated. He wallowed in his wicked reputation. His own people hated him. During a skirmish with Alizarin's raiders a Navayan crusader named Matthias of Camargha tried to kill him from behind with a mace. At the critical instant their horses stumbled over a wounded infantryman. Both lost their seats.

Matthias surrendered to Alizarin rather than endure what awaited his return to Gherig. Du Tancret suffered a broken right shinbone.

Matthias was one hundred percent cooperative with his captors but would not change religion. Nassim drained him of what he knew about Gherig and Black Rogert, gave him a horse and passage money, and let him go.

Disaffection inside Gherig ran bitter and deep. The Brotherhood of War barely cooperated with the castellan. Servants who lived outside the fortress were no longer unwilling to talk to enemies of Rogert du Tancret.

OLD AZ RETURNED FROM A FIVE-DAY ESPIONAGE MISSION. "GENERAL, the good news is that Black Rogert's leg is mending poorly."

"Good to know his luck sometimes runs shy of perfection. Unless he's just ducking the risks of joining his patrols."

"An excuse?" Du Tancret's combat shyness had been bruited for years but Nassim did not credit it. The man had too much luck.

"Are the servants so angered that they'll help us get inside?"

"That won't happen. They're more scared of Rogert than of God and the Adversary combined. They see the cost of inspiring his ire every day."

"Uhm." Nassim reflected briefly. Overall, today had been a good day in a good week. A new four-pounder had come through from Haeti, accompanied by twelve twenty-five-pound kegs of firepowder. That was not as good as the powder made by the Devedians in Rhûn but it would do. The best stuff could be hoarded against a day when reliability would be critical. "Good news, I suppose. Azer, could we trick someone into doing deadly work for us?"

"For example?"

"We know the servants who live outside are searched at Gherig's gate, heading in either direction. But the incoming searches are perfunctory. Rogert is mainly worried about theft. It shouldn't be hard to smuggle firepowder in, one ounce at a time, using people who don't know what they're doing. A charge could be built at a vulnerable point and sparked."

The Mountain's companions fell silent, stared. This was the man who had gone through moral convulsions after his attempt to assassinate Black Rogert, using firepowder. That time he had used a true volunteer.

Old soldier Bone asked, "Have you become that fixed on ending du Tancret's black tale?"

It took Nassim a moment to comprehend the universal response. He felt mildly shamed. But only mildly. The people his plot put at risk would not be known to him.

"I see your point. No. I'm not obsessed. Yet. Still, let's examine our chances of establishing a cache of firepowder inside Gherig."

Men shrugged. The notion inspired no real enthusiasm. Easier to breach the wall from outside.

"All right. Az, look into it. And keep trying to establish active agents inside. We need better intelligence. Rogert has a plan. Once he's healthy . . . I don't want to be surprised."

SURPRISES CAME. A MOVE BY ROGERT DU TANCRET WAS NOT ONE OF them. His villainy was overshadowed by events.

Az reported, "A new company of Brotherhood fighters has moved into Gherig. The most dangerous sort, committed newcomers."

"How many?" Nassim asked. "Will they make du Tancret too strong for us?"

"Thirty-four lances, the way they figure. Meaning about a hundred twenty fighting men, plus a few servants who could be armed if necessary. They're all veterans of the Calziran Crusade or other campaigns. But they may not actually strengthen Black Rogert."

"Uhm?"

"Word is, they're here to keep him under control. The Brotherhood couldn't keep him from returning to Gherig but they intend to control his bad behavior now that he's back. His leg was the excuse they needed to send these men."

"Interesting," Alizarin mused. "His own kind want him leashed."

"The captain of this new band is supposed to be humorless but capable. I couldn't learn much about him except that he is here at the express will of the masters of the order, coming from the Castella Anjela dolla Picolena itself."

"Uhm? Then some of his followers might be Special Office. Meaning he really is here to wrangle Black Rogert, not to deal with us pesky bandits."

"If the Special Office is involved they must suspect du Tancret of trafficking with the Night."

"There was a rumor about him having a pet sorcerer." No one ever found any evidence to sustain it, though.

The world wanted to believe the worst of Rogert du Tancret.

The Mountain said, "You will, of course, find out everything you can about these new men."

FOUR DAYS LATER TEL MOUSSA RECEIVED WELCOME COMPANY. AZIM al-Adil ed-Din stopped in while on his way home from Dreanger. Young Az was popular with the garrison and had won a place in the old general's heart.

Young Az told Nassim, "I'll stay tonight. I have dispatches for the kaif and those drones in Shamramdi."

"Five minutes is a blessing."

"I've brought two things for you, Uncle," using that word as an endearment. "Gifts from my granduncle. Though we should review them in private."

"Let's go up and watch the stars."

The sun had not yet set and the heat had not broken but Nassim did not mind. He needed more warmth these days. And the parapet could be as private as he liked.

He settled in the shade, into a western-style wooden chair. It was hard to get up from the cross-legged position these days. The wood was hot. The polite young warrior awaited an invitation to settle, despite his status.

Nassim observed, "These gifts must not be so large if you can carry them in your purse."

The boy folded his hands in his lap and stared at them for several seconds. "Before the gifts, the warning. The wicked sorcerer of al-Qarn survived the fighting. He eluded the hunters. He's headed this way, but not openly. Indala offered a large bounty. Some who tried to catch him ended up dead. Nastily. But the prize is big. All the tribes will try to claim it."

"We heard rumors that he was headed north."

"It's a fact. We don't know why. The clerks he left behind say he blames you for Indala's success."

"Which sounded painfully expensive. What good unification if no one survives to battle the true enemy? If the Sha-lug continue fighting . . ."

"Which brings me to the gifts." The boy produced a twist of long blond hair.

Nassim stared, understood, refused.

"You aren't pleased?"

"Truthfully? No. Gordimer was Marshall of the Sha-lug. You would have to be Sha-lug to understand what that means and what I feel. Better information concerning er-Rashal's whereabouts would be a finer gift."

"Then my second gift won't be welcome, either."

"Far from it if it's what I expect."

"Yes?"

"Indala never understood what it means to be Sha-lug."

"No one who isn't Sha-lug does, apparently. The other gift would be the post of Marshall."

"As I feared. He had me stashed away so he could make me his puppet once he achieved his ambitions in Dreanger."

"And?"

"I am content to be here. We have been enjoying some success. We expect more. I'll stick with this little war until he relieves me."

Young Az admitted, "He won't be pleased, though probably not surprised. I expect he'll accept your decision."

"Sha-lug Marshalls aren't chosen from outside. They're elevated by the men they command."

In reality they were elected by senior officers and masters of the training schools, choosing from among themselves.

"I won't try to convince you, General. You have to be who you have to be. So. Now. How has it been, having Black Rogert back?"

"Miserable. For everyone. Though it could be worse. He's injured and the Brotherhood of War have sent men to keep him under control." The subject occupied them, and kept Nassim from worrying about Indala's reaction to his refusal. The Great Shake could be fierce when thwarted.

"THE KID DIDN'T RIDE OUT HAPPY," OLD AZ SAID IN THE MORNING, beside the Mountain in the parapet. The general watched the dust raised by Young Az's band move northeastward. "What did you do?"

"I wouldn't let Indala make me his tame Marshall."

"Ah. We did see that coming."

"It seemed obvious."

"You really won't take the post?"

"Not from Indala. It isn't his to bestow."

Old Az chuckled. "I see. If the commanders of the battalions and masters of the schools call, Nassim Alizarin will be right there."

Nassim dissembled. "They've forgotten Nassim Alizarin. In any case, that call would place a wild strain on our loyalties."

The Master of Ghosts grunted. "Indeed." Indala would go on thinking they should be his. The Sha-lug would expect them to be Sha-lug before all else, Dreangerean second, faithful to the kaif of al-Minphet third, and enemies of the invader always.

Az said, "Princes don't like to be refused."

"This one is more reasonable than most. And he loses nothing by leaving us here. We do stifle the worst excesses of yon festering boil on the Adversary's arse."

He feared he was whistling in the dark, though. Indala might rid the world of every Sha-lug chieftain who refused to adapt to his new order.

Nassim could not help wondering if he should not have given the offer more consideration.

*   *   *

THE MOUNTAIN TOOK TO STAYING UP TO STUDY THE STARS. THE nighttime sky was like God Himself, vast and unchanging, and yet each time Nassim visited the parapet he saw something new. He was especially fond of shooting stars. There were a lot of those lately. They worried the more superstitious soldiers, who feared they portended great evils.

There was no apocalypse promised in al-Prama but the end of the world did feature in the Chaldarean, Devedian, and Dainshau faiths. In this messed-up corner of the world everyone knew something about his neighbor's beliefs, usually just enough to justify banging him over the head.

For Dainshaus and Devedians the apocalypse was only a potential. It could be avoided by keeping the law. For Chaldareans, though, the fire was guaranteed. There was no other way the world could be cleansed sufficiently for the establishment of God's Kingdom Eternal on Earth.

Nassim counted stars till midnight, challenging himself to enumerate those he had not counted before. Finally, he fell asleep where he sat.

He needed less sleep as he aged, but, still, late nights meant sleeping late. On days when he was not going on patrol himself he sometimes slept till noon.

The roar of falcons was an eye-opener any time. By the third bark Nassim was in motion.

There was no fourth roar.

A Lucidian met him as he headed for the gallery above the gate. "It was that sorcerer, sir! But we think we got him."

Scowling, still wrestling sleep, Alizarin shambled into the vantage of the gallery. The stench of burnt firepowder left him gasping. This gas was much fouler than that of the Devedian powder. The crews of the two lighter falcons had finished cleaning their weapons, had checked them for cracks, and had reloaded. Now they stood around looking smug.

Nassim asked, "That deeper roar. Was that our new friend from Haeti?"

"It was, sir. You will be pleased with its work."

The desert sun had yet to hoist itself over the horizon. The light outside included a lot of nighttime indigo. But there was illumination enough to reveal a scatter of men and horses who, to their astonished disappointment, had heard Tel Moussa's falcons speak.

A Lucidian officer said, "The sentries were as alert as we could possibly hope, sir. The instant they knew something was wrong they let the sorcerer have it."

"Excellent." He studied the world outside, saw dead men, dead animals, and a slope reverberating in its silence. Nothing moved. It felt like nothing dared. "Has anyone gone to pick up the pieces?"

"Just waiting on permission to open the gate."

The Mountain grunted that permission. He wondered who his men had killed. Nobody with connections, he hoped. He was in bad enough odor already.

Those dead men could not be er-Rashal and his cohorts. The Rascal would know better than to just walk up . . .

Mohkam soon reported, "They were yards short of the gate when Yudeh fired. Mowfik says none of them spoke. They wouldn't stop when they were challenged. Abd Ador on number one says he knew they were up to no good and if Yudeh hadn't fired he would have. He'd already decided. They all say there were six riders on six horses trailing two pack camels and two spare mounts. The camels bolted. They probably weren't hurt. But there are blood trails. Gamel al-Iriki has his troop ready to go after them."

Nassim dreaded the answer but had to ask. "Who were they?" That drew surprised looks from everyone.

"The Rascal and his gang. Didn't they tell you?"

"They did. But that isn't possible. Er-Rashal wouldn't just ride up and let himself be blasted."

Irked, Mohkam spat, "He didn't let anything. Sir. We did it to him. He wasn't expecting us to be alert and suspicious and he wasn't expecting our falcons."

Nevertheless, Nassim refused to believe er-Rashal's stupid move till he saw the dead for himself. Only then did he give up his high opinion of the Rascal's caution and intelligence.

He recognized two of the dead. They had crept around in er-Rashal's shadow for decades. They affected shaven skulls like er-Rashal, too.

The Mountain caught the hunters before they left. "Gamel, be careful. You'll be stalking the most dangerous man alive."

Gamel was not convinced. He hailed from some village in the eastern reaches of the kaifate. He knew er-Rashal only through the renegade Sha-lug. He did not credit most of what he heard.

Nassim said, "You don't have to believe me. But, for the sake of the men with you, pretend it's true. Go with God. We will shield you with our prayers and I will honor you in the highest if you place er-Rashal at my mercy."

Nassim watched his followers examine the dead, men and animals alike, looking for plunder or intelligence. They came up with nothing but the obvious. Horse meat would be on the menu till the carcasses went bad.

The dead had not been living well. Maybe starvation had made er-Rashal incautious.

Nassim climbed to the parapet to watch al-Iriki's hunt.

The chase soon split. One fugitive, leading two injured horses and a camel, fled toward Gherig, making no effort to go unnoticed. The pursuit overtook him quickly. The hunters, however, had to flee an Arnhander patrol. They returned with only one piece of good news. Nobody had gotten hurt.

The others were less fortunate. They caught er-Rashal.

Smoke and silent lightning marred the wasteland northeast of Tel Moussa. Then, after ten quiet minutes, it happened again, farther away.

Four men survived. They brought the fallen in aboard mounts gone half mad. Gamel al-Iriki still lived, but barely. His left side had been charred till bits of burnt bone were visible. His face, though, remained unmarred. He ground out, "When the General speaks the fool fails to listen. That Rascal may not be the most dangerous man in the world but he was dangerous enough to kill Gamel al-Iriki. But al-Iriki will have his revenge. Al-Iriki killed his horse and his camel and hit him with poisoned darts."

That said, the overly bold officer closed his eyes.

Nassim said, "We'll need to follow up."

"Bone is on it," Old Az said. "Poisoned arrows and javelins won't be enough."

"No. They won't. But he is on foot now, wounded, in country he doesn't know. It could be as simple as waiting for him at the water-holes."

Al-Azer er-Selim loosed a long sigh. "I'll go. I'll be more careful than al-Iriki was."

"Do be. I can't manage without you."

Bone and the rest of that old company sneered at that claim as they rode out seeking revenge for all that had been done to them.

ON EVEN THE LEAST DEMANDING DAYS SOME WORK DETAILS COULD not be let to slide. Most critical, the cisterns had to be kept topped up, and cleaned frequently so the water did not become foul. Mounts had to be tended, manure removed, and fodder stocks maintained. Goats and sheep had to be grazed and protected and kept ready to fly to safety should Gherig become aggressive.

And, least desirable of all, graves had to be kept prepared. Hacking those out of the hardpan earth was a semi-punitive detail. The day the Rascal came Tel Moussa filled all its ready graves but one.

Fallen horses did save many a goat and lamb from an early encounter with the butcher.

14. Antieux: Instrumentality

Brother Candle was not accustomed to petitioning the Good God for much but strength to stand firm in his faith. He found himself doing that with painful frequency, and as often tried to intercede for Kedle Richeut.

The Connec east of Castreresone was afire, figuratively. Two minor Arnhander forces, of fewer than a hundred men each, were hanging on in hopes that Anne of Menand would send help. Kedle had driven both behind walls. Each day there was a story about another savage ambush that claimed Society brothers or Arnhander soldiers.

And Socia smoldered with jealousy. Brother Candle strained to keep her focused on being a mother and master of Antieux.

Bernardin Amberchelle encountered few challenges to Socia's rule. The military class loved her. The people were accepting.

It was a time of incipient prosperity. Military success made that possible.

SOCIA TRAPPED THE PERFECT over a late evening meal, in a side chamber off the kitchen where each often ate in private. She had had a trying day. "Master, do I have the power to create law by fiat?"

The old man's spoon paused an inch from his mouth. "Excuse me?"

"I want whining made punishable by flogging. And stupidity made a capital offense. The things these people want me to decide! They're idiots! It's ridiculous! They all act like spoiled four-year-olds."

Brother Candle said, "They throw tantrums?"

"Why can't they use a brain? Why can't they take some responsibility for themselves?"

The Perfect kept his own counsel.

"Why are you looking at me like that? Oh. Oh, no you don't! You aren't turning this around on me!"

Again the Perfect said nothing.

"It's different!"

His smile said, of course it was. When Socia Rault whined, that was important. She was not some shopkeeper or artisan who just wanted a little respect.

"God damn it! All right. You win. I might have to bare my back to the cat, too. But, even so . . ."

"You will find, as you mature, that most people are weak. And lazy. Weak, lazy people whine and complain. Otherwise, they would have to take a risk to make things right. And the wrongs they suffer often don't need righting because they exist only inside their minds."

Now Socia began to sulk.

"It takes special strength to do the right thing and a good eye to recognize it."

"Life lessons. With you it's always life lessons."

"That is my calling, girl. I am supposed to be a teacher."

"Yeah? Well, you take it too damned serious. Listen. You weren't there for the petty assizes." She regaled Brother Candle with tales of trivial petitions.

He replied, "I see why Raymone was always off risking his neck. Why, though, do such matters get past the neighborhood magistrates? Ask. Strongly. Because those problems ought to be handled by parish priests and justices of the peace."

"Easy to see why priests dodge issues. They'd put themselves on record. That could haunt them down the road, if the Church ever has its way with Antieux. The justices probably don't want to offend their neighbors so they pass everything on to me."

Brother Candle nodded. This whine did merit attention. He might drop a word to Bernardin. To be successful Socia needed her government to perform at every level.

Yes. In this Bernardin's special talents might be especially useful.

Speaking of that particular devil . . .

"Master. Look! There's something wrong with Bernardin."

THE SIDE CHAMBER BROTHER CANDLE SHARED WITH SOCIA WAS NOT large. They had been alone till Bernardin appeared, though Kedle's cousin Guillemette had been in and out, bringing drink and clearing dirty platters. In the scandal-ridden Connec, with its traditions of romantic love and casual infidelity, even prigs did not lose sleep over a sixty-eight-year-old Maysalean Perfect being alone with their Countess.

Bernardin did appear to be in a trance.

He was not alone. A woman followed him. Or, on closer examination, a girl fifteen or sixteen but so stunning her youth was not instantly obvious.

She was tall. She was slim. Her eyes were big and blue. Her mouth was wide and her lips puffier than most. In one hand she carried a metal bucket. In another she held a five-foot staff with a one-foot T-top. In a third hand she carried a quartzlike crystal a foot long and two inches thick. A dark green shadow stirred inside. And in her other hand she carried another bucket, this one made of wood.

Brother Candle hardly noticed the extra hands. He could not rip his gaze away from that captivating face, surrounded by that cloud of wild blond curls, long enough to examine the semiprecious stone rosary she wore. She had a small spot just above her lip, on the right side. It was the most fascinating dot in the universe.

Though he could not check he suspected that Socia was equally enthralled.

Bernardin gobbled out noises to the effect of, "*She* has brought gifts."

Brother Candle grunted.

Then, slowly, he reddened, betrayed by a response that had not troubled him in decades.

He had an erection.

The girl smiled, showing impossibly perfect teeth. She knew.

Neither the Perfect nor the Countess challenged her presence. The demon—she had to be a devil, if not the Lord of Darkness Himself—settled her burdens on the supper table.

Brother Candle finally tore his attention away.

It shifted to the metal bucket, looming as large as a farm pond. Four whale-shaped fish a foot long swam lazily there. All four rolled over, revealing pus-yellow bellies, round mouths that seemed to be laughing, and bulging, side-mounted eyes. The demon grabbed Bernardin's shirt, pulled him close. He panted like he had just run a mile.

She removed his shirt. Bernardin shuddered as though she gave off epic static sparks. She took a fish from the pail and pressed it against his chest, then grabbed another and another till all four had attached themselves. They sank slowly into Amberchelle's flesh.

"Thou wilt know their time. Don thy shirt." There were no signs of the fish beyond savage purple scars.

Numbly, slowly, Bernardin dressed.

The girl turned on Brother Candle. She was a devil for sure. Succubus came to mind. Never in his wildest younger years had he imagined such intense temptation.

He remained rock hard.

"Take up the staff."

He did as he was told. The staff looked like planed laths painted white, actually rather goofy. The top of the T was at eye level. The demon girl thrust a hand into the wooden bucket, came out with a pair of snakes too large to have fit while another serpent lifted its head a foot above the lip of the bucket. The girl draped the first two on the staff.

Brother Candle blurted, "You're making me look like Asclapulus. Or Trismagitarus." He mispronounced both names but did not know that. At least one of those classical Instrumentalities had something to do with snakes.

"Undress thyself."

He did not want to do that. He could not find the strength to disobey. In a minute he had become a bony, withered old thing shivering while his manhood determinedly proclaimed itself. Bad enough, that, but, worse, Socia's gaze had become fixed upon it. He was a freak, like a man who had lost his ears and nose.

The devil girl took a snake from the T and laid it along the length of the outside of his left arm. It felt cold but neither damp nor slimy. Then he felt nothing at all.

Socia blurted, "Oh, my God!"

The snake melted into his skin. Unlike Bernardin, he suffered no scarring. The serpent became a ferocious, multicolored tattoo with its grimly fanged business end on the back of his left hand.

Before he got over the wonder the girl laid another snake along his right arm. Then she drew a third from the wooden bucket. She eyed his embarrassment, developed a mischievous look.

"No!" he croaked.

A shrug. A diabolic grin. A step round behind and a snake tattoo took up residence on his back, its angry head visible on the right side of his neck.

A fourth serpent ended up on his chest, coiled to strike.

"Dress thyself." After a last amused glance at his aching manhood.

The girl turned to Socia. "Thou mayest be what thou wilt." She took up the crystal. Brother Candle struggled with his clothing. When the girl turned away his brain began to work again, slowly. Why did she use an antiquated, formal form of speech? That seemed more peculiar than any accent might have.

"Think thee of the shape thee wouldst fain take, clearing all else from thy mind and cleaving only to the form of thy desire." The girl swept the crystal down in front of herself, from head to toes. She transformed into a leopardess no less alluring than the girl she had been before. The leopardess crouched in a pile of fallen clothing. It considered Bernardin and Brother Candle, for a moment purred like a lap cat.

Then it did something with the crystal and changed back into the girl, now wearing nothing to get in the way of male appreciation.

Brother Candle groaned. "No." At his age.

She was more toothsome than wickedest imagination could conjure. The ache worsened.

He wanted to whimper because she was dressing. At his age. And him being who he was.

Bernardin gurgled and fainted. Brother Candle abandoned all desire to be one of the Good Men. He worshipped the devil with his eyes.

The girl whispered to Socia, telling her how to use the crystal. Brother Candle caught a key point. You could become human again whenever you wanted but if you did it in public you would do it in all your naked glory. Whereupon the devil made Socia humiliate herself.

Bernardin's luck was in. He remained unconscious. He would never bear witness.

Seeing the woman he considered a daughter unclad opened Brother Candle's interior eye to a facet of self that he never suspected was there.

Unclad, Socia was deeply reminiscent of Margete, in the early years of their marriage. Not that the man he had been, Charde ande Clairs, had had many opportunities for so plain a view.

The demon made Socia practice till she had the knack. Till Brother Candle was confident they would all end up on the stake. The Church would be making nothing up when it rendered accusations, now.

"Most excellent. Thou hast mastered it, milady. 'Twill be thy gift. Be not profligate in the way thou useth it." The girl tugged at her apparel, made it hang more comfortably. Then, " 'Tis time. Be thou good soldiers in the struggle that cometh, all." She collected the buckets and T staff, headed for the door.

"Wait. Who? What?" He could not get a real question out.

Temptation turned, gave Brother Candle a wink. And he, unable to believe that it was possible to become any harder, felt agony as his erection strove to burst through his trousers.

The demon giggled like a silly girl, came back, kissed him lightly with those wondrous lips.

He exploded.

"I HAVE TO GO CHANGE."

"Sit. We have to figure out what just happened," Socia said.

"But I need to . . ."

"Sit down! Bernardin. Can you think yet?"

"Yes. Barely. What the hell was that?"

"You brought her here. Who was she? Where did she come from?"

Bernardin shrugged his massive shoulders. "I have no recollection."

"It would seem that the Captain-General did not get all the Dark Gods when he was cleaning up revenants. Master. Stop fidgeting."

Brother Candle was sure she knew. She was upset about that and angry because he had seen her unclad, though there had been little modesty between them back when they were fleeing the Captain-General. Modesty had been too much of a luxury then.

Socia remained businesslike. "That was no natural being."

"Genius," the old man said.

"If you're going to get petty . . ."

"You're right. I'll stop. We were all embarrassed."

"You have no idea, Master."

"Socia?"

"Your response was dramatic. Bernardin's must have been, too. I felt it myself. And I've never, ever, considered a woman that way. So. Pardon me my stare. I was amazed. Oh, Aaron! Oh, Lalitha! Preserve me. Guide me out of this fog of wicked obsession."

Brother Candle said, "We need to shake that part of it or we'll never pull ourselves together enough to work out what really happened."

Bernardin said, "She forgot something." His voice was that of a little boy distracted.

"What?"

"Look." He used his toe to stir something under the table, then eased it out. He could not yet bend comfortably. The demon had not kissed him.

"Socia, you'll have to get that. These old bones aren't that flexible anymore."

The Countess forbore comment. She retrieved what Bernardin had found. "Her necklace. She lost it when she changed shape. She must have missed it when she got dressed again."

Bernardin croaked, "She got naked?"

"Easy, boy. She did. As a leopardess."

Amberchelle looked to Brother Candle for confirmation. The old man nodded. How could they break the demon's hold? Maybe Mistress Alecsinac would know.

Bernardin said, "It looks like a rosary."

It was not but it did resemble one put together using oversize beads.

Socia wondered, "Did she really forget it? Or are we supposed to think she forgot it?"

Brother Candle shrugged. Either seemed plausible. She might have forgotten it because she was focused on driving an old man mad.

Socia said, "I have a feeling neither of you know what happened any better than I do."

Brother Candle said, "A demon came. It englamoured us. It tempted us."

"Really? Aren't you supposed to be a Seeker After Light, not some superstitious peasant who still believes in all the dark spirits and agents of evil that ran around during the God Times?"

"You are correct, woman. I am a teacher and supposed Perfect. But our faith never prepared me for what we just went through."

Bernardin Amberchelle said, "I don't think our faith mattered. If we'd had a Deve, a Dainshau, a Praman, a Maysalean, and every kind of Chaldarean here, none of them would have known her and none of them would have responded differently than we did. That fiery slip was a destroyer of faith. Any faith."

"What do we do?" Socia asked. "Whoever she was, whatever she was, she just dragged us into a new age. She made new people out of us. She gave us terrible gifts with no explanation. We have no idea why, nor any notion what those gifts may cost."

Massaging his chest, Bernardin said, "I want to forget it. I want to go to the baths and scrub myself clean."

Which presented an opportunity for an off-color jest. The Perfect resisted. Socia did the same. Amberchelle departed, preoccupied. Bemused, Socia asked, "Could any mortal girl be like that?"

"One in a generation might. I need to go change."

"It may be hard to face one another, now, but we still have to decide how to deal with it."

Sourly, Brother Candle said, "We need to find out what Instrumentality that was. Her attributes and aspects will tell us a lot. But not why, and not why us."

"I don't know where to start."

Sadly, neither did the Perfect. Everything he knew and believed had become suspect. "I have to go change."

"Go, then. Explore your wonderful fantasies. We'll work out how much we'll let what happened change our lives tomorrow."

Brother Candle grunted agreement. He had to flee this scene of embarrassment.

He knew he would not get much sleep.

Questions and fantasies alike would rule his night.

He went wondering if all that really had changed his world. It might all be surface flash to the cranky old Perfect inside. Anyway, he was much too old for more drama.

But he had looked into the eye of the living Night.

There must be a reason.

That inspired an abiding dread.

15. Alten Weinberg: Gathering

The Righteous waited outside Alten Weinberg for a day. The city needed to ready itself.

Naysayers plagued the new Empress, vainly hoping she would end the insanity begun by her sister. The last thing the great lords wanted was a standing army at the beck of the Imperial Will. The barons cherished their ability to defy the central authority.

Few had done so since the first years of the Ege dynasty but the inclination never faded.

The baronial class saw power only in terms of what they would do if they had it. Never mind that the Righteous had been created strictly as a spear to hurl into the Holy Lands. Katrin had used it for personal war. What oath would keep the new Empress from doing the same? The Commander of the Righteous claimed he would not be a political instrument but was clearly bedazzled by the younger Ege chit.

They knew the way of the world, those old men. They knew.

The Commander wished those old men would let him be apolitical.

It would help if Helspeth showed strength often hinted at but which seldom surfaced.

She might begin to trust it, supported by Captain Drear, Renfrow, and the Righteous. They could make firm political statements for her.

She had done well, so far. Of course, she had learned of events in Brothe before anyone else. She had been prepared. She had kept order.

Another sorry Ege death.

Johannes had lost three wives, none heroically or elegantly. His own death had been an anticlimax, a premature footnote. His sickly son and successor, Lothar, had survived longer than the most optimistic projection but still had died a child.

Katrin had not been a bad woman but hers had been a bad reign because of a bad choice in religion and a bad marriage to a bad husband who died a bad and needless death because of his own bad thinking.

Katrin and the Imperial office suffered. Expanding prosperity was a mark of her brief reign, though. There had been no calamities, neither plague nor drought, flood nor famine. Her wars had been far away and successful.

The Righteous waited but Hecht had agents in the city already, visiting those Righteous who had remained in place at the inception of the campaign. Rivademar Vircondelet, one of Titus Consent's favorites, led the infiltrators. Buhle Smolens commanded the left-behinds.

Smolens had been with Hecht a long time. He was no longer entirely trusted because he had stayed with the Patriarchal forces for a while after Serenity dismissed Hecht as Captain-General.

Most of Hecht's staff had questions orbiting them. He still was not fully confident that Titus Consent had truly converted to the Chaldarean faith. Nor was he sure that Clej Sedlakova and others with the Brotherhood of War in their background did not retain that ultimate allegiance.

They had their reservations, too. They watched their Commander closely. It was seldom possible for him to enjoy a visit from family.

As they had in the past, Hecht and his staff holed up in the mansion of Bayard va Still-Patter, the Empire's ambassador to Brothe. Bayard was the son of Ormo va Still-Patter, Grand Duke Hilandle, a key member of the Council Advisory. The Council evidently existed to bully the children of Johannes Blackboots, each of whom, in turn, grew to loathe those meddlesome antiques. The meddlers, no doubt, meant to go right on jostling those at the tiller of the ship of empire.

Most of the Council had hared off to join in the humbling of the Patriarchy. They were not yet back. Helspeth had some time.

Bayard va Still-Patter was a friend of the Righteous and their Commander. His father, decidedly, was not.

Hecht was still trying to shake the dust off when one of Consent's clerks told him, "We're getting buried in requests for visits, sir."

"And you would like suggestions."

"It's your time, sir. Mr. Consent says we can't give it away without your approval."

"Make it sound like I'll see everybody as soon as I can. To make it fair, we'll draw lots."

"That's sure to piss off the ones who think they're important, sir."

"They'll be even more irked when they find out the lottery is rigged."

The clerk took several seconds before observing, "You shouldn't provoke anyone deliberately, sir."

"Good point. Maybe success has gone to my head. I need to remember that nobody cares what we did last month. They care about what they can wheedle today and tomorrow."

"Yes, sir. Sir, I brought a list of who wants to see you and what they say is why."

"Good. Leave it. I'll look it over. If any are waiting around, tell them I won't see anybody before tomorrow. I'm too tired."

He *was* tired. Lately, he was tired all the time.

High on the list was the Princess Apparent.

Among others, two names stood out: Ferris Renfrow and the Graf fon Rhejm. The latter was one of Katrin's uncles. Hecht had not met the man formally. Fon Rhejm was not a regular in Alten Weinberg. A meeting might be useful.

"Cantata."

"Sir?" The clerk had been about to slip out.

"A change in instructions. I'll see Ferris Renfrow as soon as he can manage. Then arrange for a visit to or from the Graf fon Rhejm. I'd rather see him here but I'll go to him if he insists. Once you've handled that, tell Vircondelet and de Bos that I need this list annotated. I don't know who half these people are."

"Very good, sir."

FERRIS RENFROW ARRIVED WITHIN THE HOUR. HE WAS NOT ALONE. Asgrimmur Grimmsson accompanied him. Hecht's protectors did not want to expose him to the ascendant. They sensed a wrongness.

Hecht said, "If it makes you more comfortable, Titus, sit in. You won't like what you hear, though."

"Why let Grimmsson in? He smells dangerous."

"He is dangerous." Hecht was puzzled. Consent had seen Grimmsson before . . . That might be it. His recollections of the ascendant harkened back to before a few rounds of godshot shredded Asgrimmur's Night-madness.

Hecht asked, "Are you bothered because of who he used to be? Don't be. He's with us, now."

Consent just looked puzzled.

"Bring them up, Titus. And have the quiet room checked. We may need it."

Renfrow and the ascendant arrived accompanied by Consent and two large, well-armed soldiers who posted themselves inside the entrance. Hecht accepted their presence, though they could do little if either visitor had evil inclinations.

They let Titus relax. That was good enough.

"Look at you, Asgrimmur!" Hecht said, noting that the ascendant had not yet figured out how to grow a new hand. "You've gone modern." A good stone of hair had gone away. What survived was oiled and combed. A ghost of a mustache and a little triangle of hair on the man's chin were the sole recollections of a once formidable tangle of beard. The ascendant's clothing had undergone an upgrade, too. "Welcome to the Thirteenth Century." Hecht glanced sidelong at Ferris Renfrow. Did the Bastard have anything to say about the new Asgrimmur?

Renfrow shrugged.

"Everybody grab a chair, drag it over here. Form a square. Settle. We'll talk."

They did so, Titus included. Grimmsson and Renfrow waited for Consent's presence to be explained.

"Titus needs to know what's going on. I've kept him in the dark."

Renfrow observed, "You've never been forthcoming with anyone."

"Justifiable. Consider the people I deal with. Titus. You know these men. You've probably fantasized some interesting theories about them."

Nervous now, Consent nodded.

"It's worse than you think." Hecht glanced at the lifeguards at the doorway.

Renfrow said, "They won't understand us. Any other eavesdropper will be both related to you and better informed than you are."

"I'll take your word. Here's the story, Titus."

Hecht sketched the facts. He skipped some key points, like his death from that assassination attempt and an explanation of how he had survived.

Consent muttered, "We didn't need to take this to a quiet room?"

Renfrow had done something. Bits of darkness were on patrol.

Asgrimmur said, "Find work for the Old Ones. They're getting into mischief because they don't have anything to do."

"Tell them to stop. Bad behavior isn't productive. And it attracts attention."

"Just like that?" the ascendant asked. "When they haven't seen the middle world in ages?"

"They need to understand that this isn't the middle world they knew. In this middle world people know how to kill gods. In this middle world some people have dedicated their lives to that."

"You want to threaten them when they've already agreed to help you?"

"No. I want them informed. They can call Heris or me Godslayer. We earned it. But we weren't doing it for sport. They need to understand that some people want them exterminated because their existence threatens them. The Special Office, for example. Those people saw what happened in the Connec. They were there."

Renfrow said, "With the wells of power so weak no new gods will arise. If the Old Ones feed on other Instrumentalities they won't get stronger, they'll just buy time."

Hecht said, "If the wells don't come back the Special Office will get what it wants without lifting a finger."

"In the sense that the Night will keep getting weaker. The Instrumentalities will never go away completely. Unless they get on the wrong side of your sister."

Asgrimmur said, "Some are clever. They may find ways to beat the drought."

Hecht had a thought so disconnected he shook his head as though to dislodge it, or, at least, to shake loose an explanation of why it had gone off ninety degrees to nothing.

Titus stood. "Boss? You all right?"

"I don't know. Strange ideas just bubbled up out of nowhere. I'm not used to that."

"Huh?"

"See, I had this sudden notion that we have to do everything we can to get hold of Grinling."

His companions all made puzzled noises. Consent went a step further. "Evidently another mystery where I'm no initiate."

"Grinling is a magic ring. Built by the Aelen Kofer. It got lost in our world ages ago. Dumped into the Shallow Sea, or maybe the Mother Sea. I don't know much about it so I don't know why I'd think about it now."

The ascendant said, "If you knew how to work it you could use it to control the Shining Ones and make yourself Master of the Nine Worlds."

Again Titus expressed confusion.

"The Shining Ones, or Old Ones, were always collective names for the old northern gods," Renfrow explained. "To confuse things, these days country people call elves and other minor Instrumentalities the Shining Ones, too."

Consent said, "I was angry about being left out. Now I'm not sure ignorant wasn't best." He looked desperate. "Boss, how do you get your head around all this?"

"Sometimes I can't. Mostly, I just remember that it's the Night. You shouldn't have trouble adapting. You handled the revenant hunt in the Connec."

"Oh," Renfrow said. "The Connec. Bad news out there. Count Raymone caught a gang of Arnhanders trying to sneak Serenity through to Arnhand. He got hold of the dirty end."

Hecht demanded details. Raymone was neither a friend nor an ally but he had thought well of the man. And the Count's determined enemy, Bronte Doneto, seemed equally determined to be an enemy to Piper Hecht.

Renfrow had few details. He had seen nothing himself. He had visited the scene days after the event.

"No Anselin?" Hecht asked.

"No Anselin. That rumor may have begun as a lure for Raymone, but I doubt it. The Arnhander force wasn't that strong. It was one of those shit happens things. Serenity was lucky to get out with his ass still attached. He was badly hurt. You really want, send the old man to cut his throat. He's nowhere near Salpeno yet. He'll move slowly because of his wounds."

Hecht had traveled with a recuperating Bronte Doneto, escaping the Connec early on. "He'll be making somebody miserable. He doesn't handle pain well." He ignored the suggestion about loosing the Ninth Unknown. "You're on the inside, now, Titus. Forget what you believed before you sat down. Open your mind to what is." Then, "I know that isn't much help. I have trouble and I've lived with it for several years."

Renfrow said, "I have for seven hundred. And Asgrimmur has for three hundred."

The ascendant disagreed. "It must have been longer than that. I was asleep in the Realm of the Gods for ages. The dreams weren't pleasant."

"Easy," Hecht said. The old insanity had begun to surface, there. "Here's a thought. If the Shining Ones need to stay busy have them find Grinling for me. Have them find Anselin. He's got to be somewhere."

Asgrimmur said, "I'm sure they're looking for Grinling already. Whoever finds it would have a leg up. You might've noticed that they're not team players."

Hecht said, "I'll see the Empress soon. Till I get different orders, Titus, assume that we're still headed for the Holy Lands. No big thing for you, Renfrow, but our livelihood for the rest of us."

Grimmsson stirred uneasily. "I said I'd help once my other business was done. It is. What should I be doing?"

"Running my special operations force." It came smoothly, without forethought. "You'll manage our rescued friends, plus Zyr and Red Hammer if Heris can get them back."

"I understand you lost the Zyr egg."

"No, I didn't. But while we were transitioning it changed somehow. Heris is trying to work out what happened." But he feared that whatever had, it could not be undone. Zyr might be gone forever.

The ascendant said, "I transitioned with Heris before. It was so awful I won't ever do it again."

"It was never easy for me, either. Renfrow. Your part is done. What're you going to do now?"

"What Ferris Renfrow always does. Stay out of sight. Be a phantom threat that protects the Throne and spies on its enemies."

"Who do not include the Righteous."

"At the moment. Times keep changing."

Hecht betrayed his irritation.

"Easy, Commander. A jest, no more. I foresee no problems."

Hecht caught a glimmer of motion in the corner of his left eye. He turned. So did Renfrow and Grimmsson. There was nothing to see. Renfrow's black beads did not become active. Hecht asked, "Titus, how much do the men know about Asgrimmur?"

"Enough to be nervous."

"How about we don't tell anybody who he used to be? We could come up with a hook or a claw, couldn't we?"

"Well . . . call him Sweetling, keep him from going all hairy and rustic again, make him dress like he's from this century, he can get by. People who have to depend on him will want some sense of who he is, though."

"We're mercenaries. We lie about who we used to be. We lie about where we came from. Trust we earn now."

Asgrimmur might not have been listening. "The Old Ones will have their hands full dealing with Vrislakis and Djordjevice. We didn't get the cream of the Shining Ones."

Piper Hecht steepled his fingers in front of his chin. "I'm going to let you explain that."

"What?"

"Back when, the implication was that you put the whole gang out of business. Permanently. Plus, the top god and the Exile are gone. Right? So. Some were trapped, but not the whole bunch. Right?"

Asgrimmur nodded. "Twelve, about half of them not first rank."

Hecht grunted. "And the others? I could probably think of seven or eight more names."

"They were away when the Aelen Kofer closed the gates between the worlds. They're in Eucereme, now, where they'll stay till the end of time unless the dwarves reopen the ways. You met Iron Eyes. Will he suffer a change of heart when there's nothing but servitude in it for the dwarves?"

Renfrow said, "Commander, you're fussing about things in need of no fuss. We have plenty to occupy us." He spun in his chair, stared into a corner, snarled something inarticulate. His black beads rolled around but accomplished nothing obvious.

Grimmsson watched the same corner, staring slightly to the side.

Hecht thought he knew what was happening. "I don't know which one of you that is, but come on out. Now."

A shimmer. A sharp vertical line. A two-dimensional form that turned to become Lila, red-faced. "Are you sure, Father?"

Hecht glanced at the bug-eyed guards, who fumbled with their weapons. He had miscalculated. He should have let the girl be. Now he had to come up with a believable explanation. "Always thinking, our Piper," he muttered. "But too late, now. Why are you here?"

"Just keeping in touch. Making sure you're all right."

"Checking up for your mother?"

"No. For Heris."

"Heris?" That was startling. And that was Lila, talking straight up.

She said, "Strange things have been happening in Brothe. All over Firaldia, actually. Heris says it's the Old Ones playing pranks. She would very much like to see you." Lila pointed at Grimmsson.

Titus Consent's eyes kept getting bigger as he worked out the truth behind all those mystery midnight visits. "This isn't possible! None of this is possible!"

"Stop thinking that way," Hecht told him. "Possible or not, this is part of our business, now. And it will get worse."

Renfrow nodded. Asgrimmur was involved in a side conversation with Lila. The Commander of the Righteous glanced at his lifeguards. They were confused. They recalled something happening but no longer knew what it was.

Renfrow murmured, "The alliance is holding." Whatever that meant.

Asgrimmur said, "I'll flap down and see what Heris wants. Where is she, Lila?"

"She was at Anna's house when I left."

Hecht demanded, "What? Anna was supposed to stay safe in the Castella!"

"Calm down, Dad. Those troubles have died down. It's safe. Except if a giant bird lands on the front stoop and turns into a naked man."

"You said strange things . . ."

"I did. I didn't mean riots. Wait. That's not right. There are disorders. But not where our house is. Heris says those Instrumentalities are looking out for Anna, anyway."

"Why?" Hecht addressed the question not just to Lila but to everyone.

The ascendant reminded him, "The Old Ones are totally selfish. So Anna's fortunes must be important to them." While Hecht puzzled that, he added, "I'll be back in a few days. I hope with my commandos rounded up."

"Put them to work. Aren't they supposed to be focusing on the Windwalker's cousins?"

"They are. Count on it. Just don't expect fire in the sky over the northern horizon."

Renfrow and Grimmsson slipped past the two lifeguards. Those men seemed to have concluded that the Commander of the Righteous no longer needed guarding. They followed.

Hecht caught Lila wearing a smug smirk. "What did you do, girl?" Getting nervous. She was too deft at all this stuff.

"It's simple, really. And handy when your parents are getting on your nerves . . . Whoa! Just joking. We're careful not to get caught. Except for Pella, who doesn't think ahead."

Hecht did realize that she was teasing before he exploded. He kept the darkness out of sight and silent. Lila was less hard than she pretended.

Hecht said, "I understand that young people feel obligated to irritate their elders. And I'm not used to young people. So try to clamp it down."

Lila eyed him hard, maybe cataloging his thoughts and impulses. "All right. Sorry. I need to remember that you and Anna don't know much about kids because neither of you ever got to be one."

"Thank you. I think." Recalling that Lila had never been one, either.

"Great. Stiff old stuff all done. Who do you want me to spy on, Dad? What do you want me to steal?"

"You didn't keep yourself very low-profile when you got here."

"Sorry. I was trying to get onto the third floor of someplace I've never been before. The up and down stuff is hard! That's where I messed up. I was two feet too high. I had to keep from falling. That's why everybody noticed."

"And now even Titus knows what you can do."

"Good for him. He'll keep looking over his shoulder."

Inasmuch as Consent was still in the room, still in his seat, Hecht expected an excited response. But the man's eyes had glazed over. His breathing was shallow and slow.

"Lila. What did you do to him?"

"Nothing. I didn't have any reason . . . It's the old man. It has to be."

Cloven Februaren rotated into existence. "She's a fast learner, Piper. But she needs to keep a sharper eye out. Check your back trail once in a while, girl. Something might be gaining on you."

Februaren made several small, odd, complicated hand gestures. Black beads rolled out of shadows and out from under things. They mustered in front of Februaren, who told Lila, "Scoop those up for me, darling. I have trouble bending."

"No."

Startled, Hecht blurted, "Lila!"

"He's being a jerk, Dad. They'll sting me if I touch them with my bare hands."

Hecht eyed the old man. Februaren grinned. His right eyebrow went up. "She's right. So she has been paying attention." He bent and scooped. The black beads hopped into his hand. "They say keep your friends close and your enemies closer. You got to wonder which is which, sometimes."

"I do every day," Hecht said. "Is there a reason you turned up?"

"Keeping an eye on Lila. This was an extreme-range solo. I wanted to be handy if she got into trouble."

Lila looked pleased and put out at the same time.

Hecht said, "Can you unspell Titus?"

"Not yet. I wanted to let you know that our divine friends are up to something. I don't know what, yet."

"I've had that feeling all along. But I can't grasp the motivation. All they need to do is wait. We won't demand much of them."

"I think they can't help it. I think they all have a little Trickster in them. In any case, they'll have convinced themselves that they aren't violating the letter of their contract."

"So what are they doing?"

"I don't know. It isn't obvious. Mischief, mostly around churches."

"Vandalism?" The West had a standing tradition of majorities desecrating minority houses of worship.

"Sort of. I'm not sure how. They aren't busting stained glass windows or stealing candles. It's more like they're sucking the holiness out. Though holiness isn't the word I want. It's whatever brings on that feeling that you're in a consecrated place," said Februaren.

"And you a Prince of the Church."

"Yeah. I should pay more attention to the business end of religion."

"Have you ever celebrated a mass?"

"No. But I'm not unique. The Collegium is all political. God, and God's work, doesn't have much relevance."

"Call me weird. I don't think God would agree."

"God gets along. How often do you see Him disagree with the Collegium? Or any Patriarch?"

"I don't much care, honestly. Religion has abandoned me so I'm no longer inclined to respect my end of the bargain."

"Just a heads-up," Februaren said. "Watch out for weird stuff happening. Now, besides keeping a lookout on the wonder girl, here, I wanted you to know that Heris and I won't be around for a week or two. The Shining Ones have come up with a lead on Vrislakis, or one of those."

"Then the Shining Ones shouldn't be getting into much trouble. They'll be helping you."

"That's my plan. We'll see. But the Old Ones strive hard to be difficult. They don't want to communicate directly, but don't want to go through the ascendant or the Bastard, either."

"Don't put up with it. Just tell them what they're going to do."

Februaren shrugged. "Lila, girl. I don't see any reason why you can't operate on your own, now. Just be careful. From now till Heris and I get back you'll be your father's guardian angel."

Februaren turned sideways. The air whooshed into the space he had vacated. But then he popped right back, four feet from where he had been before. "Piper, the communication pendant. You haven't used it for a while. Do you remember how? In case . . ." He stopped. Consent showed signs of shaking his torpor.

"I must have lost it. I have no idea when. Last time I . . ."

He did remember. During his sordid encounter with Empress Katrin in the Krulik and Sneigon falcon manufactory she had insisted that he get rid of the pendant. It kept hitting her in the back of the neck.

"I'd forgotten all about it."

"And yet you've made it through everything. Maybe you *are* beloved of the gods. What about your amulet? Have you lost that, too?"

"No. Right here." Hecht raised his left hand, squeezed his left wrist.

He forgot the amulet most of the time, too. But not lately. "It's been driving me crazy. It itches all the time."

The old man's gaze was, suddenly, so intense that Hecht took a surprised step back. "What?" Hecht said.

"The god hunt might get off to a slow start. If it does, your sister might turn up here. Don't expect her to be in a good mood if she does."

The Ninth Unknown rotated again.

Consent had recovered enough to understand what he was seeing. "Boss, I don't know if I can handle this."

"You get used to it. The hard part is remembering not to talk about it around people who don't need to know."

"Nobody would believe me, anyway."

Hecht thought Titus might be surprised.

ALGRES DREAR AND A DOZEN BRAUNSKNECHTS TURNED UP TO TAKE the Commander of the Righteous to see the Empress. Hecht's staff were nervous but he was confident of his safety.

Lila had been hard at work eavesdropping. She had had a good time, with no trouble. Only Ferris Renfrow was a problem. Hecht had told her to stay away from him.

She had not done so, of course. Her ration of youthful over-confidence had been well fertilized by her Construct-supported skills.

Renfrow taught her a lesson Hecht did not hear of till much later. Lila spent a few hours inside a soundproof, lightless quiet room in such perfect repair that she was unable to transit out.

Hecht's past visits to Helspeth had taken place at the Ege family mansion or other private venues. Seldom had many others been present. This visit was supposed to take place in the privy audience of the Imperial Palace, the official residence of the Grail Emperors. He found people in the halls and grand ballroom. Scores of them. With servants and guards, maybe hundreds. At least a score were Braunsknechts, big, hard men dedicated to protecting the Imperial person. They wore excellent armor, carried excellent weapons, and, Hecht noted, each bore a brace of handheld firepowder arms. They looked like they might be asked to break a siege at any moment.

Hecht asked Drear, "Is the mood here as crazy as it seems?"

"It's worse. What happened to Katrin was the last thing anyone expected. The Empire was resigned to an inauspicious reign. Important men had their appointments and expected to milk them once the war in Firaldia sputtered to an end."

"What?"

"Those wars always did. Even when Johannes was successful, something always happened. Something happened this time, too, but you were ahead of it. So Alten Weinberg is in chaos. Nobody had warning enough to pick sides and decide on a preferred form of obstructionism."

Hecht grunted. He studied the people around him, saw more resentment and calculation than inclination to build a better future. "The Righteous have acquired new tools for handling deliberate obstructionism."

Drear did not respond. The set of his shoulders said he thought Hecht was posturing.

Hecht said, "I'm sure it won't be long till someone earns a demonstration."

"Commander, what you'll face here will be petty. Mostly trivia like jealousy over your access to the Empress."

Access was always invaluable around a court. It was coin—or the lack thereof—in a political sense. The Council Advisory had profited immensely by controlling access during the reigns of Katrin and Lothar.

"You see a lot of Helspeth, Captain. Is she talking major changes?"

"She'll let you know what's on her mind." Stated sharply.

Constant stares from palace denizens. Hecht pictured hungry lizards with long tongues darting.

He shuddered. Creepy. They had the eyes of lizards, too.

He considered each face, sure he smelled their hidden thoughts.

He smelled coffee as he approached the privy audience.

Three people waited with the Empress, who had taken steps to appear Imperial. There was the inevitable Lady Hilda, the Graf fon Rhejm, and Archbishop Brion of Urenge, the latter not in his ceremonial apparel. Lady Hilda was occupied with the coffee. Empress Katrin's uncle seemed older and more massive than Hecht remembered. He had the eyes of a raptor. The Archbishop had the eyes of a vulture. But that was not fair. Hecht did not know the man. He had a better reputation than most of his peers. No scandal attached to his name.

Both men had appointments for private visits.

Captain Drear joined them. Drear seldom strayed far from his Empress.

Hecht performed the obeisances due the Imperial personage, did the same for the Archbishop, then accepted coffee from Lady Hilda, who delivered the wondrous beverage in a beer mug accompanied by a flirtatious flutter of lashes. He smiled back and would have winked if unsmiling eyes had not been watching.

The dignity of her new estate had possessed Helspeth already. She perched on her audience throne quite regally. She rose, stepped down to greet Hecht, let him kiss her massive Imperial signet ring. She chose to wear that where married women wore a wedding band. A statement? In a faint whisper she said, "I'm desperately trying not to giggle."

He lifted his gaze.

The magic was still there. Whatever else she might be, she remained the woman who liquefied his spine and turned his knees to butter.

He recognized the same response in her. He did not trust his mouth with words.

Helspeth stepped back. "Let's all sit and enjoy our coffee."

A sizable table had been brought in for the purpose. Helspeth assumed the seat of honor, assisted by Captain Drear, who took station behind her right shoulder. Lady Hilda guided Hecht to the far end of the table, facing the Empress. After pouring coffee she took station behind his right shoulder. Archbishop Brion and the Graf fon Rhejm settled on the long sides of the table, nearer Helspeth, the Archbishop taking precedence to her right. Neither he nor the Graf said anything.

"So here we are," Helspeth said. "Where I never expected to be, nor am I yet sure I belong. Commander of the Righteous. You saw what happened with Katrin. Tell us. Spare me no detail."

He told it, sparing Helspeth the more sordid details. He would take those into the Night unshared with anyone.

"Thank you, Commander. Much as I hated to listen, I had to hear that. So: where do we go from here?"

That sounded rehearsed. Hecht did not respond. His silence did not disappoint her.

She continued, "There will be changes. Fewer and smaller than some fear, not as many or as large as others hope. I mean to step back from Katrin's romance with Brothe. My policies will more closely align with those of my father. But I do intend to fulfill Katrin's promise to liberate the Holy Lands."

Helspeth reminisced about her father's hope to take the crusader mantle, which was where Katrin had gotten the idea.

"We're capable financially. Commander Hecht's recent campaign, though costly, did not strain the treasury. And we can count on considerable external support. The Church has wanted a new crusade since the Battle of the Well of Days. Commander, go on doing what you would have done if misfortune hadn't overtaken my sister."

She still sounded rehearsed.

Hecht bowed in his seat, pleased. He had a job. It would keep him in Alten Weinberg, near Helspeth Ege.

With an adopted daughter lurking.

Lady Hilda startled him by stepping forward to fill his cup. She got a little close when she did. She and Helspeth were playing at something.

The Archbishop squirmed. Lady Hilda did not refresh his coffee unasked and he was not pleased by what he had heard. But a new wind was sweeping the Brothen Episcopal Church and that threatened to become tornadic.

Gervase Saluda talked a good game when he blustered and roared about the Church's need to extirpate corruption. How sincere he was remained to be seen. If he meant it he would have to move fast, before inertia defeated good intentions. Cronyism, nepotism, simony, and abuse of the power to confiscate the properties of heretics were all time-honored perquisites.

Archbishop Brion dared not stand in favor of all that. That could cost him any chance for future gains. He was no Chaldarean fanatic. He was a functionary in the Church bureaucracy.

Hecht glanced at the Graf. The man's steadfast silence made him uncomfortable.

Helspeth said, "Ferris Renfrow tells me you've acquired new personnel resources, Commander. He didn't go into detail."

Good for Renfrow. "We have gained the assistance of a small group of refugees with unusual skills and talents. They should be a great help."

"Can you tell me more?"

"No, Majesty. Not now. If you really need to know more, consult Renfrow. He knows them better than I do."

"He won't talk. So, other matters. In particular, Count Raymone Garete of Antieux. What does his passing mean? Is it important?"

"Extremely. He resisted every encroachment from Arnhand and all of the Church's bullying. If Arnhand had a king in place I'd expect the Connec to be invaded again. But there is no king. The new Patriarch is not obsessed with the Connec. And the Connec has Count Raymone's wife. I hear she's friendly with the madwoman who killed Regard. Those two, and Count Raymone's cousin Bernardin, seem determined to baptize the Connec with foreign blood. I'm quite happy not to be Captain-General anymore."

Helspeth said, "Arnhand's ambassador has asked for troops to 'Silence the heretic rebellion.' "

"And?"

"And nothing. It was a blatant show of arrogance. Since Anne of Menand got her talons into Charlve the Dim's vague soul . . . No matter how much she's embarrassed, no matter how heavy the cost in castles, towns, treasure, and lives, Anne goes on like she's queen of the world."

Everyone stared, surprised by her intensity.

Helspeth Ege did not become exercised about events in foreign places. Helspeth seldom became heated about anything. She had been schooled by years spent concealing her thoughts and feelings.

The Empress sipped coffee, asked, "What's become of Anselin of Menand? Is he really missing? Renfrow says people have started looking. He could become important."

Hecht shrugged. He had no idea. The Graf and the Archbishop apparently did not care. Algres Drear did but it was not his place to comment. Hecht made a mental note to find out if the Shining Ones had made any progress toward finding Anselin.

"Commander?"

"Excuse me. My mind wanders. I was pondering how we could communicate across the distances we'll face next summer."

Helspeth and the Archbishop scowled. Graf fon Rhejm seemed indifferent. Helspeth said, "Archbishop Brion asked what role you see for the Church in the coming crusade."

Hecht did not respond honestly. He wanted the Church to stay out of the way. "There'll certainly be a need for chaplains and healing brothers and someone to bless the men before battle and provide last rites to the fallen."

"Commander, that isn't what he meant."

"I feared as much. I'll try to state this politely. The business of the Church is the care of souls. The business of the Righteous is war. Whatever the goals of our enterprise, they will be achieved by military means. I won't accept interference in military operations by persons not military. I, and the fighters who go, won't be walking all those miles, suffering alien weather and climate and new diseases, nasty insects and enemy resistance, to feed the whims of anyone. I expect our goals to be stated clearly before we march. I expect to be left alone to attain them. That was the understanding the Righteous had with Empress Katrin. We have chartering documents stating that. Is that clear enough?"

Apparently so. But, predictably, the Archbishop was not pleased.

Hecht told him, "We have our appointment tomorrow, Your Grace. I will be pleased to discuss this further then."

Helspeth glared. "You have a private meeting with the Archbishop, Commander?"

"Yes, Majesty. Much of my time, for the foreseeable future, is committed to meetings with individuals who insist they need a slice of that time." He did not glance at Graf fon Rhejm. He had asked to see the Graf.

"I see."

He thought she did.

He did not mention it but he planned to send her transcripts of his meetings.

Helspeth said, "Brion, was there something you wanted to discuss with the Commander that can't be handled here? I'd rather he didn't waste time on people who have no part in his project. We're behind. He lost months taming Firaldia for my sister."

Hecht allowed himself a private smile. The girl was donning the role, and she was her father's daughter. She had made it clear that outsiders could approach the Commander of the Righteous only on matters pertinent to the coming enterprise.

Helspeth continued, "Commander, don't waste time on the posturing and backbiting Alten Weinberg so loves. I know you're a polite man. You don't feel comfortable turning people away, so I'll stand in as the rude one when the need arises. If the fleas can't stop biting I'll move you out to Hochwasser."

Brion's visage kept darkening. Graf fon Rhejm went on having a lot of nothing to say. Hecht wanted to argue. Hochwasser was not far, yet too far to lend quick support in an emergency. Still, he held his tongue. Helspeth was trying to insulate him from Imperial politics.

She did not yet understand that politics could not be avoided. He was not sure he grasped that fully himself. He did resent the loss of time it cost.

The Archbishop started to say something. He made an inarticulate sound, subsided when everyone looked at him. He shook his head.

Hecht decided that the man was not a villain. That kind, like Bishop Serifs and Bronte Doneto, were never shy, however hostile their audience. He glanced at Algres Drear.

Drear had, probably, thrown Serifs off a cliff in the Ownvidian Knot, for being himself. Bronte Doneto was a survivor of that same journey.

Hecht had seen nothing, ever, to suggest that Drear's conscience bothered him.

The captain shifted slightly, made uncomfortable by Hecht's regard.

Lady Hilda started to pour more coffee. Hecht raised a hand. "I've had enough." But only because neither the Graf nor the Archbishop had been offered any, nor had the Empress herself been before the Commander of the Righteous. Hecht caught a fleeting smile from Helspeth.

She said, "You will receive every support that Katrin provided, Commander. Her great work must go forward. Also . . . the Graf fon Rhejm wishes to speak. A family matter. Uncle Albert?"

Fon Rhejm's was not a voice made for oratory. It alternated between gravelly growl and squeak. He had taken a blow to the throat at some point. "Ferris Renfrow salvaged Katrin's secret papers before the Grand Duke or his ilk could seize them. He managed to get them here before the old gentlemen of the Council Advisory could arrive. Among those papers was her will, properly executed, attested, and witnessed while she was staying in the Penital, just hours before her deadly ride."

Guilt pierced Hecht. And terror followed.

He must have shown something. The Graf said, "She must have had a presentiment. She used the document to beg forgiveness of everyone she hurt. She confirms Helspeth as her successor, in accordance with Johannes's wishes. She asks specific forgiveness for having been so cruel to her sister. She commands the lords of the Empire to be faithful to Helspeth. There is advice to Helspeth about being a careful and wise ruler, never forgetting that she is Empress of all the people, not just the loudest factions.

"As an aside, I find that uncharacteristic of my niece."

Hecht said, "Starting when her baby was born dead, she went through some bad emotional seasons. When the news about Jaime arrived she turned into a different person. Her lifeguards were afraid she would harm herself. She didn't, though, till that wild ride. That took everyone by surprise."

"So we understand. Renfrow says he found nothing untoward."

Hecht felt some relief.

"The rest of the will concerns you."

The terror again. "Sir?"

"She was convinced that you and the Righteous could buy her entry into Heaven. She wanted to make sure you could keep on with what she called 'the Enterprise of Peace and Faith,' which is Churchspeak for 'crusade.' She left her titles and properties to you, for the use of the Righteous, till the crusade is done. She saw something in you she trusted."

"She can't do that!" Hecht said. "We talked about that. She shouldn't have done that." He could not begin to imagine the peculiarities that had roamed that woman's mind. "What *did* she do?" This could get him killed.

Graf fon Rhejm said, "You now control the incomes from her possessions. You are now one of the Empire's richest men. You are now lifetime lord of Eathered and Arnmigal, but not of Kretien and Gordon. You can't have them. That would elevate you to Elector. The other Electors wouldn't tolerate that, and she knew it."

Hecht could not speak.

"My niece had great faith in you."

Hecht shook his head. Eathered and Arnmigal, way north of Alten Weinberg, were among the richest constituents of the Empire.

"It's not hereditary, Commander. After the crusade, and your passing, properties revert. Those Katrin received through the Ege line will turn back to the Eges. Those received through her mother's line revert to us. But, still, Eathered and Arnmigal will be yours for life."

"Aaron preserve me!" Hecht swore.

"The danger will be less than you think. Possibly less than it was before. Katrin's family will honor her wishes. In death, at least, she'll have something she wanted."

Hecht wondered how the family would benefit. This was the kind of will that vanished on discovery if disadvantageous to those who found it.

He wanted to protest. He wanted to refuse. Those options would not be granted.

Fon Rhejm said, "Your new titles won't add to your workload. You won't need to be present in Grumbrag. You needn't deal with routine work. Those uncles and cousins who handled the castles and estates for Katrin will do the same for you. Most were honest serving Katrin. I expect the same moving into the future. Again, it's all Katrin's way to make sure you have the status and income to fulfill her dream and guarantee her memory."

Hecht glanced at Helspeth. She wore what looked like an honest, happy smile. Could this news explain Lady Hilda's new warmth?

A glance at Daedel showed her looking poleaxed.

As did the Archbishop, who was flustered, then outraged.

Hecht said, "Lady Hilda, I've changed my mind about that coffee," stalling while he tried to identify fon Rhejm's angle. Katrin's uncles had been a threat in definite need of consideration if one schemed against Katrin while she reigned.

Helspeth said, "Commander, consider changing your beverage to something that won't make you shakier than you already are."

"Excellent advice, Majesty. Thank you. I've changed my mind again, Lady Hilda. Graf, I don't know what to say."

"Say nothing. The Empress and I believe that a public announcement should wait till after Katrin's funeral, which is up in the air. Those bringing her home are having trouble."

Helspeth said, "We'll inter her beside my father and brother."

Funeral talk stirred thoughts Hecht preferred not to be there, like wondering how it had been for the men who brought Johannes back from al-Khazen. It had been daunting enough dragging those mummies from Andesqueluz to a shore where they could be put aboard a coaster headed for al-Qarn, and the stink had been out of those for fifteen hundred years.

"Commander?"

"Yes, Majesty?"

"You're daydreaming again. Not the best way to assure the affection of your sovereign."

"I beg your pardon, Majesty. I became entangled in the impossibilities. Twenty-five years ago I was a boy, living no better than most peasants, on the pagan frontier. Now I'm come to this."

"You'll come to immortality if you liberate the Holy Lands."

Yes. Well. That would make an especially interesting legend once the full facts were rooted out by the historians.

Helspeth rounded on the Archbishop. "You've heard things I didn't expect you to hear. You will not repeat them to anyone."

"As Your Majesty commands." Brion bowed but not as deeply as he ought. Plainly, he did not consider the occupant of the Grail Throne more exalted than an archbishop.

Everyone noted that. Brion noted them noting it. He reddened, became flustered again.

Helspeth let him off. "Brion, begin arranging the coronation. Keeping in mind what we've discussed. Low key. Inexpensive. We've had too many coronations lately."

The Archbishop delivered a deeper and, possibly, more sincere bow. "I understand. Though the Ege successors have set a standard . . . No. Not my place."

He wanted to criticize the children of Johannes for their parsimony. Lothar had not enjoyed a major coronation. Katrin's had been more gaudy but she had restrained the extravagance where she could.

"No. Definitely not your place. Your job is to administer the oath and put the crown on my head." Helspeth faced Hecht. "No trip to Brothe for me, though the Patriarch is welcome here."

That was, inelegantly, a message to Brion. His status could be adjusted if he steered a course at variance with that set by the Grail Throne.

Helspeth meant to catch him in the notched stick occupied by pro-Patriarchal clerics during the reigns of Johannes and Lothar.

The Archbishop developed a tic. His right eye looked like it was attempting an incompetent wink. He could not stop it despite vigorous rubbing.

Helspeth said, "Brion. Your eye. Is something wrong?"

The Archbishop stared at something remote, that only he could see.

"My God!" the Empress swore. "He's having a stroke! Captain Drear. Find me a healer."

Hecht suspected he knew the real nature of Brion's affliction.

Lila. Playing around. Or trying to look out for him.

Graf fon Rhejm said, "I don't think that's it, Helspeth. I think there's something in here with us. And he can see it."

The Empress grew paler. Hecht could not reassure her. Nobody needed to know his daughter could slide in and eavesdrop.

If that was it.

He saw nothing himself.

The something might not be Lila. Nor the Ninth Unknown. That old man would not resist a practical joke once his presence was suspected.

Graf fon Rhejm said, "I'm beginning to sense it, too. Helspeth, let's take this up after you have Renfrow exorcise the room. The time-critical issues have been covered."

"I don't think Renfrow owns the right skills, Uncle Albert."

"Then find someone who does." Fon Rhejm headed for the exit.

Lady Hilda fussed around Helspeth, trying to get her to leave, too.

"Hilda! Stop it! If an inimical spirit was after me, I'd be had. Anyway, what good will running to another room do?"

"I'd feel better."

"Commander!"

Helspeth's shout got his attention, and that of the Archbishop, and stopped the Graf fon Rhejm at the door.

"Uh . . . Majesty?"

"You're daydreaming again. We have a problem."

"I don't see anything. But I'm to Night things like a deaf man to a song."

The Graf said, "I don't feel it, now."

The Archbishop, despite his tic, pulled himself together.

Hecht came up with a more disturbing suspicion.

One of the Old Ones had been eavesdropping.

THE COMMANDER OF THE RIGHTEOUS ASSEMBLED HIS STAFF. HE SUR-veyed faces. These men were not as excited as once they had been. But they were attentive and professional. And ardently tired.

"Some of it was no surprise." He settled his behind against a tall stool. His wounds from that last assassination attempt were remind-ing him that he was still mortal and that they still needed further healing—however little they had bothered him recently.

"We'll have the same backing we did when Katrin was Empress. Plus." He scanned faces again. Could they keep their mouths shut? "None of you have given me reason to mistrust your discretion. So far. I need that to continue. What I'm about to tell you can't leave this room. If it does, I'll know exactly how and who. All right, then. Em-press Katrin willed the incomes from her properties to us for as long as it takes to liberate the Holy Lands."

That caused some chatter. Hecht let it simmer. He answered no questions. "Now, the final point. So we'll have more pull with the knightly and noble classes, Katrin also assigned me her title as lord of Eathered and Arnmigal. Her mother's family will back that."

Titus Consent said, "I see an assassination attempt hours after we're declared successful."

Hecht nodded. "I wouldn't be surprised. On the other hand, we'll have some outstanding, if slippery, associates working with us. They'll let us know if treachery is afoot."

Carava de Bos said, "You and Titus keep talking about some stud new folks coming on board. Who? When do we get to meet them?"

"It shouldn't be long."

Just fifteen minutes, in fact. A messenger from the sentries at the street door reported arrivals who insisted they had an appointment with the Commander of the Righteous. They looked important and were impatient. What to do?

The messenger was both terrified and starry-eyed. Hecht told him, "Bring them up."

Five Shining Ones entered the meeting room: Hourlr and Hourli, Sheaf and her daughter Aldi, and Eavijne. Eavijne looked lost, Sheaf and Aldi as though they wanted to vamp the world. Hourli told Hecht, "The others will be here soon. They haven't yet seen all the wonders."

"And Vrislakis and those?"

"Djordjevice the Foul is no more. Your Heris is doom itself. The rest will be undone soon."

"Excellent!" Hecht considered these five. They had done well making themselves look human—but not the sort who faded into a crowd. They were beautiful, radiating power and a weird and dynamic tension between lust and dread. The men began selecting goddesses for slavering devotion.

Hecht was not immune. "Hourli, you see what's happening?"

"See it and smell it. They don't do it on purpose. It takes a conscious effort to control." Her eyes rolled up. Her face became an indeterminate shimmer.

The sensual charge in the air declined to a level not unusual for a room full of younger men suddenly exposed to a clutch of attractive women.

Hourlr had fun watching.

Hecht told Hourli, "We'll never get anything done if you can't keep those fires banked."

"They understand in here." Hourli knocked herself in the forehead. "But it's been ages since they've been able to run wild. Nobody knows them. Nobody fears them anymore. They don't yet understand in here, or here." She tapped herself over her heart, then her crotch. "But don't despair. They're working through it. Now they're all excited about helping you."

That sent a chill down Hecht's spine.

Hourli touched his shoulder. "I wish you would trust us."

He smiled, weakly. He was not yet entirely convinced that he dared believe they existed.

"Tell us what you want done. Work will keep us out of mischief."

He sometimes fell asleep worrying that. How could a mortal manage indentured gods? He had a list of chores, of use but not especially imaginative.

Hourli whispered, "Interesting game you have going with your Empress. Is the object to see who goes mad from self-denial first?"

Hecht nearly panicked. But only he had heard.

His staff were still distracted by hormonal hangovers.

Hecht said, "Gentlemen, these people get immediate access to me. Unless I'm sleeping. More will show up eventually. You'll know them when you see them."

THE OTHERS TURNED UP NEXT AFTERNOON, DURING HECHT'S MEETING with Archbishop Brion. Brion pressed the usual Brothen Episcopal agenda. His heart was not in his bullying, though. He knew he was wasting his breath.

He understood more soon after Titus leaned through the doorway to announce, "Three ladies to see you, Commander. The ones you told us to expect."

Hecht felt their presence before they came in, as did the Archbishop, who nearly whimpered when he saw them. They had no special look, though. They had taken the semblance of middle-aged tradesmen's wives.

Wife had done an especially fine job making herself into a dowager milliner. But there was no stopping the feeling of Night coming off her.

"Greetings," Hecht said. "I see you've been eating well."

All three were less tenuous than they had been.

Wife considered the Archbishop. "This one is sensitive."

Brion croaked, "Demons! Commander . . . are you trafficking with demons?"

"Instrumentalities. Which the Church does, too, when it's convenient. This lady became a national saint in Andoray a century ago." In the thinnest disguise.

Brion's tic returned, with a palsy added. He had some historical training. He worked out the identity of the milliner's wife.

She offered him a benevolent smile.

He nearly melted in terror.

All Shining Ones had their dark sides. Each figured in some tale where wickedness got done to mortals or denizens of the other worlds. It was no great matter that the Instrumentalities might be responding to bad deeds done them with deeds more wicked. The deeper truth was that the Shining Ones decided what deserved divine retribution.

Viciously senseless divine behavior was central to all religions birthed in the Holy Lands. The God of the Dainshaukin was especially irrational and cruel.

Those Instrumentalities seemed starved for the fear of mortals.

Some mortals now offered fear back.

Piper Hecht did not feel good, thinking that.

He asked Brion, "Do you know the old northern gods the Church pushed aside?"

Brion croaked, "Yes. Some."

"Despite Church doctrine, the Shining Ones existed. Now they're the Old Ones to people up north. And they're still around." Hecht gestured at Wife and the Choosers. "They're indentured to the Righteous. They'll help liberate the Holy Lands. And you, my friend, will keep that to yourself. While being the best damned Archbishop you can. Understand?"

The Choosers moved out of Hecht's sight. They showed Brion something that served up another helping of terror. He babbled assurances that no one would hear a word from him.

"I do hope that's true," Hecht told him. "For your sake, I do."

THE LAST VISITOR HAD GONE. HECHT COULD RELAX WITH SOME ROUtine administrative work. He told Consent, "When you're young you daydream about being a famous warlord. But once you're there you find out that mostly you do political stuff."

Consent shrugged. "Not something I'll ever have to worry about. You needed something?"

"Not exactly. Lila was here today. I didn't see her. She brought mail. There's something for you from Noë."

After an instant of excitement, Titus grumped, "She's probably knocked up again. I don't know how she manages."

"You really need me to explain?"

Flicker of a grin. "Maybe. How the hell does Anna keep from getting pregnant?"

"My guess is, she can't. Or maybe she just doesn't want to. Noë doesn't seem to have any problems having babies."

"No kidding."

"I did mean intellectual reservations."

"Not that, either. I'm lucky I don't see her more than I do. She'd be dropping one every ten months." Consent reddened slightly. Despite years around coarse men he could not lay his private affairs out in common view.

Carava de Bos came in. "One of your new friends wants to see you, Boss."

"I'm going to regret saying they could drop in any time. All right."

De Bos stepped aside. Hourli pushed past. De Bos shuddered. Hecht wondered how he responded to Eavijne, Sheaf, or Aldi.

The goddess announced, "We found your missing king, Commander."

16. Tel Moussa: Misfortune

Nassim Alizarin was enjoying a chilled pomegranate. Azim al-Adil had sent a dozen from Shamramdi. A warrior came to his cell. "Arnhanders are approaching bearing a palm branch, General."

"What?" The Mountain could not have been more surprised had Old Az come back from his hunt with the Rascal chopped up and stuffed into bags, though the real surprise there would be that er-Selim had not instantly burned the fragments in a dozen scattered fires before the meat had cooled.

The Master of Ghosts was not inclined to take chances.

"What I said, General. A party has come from Gherig. Twenty-five knights. They stopped just outside falcon range. Their banners are Brotherhood of War. Black Rogert isn't with them."

"To the parapet, then. And have my advisers join me."

NASSIM LEANED OUT, LOOKED DOWN. TWENTY-FIVE MEN EXACTLY, formed neatly, armed, but not looking for a fight. A fight would not go their way. If they wanted to gain the Mountain's attention they had found the perfect means. He would not be able to control his curiosity. The situation suggested so many possibilities, some potentially positive. "Heads together, here. Anybody. What does this mean? Are they trying to lure us out?"

Bone suggested, "They want to talk."

"Why?"

"They have something on their minds."

"Bone!"

Bone pointed. "The pennon on the lance of the man beside the herald with the palm frond proclaims him a Master of the Commandery."

"The scarlet pennon with the white-accented blue stripe down the middle?"

"Exactly." With a touch of exasperation.

"We haven't seen one of those since the Battle of the Four Armies."

"We have not. They're rare. There are only four. One in Brothe. The senior one, in Runch. The second most senior, in Vantrad. And the one in the Brotherhood fortress in the harbor at Triamolin."

"Not much chance we'll see either of the first two."

"Nor either of the others."

"Bone? You saying this is a trick?"

"Those banners and pennons, and the devices on the shields, aren't ones we're used to seeing."

"So they're the new people at Gherig. Let's go see what they want."

"It was me, I'd let them broil in their armor a while, then hit them."

Nassim chuckled. It took Bone a while to work up a case of blood-lust, then longer to let it go.

It took a while to get downstairs, get armed up and mounted, then get out the gate. A brace of falcons rolled out behind Nassim and Bone. They took positions where they could snipe at the outlanders at long range. Their support would give the Mountain and Bone a running start.

The falcons crews did not sneak. Neither did they make a show.

The Mountain wished his Master of Ghosts were beside him. But Az was still hunting er-Rashal. Nassim had begun to worry.

Bone remarked, "This might be a bad idea. Two of the men in the front rank are Special Office."

"Sorcerers?"

"Possibly."

"Let's hope this is an honest effort to talk, then."

"I've been hoping that since they showed up."

Nassim grew more comfortable as he moved closer. None of the westerners wore helmets. Most had eased the fit of their armor so air could circulate a little.

It was miserably warm for men newly arrived from cooler climes.

Nassim halted ten feet from the two out front of the westerners. "I am Nassim Alizarin, sometimes called the Mountain. I hold this fortress in the name of the Great Shake Indala al-Sul Halaladin and the God Who Is God." He did not include his father's name or a place of origin when identifying himself. If these Arnhanders knew the east they would understand that they faced Sha-lug.

"Madouc of Hoeles, Brotherhood of War." The man in charge spoke the Lucidian dialect with little accent. "Master of the Commandery in Gherig on behalf of the Brotherhood, the God Who Is the One True God, and all His saints."

Nassim saw no emotion in the crusader's cold gray eyes. He might have come to buy sheep.

Nassim must have betrayed his surprise. The Brotherhood warrior inclined his head. "The Council in Runch have decreed the founding of a new Commandery at Gherig. I have been directed to be its Master. I wanted to introduce myself. I wanted to make it known that there will be changes. And I wanted to offer you an opportunity to evacuate your tower with your lives and possessions intact."

"A generous gesture. So much so that I find myself compelled to respond in kind. I extend the identical offer to you and the folk of Gherig, good till the rising of the new moon."

The Arnhander smiled.

Bone whispered, "We've seen this man before."

"Yes. On Artecipea. He was the Captain-General's chief lifeguard. Possibly as cover for something more sinister."

The outlander heard, understood, and appeared puzzled. He did not recall having seen them before. But they had been minor players at Arn Bedu.

The westerner said, "Though never hidden to the attentive eye, Indala's strategy has become manifest. The Brotherhood of War will not allow him to succeed."

Clearly, the man not only meant what he said, he believed it and wanted to save those who must perish if Indala persisted.

Nassim took care to sound neutral. "The truth will be known when God reveals His hand upon the field of battle."

"You were at Arn Bedu? The man who felled Rudenes Schneidel, who destroyed the demon god Seska, and who brought down the walls of unassailable Arn Bedu, is coming. The vastness of his host will be incalculable. Those wise enough to make peace now will find that season condign. Those who do not will be extinguished."

"Is he in for a surprise," Bone muttered, probably to himself.

Nassim was less certain. Else Tage had been given no reason to remain faithful to Dreanger, al-Prama, or even the Sha-lug.

The westerner asked, "You won't take advantage of my generosity?"

"Your generous grant of an opportunity to oppose the enemies of God? We will take every advantage. I promise."

The Master of the Commandery of Gherig sat quietly, as though unable to believe what he had heard. "As you wish, so must it be." He turned his mount and rode slowly to and through his companions. One by one, they turned and followed. The herald with the palm frond went last.

Bone asked, "Did we miss something here, General?"

"That could be. Maybe they thought we knew something that we don't. Find out. Those men are absolutely certain of the future."

Nassim did not move till the last Arnhander passed out of sight.

AL-AZER ER-SELIM RETURNED. HE HAD NOTHING GOOD TO REPORT. Er-Rashal had escaped into the wild Idiam. His soldiers, Lucidians familiar with the horror stories about that country, flatly refused to go after the sorcerer.

Old Az took over trying to figure out why the crusaders felt so confident. He discovered nothing useful.

The Mountain called Bone to the parapet. "Bone, I have another journey for you. I'm asking because you're the only man who can do this."

The only man did not conceal his distress. "Chances are, I wouldn't survive another journey."

"You'll outlive me by twenty years. This time you won't go alone. Take a dozen men with you. Anybody but al-Azer."

Bone awaited his sentence.

"I want you to go to al-Qarn."

Bone asked no questions.

"Find our brethren and explore their attitudes toward the current situation. Find out how successful Indala has been at unifying the kaifates. Also, find out what became of Captain Tage's family. And my wife."

"The Captain's wife explains why me, I suppose. We've looked before. We had no luck."

"Men were told to look. They took no risks. They didn't want to attract attention."

"Things should be more relaxed, now. And I've actually met the woman, though that was a long time ago. Do you have something in mind?"

"Nothing so wicked as what you're imagining. They're owed. And their appearance in the Holy Lands might remind the Captain of his roots. He seems to have lost touch."

"Oh, he has, General. If he'd taken us with him we all would have."

Never having been part of an isolated and intimate company like Else Tage's, Nassim did not fully understand the bonds those men had forged. But he did understand that war made families of men who became alloyed far more solidly than any conventional family.

That had begun to develop here at Tel Moussa several times. It never fully ripened because Indala did not leave his Lucidians in place long enough. Tel Moussa was a sorting house. Here the best men got blooded and the worst men got dead before they became liabilities in a larger arena.

"I can't order you to go," Alizarin said. "I have used you too hard."

"Stop. Don't pluck my guilt strings."

Nassim stifled his protest. "No need to rush. And no need to take risks."

Bone did not respond. There was nothing to say. This was the life he had chosen. Out of it, someday, would come the death that was implicit in his choice.

"Don't put yourself in harm's way if the family is still a touchy matter. Same thing with anything else of interest to us."

"The Great Shake's men could object to us sneaking around like we're part of a conspiracy."

"If they press, tell them the truth."

"And that would be? For these purposes?"

"The truth is, though I won't become Marshall if I'm beholden to Indala, I do want to encourage the Sha-lug to join Indala's new Great Campaign to oust foreigners from the Holy Lands."

Bone slipped into a sour, sarcastic mood. "Would that include Dreangereans, Lucidians, or tribal groups out of Peqaa?"

The Mountain snorted, mildly amused.

17. The Connec: Gifts

Brother Candle, Socia, and Bernardin Amberchelle gathered each evening to share what they learned about their remarkable visitor, always a great deal of nothing. No one had seen her, no one knew anything about her. Even Mistress Alecsinac, after studying the Perfect's tattoos, Bernardin's scars, and Socia's massive crystal, which she now carried in a sheath like a dagger, could tell them nothing. Nor could she explain the forgotten necklace. She saw nothing special about it.

Mistress Alecsinac was younger than Brother Candle but still of considerable age. And she was frightened. "These are great potencies, Lady. No known Instrumentality answers your description. No Instrumentality takes such an avatar. Our significant Old Ones—the ones that started to come back—were all destroyed by the Captain-General. This will be something different. This will be something the Connec has never seen."

Bernardin Amberchelle unleashed one of his occasional intellectual surprises. "Any chance she could be a new goddess?"

Mistress Alecsinac considered. "New to the Connec, certainly. But you said she spoke an old version of the language. She may belong to an elder generation of Instrumentalities."

Brother Candle had spent as little time as he could with the witch during Socia's pregnancy. Even Seekers After Light had no room in their faith for such people—except when her special knowledge might ease a birth or help the sick. Despite her bizarre connections, though, Mistress Alecsinac was reasonable, rational, and articulate where Brother Candle would prefer a raving madwoman.

The Perfect said, "We know a lot of old, dark entities were awakened by Rudenes Schneidel. The Captain-General dealt with those and Schneidel but maybe Schneidel wasn't the only sorcerer stirring up revenants. The world was infested before the Old Empire culled them."

Mistress Alecsinac asked, "Do any of you have any idea what she did to you?"

Brother Candle did not confess that he felt more alive than he had thought possible earlier, or than was seemly for a man of his years. The old woman cared only about tattoos and scars. "No," he said. "And I'm starting to scare children."

Socia said, "That's what crazy old men do."

"Socia?" the Perfect said. "Is there something you don't want to reveal?"

SOCIA FELL IN LOVE WITH HER DEMONIC CRYSTAL. SHE ABUSED ITS power immediately and often. Denizens of the citadel began muttering about ghosts and demons. The Perfect heard of monster hounds seen from the corner of the eye, of great cats gone in a blink, of unfamiliar men and women stalking corridors by night and refusing to answer challenges. There was also talk of a huge bird, possibly an eagle, seen leaving a window up near the Countess's chambers. Her people were worried about her safety.

The Perfect asked, "What don't you want to share?"

Socia confessed, "I've been changing shape. A lot. More to do practical jokes than anything useful."

"Useful?"

"I can go anywhere I want if I take the right shape."

"Ah. I see." Now that he knew he could worry about the trouble into which she could get. He imagined a dozen ways with no effort at all.

"I'll bet. The demon said use the crystal sparingly. Probably to avoid attracting attention but, maybe, too, because it has limits. Maybe you only get twenty changes, then it dies."

"We don't know that."

"My point exactly. We don't know anything about any of the gifts she gave us. We have to figure them out for ourselves. She was, by any reckoning, a devil. And it's a given that things of the Night aren't always what they seem. Gifts especially."

Socia could say nothing to change that. "I just got overwhelmed. But I did find out some useful stuff, Bernardin. I flew out to see Kedle. I did some scouting for her. That woman . . . Five minutes after I showed up she was already coming up with wicked things we could do to our enemies."

Brother Candle had no trouble believing that. Kedle was quick, opportunistic, and brutal. Socia's tone suggested that they had done something wicked already. "Wondrous as the practical applications may be, we really should know more before we assume what could be deadly risks."

Reluctantly, Socia conceded his point, but then began telling Bernardin about a conspiracy she had unearthed while prowling.

"Ah. I did think that the Raisen brothers were tainted but they never gave me an excuse for bringing them in. Now I have one."

"What will Kedle do if I stop going to see her?"

"Without you."

"But . . ."

"She managed before. You probably gave her enough so she can work her wickedness for weeks."

"But . . ."

"You just want to be off having adventures instead of governing. But you aren't Raymone Garete. You can't get away with leaving it to others. You have the assizes coming up."

"There's always assizes coming up. But you're right. I just want to get away." She sighed, resigned. "There is one thing, though. That demon might be following Kedle around."

"Why do you think that?"

"Kedle says strange stuff happens whenever it looks like there might be a fight."

"Like what?"

Socia shrugged. "Just weird things. Illusions. Apparitions. And things always going easier than they should."

Bernardin said, "I'm getting some creepy feelings here, Master. What have we stumbled into?"

Brother Candle had his own creepy feelings. "That's what we need to find out."

"How?"

The Perfect had no idea.

THERE WAS A SMALL DEVEDIAN COMMUNITY IN ANTIEUX, ALONG WITH a minuscule Dainshau presence. Having learned nothing useful from fellow Seekers, Chaldareans, or pagans, Brother Candle took his inquiries to their holy men. He did so of an evening, after having found out who to consult and having arranged an appointment. He went without concern for his own safety. With Bernardin Amberchelle in charge, it was said, a toothsome virgin could stroll through town naked without fear.

Bernardin did take a draconian approach to law enforcement. His heavy hand inspired protests from no one but Bishop LaVelle.

Most Deves and Dainshaukin now lived outside the wall, in a growing suburb on the west bank of the Job. Commerce developed fast when the wolves of war ignored the region for even a few months.

Having landed there from a small coaster, once, Brother Candle thought he knew the waterfront. But he lost his way twice, which left him worried that he would be late. The darkness seemed more like a comfortable old cloak than a potential source of danger.

Trouble did not find him in the narrow ways where he became lost. It pounced when he was just yards from his destination, a small Devedian temple. He was to meet a part-time priest named Radeus Pickleu. Pickleu was known more as a surgeon than as a priest. He had traveled and had a reputation as a student of comparative religion and religious history. Brother Candle had met Radeus Pickleu before. Pickleu had been a surgeon in the Connecten expeditionary force that participated in the Calziran Crusade. The Perfect had been a chaplain. Pickleu had had a knack for communicating with the pagans of Shippen.

A man stepped into the Perfect's path. He may have been waiting, or may have been tracking an obviously old Maysalean. In the weak light from the temple's open doorway the Perfect saw that Bernardin's oppressions had been inadequate outside the wall. This thug was almost stereotypically Society. He wore a cassock with the hood up and had a black cloth tied across his face.

"Good night, heretic. Well met."

"Indeed?" Brother Candle was shaken. "I doubt that." The man had spoken with malicious sarcasm.

"It is a good night for us. We know you. You'll give us leverage on the Rault bitch. She'll call off her hounds to save you."

Brother Candle knew the opposite would be true. Socia would slaughter Brothen Episcopals, man, woman, and child, till she got her own back. Probably on the steps of the cathedral, where many good folk had died the first time the Church tried to scourge Antieux. "You're making a mistake you won't have long to regret." Brother Candle noted that "we" meant a party of four, two behind him and one a dozen yards to his right, younger and reluctant to become involved.

The old man spoke considering the resources Socia now commanded. He saw no active role for himself in what was about to happen. His part had to be avoidance of offering excuses for bad behavior till Socia could bring the hammer down.

The men behind the Perfect seized his arms. The one on his right leaned in to whisper something cruel. Brother Candle never heard specific words.

The old man felt a cold surge of motion up his back and neck, to his cheek. He rocked. Whispering Man screamed, reeled away clawing his face.

Brother Candle's left arm shuddered and surged, sideways and back. The man there shrieked. He began flailing his right hand as though trying to shake off a handful of coals.

The old man heard a hiss beside his right ear, sensed weight and motion there. Likewise at the end of his left arm. And now his right reached for the man who had blocked his path. The Perfect saw the snake strike at the thug's right hand, which had begun rising, gripping a club.

Another shriek.

All three thugs went down, shaking, then going into convulsions. The fourth remained rooted, eyes huge, indecisive. Brother Candle shouted, "Run, boy! While you have the chance."

People poured from the temple, shops, and houses.

The boy ran. Brother Candle hoped fear would sear away any inclination to continue his night-crawling career.

The screaming faded into gasps of strangulation.

Brother Candle felt the weights of the snakes fade. His mind seethed with guilt and insane speculation.

The first neighbor arrived. He saw nothing to set the Perfect apart, except for the old man's trembling. The snakes were tattoos again, though Brother Candle imagined their cold muscles flexing under his skin.

Every passing moment left him more appalled.

One nagging, irrelevant thought insisted on slicing through the chaos. One tattoo had not wakened at all.

Radeus Pickleu arrived, deeply concerned, and put the question the gallery wanted answered. "What happened?"

"The Night . . . Those men meant to attack me. Something struck them down."

The evident ringleader, twice bitten, arched his back, suffered one final vicious convulsion, and died. The others continued to shake, foam at the mouth, and make noises that sounded like faltering speech in an alien tongue.

Pickleu stared a moment. "You'd better come inside. Did they hurt you?"

"They never touched me."

"Any idea why they came at you?"

"The one who died called me a heretic and said they meant to use me to make the Countess do what they wanted."

"Oh. Society scum. They breed like mosquitoes. I should've realized when I saw them."

Hands urged the Perfect toward the open temple door. He tried looking back, could not see the fallen men. They were surrounded by neighbors now, including several in the queer black garb of Dainshaus. He did not see a healer.

A half-dozen men lifted a body, headed down the dirt street toward the river. Brother Candle thought he saw the man struggle feebly.

Pushing hands forced him inside the temple.

Pickleu said, "Sit. Relax. Talk about why you're here. What's that on your face? I didn't think you were the tattoo kind. That isn't some secret Maysalean symbol, is it?"

"No." Brother Candle had forgotten how this dark, trim little surgeon could chatter. Conversations tended to be lopsided. "But tattoos are one reason I wanted to see you."

"Your message said you had questions about old religions."

"Questions about a particular Instrumentality that I haven't been able to identify." He raised a hand to forestall Pickleu's rattling and prattling. "I'd rather not perform for a crowd." There were twenty people within earshot, some not Devedian.

"I take your point. Everybody. All of you. Clear out. The Perfect came for a private conversation."

The gallery cleared off. "Thanks. Let me explain before you ask questions. That should save time."

"It's true, more gets done when Pickleu isn't talking."

Brother Candle gave an edited version of the visit from the blond Instrumentality. He included his tattoos and Bernardin's fish but said nothing about the tattoos coming to life. He mentioned Socia's crystal but not what she did with it. "And she dropped this." He produced the necklace. Or rosary. "Which may have been accidental or deliberate."

"Four arms?"

"Four. But now that I'm concentrating, only when she came in. She went down to a normal complement right away."

"The physical description doesn't match any Instrumentality I know about. The tattoos and fish aren't familiar, either. The crystal rings a bell. I can't recall any details. The necklace must be significant. The pattern of the stones matches that of those in an obscure necklace from the old northern mythology. This is a copy. The real Brising Stones would be so heavy no mortal could lift them."

"I know nothing about those Old Ones. I knew only a little more about the home-grown devils that popped up last year."

"The Shining Ones were part of Connecten history, too. Obliquely." Pickleu provided a quick tutorial. "I wouldn't swear that you've got a revenant from that pantheon, but the necklace is suggestive. Your Instrumentality wouldn't be one of the famous ones—though they all liked to disguise themselves to have fun tormenting mortals."

Brother Candle was instantly confident that he would never find a more sensible theory.

"Where do I find a priest? Or an expert?"

"You don't. Those gods are gone."

"That's what we thought about Rook and Hilt. So? Somebody who knows more would be a big help."

He got more history. More obscure mythology. Nothing really useful. The religion was dead. Only confused parables lingered. He thanked Pickleu for his efforts, educational and medical, but could not conceal his disappointment.

"There's nothing more I can contribute, Master. And I know of no one who can tell you more. But we do hope you will do us a favor in return for our efforts."

"Of course."

"We need a policing presence out here. Just a couple of men, after dark, to make it understood that the Countess knows we exist. Amberchelle has imposed rigorous control inside the wall and out in the countryside but he hasn't done much for us here. The villains move in to be safe. The one who died is an example. We'll count his passing a blessing. But there are more like him."

"I'll let the Countess know." Though that would cost him moral anguish. Bernardin would be thrilled to come onto a rich new shoal of villains. "I guess I'll have to catch my Instrumentality and ask her if I want to know what's going on."

"It's worth a try. My son Merak will walk you back. The kid who ran away may have friends."

"I VISITED A DEVE SCHOLAR WHO STUDIES LOST RELIGIONS," BROTHER Candle told Socia and Bernardin, over breakfast. "He wasn't much

help. He did ask me to tell you that the suburb on the riverbank is infested with Society types. They're involved in criminal activities in order to raise funds."

"The end justifying the means."

"Essentially."

Socia said, "Deal with that, Bernardin."

"I will. A lapse on my part, there. I never thought the area needed
special attention."

"The Society is like dysentery. Or mold. Or rats. It will get in anywhere where we're not trying to keep it out. Not even the Patriarchs
can control it anymore."

Brother Candle pushed back from his austere breakfast. "Not to
make your mood any more bleak, Socia, but it's time to hear the assizes."

Bernardin added, "Bishop LaVelle will be an early petitioner."

"Isn't he always?" Socia pulled a sour face. "But I do admit that he
has guts. When every other Brothen priest is on the run our bishop
hangs in there, doing his best."

Bernardin grumbled, "And doing it honestly."

Socia said, "Come along, Brother Serpent. I can maybe use a snake
man to look out for me today."

The Perfect did not appreciate the humor. He could not make peace
with the fact that three men were dead because of what the Instrumentality had inflicted upon him.

18. Alten Weinberg to Cholate: For the Prize

Alten Weinberg did not boast a large Devedian community. The
one that existed was prosperous, cultured, and strove to be included in Imperial society. Devedians were prominent in the state bureaucracy.

A Devedian scholar named Rodolof Schmeimder was his people's
spokesman to the Righteous. He had appointed himself back when
Carava de Bos returned with captives and plunder from the raid on
the Krulik and Sneigon manufactory.

Schmeimder asked to see the Commander.

Titus Consent argued, "It can't hurt to see the man."

"Special pleading for a member of the old tribe?"

"No. I only met the man once before. He rubbed me wrong. I sent
him back to de Bos. Carava thinks he'd be a valuable friend."

"Why does he want to see me?"

"Because he can't get what he wants from de Bos or me if you're going to fly off the handle when we do our jobs. You can't second-guess us like that if you don't actually know the people involved."

"I see." This went back to a blow-up he had suffered on discovering that Deve craftsmen from Krulik and Sneigon, now restricted to a controlled access section of the Hochwasser canton, had been allowed to send letters to their families. Mostly those were in Brothe, where Piper Hecht had enemies. "So. This is punishment for me having overreacted."

In the calm following his outburst Hecht had taken a moment to examine their logic. It was no secret what had become of the people taken in the raid. The craftsmen, their outrage spent, seemed content to pursue their careers in their new surroundings—so long as they enjoyed some basic freedoms, kept their dignity, were paid, and were not badly treated.

"I did overreact. I was too paranoid. What could they tell the world that it doesn't already know? What does Schmeimder want to nag me about, specifically?"

"He'll have several things. The biggest, I think, will be permission for the falcon makers' families to join them."

Hecht felt his anger rise. But, why? He stilled it, more easily than he had before.

Titus continued, "It makes sense. If their families are here they will be less inclined to make trouble or try to get away."

Hecht tried to recall when he had begun suffering spells of irrational anger. Normally, he calculated carefully before exploding. Consent and de Bos had been taken aback once they realized he was not acting.

Titus said, "He'll also ask for their confinement to be relaxed. I don't see much worry about them wandering off."

"If we let their families come here."

"Yes."

"What's their productivity like?"

"Feeble. They do just enough to get by. Quality isn't what it was before, either. Plus, we're having problems providing ore and firewood. Hochwasser isn't well located for those things."

"Bring them smelted iron and charcoal already burned."

"And sulfur? And saltpeter? We should consider moving the craftsmen to the resources instead of doing it the other way round."

"Then look at that. Making sure we don't give up anything." The critical result of the Krulik and Sneigon raid was not that he had acquired those master weapons makers but that he had denied their products to everyone else. Those firepowder weapons he encountered in battle would be second grade.

Titus Consent listened but did not respond to his concerns. "Schmeimder will also want permission to raise a Devedian and Dainshau regiment to join in the liberation of the Holy Lands."

"Are you kidding me?"

"Their faiths were born amongst the Wells of Ihrian, too. Long before ours."

RODOLOF SCHMEIMDER WAS NO STEREOTYPICAL DEVE. WHAT HAIR he had was vaguely blond. His eyes were the blue common to half the subjects of the Grail Empire. And he smiled a lot, which was not characteristic of the portrait of the species Hecht had built inside his head.

While Hecht took Schmeimder's measure the visitor returned the favor. "I hope you don't think I'm out of line, here, Commander, but your aura suggests that you've been touched by the Night."

Consent, keeping notes, gasped.

Hecht asked, "How so?"

"Unfortunately, that sort of thing can't be explained like describing the good and bad points of a horse."

"So, like a fortune-teller, you can make up whatever you want. You don't have to deliver any evidence."

That startled Schmeimder. "Well, uh . . . yes. I see how you might think that if you're not sensitive to it yourself."

"I promise you, sir, my Night sensitivity is such that the Night has to smack me with a club before I take notice."

"No one has mentioned this?"

"My troops tell me I'm spooky all the time. I don't think like they do. And strange things happen around me. But that's because we're out there trying to make strange things happen."

Titus Consent kept quiet, face blank.

Hecht said, "Which is all irrelevant. Mr. Consent says you want to discuss specifics. Let's get to that. I have a meeting with the Empress coming up."

"I know. You have to decide what to do about Anselin of Menand . . . Oh!" Schmeimder blanched. He knew things he should not and had betrayed himself.

Hecht did not glance at Consent. The leak would not have come from there. The lapse would be at Helspeth's end and, likely, inadvertent.

"Spying certainly isn't the best way to win the affections of the Empress and the Righteous, Master Schmeimder."

"I'll grant you that. But I would remind you that nothing stays secret in Alten Weinberg. Only when nothing is written down and every discussion happens in a quiet room is there any hope at all. And even then, word gets out. Somebody tells his wife or lover or best friend. In strictest confidence."

That was true in Brothe, too, where conspiracy and intrigue had become art forms.

"I understand that. Some things, though, need to be kept quiet so bigger secrets aren't betrayed and lives aren't lost. The matter of the missing king features both risks."

"I've forgotten I ever knew anything I shouldn't."

"You wanted to see me why?"

Schmeimder expressed almost exactly what Titus had said he would.

Hecht asked, "Do you understand why we isolated those people?"

"I don't, sir. Not really. They were craftsmen who found ways to make better products faster than their competitors in response to the demands of an expanding market. Which is what merchants, artisans, and craftsmen do."

"Exactly. You are correct. But let me offer a counterpoint, from the perspective of the Righteous. The Shades."

"Excuse me? I don't understand."

"The main engagement of the Firaldian campaign happened at a place called the Shades."

"Oh." Still puzzled.

"A few hundred Righteous engaged several thousand troops raised by the Patriarch. The Patriarch's troops died. The tool we used to make that happen was the Krulik and Sneigon falcon. Manufactured by the men we've isolated at Hochwasser."

"Oh."

"Master Schmeimder, I do not want to take the Righteous onto any field where they'll face what Serenity's men faced. That is why those men are locked up out there."

"You want to hold the knife-maker responsible for what his customer does with his product."

"I don't want the knife-maker to sell his product to anyone but me. Which I have managed with a minimum of disruption and pain—compared to most episodes in the history of your people."

Schmeimder stopped short of arguing after recognizing the veiled threat.

Hecht continued, "My staff agree with you. Those people haven't been troublesome, just willfully slow and mildly obstructionist. If productivity and quality improve, improved conditions will follow."

"About that. About quality. I've been asked to point out that the saltpeter you're providing isn't the best."

"Maybe someone should pay closer attention during the refining process." He glanced at Titus. Titus shrugged. "In future, bring your concerns to Mr. Consent or Mr. de Bos. They will do what is best."

"The other thing, then, sir, is, can you make room for a company of free will Devedians who also want to see the Holy Lands?"

"Mr. Consent told me you might ask. You understand my natural reluctance?"

"A knee-jerk response common throughout the Chaldarean world. Deves with weapons? It raises frightening prospects. But it could prove disarming in the long run. Working in common cause, Chaldareans should become less frightened of their neighbors. And younger Devedians could improve their self-image by getting involved in something the broader society approves and respects."

Consent kept his face blank and mouth shut. Once upon a time he had been filled with that kind of naïve optimism, too.

Hecht said, "My staff is with you on this one, too, Master Schmeimder, though I'm skeptical myself. It will be a hard sell for me but I will remind everyone how well my Devedians did during the Calziran Crusade."

"Is that a roundabout no?"

"It's a roundabout yes. But prepare to be disappointed. Grand Duke Hilandle, Lord Admiral fon Tyre, and their sort won't be confused by any facts I present in lieu of prejudicial arguments."

"I see." Schmeimder remained puzzled, like he had thought the Commander of the Righteous could damned well do whatever he wanted.

"I'll present the idea and recommend a positive response. Now. This news about my agents having learned the whereabouts of Anselin of Menand. Is that out yet? Has the Arnhander ambassador heard? Or the Archbishop?"

"I think not. Not yet. But don't count on having much time. That's just too big a story."

"No doubt. No doubt." It might be time to deploy his special resources.

THE GRAND DUKE HAD BEEN BACK IN ALTEN WEINBERG JUST A FEW days. He was, he claimed, likely to die of apoplexy if many more wicked changes tumbled into his path. It was all he could do to maintain his composure in the Imperial presence. He managed that only because of the relentless pressure of observing eyes.

Lord Admiral fon Tyre was not pleased, either. But he, too, felt the watching, calculating eyes.

Those eyes were numerous but the most intent were those of Katrin's uncles. Those men had not been reluctant to spread the word that Hansel Blackboots's last child was not going to suffer what her siblings had. They had been particularly remiss where Katrin was concerned, repelled by her romance with the Patriarchy. That was over. Helspeth Ege was of age. She was Empress legally. She did not need self-serving old men bullying her.

Wherever the Grand Duke, the Lord Admiral, or the former Masters of the Wardrobe, the Privy Purse, or the Household began to show exasperation publicly, an uncle turned up.

All this Hecht learned within minutes of reaching the palace. Which, to his surprise, was overrun by the ruling class.

There might be no intimate meeting to decide about Anselin.

Helspeth had had the grand ballroom opened and lighted profligately. The excuse was, ostensibly, a celebration of Katrin's amazing success in the war against the Patriarchy.

The new Empress had had a throne brought in. Twelve Braunsknechts surrounded it. The Commander of the Righteous had brought a dozen of his own most intimidating soldiers, on the recommendation of Hourli, who assured him that of the countless plots afoot at least three meant to free the Empress of her wicked Commander of the Righteous by murdering him.

Hecht worked his way through the press, to Algres Drear. "What is all this? I expected a planning meeting."

Drear could add nothing to what Hecht had picked up crossing the ballroom. "She doesn't confide in me. I think she wants to hit these people over the head with a shovel. She wants them to go home for the winter with their heads stuffed with things to brood about."

The northern lords would move on quickly. It would be harvest time soon. In three weeks Alten Weinberg would be a ghost of its summer self.

"I have a bad feeling about this, Drear."

"A sensibly upbeat attitude."

"Trouble?"

"Let's see what she does."

Drear was right. Helspeth did want to hit people over the head. As the crowd began to relax, a Braunsknecht sounded a trumpet. Helspeth read Katrin's will into the startled silence, word for word, including a rambling excoriation of Serenity—and, most especially, her elevation of the Commander of the Righteous to the high peerage.

Piper Hecht nearly melted in the heat of the glares directed his way, heat that did not reflect directly on Helspeth. This would be recalled as further proof of Katrin's insanity, though, surely, there would be a faction that damned Helspeth for not having burned the will instead of making it public.

THE GRAND DUKE DID SUFFER HIS APOPLECTIC EPISODE WHEN HE heard that a common adventurer from the Empire's nethermost frontier had been made a prince.

A common adventurer was now, for the length of his life, one of the most important men in the Grail Empire. That was no longer a mocking, malicious, sad rumor. The Ege chit had announced it herself and was downright gleeful about the distress it caused her Council Advisory.

The Grand Duke did not yet understand that the Council had been disbanded, to be reconstituted with people selected by the new Empress.

Hilandle noted an especially oversize member of the Commander's lifeguard regarding him intently. The Grand Duke thought he seemed familiar. His frown deepened when he noted that the man had no right hand.

Hilandle chose that moment to lose control.

THERE WERE SCORES OF INVISIBLE PEOPLE IN THAT BALLROOM, BRINGing beer and wine and foodstuffs, clearing away and cleaning up. They went unnoticed but were neither deaf nor blind, nor were they immune to the influence of the Shining Ones.

By celebration's end Helspeth would become beloved of the common folk. She had defied the wicked old men whom even her father had dared not alienate. Her favor carried the new Lord Arnmigal along.

No one saw that at the moment. Nor was it obvious that Helspeth could defy the old men more easily because they were so much older today. Hilandle and fon Tyre had used themselves up trying to rage through Firaldia like youngsters still in their forties.

None of the dismissed Councilors had the fire in their bellies anymore. They preferred to get their ways by banging their swords on their shields. But an Empress with Ferris Renfrow, Algres Drear, Katrin's uncles, and Piper Hecht behind her was not likely to be intimidated.

*   *   *

"THIS IS LADY HOURLI," HECHT SAID. "SHE'S MY NEW INTELLIGENCE chief."

Eight people had crowded into Helspeth's refurbished palace quiet room. The smells of fresh plaster and fresher paint lingered. With Hecht and Hourli were the Empress and Lady Hilda, Ferris Renfrow, Algres Drear, and, to their consternation, Grand Duke Hilandle and Lord Admiral fon Tyre.

"Intelligence chief?" Helspeth demanded. "A woman?" Hourli was harvesting a crop of admiring looks from the older men.

Six people chuckled. Hourli did not. "Said the female emperor."

Hecht said, "She found Anselin. And Titus wants to try other things."

Renfrow said, "I can vouch for the lady's competence."

"Ferris? You know her?"

"A distant relative." Not strictly true. "She's brought some family members in to help the Commander. All women, except for her twin brother."

Hecht added, "And they're helping out of conviction, not for pay."

Helspeth did one of those things that would startle people throughout her reign. She dismissed the matter. "All right. Your department, your problem. Talk to me about Anselin."

Hecht glanced at Hourli. The Instrumentality deferred with a nod. He then glanced at Lady Hilda, who, this time, was not busy with coffee. War in Dreanger had interrupted the smuggling chain. Daedel winked.

"Anselin wanted to see Hypraxium on his way home." Which was common knowledge, now. "He visited the great buildings and was a guest of the Emperor, who suggested he take an overland route home in order to avoid interception by Navayan or Plataduran warships. Anselin took that advice."

But once Anselin departed Hypraxium, accompanied by one knight, two squires, a serjent, and a gaggle of servants, including a personal confessor, he had tumbled off the edge of the earth.

"Anselin's party was too big to go unnoticed but too small to fight."

"He's dead?" Helspeth blurted. "Murdered by bandits?"

"No. A false guide took him along a wrong road, into Hovacol. King Stain has him. He plans to auction him off. Stain has been behaving strangely for several years. His enemies claim that he is possessed."

The Grand Duke opened his mouth for the first time. "How could she possibly know all that?"

"Lady Hourli has unique resources."

Ferris Renfrow said, "She does."

"But . . ."

The Empress interjected, "We've been told, gently, that how the sausages get made is none of our business. Be content with the meat on the table."

"Thank you, Your Grace," Hecht said. Then, because Helspeth hated being called that if only because it had pleased her sister, he said, "Sorry. I meant Majesty. And it's true. Every profession has trade secrets."

"Do get on with it. Tell us what you plan, Lord Arnmigal." Rubbing it in.

Lady Hilda winked again. Hecht pushed that distraction aside. "I mean to take Anselin away from Stain. I need your permission."

"Do you? You must be exceeding confident that permission will be forthcoming. Buhle Smolens and Rivademar Vircondelet, with two hundred fifty men and twenty light falcons, left early this morning."

That caught Hecht off guard. "Yes. I try to keep the men sharp with field exercises."

Helspeth stared for several seconds. "A good idea, I don't doubt. The sword's edge should be kept polished. Stay a moment when the others leave." Perhaps a sop to the old men, him facing a dressing down. "I want to hear how much this perfect edge is going to cost."

"As you wish."

"Always. Proceed with your plot. Although, I'm thinking, had you dealt with Stain when Katrin asked, this situation might not have arisen."

Unfair, and even the old men saw that.

"This opportunity would not have befallen us."

It would have been a different world. The Righteous would not have taken the Krulik and Sneigon works before hearing about King Jaime. The Righteous would not have had the falcons that had made the difference at the Shades. Katrin would be alive and a prisoner of the Church. Serenity would still be Patriarch.

Helspeth stepped back. "You're right. Anselin would have ridden in here. We'd be trying to get Anne of Menand to bully Serenity into trading him for my sister."

Said sourly. Helspeth was in a contrarian mood. Hecht glanced at Lady Hilda, seeking a clue. He got another wink.

What the hell was Daedel up to?

"Hilda?" Helspeth said. "You have something to contribute?"

"The Archbishop keeps complaining about something being wrong with the churches."

Helspeth said, "Since none of these barbarians are inclined to take a cue and ask, what does that mean?"

"I'm not sure. The Archbishop has trouble making himself clear when he's excited. I think he means that the churches no longer have a holy feel."

Still no commentary. It was not clear what Hilda meant, either. Lady Hourli, though, looked uncomfortable.

Lady Hilda grumbled, "I'm saying what the Archbishop said. Maybe he meant the churches aren't blessed anymore. Maybe he meant that God isn't there anymore."

Hilda was disappointed by the numb response, obviously. Hecht suspected that she had hoped that someone could clarify Brion's complaint.

"No more snow jobs," Helspeth told Hecht when they were alone.

"Including having Hilandle and fon Tyre in so the old guard doesn't get its noses out of joint?"

"I can make that exception."

"What is this with Lady Hilda? She was flirting. Are you testing me?"

Helspeth raised an eyebrow but did not explain. "The Grand Duke of Eathered and Arnmigal is free to do whatever he considers to be in the interest of his Empress, even to rescuing the King of Arnhand. But the Empress would appreciate knowing what Lord Arnmigal intends before it becomes a public issue."

"Understood. But it's hard to keep you up to the minute."

"Really? When you have friends who pop into my bedroom in the middle of the night? Who know intimate details of things happening right now in a kingdom hundreds of miles away?"

Before he could placate her, Helspeth growled, "You want me to take you on faith but you won't trust me."

Hecht's shoulders hunched. The new, imperious Helspeth was disconcerting.

Hecht felt Hourli laughing somewhere close by.

"Very well. But you won't believe the truth when I tell you."

"Try me, my lord," said from inside two feet, head tilted back, eyes narrowed sleepily. Then she reddened.

Hecht was too pressed to respond, with humor or contact. "My Lady Hourli is the old goddess Hourli. Her twin is the god Hourlr. Also helping the Righteous are the goddesses Sheaf, Eavijne, Aldi, Wife . . ."

"Stop! You're right. I don't believe you. I can't, for the sake of my immortal soul. I know those names from when I was little. My old nurses told me stories about Donner and Ordnan, Hourli and Locke."

"Excellent. If you won't believe me I won't have to explain." He was sure he heard Hourli laughing. Being the subject of disbelief could be an advantage, sometimes. You could do what you wanted and not be blamed. "Just carry out my recommendations and enjoy the results."

"Lord Arnmigal . . . The hell with it! I have no hope of salvation if God does condemn us for sins that that we commit in our hearts."

Hecht waited.

"Hilda was doing what I told her to. I wanted to know what you'd do. But she went a little further than I wanted. She might mean it."

"Isn't that rather juvenile?"

"Yes. It is. But do I know any better? Have I had any chance to learn? I tripped into obsession at first sight with a man I saw for just a few minutes while my father was questioning a prisoner. The prisoner became Patriarch. The man who captured my imagination saved my life under the walls of al-Khazen. My lord, the only other man who ever forced his way into my mind, as a man, was Jaime of Castauriga, which repelled me. He believed he had the right."

"Uh . . ."

"He thought he had a claim on any woman he wanted. I infuriated him by refusing. So did Hilda. She's easy but she has standards. She knows wicked slime when she winds the stench."

"Helspeth! What are you? . . ."

"I'm sorry, my lord. I am Empress, now. I don't get much chance to be human. I fall apart when I try."

Hecht heard divine laughter once more. Probably his imagination. The Instrumentalities of the Night could not penetrate a well-maintained quiet room. It had to be his guilt about his own obsessions.

Helspeth Ege was naïve about the interplay between man and woman but she did know that Piper Hecht was as captivated by Helspeth Ege as Helspeth Ege was enthralled by Piper Hecht. "There will be a hasty coronation next week. We want to get it done before the grandees go home for the winter. After that I can do pretty much whatever I want."

"I know. That scares me. I'm a weak man. Sometimes I just can't do the right thing. And this could hurt people who don't deserve the pain."

Helspeth nodded sadly.

Hecht said, "That old man who turns up in odd places at odd

times would know right away. He knows my mind already. Others suspect."

He was rehearsing the facts more to convince himself than to caution Helspeth. She had crossed her last river already. She might offer him no more choice than Katrin had.

But Katrin was between him and God, now. He had been profoundly lucky, there.

Those watching Helspeth were, no doubt, circling in hopes that something damning would happen right now, tonight.

"Anything that happens will touch more lives than yours and mine."

"And if nothing happens, that will diminish lives as well."

"We have to make choices, dearest. Amongst them are, who has to suffer the hurt caused by the attraction between us. Us, by denying ourselves? Or those who . . . ?"

"Stop. I can do no more of this now. Go back to your demons. Catch Anselin. Let me get my heart under control. We'll talk Imperial business later." Helspeth had recovered.

"As you wish."

A dozen palace denizens contrived to be close by when the Empress and new Grand Duke emerged from the quiet room. Each felt a letdown. Scandal had been avoided. The couple looked like they wanted to fight.

HECHT FOUND LILA WAITING AT THE STILL-PATTER MANSION. SHE HAD brought Vali. He groaned.

Lila was quick to have her feelings hurt.

"Sorry, girls. It's been a hard day. I was looking forward to bed. What is it?"

"Nothing important. This was Vali's first long transition. We thought we'd see how you're doing. There isn't any real news except that Brothe has calmed down."

Vali said, "And a lot of priests are yammering about there being something wrong with the churches. Some say it's because God is turning away since the Church allowed a layman to overthrow an elected Patriarch."

"Wasn't the first time that happened." Hecht sighed. "It might be heresy but I suspect that God could not care less about the Patriarchy."

"We can go away if you want," Lila said.

"No." He needed contact with reality. "I don't see you often enough.

You remind me of what I have when I'm not Commander of the Righteous."

Both girls were pleased.

Vali said, "We saw Pella on the way. Him and that dwarf are only about forty miles from here, now."

"Dwarf?" Startled.

"Oh. No. Not like Iron Eyes. That Armand creature."

"The freak," Lila opined.

"Girls. Armand can't help being Armand."

"Yes, he can," Lila said. "People have choices. Maybe limited, like ours in that place where you found us. But nobody has to embrace their own humiliation. Armand is a freak because he does. You'll see. He gets here, he'll find himself a keeper who'll treat him like shit."

Vali said, "That's why he split with grandpa Muniero. Grandpa treated him too good."

"May be, but I don't care. Tell me how Anna is."

Neither girl seemed eager to address that. Vali finally said, "She's just Anna Mozilla while Piper Hecht is away. She goes along in kind of a daze."

Lila said, "She's doing better now that she's back in her own house."

Another twinge of conscience. But they had worked that out at the beginning.

Anna did not expect him to be faithful. She was a mistress, not a wife, and he was a man. But she would surely suffer from anything as public as a liaison with the Grail Empress.

"When you get back I want you to remind her that I think of her all the time."

"We could take you."

"That won't happen, girls."

"Fraidy cat," Vali said.

"Absolutely. Now scoot on out of here."

They went, but not before needling him with observations between themselves about how attractive some of the younger officers were, especially that Carava de Bos.

De Bos had a definite reputation.

PIPER HECHT DID NOT PARTICIPATE IN HELSPETH'S CORONATION, EVEN as a witness. He and his key staffers avoided the end of the political season by joining the expedition to Hovacol. Pella accompanied him.

Asked politely by a purported ambassador—Hourlr in mortal guise—King Stain refused to surrender Anselin. He summoned his host.

Perceived bullying by the Grail Empire guaranteed an excellent response despite Stain's recent lack of intimacy with rational thinking. More than five hundred horse and a thousand foot awaited the Righteous in a sound foreslope position behind a stream spanned by a wooden bridge eight feet wide.

The consensus of Hecht's staff was, "Oh, shit! What have we gotten into here?"

Kait Rhuk suggested, "Roll the falcons up to the riverbank. Take them under fire. That will make them come at us."

Drago Prosek nodded. "I'm considering starting with half charges so they have time to watch the shot come in."

And Rhuk: "Keep the falcons near the bridge so we can concentrate fire when they charge."

"All good thinking," Hecht said. He glanced at the sky. "We have two hours of light left. Pity that ridge is behind us. It wasn't, the sun would come down in their eyes. Vircondelet. Break out twenty men. Start making camp. We'll stay here tonight." That should buoy their confidence. He checked the shadow of that ridge. It was creeping eastward.

The men set to work siting falcons and raising berms to protect their crews. Stain's men first seemed puzzled, then uneasy. The invaders were behaving strangely. They should have turned back once they saw what awaited them. But the Righteous were, all workmanlike, preparing to become unpleasant.

Hecht summoned Kait Rhuk. "Kait, did you put my kid on a crew?" Pella loved the smoke and thunder.

"Over there. Last on the left. He's the powder boy."

"All right. Good." He sighed. Powder boy was a dangerous job. On the other hand, Rhuk had sent him to the weapon farthest from the bridge.

The shadow of the ridge passed the Righteous. Hecht tightened his cinch, mounted up. "Be back in a minute."

He crossed the wooden bridge and headed for the waiting army. Some looked like veterans. Their arms and equipment were better than he expected. King Stain might know what he was doing.

Hecht stayed behind the line of shadow, halted beyond bowshot. The men ahead did not know what to make of him. Had he come to parlay?

Hecht did not know himself. Intuition moved him.

The shadow began to claim the men of Hovacol.

Hecht raised his right hand high. "Now."

Thunder rattled off the hills. A pair of horrors twice man-size swept out of the shade behind the Righteous, hurtled toward King Stain. Their shrieks melted spines.

Hecht felt himself being pulled in the ferocious psychic wake of Fastthal and Sprenghul, the Choosers of the Slain, this time come before the fight, spreading terror. Those men up ahead would not recognize them but would imbibe the dread surrounding them.

The animals were more frightened than the men. The formation began to crumble.

The Choosers came round again, sweeping in from the ends of the Hovacol line. That fell apart. Only King Stain stood his ground.

Hecht lowered his hand. He was confused. How had he caused all that?

Brokke, Sedlakova, and Consent joined him. Behind and below, the Righteous crossed the bridge.

Consent, eyeing bewildered stragglers ahead, blurted, "What the hell just happened?"

"What do you mean?"

Brokke said, "Something happened to you up here, Boss. And it was damned scary."

Consent said, "You turned into a pillar of shadow. You had lightning in your hair."

"I did not. Stop messing with me."

Sedlakova said, "Boss, you ain't going to bullshit nobody about this. Everybody saw it. On both sides."

A makeshift lifeguard assembled around Stain, up the slope. The King of Hovacol was not short on courage.

Hecht was inclined to argue. "I don't remember it that way." He did not remember at all. "Clej, go up there and make sure they don't have a surprise waiting across the ridge. Catch me a straggler. I want to know what *they* think just happened."

He had an elusive recollection of the Choosers. Startled, he looked around, saw nothing remarkable—except the attitudes of his companions.

"Hagen, go on and finish making camp. Let the creek be our moat. We'll move on tomorrow. Drago. Kait. They're not here? Remind me to tell them to watch their powder. It might rain."

There were but a few wisps of cloud, set ablaze by the sun beyond the western ridge.

Hecht's companions looked him askance again, probably more because he wanted to caution Rhuk and Prosek than because he was predicting the weather. Those two needed no advice in their chosen field.

Hecht said, "Gentlemen, the rest is yours. I'm going to lie down."

HECHT WAS LOOSENING HIS BOOTS WHEN PELLA SLIPPED INTO THE tent. "You all right, Dad?"

"Just worn out."

"What happened?"

"I don't know. I wish people would stop asking."

"Are you scared?"

He was. He did not like not being in complete control. "I'm just tired. I just need to lie down."

"All right. I can take a hint."

Hecht fell asleep concerned that he was pushing people away by keeping his thoughts and feelings to himself.

KING STAIN'S TROOPS DID NOT GO HOME. THEY MANEUVERED. THEY tried to draw the Righteous into traps. They performed well but got no chance to take advantage of their numbers.

The Commander of the Righteous intuited their every move. The Choosers did not reappear. They were not needed. A vigorous cantata from the falcons discouraged every ambush.

Cholate was King Stain's seat. The walled town sat on a short hill in a tight bend of the Vilde River. That hill rose just thirty feet at its highest. The Vilde was fifty feet wide, deep, and slow, a fine natural moat round the northern third of the town. Once, probably in antiquity, a canal had been dug round the other side. It had not been kept up. Today it was boggy ground backed by a wall that had not been maintained, either. Crude palisades had been thrown up in gaps where the stonework had collapsed or been plundered for building materials. The population and country alike were stunned by the appearance of invaders. Enemies visiting Cholate seemed vastly improbable.

A plain fronted Cholate outside the bog, with heavy forest in the near distance, to the right and down the Vilde. When the Righteous arrived the locals were salvaging what crops they could. King Stain's army stood ready for battle between them and the invaders.

"Same tactics," Hecht told his officers. "Get as close as you can, then dig in."

Brokke asked, "You're not going to attack?"

"I'm going to be flexible. They have the numbers. If we have to fight I want them to come to the falcons. Through pits, trenches, caltrops, tangles, and whatever else they give us time to prepare."

Local soil was easy to shift. There was plenty of timber nearby. The Righteous trenched and raised ramparts. They made the ground bristle with sharpened stakes meant to break up and channel a mounted attack.

King Stain did nothing to hamper the work.

Titus Consent said, "They can't decide what to do."

Hecht replied, "They've never seen anything like us. And they don't want to be part of another Shades."

"Then they should try maneuvering. The falcons don't get around so fast. And we only have so many."

"Excellent thinking. Stain should find a way to come at us so our falcons don't negate his numbers. Instead, he's waiting for us to come to him."

"That would work if we took the bait."

"We won't. Drago." Prosek was passing. "Once we're ready to receive an attack I want you to begin bombarding their formation."

Prosek grinned. "Any special targets?"

"Equal opportunity, top to bottom and left to right. They're rattled already. Let's make them think even more. And be ready for a charge."

Absent the grin, Prosek asked, "Should I have godshot loaded or standing by?"

"Standing by. Wait. Charge one falcon. Let's make that doctrine. One weapon always ready for the improbable."

Prosek nodded. So did Consent. Neither appeared comfortable with the word "improbable."

Nobody was comfortable around Hecht anymore.

Falcon fire provoked anger but no aggressive reaction. At extreme range the weapons did little damage. Hecht expanded his earthworks till they shielded the Righteous on all sides. His officers worried that he might let them be surrounded.

There was no ridge behind the Righteous. No shadow to roll across the land. But Hecht had positioned himself so the sun would set behind him.

He gathered his officers. "Got a volunteer to carry the olive branch over to those people?"

Silence.

"Somebody needs to go. You don't want me to do it again."

These men were more worried about Lord Arnmigal than they were about Stain of Hovacol.

"I'll take it, Dad."

Startled, Hecht asked, "Can you ride? You'll have to ride." Which seemed the stupidest question possible, though an approach on foot would insult members of the cavalier class.

"Just put me on a good-looking horse."

"Forget that," Clej Sedlakova said. "Send the one-armed man, Boss." Pella used a hand to conceal a smirk. The sneak.

"The one-armed man's gesture is appreciated but the job calls for someone who can carry a banner and steer a horse at the same time."

To which Pella said, "I'll carry the banner. Or the olive branch. He can do the talking."

"All right. Clej, remind them that Anselin is all we're interested in. They hand him over, we go away. They don't, we take him. But say it politely."

Hecht ground his teeth as Pella and Sedlakova rode off. Hagen Brokke muttered something about the boy growing up.

The encounter was brief. The locals were not demonstratively antagonistic. Sedlakova headed back. Pella lagged a moment. Hecht grumbled, "I hope he didn't just say something obnoxious."

Sedlakova did not bring good news. "The interpreter says everybody but the King is willing to give Anselin up but Stain has been more strange than usual, lately, and refuses to cooperate."

Hecht grunted. He looked at Pella. The boy said, "I didn't say anything, Dad. I just gave them the hard-eye."

"Really?"

"It's psychology. I'm just a kid. If I'm not worried . . ."

"Maybe. Clej. Find a way across the river. Pella. Go back up there. Tell them I'm challenging Stain himself."

"Boss?"

"Dad?"

"Don't argue. Do it." Stain would be too cautious to accept. He would not test himself against a complete unknown.

HECHT'S CONFIDENCE WAS MISPLACED. PELLA BROUGHT WORD THAT Stain would meet the Commander of the Righteous tomorrow afternoon.

"I fooled myself," Hecht confessed. But he felt no anxiety.

Not so the others. They wanted him to weasel out. "That's what he's counting on." Hecht did believe that. "He called my bluff. Now I'll call his. Rivademar, you can be a half-ass diplomat when you want. Make the arrangements. Avoid any mention of a truce."

This would be a good time for the Shining Ones to contribute. Something. Anything. Where the hell were they?

Pella protested, "Dad, you don't have any armor, or anything."

Hecht shrugged. "The die is cast. Vircondelet. Go."

"Yes sir, Boss." Grinning through the dark brush that had sprouted on his face during the march.

Pella asked, "What are you up to, Dad?"

"Events should make a face-off unnecessary." He wondered at his own confidence.

CLEJ SEDLAKOVA, UNWITTINGLY GUIDED BY FRIENDLY SPIRITS WHOSE invisibility had Lord Arnmigal muttering, located an unguarded bridge. Hecht sent his cavalry and four falcons across and downstream, to face Cholate from the north bank of the Vilde. A stone bridge spanned the river. The last ten feet, however, consisted of a heavy drawbridge. The citizenry had tried to raise that. It had become stuck partway up. Sedlakova installed his falcons at the head of the bridge and raised earthworks to protect against a cross-river sortie.

His falcons did not speak. He believed they would be more intimidating, waiting quietly.

SEDLAKOVA SENT HIS COMMANDER A MESSAGE IN THE HEART OF THE night. The courier crossed the river by means of a taut rope running from bank to bank. Soon afterward forty men used the rope to cross in the opposite direction. Titus Consent led them. Lord Arnmigal tagged along, just to observe. Weapons, clothing, and gear crossed in captured boats. The noise seemed loud enough to disturb the dead but Cholate sounded no alarm.

Hecht stood by while Titus crouched with Sedlakova, considering Cholate's river gate. "When did this happen?"

The gate was open. The drawbridge was down. A man who had stolen across reported that neither portcullis had dropped.

"That's the creepy part. I'm not sure. Schacter scouted it as soon as we noticed it. He got out as soon as he saw that it was all open."

"Think it's an ambush?"

"I'm thinking it's something else altogether." Sedlakova glanced back. "How could that stuff all happen without making any noise?"

"No noise? Sounds unlikely."

"Not unlikely, impossible. It makes me nervous." He looked back again but referenced no other recent unlikely events.

The Righteous operated in a fog of unlikely events.

Hecht observed, "It would be a sin to ignore that invitation."

"But if it's an ambush . . ."

"I'll trigger it myself. Titus?"

"Ready." Consent's voice squeaked. Those nearby chuckled. Forcing his voice deeper, Consent said, "Make sure your gear won't rattle, then let's go."

A rind of moon sometimes peeked through gaps between scurrying clouds. Its light seemed unable to reach the bridge, though it glistened off the river. Hecht moved ahead, sliding through the shadows. Those who followed maintained a silence no commander could fault.

Hecht's confidence grew. He understood after he stepped into the darkness of the passage through the wall.

Three Shining Ones awaited him, invisible till he came within a few feet. Their semblances were not rigorously human tonight. He recognized Hourlr and Sheaf, barely. All three faded. Hecht covered Consent's mouth, in case. No one else saw the Instrumentalities.

"Go on," Hecht whispered. "I'll watch."

Titus sent men to find the gate guards. They were in a sleep so deep they seemed frozen in time. Consent had them restrained, then moved on.

The story was the same everywhere.

Soon all the men were inside and headed toward the citadel. Sedlakova grumbled, "I hope nobody kypes the falcons."

Hecht assured him, "They're safe."

Consent demanded, "Everyone keeping their matches out of sight?"

Most of the men carried handheld falcons. For no reason obvious to Lord Arnmigal soldiers operating in the dark were more confident when armed with those.

A soldier impressed with how well things were going murmured, "The gods are with us tonight."

Consent sent a team to see if a gate could be opened for the main force. The rest he led to the citadel, where that gateway was open, too. And the garrison, to a man—all three—were snoring.

The place contained neither King Stain, any of his court, nor Anselin of Menand. Nor was there any sign of the knights, nobles, and men-at-arms who made up Hovacol's army.

"Colonel Sedlakova!" the Commander of the Righteous growled. "Come here! Tell me how Stain made a whole army disappear."

"I want to, Boss. But I can't. It'd be a handy trick to have. Maybe he has unseen friends, too."

It was too dark for Sedlakova to enjoy his commander's scowl.

"Titus, have you sent warning to the camp? Stain may be considering a surprise of his own."

"I did send word when I saw that there were too few people around."

"Would you care to exercise your imagination? Where is Stain?"

"We didn't push hard because he did what we wanted by backing up instead of fighting. My guess is, he went in the gate we could see and right on out the one we couldn't, up the river and into the woods. He hasn't let any fires be lighted so he hasn't attracted attention that way. I'm surprised he hasn't launched a night attack. I would have."

And would have charged straight into the talons of the Choosers. But Hecht could not admit that. Why had his supernatural associates not passed on the facts about the actual state of affairs? Though when they could have done so without attracting attention made for an intriguing question.

He had a sudden notion that he should have anticipated Stain.

He shook his head as though trying to rid it of cobwebs. "Gentlemen. Ideas. What is Stain trying to get us to do? He's not stupid. He's enjoyed a lot of military success the past few years."

Sedlakova shrugged. "I'm out of my depth, Boss."

"Titus?"

"Could he want to put us on the inside so he can close us up and starve us?"

Sedlakova liked that. "That would reduce the advantage of the falcons. They're too clumsy to handle a shifting axis of attack. And, being on the outside, he'd have his whole kingdom to provide men and supplies."

"That must be it." Though it did not feel entirely right. "So let's disappoint the man."

The Righteous drove the remaining population out into the gathering dawn, allowing them to take nothing but their clothing. Let King Stain carry the burden of so many women, children, and old people. Let him look homeward to see Cholate's able-bodied men demolishing churches, walls, and public works. Let him watch the resulting debris be used to render the Vilde unnavigable.

Meantime, Hagen Brokke would create more tangles and pitfalls around the Righteous camp.

Lord Arnmigal kept most of his men there. He preferred to face any attack there, though he remained unsure of the advantage. He had found a flaw in Consent's analysis of Stain's intent. Stain did not have men enough to properly invest Cholate. The Righteous could escape using the bridge to the north bank of the Vilde.

HECHT WAS NAPPING. HE DID THAT WHEN THERE WERE NO CRITICAL demands on his time. Pella interrupted. "Wake up, Dad. You need to get up."

"Huh?" He had been deep into a strange dream where he roamed an unfamiliar cold waste with a band of blood brothers, hunting. Their quarry might have been a man. Might once have been a friend. Might have been the father of one of the blood brothers. The hunt might have taken place in the wild country Piper Hecht called his homeland. A lot of might-have-beens wisped away like breath scattering on a winter wind.

"It's almost noon. That Stain guy says he's ready to fight."

Hecht could not help being confused. "I thought he went away."

"He came back. He says he's chosen lances."

Hecht shook his head. "Lances?"

Pella explained. Lord Arnmigal had issued the challenge. The challenged got to choose the weapons. After that the outcome was in the hands of God. "He probably picked lances because everybody knows you don't fight on horseback."

"Not lately." He consulted his nerves. He had none. He should have had, but he was dead calm. "I want to see Mr. Sedlakova."

"Dad? You're not gonna . . ."

"Of course I am."

"But! . . ."

"Get Sedlakova, boy! Now!"

IT TOOK CLEJ A WHILE TO COLLECT EVERYTHING BUT HECHT DID GO to the contest equipped the way he wanted. He rode a small, agile horse instead of a charger. Nor did he carry the heavy lance westerners preferred. His choice was ten feet long, thin, light, like the lances used by the Sha-lug. He bore a small round shield on his left forearm. His helmet was light, too. For armor he wore a borrowed scale shirt over his own link mail.

The mind inside the head inside the light helmet, still glacially calm, wondered if his muscles would remember the moves they would have to make.

He sensed uncertainty at the far end of the field. Those people had not expected him to show up looking confident. There was uncertainty at his own end, as well. None of his people thought him even a rudimentary cavalryman.

He considered Pella and Titus. Titus held another two lances. If Hecht broke three he would be in trouble. Stain, yonder, had a more generous supply.

Pella was pale and shaking. He could see no good coming from this.

Time stopped.

Hourli and Hourlr stepped out of nothing. The goddess extended a hand. Her brother did the same. His held a short black spear. Hourli said, "Trade."

It did not occur to Hecht to do anything else. He knew that spear. He surrendered his lance.

The spear was heavy. It dragged his arm down. It changed as he forced it back up. It became a light cavalry lance.

The Shining Ones vanished.

Time resumed.

Hecht endured the pre-fight ceremonies, though he saw no point to them. Hagen Brokke sidled close. "Boss, get him early. He'll start out just trying to knock you off your horse. If he sees that you're going to be stubborn he might decide to kill you. He's had a bad temper the past few years."

Hecht grunted. That agreed with what the Shining Ones reported.

Still, the Enterprise would come this way next spring. Stain ought not to provoke its backers.

The Enterprise would come. There would be a Commander of the Righteous and a mission to liberate the Holy Lands. Crusade fever had begun to course through the Episcopal Chaldarean world.

Piper Hecht had to stop woolgathering. King Stain had taken his position. He and his mount alike were richly caparisoned. His charger was immense. A feather plume wobbled in the breeze above his helm. "A noble vision," Hecht said. "A shame to ruin all that finery."

Men from both forces lined the edges of the field. Officers tried and failed to keep them out of the barley nearby. A priest in the odd raiment of the Eastern Rite stepped to the middle of the field. He carried a pole with a white pennon attached. He swung that down as though to punish the earth, sprinted off dragging the pole.

Horns sounded, Hecht supposed for the benefit of the blind. He consulted his courage. He remained unafraid, relaxed and confident, and that made no rational sense. His opponent was famed as a tiltyard bully and scrapper.

He urged his mount forward.

In these passages knights crossed their lances behind the necks of their mounts and tried to unseat one another as they passed left side to left side. Thus, their lances did not cross and become entangled. Hecht had witnessed a few tournaments. He had not understood the formalities. Tilts were, at their base, practice for war. In war the rule was, you strove to be the man still standing when the fighting came to an end.

Stain was a traditionalist. He couched his lance under his right arm and crossed it behind his mount's neck. His form was exquisite.

Hecht grasped his lance two-thirds of the way back, shaft tight against his forearm, the whole raised to shoulder height, arm cocked back to thrust, lance head slightly low. When Stain drew close he swerved to pass right hand to right hand. He drove his lance's head at Stain's face.

In the Vibrant Spring School a lancer learned to use the tip of his weapon to snatch rings off moving targets. Else Tage had been a magnificent student. Piper Hecht was fifteen years out of practice. Heartsplitter did not find the gap in King Stain's visor.

Hecht did push the man backward in his saddle. He did remember to whip his lance round so the sharp edge of its head scored the flank of Stain's mount. Not done to perfection, but done.

He trotted on, unaware of the uproar from the sidelines.

His mount seemed to approve of the proceedings so far.

He turned, let the beast catch her breath. Yonder, Stain was complaining. Hecht waited. He remained comfortable and confident but doubted that he had yet made his point.

Stain readied himself for another pass. His gelding was not as engaged as he. It favored its right rear leg. Blood stained its white caparison.

Hecht waited.

Stain refused another pass to the right so Hecht gave him what he wanted.

As he closed with the King, he swerved right, increasing the angle Stain must use to place his lance on target, took its head on his shield, pushed it past him. At the same time he drove his own lance down at the outside of Stain's left thigh. The King's mail took a long, deep, smoking, cherry-red score but held. Heartsplitter skipped to the gelding's caparison, opened a gash in its side two feet long.

Stain's mount stopped. It screamed. It dropped its rear end as though it meant to sit. Then it tried to throw Stain.

Hecht slowed, turned in a tight circle, came back, gave Stain a solid thump in the back of the helmet with Heartsplitter's butt. He circled again. Stain tried desperately to control his gelding.

Hecht passed right side to right side. Stain could not get his lance up nor his shield across. Heartsplitter penetrated Stain's mail, pierced his right shoulder to the bone. Hecht withdrew to his end of the field. Sedlakova and Pella stared, eyes wide. The uproar along the sidelines was deafening. Hecht did not hear it. He faced King Stain, waited.

He sensed disbelief behind him. Sedlakova found his voice. "That was amazing, Boss. You made it look easy."

"Let that be a lesson. Don't underestimate me." As Stain finally got his mount under control, Hecht asked, "Is he stupid enough to keep on?"

"He won't see that he has much choice."

Some unfathomable western pride stuff must be at work. "I don't want to kill him, Clej. He's able. He could be a valuable ally. Go ask them not to make me kill him."

Sedlakova was confused. "What are you talking about, Boss? This isn't about anybody killing anybody. It's about getting somebody to yield."

Hecht said, "I said go tell them I don't want to kill him."

"All right."

Pella took off running up the left side of the field. He did not reach the far end in time.

Stain got his dappled gelding moving, slowly. The animal no longer wanted to play.

Hecht sighed. Neither did he. Could he manage this without killing Stain or doing the gelding further injury?

Stain cast his lance aside, drew his sword. Hecht suspected he was expected to do likewise.

He retained Heartsplitter. Trotting, he closed and thrust at Stain's face again, which the man expected. He chopped ferociously, sword ringing as it bounced off the divine spear. Hecht spun that, to use as a club. He whacked Stain on the back of the neck, leaving him wobbly.

Another brisk passage, sword against spear. Stain could not force Hecht to his shield side. And Hecht had the reach by a yard.

The mare seemed to read Hecht's mind. Every move she made was exact and perfect. Hecht thumped and poked, hit the King's feet, knees, elbows, hands, and prodded the gelding's wounds. He wanted to limit the harm he did but feared those watching would think he was toying with Stain. That would not be good.

He landed a solid blow behind Stain's right knee, poked the gelding's worst wound. It screamed, reared, successfully shed Stain this time, limped off and refused to let anyone come near.

Hecht dismounted. Stain got his feet under himself and tried to get himself up but when he lifted his shield his right knee buckled. He dropped again, supported himself on the shield.

"Do you yield?" Hecht asked.

"Never. You did not fight as a gentleman."

"I'm not a gentleman. I'm a soldier. Combat isn't play. That's the lesson here. I will win. Yield."

"I will not. I won't dishonor . . ."

"You mean to die over this?"

"Kill me here. Otherwise, I won't rest until . . ."

"If that's the way it's got to be." Hecht raised Heartsplitter. "I don't want you haunting my back trail." He thrust.

Stain managed to deflect the spear. Heartsplitter itself seemed surprised. So. Stain *was* more than just a man.

A circle formed. Men from both forces begged the combatants to stand down.

Hecht said, "He insists that I kill him. He won't stand for anything less." He thrust again. Then again, and pushed through Stain's guard. Blood leaked from all of the King's wounds. The thing that possessed him could not stop his flesh from growing weaker. "He has a bad case of the stubborns." Hecht saw no need to note that Stain had surrendered himself to the Will of the Night. Behind the wicked presence Stain felt like a good man worth saving.

Clej Sedlakova said, "No doubt he finds all this hard to believe. He has a huge reputation. You have none."

Hecht delivered a butt stroke that turned Stain's helm sideways. The man could no longer see.

Pella said, "Step away, Dad. Let it go."

A shadow swept across the field. A lone, massive thunderhead moved in front of the sun, pushing a frigid gust front. Men of every allegiance cursed it.

The cold was bitter around the King. Stain straightened his helmet. He looked around wildly.

A woman stepped round Hecht and approached Stain. Hourli. Men asked, "Who is that?" and, "Where the hell did she come from?"

Good questions both, sure to rattle the Righteous further.

The thunderhead stopped moving. That distracted attention from Hourli.

Stain strained to raise sword and shield. He could not. His knee gave way again.

Hourli rested a hand on his shoulder. He released a long groan. An icy spin devil swirled round the pair, snatching up leaves and bits of grass. A fading shriek startled everyone. The baby whirlwind raced toward the nearby woods as though desperate to escape. Traces of dark smoke twirled inside.

Rain began to fall. It included bits of ice.

Stain found the strength to rise. He removed his helmet, shambled forward, dropped to his good knee, presented his sword to the Commander of the Righteous. "An end to this, Lord Arnmigal. I yield without reservation. God's Will is clear."

Lightning flashed. It smashed into the wood, shattering trees. The rain grew heavier and more hail-laden. Hecht told Stain, "We need to get in out of this before that lightning walks over here."

A dozen blistering bolts had struck the forest already.

Somebody asked, "Where the hell did that woman go?"

Another immediately demanded, "What about the mare the Boss was riding? Where the hell is she? Did the thunder scare her off?"

A carronade hammered the woods. Stain said, "I have to get my people under cover." Two were helping him keep his feet. He seemed a different man.

Hecht's were headed for shelter already.

The downpour increased. Hailstones made the footing treacherous. Hecht joined the general flight for shelter.

The lightning pounding the forest moved away from Cholate.

He wondered who was wielding the hammer. Then he wondered why he was wondering that.

19. Tel Moussa: Growing Despair

Al-Azer er-Selim settled beside Nassim Alizarin to watch another sunset. Distant clouds, over the White Sea, burned like hellfire. Nassim observed, "You seem glum. I suppose that means bad news."

"After a fashion."

"You're going to tell me why that sprig in Gherig is decorating our graves."

"After a fashion."

"Az, I don't have the patience."

"I've put together a notion based on what isn't there to be seen."

"Yes?"

"The Brotherhood is taking Indala deadly serious. They began working against the Shake's plan before he left for Dreanger."

"So they knew, despite our efforts."

"Yes. They were distressed when Black Rogert came back to Gherig. They tried to stop that. They failed. But they found an alternative. Technically, Gherig belongs to the Brotherhood. By making it the fifth commandery they could install a Master senior to the castellan assigned by the King of Vantrad."

"Reducing du Tancret to the job of housekeeper. Clever. But that doesn't explain their absurd level of confidence."

"How have we done with the new men?"

"They may be new to the Holy Lands but they aren't new to war. The men we're sending out there are."

"And they have strong support from their Special Office. Which gives them intelligence resources we can't match."

"Could that be why they're so confident?"

"There's more. Something to do with the Night. The details are obscure. It might have to do with the Wells of Power."

Nassim grunted. The Wells of Ihrian. The dying wells. The nearest was the Well of Days, which had lent its name to Indala's great triumph over the crusaders, years ago. That well lay just beyond today's tacit frontier.

The Wells all lay inside the Crusader States.

"Are they counting on a resurgence in power?"

"I couldn't say. There was a rumor that Apparitions had been seen, then another about the Brotherhood considering fortifying the Wells."

Fortify the Wells? Could they? That idea had not surfaced before.

Then bad news arrived, twice in quick succession. A force patrolling the road to Shamramdi had been wiped out eight miles back toward the Lucidian capital. Then a daring band of youths who had found the courage to go into the Idiam after er-Rashal had the misfortune to find him. Only two made it back to Tel Moussa. Both were mad.

NASSIM ENJOYED A LEMON WATER SWEETENED WITH HONEY. HE watched the sun settle toward the distant White Sea. He was the picture of contentment. His enemies would have been unnerved.

He was anything but content, though. His world was falling apart. Disaster circled ever closer, patient as a vulture.

Az would not let him wallow in self-pity. Az would kick his behind till he banished defeatism. The Mountain had to remember that he was Sha-lug. Az said, "There was a messenger from Shamramdi. From Indala's uncle. They've finally heard us. Reinforcements will be sent."

"For all the good that's likely to do. Double the number of grave diggers."

These days the burial ground often had immigrants waiting for a place to lie down.

Tel Moussa gave as good as it got but the crusaders did not mind losing their hired foot soldiers.

"What are they doing, Az? Why are they doing it? How does this constant engagement advance their design?"

"That I can't tell you, General."

"Lack of good intelligence."

"Lack of any intelligence. Their Special Office operators do a great job keeping us ignorant."

"Might they be pressing just so they can find out about me?"

"That could be. However . . ."

"Yes? More bad news?"

"Not exactly. Our friends do hear things."

"Make me happy, Az. Tell me something useful."

"Useful won't make you happy. The foundation of the Master of the Commandery's strategy is his expectation of the arrival of the new crusader army. Then they'll begin fortifying the Wells and sources of water."

Nassim groaned. He did not believe the new crusade would be anywhere near as big as predicted. A few thousand at most, not some vast horde of many tens of thousands. They would be commanded by one of the most promising warriors ever to come out of the Vibrant Spring School. The only possible outcome was a Praman triumph grand enough to be celebrated for a thousand years.

The Mountain turned a bit less pessimistic.

Az would not have that. "Do you have an evacuation plan?"

"For here? What the hell?" He noted the twinkle in the other man's eye.

Az was determined to drive him out of his bleak season.

"No. There's no reason to think there'll be any need. How can they possibly make us abandon this place?"

"I don't know. I'm with you. We have food, water, loyal men, and our falcons. What can they possibly do against that? But."

Nassim grunted.

Az said, "They have a plan. They expect it to work. We should create responses to put into effect if they do achieve success."

The Mountain said, "We do have a plan. I just haven't seen any need to put it out there."

Az watched the light fade, let darkness gather some before saying, "Please prepare for the worst."

"What do you know?"

"Nothing for sure. I don't have the skills to unmask the future. But I am sure that bad times are on their way."

Displeased, the Mountain turned to a less dismal topic. Er-Selim was not interested. He produced a plausible excuse for taking himself elsewhere.

Er-Rashal al-Dhulquarnen made himself master of Andesqueluz. He had no rivals. He was the only live human being on the mountain, Asher.

The Rascal's doings reached Nassim's ears in, at most, two days.

He had new allies.

Small clans of wild men lived in the Idiam. Outsider dread of the haunted desert shielded them. They adhered to none of the self-certain religions of the surrounding world. Fewer than a thousand subsisted in a land that, barren though it was, could have supported several times their number.

The world knew them as the Ansa. They called themselves the Eath. Most spoke Lucidian with a guttural accent. No outsiders spoke their language.

Two of these Ansa approached Az as he sought a way to approach the Dreangerean sorcerer unnoticed. They were not pleased with er-Rashal. They had discovered, suffering some pain in the process, that they could not correct the abomination and horror of his presence.

He had swatted them good.

They knew the situation outside the Idiam. In the main, they did not care. They cursed all outsiders equally. But they found the Mountain least repugnant of all the warlords not blessed with having been born to the Eath.

They wanted what Nassim Alizarin wanted, shot of the diabolical outsider in the city of the dead. They understood "enemy of my enemy." They proposed an alliance—exclusively for the purpose of expunging er-Rashal al-Dhulquarnen.

So the Mountain knew, always quickly, when the Rascal was on the move. But he could discover no way of doing anything about that.

Er-Rashal would not let him.

Nor would the new gang at Gherig.

Madouc of Hoeles was the most vigorous opponent Nassim had ever faced. He was clever and relentless. His war of attrition never ceased. He appeared to have a definite strategy. Most nights the Mountain fell asleep cursing as he tried to figure it out.

Clearly, the Master of the Commandery was isolating Tel Moussa, little by little, as Nassim hoped to do with er-Rashal.

He could not reach the sorcerer so had the Ansa watch and summon aid whenever er-Rashal tried to reach the outside world. The Rascal was vulnerable only in that he required food.

Tel Moussa needed food and water, too. Madouc of Hoeles did not set a formal siege. He did not have that much strength.

"He always knows what we're doing," Bone complained. "Every convoy has to fight." Tel Moussa had become dependent on caravans from farther east. Gherig now denied it the ability to defend its flocks and hidden gardens.

Some oft-promised and as often delayed reinforcements finally did arrive, two hundred fifty veterans of Indala's campaign in Dreanger. The Master of the Commandery, with every able-bodied man available, including crippled Black Rogert, met them within sight of Tel Moussa and drove them off before Nassim could send help.

Sorcery must have been involved, Nassim thought. No other explanation made sense. "This does not bode well, Az," he grumbled. "We can look forward to a long and unpleasant winter."

"You are surrendering to despair again, General. To the Will of the Night. You know Indala himself will turn up here someday. He'll need to be here when the crusaders come."

True. But would the Great Shake bother rescuing the garrison of Tel Moussa after their commander had denied him what he wanted?

"I wish we could make this Madouc understand how important it is to make the Rascal's life miserable."

"You could go explain. You could ask the Ansa to show him."

Nassim scowled, aware that the Master of Ghosts was not serious.

Az said, "You make too much of that asshole, General. You grant him too much respect. What scheme of his has ever actually succeeded?"

"None. But only because somebody always got in the way."

Al-Azer er-Selim was not impressed by anything but bottom-line results. Er-Rashal al-Dhulquarnen had few of those to back his boasts. His greatest triumph, development of a workable falcon, was a matter of indifference to him.

20. Antieux: Last Happy Season

Brother Candle felt no different—except for enduring the endless horror of knowing he had been involved in multiple deaths. The dead had been bent on hurting him. He had been but a vehicle for those deadly serpents. But the guilt persisted.

And he knew, as soon as he hobbled out behind Socia, into that hall where she decided who owed what to whom, and who the chicken belonged to if it laid eggs somewhere other than in its proper coop . . .

The logic people brought to these sessions boggled a rational mind.

He knew the news had raced around the city, growing fat on the popular imagination. Everyone became nervous when they looked at him—Bishop LaVelle being a serious exception.

The Bishop lived life in an alternate reality.

Brother Candle wanted to cringe away from people who looked at him the way they looked at Bernardin about to go on a rampage.

The assizes started as they always did, with stupid arguments that had no business being brought before the Countess. All three cases should have been handled at the neighborhood level.

The Perfect leaned down to one of three scribes recording the proceedings. (Three because one could not scribble fast enough by himself. The trio would later unify their notes into an official transcript.) "Tomorrow. Noon. In this hall. I want every justice of the peace and local magistrate. No excuses. Understood?"

"Yes, sir." Scribble scribble. "It shall be done." So this was what power felt like.

Better get shot as soon as he could. Even this small taste was seductive. What wonders might he perform if no one dared deny him!

The cases were the usual nonsense. Bishop LaVelle's matter was not unusual, either. He was so confident of the righteousness of his Church's doctrine that he argued that it should be the basis of all civil law. At the moment he had a problem with fines levied on a church that had granted sanctuary to three brothers convicted of multiple murders, arguing that the killings could not be considered crimes because they had been done on behalf of the Church.

The brothers belonged to the Society.

Though LaVelle was frustrating he remained untouched. He was the least villainous bishop in living memory.

"Your time is nearly up, Bishop," Socia said. "Your petition says nothing about these matters. Are you here to present a false case?"

False case meant a case sneaked into proceedings without prior warning, not a case based on lies or deception. Those were part of all trials.

This time the Countess allowed some leeway. Complaining publicly filled the Bishop's need to do something. He stirred no trouble elsewhere while he was free to vent in court.

"My heartfelt apologies, Ladyship. Again I let myself drift from the critical subject. I meant to protest the vandalism in the churches."

"Vandalism?"

"Yes, Ladyship."

"You have two more minutes. Don't waste them. Vandalizing a sacred place is something I won't tolerate. Speak."

The Bishop did so but failed to articulate clearly the reasons for his distress.

Socia said, "We've heard all this before. That isn't vandalism. You haven't identified any actual damage. As the Church reminds me frequently, sacred matters are none of my business. But I will, for thoroughness's sake, ask: what did you think I could do to help?"

Bishop LaVelle had no answer.

"All you do is register complaints. Bring specifics. What happened? Where did it happen? How do you know it happened? None of this vague, 'it doesn't feel right anymore' stuff. Do you understand?"

The Churchman filled with new hope simply because Socia had listened and given instructions.

Clever girl, she said nothing that LaVelle could not have worked out for himself.

The bailiffs brought the next matter forward, a classic concerning the ownership of almonds fallen from branches extending over a fence.

BERNARDIN SAID, "I NEED YOU TO COME WITH ME, MASTER."

"Where? Why? For what?"

"We're going church hopping to see why the Bishop is upset."

"All right." Though he felt uncomfortable leaving the citadel. He might run into somebody whose enmity would waken his serpents. "Have your tattoos done anything, Bernardin?"

"What? Oh." It took a moment. "No. They aren't tattoos, though. They're scars."

"Whatever. No unexpected behavior?"

"Not yet. Quit stalling."

Brother Candle realized that he was, indeed, stalling. "I'm ready."

Bernardin started with the nearest chapel.

"There's definitely something not right here," the Perfect said immediately. "I can't say what, though."

He roamed the place, touching, sensing. Bernardin trailed him. He felt the wrongness, too, though less sharply. "There's no pastor here anymore. The last one turned out to be a Society don."

They and their bodyguards visited a dozen Episcopal Churches. Most had been abandoned by their parishioners. Each had the same dead feel.

Bernardin's answer was not original. "It's like the holiness has gone away. I know. The priests keep saying that. I guess it's true, even if we never considered Episcopal churches true holy places."

"We need to visit churches that aren't Brothen Episcopal."

"Good idea. There aren't so many of those."

"Let's start with some that recognized Viscesment instead of Brothe."

That made no difference. Every church was the same. Each was just a building, now.

Brother Candle grew increasingly depressed.

Bernardin said, "We should check the temples of the Deves and Dainshaus, too."

The Perfect understood his own mood, then. He was afraid they would find Maysalean holy places barren of grace, too. His faith was not secure enough to defy a Night that penetrated the fastnesses of his own religion.

Bernardin headed for the Devedian temple where Brother Candle had consulted Radeus Pickleu.

The story remained the same.

The Perfect observed, "It wasn't like this the other night."

The beadle explained, "The sanctification went the morning after you visited us, Master, some think because a nonbeliever was allowed inside."

Bernardin said, "It's happened at every church in town."

"Pickleu made that argument. We're not superstitious savages like Pramans."

Pramans did believe nonbelievers polluted a temple just by entering. The temple so fouled had to be cleansed and consecrated anew.

"A loss of consecration?" the old man muttered. "Is that what it is? Assuming all things are possible inside the Night . . ." He was not sure where he was headed but knew he was tramping alongside the frontiers of enlightenment.

How could a holy place become unconsecrated without the collusion of its priests and congregation?

"No choice now," Brother Candle said. "We have to check meeting places used by Seekers After Light."

"Want to try the Dainshau place?"

"No. They're worse than Pramans about pollution."

The beadle said, "They are. But they do have the same problem. Their holiness went the same day ours did."

The plague had not spared the meeting places of the Seekers After Light.

Brother Candle and Bernardin returned to the citadel, to the small room off the kitchen, for supper. The old man toyed with his food.

Spiritually, he was devastated.

Bernardin finally hazarded, "It must have something to do with that woman. That Instrumentality."

The Perfect grunted.

"The changes started after she visited us."

"So she's the real, true God?"

"She's the bull Instrumentality around here, right now. That's all."

Maybe. But how could one weird adolescent be more powerful than any traditional deity? Assuming all things were true in the Night—a premise no established religion entirely accepted—faith alone should leave even the God of the Dainshaus able to withstand the demon. Unless every established religion included a fatal flaw in its foundation.

The absolute, root question would be, how could an omnipotent, omniscient, omnipresent God fail to deal with some previously unknown entity possessing the ability to amble in and suck the holiness out of His consecrated sites?

Socia was nowhere to be found.

Bernardin grumbled, "I'll bet she sneaked off to see Kedle. She didn't have any other obligations today."

"But she . . ."

"Really, Master. Socia Rault? Who knows her better than you? Will the woman let good sense get in her way?"

Guillemette had just come to see if they needed anything. She snapped, "The Countess spent the morning with Lumiere. After lunch she went to the audience hall to deal with a gaggle of magistrates who claimed they'd been ordered to a general assembly of city judges."

"Damn me!" Brother Candle swore so seldom that Bernardin and Guillemette alike were stunned. "I forgot! I was going to upbraid them for wasting Socia's time with petty cases. I blame you, Bernardin. If you hadn't dragged me out . . ."

"My fault? You could have said you had something going."

"You made it sound like Socia wanted it handled right now."

"It could have waited. Getting those chickenshit justices to look down and find their balls would be more important than any silly-ass running around we did."

Exasperated, Guillemette said, "And you're the men the Countess considers the backbone of Antieux. Is there something you want? I'll only be here a few minutes more."

Bernardin said, "You could tell us where the Countess is. So we can tell her what we found out. And so the Master can apologize."

Brother Candle rolled his eyes.

Guillemette made a growling noise. "You can get your own supper." She headed for the nearest doorway, but halted, framed there. "She's probably enjoying dinner with my cousin in Arnhand." Then she was gone.

Half a minute later Brother Candle said, "Bernardin, I'm too old. I should have been one with the Light years ago. I feel more like I'm not in my own world anymore, every day."

"You know too much. Everybody we saw today would feel just as lost if they knew what you do."

Bernardin had misunderstood. Deliberately? Maybe not. Amberchelle's worldview was simpler. "No doubt. No doubt."

"What I'm thinking now is, we're missing something. Something that might be obvious to an outsider but you and I can't see because of what we believe."

"Bernardin . . ." This was one of those times when Amberchelle amazed and perplexed him by being deeper than seemed possible.

Talk of the devil conjured her. Socia wandered in, looking exhausted. An attentive Guillemette rematerialized.

"Thought you were going away," Amberchelle grumbled.

"I lied. I had to get away from you children."

Socia volunteered, "I went and saw Kedle."

Brother Candle grunted. He wanted to mention the obligations of motherhood but did not, recalling what Guillemette had said about how Socia had spent her morning. It would be breath wasted, anyway.

Amberchelle responded, "And? They haven't hung her yet?"

"No. I'm getting worried about her."

"Really? Why would that be?"

Socia did not catch Amberchelle's sarcastic tone.

"Because she's running wild. She's killing people. She doesn't care who. If they aren't one hundred percent our friends and willing to exterminate anybody who doesn't think the way we do . . . She's in Arnhand, now, being more cruel than the Arnhanders ever were. Yesterday she overran an estate belonging to one of Anne of Menand's cousins. She killed everything, including mice and sparrows where she found them. She burned everything burnable. She poisoned the wells. Her men never argued. They believe she was chosen by God to punish Arnhand. They idolize her."

"And you're jealous?" the Perfect asked.

"Not anymore. Now I'm terrified she'll start believing what her men say. That she'll decide God really is with her and it's perfectly reasonable to think she can subdue Arnhand with just a few hundred men."

Bernardin muttered something about more men slipping away every day to join Kedle. He did not mean to be heard.

Brother Candle said, "You're worrying too much. Kedle is stubborn and willful but she does have a sense of proportion. She'll just harass Arnhand. She won't get into any real fights."

"You sound like you're behind her."

"I'm trying to tell you what I think she's thinking."

Bernardin shifted talk to what they had learned about the problems in Antieux's churches.

ANTIEUX ENJOYED A HALCYON SEASON OF SEVERAL WEEKS' DURATION. The entire city seemed happy and content. Even Bishop LaVelle's complaints were infrequent and random.

The magistrates, justices of the peace, and remaining parish priests began taking care of the trivia they should have since Socia's ascension. They learned that she would not overrule them even where she disagreed with their judgments.

Then came news concerning the improbable events at Vetercus.

21. Alten Weinberg: Winter

The Righteous reached Alten Weinberg on an afternoon when random snowflakes swirled, proclaiming the end of the campaign season. There had been enthusiastic welcomes along the way. Common folks, for some reason, seemed to feel included in the triumphs of the Righteous.

The nobility were more restrained. A common adventurer, however favored by the Ege sisters, was poaching in their preserve.

Hecht did his best to charm those he met along the way. Possession of Anselin of Menand helped, but not a lot.

Although holiness had abandoned more and more churches the hunger for crusade was rising, a communal insanity taking hold of the Chaldarean world. Hecht began to worry about the whole becoming too big to control.

He worried about the Shining Ones, too, though they respected their contract and remained disguised. The more compliant they were the more nervous he became. The core him, hammered into shape in the Vibrant Spring School, did not want to believe any good could come of traffic with devils.

As much as he worried about them, his staff worried about him more.

Events in Hovacol had rendered less striking his apparent return from the dead. He had been strange after that, but only somewhat and only for a short while. He had appeared normal enough in Brothe. His turning up unconscious on the road into the Remayne Pass was troubling, but . . .

Lord Arnmigal was downright weird. He called devils to the battle-field. He did not break a sweat while conquering a renowned brawler. He had driven a demon out of said brawler.

None of which had been explained to anyone's satisfaction. Lord Arnmigal was as concerned as anyone else.

Always clever, he had become smoothly facile tactically. He knew what his opponent would do before that opponent moved. He seemed incapable of error and equally incapable of understanding why monstrous competence scared those around him.

He had every characteristic desirable in a Commander of the Righteous on the eve of a history-defining effort to cleanse the Holy Lands of unbelievers, heretics, and other abominations in the eye of God.

On the other hand . . . Piper Hecht was frightened. He could not shake a conviction that he was not the man he had been. The Hovacol raid had changed him. Again.

Else Tage had become Piper Hecht. Piper Hecht had settled in so comfortably that Else Tage was scarcely a reminiscence. Piper Hecht had become so real that he had memories of his manufactured Duarnenian past. It took an effort of will to recall the Vibrant Spring School.

When he did ferret out those elusive recollections he banged up against the realization that he had been another someone before he became Else Tage, the boy Gisors, whose natural father was a lord of the Brotherhood of War. Gisors had had a family. Piper Hecht had found that family again—and right now very much wished that the member called the Ninth Unknown would show up and help navigate the stormy emotional seas.

Where was that old man? For that matter, where was Heris? Where were Lila and Vali? His only family was Pella, who went round in a slack-jawed daze, constantly frightened.

The boy had been unable to get both feet on the ground since the confrontation with King Stain.

Hecht wished he could summon Hourli and find out what was going on. Which sparked a faint touch of good humor. "No matter what I have I always want more." Then he felt a sudden conviction that he needed only lift his arms and the Choosers would respond. That Sprenghul and Fastthal were up to no mischief because only Arlensul had known how.

Hecht and an escort left the column in response to an Imperial summons that included Anselin of Menand. Hecht felt a twinge of jealousy.

Suppose Helspeth fell for Anselin the way Katrin had for Jaime of Castauriga? Anselin was handsome, young, confident, and personable. He might make a good king if he eluded his mother's machinations.

"Pella. Come with me."

"Dad?"

"You may never get another chance to see the inside of the palace."

THEY DID NOT GET FAR INSIDE. HELSPETH MET THEM IN A ROOM NORmally used to assemble the palace guard. Braunsknechts filled the corners. The lighting was bad except around the Empress. She was developing a taste for drama. Also, her pleasure at seeing Hecht was so obvious that even the densest witness had to wonder.

His jealousy slithered down into the fetid deeps.

Helspeth had a dozen women and functionaries with her. She could do nothing now. She turned to her guest king.

Anselin's attitude remained guarded.

Hecht had seen little of the man in transit. He had not acknowledged Anselin's status, nor had he treated the man with more deference than others who traveled with him.

Anselin's companions had given no trouble. Perhaps durance in Cholate had been less pleasant than the prospect of the same in Alten Weinberg.

Helspeth sparked off orders to people who had been rehearsed. Hecht noted her wary glances at Pella.

This might, indeed, be the boy's only chance to see the inside of the palace.

Helspeth said, "It pleases us to see thee returned hale and successful, Lord Arnmigal." She sounded imperially remote. From behind her, Lady Hilda showed Hecht a ghost of a wink and spectral smile. And he understood.

Daedel would be Helspeth's avatar. She would do what Helspeth dared not do herself. He returned Lady Hilda's ghost wink. Helspeth saw and ghost-smiled herself.

Less formally, the Empress said, "We understand that you are anxious to see to the welfare of your soldiers and would like a chance to shake the road off, Lord Arnmigal. Now that we have satisfied our eyes we will not keep you. Captain Drear will arrange an informal audience for tomorrow. We will expect grand tales of adventure. Anselin of Menand, a suitable suite has been prepared for you."

Hecht caught a speculative look in Daedel's eye as she considered that handsome youth.

He wished her luck but thought she might be disappointed.

Anselin of Menand had proven himself a formidable warrior in the Holy Lands. He had revealed unexpected skills as a commander. He was tall, blond, pretty, played the lute and had a good singing voice. He was the perfect knight in every way and everywhere but in the tilts of love.

Not once had his name been coupled with that of a woman, neither high nor low. Which left Hecht the more puzzled by his own jealousy.

Ah. It was not Anselin but what Anselin represented that sparked the emotion. The attraction between him and Helspeth remained, as powerful as ever, but now she was Empress. Socially, she was further away.

Back in the street, Pella asked, "Dad, how come the Empress was so rude? I thought you were friends."

Hecht settled into his saddle. Snowflakes wobbled into the light of lanterns and torches. "She was being the Empress Helspeth, not Helspeth Ege. She can't be just a person anymore, she has to be the personification of the state. She wasn't trying to be rude."

"I think it stinks."

Lord Arnmigal, Commander of the Righteous, did not disagree. "You're right, Pella. That shouldn't make a difference. But it always does. It's the way the world works. It's the way people are made."

ALTEN WEINBERG REMAINED ALTEN WEINBERG, EVEN IN WINTER. THOSE who did not return to their estates remained doggedly political and contrived to cross paths with the Commander of the Righteous. Lord Arnmigal gained a reputation for being short-tempered. He did manage to deal respectfully with Archbishop Brion, Katrin's uncles, Rodolof Schmeimder, Arnhand's ambassador, and Algres Drear. The pressure of Imperial politics was severe. The role of Commander of the Righteous had accumulated considerable gravitas. The princes of the west were sending commissions, observers, representatives, or ambassadors to look into possibly joining the Enterprise of Peace and Faith—while much of the Grail Empire nobility insisted the crusade was a smoke screen masking the tyrannical ambitions of the Empress and her Commander of the Righteous.

Lord Arnmigal sometimes roared in frustration but as often was as thrilled as a boy who had successfully executed an amazing prank.

He had advantages enjoyed by no warlord before him.

HECHT ENTERED HELSPETH'S QUIET ROOM WARILY. THE CUSTOMARY band had gathered beforehand: the Archbishop, the Graf fon Rhejm, Ferris Renfrow, Lady Hilda, and the Grand Duke. The Empress had, in Hecht's absence, won that crusty old warrior over.

She could be a charmer when she tried.

Renfrow shut the door. Captain Drear did not remain inside.

Lady Hilda began serving coffee. The smuggling routes had recovered. She was brisk today, absent all flirt. She looked worn out. Hecht lifted an inquiring eyebrow when she was behind the Archbishop. She responded with a weak shrug.

Renfrow, checking the room's integrity, caught the exchange. "Our lady paladin of the night tilts has been defeated." For which Lady Hilda gave him a look braided of purest venom.

Hecht observed, "The good Anselin has the makings of a perfect monk."

"The makings of a Perfect," Renfrow said. "I believe he could resist the blandishments of . . ." He stopped but Hecht understood. Anselin would remain indifferent even to Eavijne, Sheaf, or Aldi. "I have a final test in mind."

Helspeth said, "Anselin is the perfect guest. By now news of his presence here will have reached Salpeno. He plans to deliver some exquisite pain once he gets back there." ·

All eyes turned her way. "I paraphrased something he told the Compte de Longé. Lord Arnmigal. You're the reason we're here. I want to hear every smelly, sordid detail of your romp through Hovacol. My spies tell me strange things happened."

Hecht glanced at Renfrow. Renfrow had not been out there. "Lord Arnmigal? You seem distracted."

"I'm tired, Majesty."

"A feeble excuse. Tell the story. And don't leave stuff out."

He told most everything, failing only to explain that the Shining Ones—never mentioned by name—were Instrumentalities from olden times now serving the Commander of the Righteous on a lifetime indenture.

Archbishop Brion would have had another stroke.

Brion had yet to say anything. In fact, there was a conspiracy of silence between him, the Grand Duke, and the Graf fon Rhejm. They asked nothing and offered nothing.

Hecht talked. Helspeth asked questions. Indeed, she pecked at every detail, sure he was holding back.

Renfrow enjoyed his discomfiture. The spymaster sipped coffee, smiled occasionally, and left Hecht wondering what Renfrow had actually reported.

Helspeth kept after the duel with Stain. Once he finished, she said, "I've heard the story three times, now. It seems like no two people saw the same thing."

"Witnesses to an emotional situation seldom agree about the details, Majesty," Archbishop Brion observed. "Reports I've heard made it sound like His Lordship had a guardian angel." The edge to his voice, nearly hysterical, implied that Brion knew any such angel must be one of the fallen.

Hecht said, "If you said that right after, I might have agreed. Things did get strange. But if anything is watching over me it isn't for my sake."

With amused admiration, Renfrow said, "Masterful, Lord Arnmigal. Masterful."

Helspeth demanded, "Are you two playing a game without including the rest of us?"

Renfrow replied, "Every day, Majesty. Every day. But it's just boys will be boys. Now, unusual as Lord Arnmigal's adventure was, there are other things that need attention. For example, the question of what to do with Anselin of Menand."

Helspeth said, "I foresee serious concessions from Arnhand in exchange for his return."

The Grand Duke grumbled, "Sell the pretty shit."

"Milord?"

"Do what that absurd Stain meant to do. Put him on the auction block. Isabeth of Navaya might cede Calzir and Shippen in exchange. The Connectens, if they had anything, would beggar themselves to claim him. And his mother might be forced to finance your Enterprise. Make her pay. Make her pay big. Keep her paying till she bankrupts Arnhand."

Renfrow observed, "Anselin is worth a fortune in political capital just sitting here doing nothing, too."

Helspeth said, "I want your thoughts, Ferris, but first I have a question for Lord Arnmigal, which is, do we still have issues enough with Bronte Doneto to demand that his person be part of Anselin's ransom?"

"Entirely your decision, Majesty. You know what your sister would want."

"Yes. All right. Ferris."

"If you'll reflect, Majesty, I'm sure you'll see a number of ways that Anselin could be of more value held here."

Hecht observed, "The Compte de Longé seems almost hysterical lately."

Helspeth said, "He's a fool with an impossible assignment. Anne sent him here to get him out of Salpeno. The Empire was sure to collapse if it was ruled by Lothar, Katrin, or Helspeth Ege, so Alten Weinberg looked like a good place to get him out of the way. But now they want him to develop an improbable case of competence and pry Anselin loose. At no cost."

Archbishop Brion spoke up again. "The succession. Yes. That must be addressed at the earliest possible opportunity, Majesty."

The men looked at Brion, amazed. Where had that come from? Though it was a fine question. Helspeth said, "But not right now. It will be dealt with in the customary manner, in the course of time, when I produce a son. Or a daughter, if that be God's Will. Till then, my father's Bill of Succession remains the law."

"But that means that if something happens to you your mad aunt Aneis becomes Empress."

"If that terrifies you, Brion, make absolutely certain that nothing happens to the Empress you have now."

Renfrow said, "Majesty, this reminds me that there is much to be considered concerning the situation in the Connec."

Hecht smiled. That was hardly a finesse. He was interested, though. Absent the Shining Ones all he knew about what was happening elsewhere was what Carava de Bos and Rivademar Vircondelet gathered from travelers.

"Strange things," Renfrow said. "As strange as what happened in Hovacol, plus local problems resembling those plaguing our good Archbishop."

"Ferris, don't you dare . . ."

"Majesty?" Renfrow was taken aback.

"Sorry. I mistook what you were saying. Proceed."

"Of course. So. These are the bare bones facts. Kedle Richeut has become a serious problem for Arnhand. Calling themselves the Vindicated, she and her men have been wasting the Arnhander countryside. They have raided within forty miles of Salpeno. They are kind to no one but are especially cruel to anyone who participated in any incursion into the Connec. Any holding belonging to Anne of Menand becomes a desert."

Hecht interjected, "The woman wants her message made clear."

"Profoundly. The Countess of Antieux is nearly as mad. She has been involved in several Vindicated actions, sometimes after having been seen in Antieux the same day," Renfrow said.

"Really?"

"Really."

"That bears examination."

"I don't have the skills. That would be a task for your Ninth Unknown."

"Or one of our new associates. None of whom have turned up lately."

Helspeth asked, "You two do realize that this isn't a private consultation?"

Renfrow said, "Yes, Majesty. We'll save that for another time. To Richeut. Though she has no falcons there are similarities between her operations and those of our esteemed Lord Arnmigal."

Hecht raised an eyebrow. "No falcons? How, then, similar?"

"Richeut routinely bests larger forces by catching them when they're vulnerable. She always knows where they are, how they're disposed, and what they plan. She won't engage unless she's confident of the outcome. When she retreats she does so deftly, avoiding complications. And, as happens with Lord Arnmigal, prodigies and miracles attend her."

This female captain had her own Instrumentalities?

"What kind of prodigies?" Helspeth asked.

"A giant bird often turns up wherever she is, only by night. A similar genius is sometimes seen over Antieux, also only at night."

Brion muttered, "More traffic with demons. You should have exterminated those people, Commander."

"They wouldn't let me, Archbishop. They were stubborn about it."

Helspeth asked, "Are these people a direct worry, Ferris? We have done the Connec no harm."

"No threat. Those starving bitch wolves only take Arnhanders and the occasional Churchman."

Archbishop Brion wanted to protest but knew he would get no sympathy.

Renfrow said, "Society brothers they treat the way the Society treated Connectens till last spring."

The Archbishop pleaded, "May I step out before I suffer another stroke, Majesty?"

"You may not. Continue, Ferris."

"That's it. Except that Antieux is suffering a rash of church desanctifications as widespread as ours."

"What is it? What causes it?" Helspeth asked.

"I don't know. I'll find out."

Hecht felt uncomfortable when Renfrow said that.

HECHT FOUND RENFROW WAITING OUTSIDE THE PALACE, FOLLOWING his own last private minute with Helspeth.

Renfrow said, "She's growing into the role."

"Fast. I just enjoyed an exhaustive review of my failings as Commander of the Righteous. So far. She's sure there will be many more."

He was not dissembling. Helspeth was not pleased that her Hammer of God could call terrible Instrumentalities to the battlefield.

"I think your job is safe."

"I'm not worried. It is troubling to be misunderstood, though."

"Isn't it? I'll walk with you a way. If you don't mind."

"I don't. But there are some sharp ears, round about."

Hecht's lifeguards had been waiting, as well. Every man of the Righteous wanted to know what was going on with the boss.

"They'll just hear mumbling. I'm wondering if you understand why the Widow is so successful," asked Renfrow.

"There's one easy conclusion, isn't there?"

"That she is favored of the Night."

"Anne of Menand will make the claim. Her own people will believe that she is beloved of God. Meaning the Good God of the Maysaleans."

"You got all the revenants when you were cleaning up out there, didn't you?"

"All of the ones we knew about. Rook was tough. I couldn't guess what might be loose out there now."

"Nor can I. I'll keep watch but it isn't critical."

Hecht said, "It can't hurt to have those madwomen suck the blood out of Arnhand."

"No. But it might be useful to have its wealth and manpower behind you if you do launch the Enterprise."

"That will happen, though I'm starting to wonder if we can be ready this summer. We keep getting distracted by political stuff."

"That'll still be true if you live a thousand years. If three people have a goal two will try to subvert the third because they think they have a better idea. Or because they see a chance to line their pockets. Or because they've been subverted by the object of the operation. Or because they're just plain stupid. Stupid is what I see the most."

"You're expansive tonight."

"Frustrated and taking it out on you. Feeling outside of everything," said Renfrow.

"You? I don't know where my family are, let alone what they're doing. The same for the Shining Ones."

"The Choosers are your guardian angels. Everyone else is at work trying to eliminate the Windwalker's brothers and cousins."

"Easy." The lifeguards were close.

"If you say so."

"That's why I've had no contact? They're tied up in a big struggle?"

"Unless they're fooling us all."

"And the ascendant? I haven't seen him, either," said Hecht.

"I suppose. Though I thought you gave him a job."

"Sort of. But he doesn't seem to get the team play concept."

Renfrow grunted. He was done talking. He turned aside and vanished into shadows. One lifeguard asked, "How did he do that?"

"What?"

"He walked into that shadow and didn't come out the other side."

"I don't know. Maybe sorcery. Let's get out of here."

No one argued.

THE FOLLOWING MONTH WAS A LONELY ONE. HECHT FELT ISOLATED even with his oldest intimates. They sensed his mood but understood it no better than he did. Titus Consent, who went back furthest of any, valiantly strove to break through. He did get Hecht talking enough to admit that his moroseness was becoming a problem.

"Boss, we can get along without you micromanaging. We like it that way. But outsiders need to see the Commander of the Righteous in charge. Just so the rest of us can feel comfortable, how about you pretend you're interested when we have company?"

They were alone at the moment. Hecht had been brooding, about what he could not have said if asked. Somehow, by word or tone or triggered nostalgia, Consent got through.

"Am I really that . . . ? Titus! I've become pathetic. How did that happen?"

"I couldn't say. But since you're here in my world for now, how about you tell me how to keep you here?"

Challenged, Hecht determined to conquer his malaise. "I can't explain because I don't know, Titus. I for sure don't like it." He caught himself digging at his left wrist, trying to kill a vicious itch. His wrist was raw, moist some places, scabbed elsewhere. "This is driving me crazy, too. I should get something on it before it festers."

"We'll need an itch balm or you'll scratch till your hand falls off."

What he needed was to be rid of the amulet, which supposedly caused itching only when he was close to some serious Instrumentality. But it itched all the time anymore.

Could a Rudenes Schneidel sort, or something like Vrislakis, be tweaking the amulet to distract him? Maybe hoping he would shed it?

Titus said, "I know a poultice that should help."

Hecht grunted.

"Whenever you're mentally present you dig at your wrist. But when you go surly and start studying your own belly button you leave it alone."

"Really?"

"Yes, really. I'll have the field doc do something as soon as I can."

Hecht grumbled sullen assent.

"While I have you animated, do you have any thoughts on how we can pull you out of this melancholy?"

"If I did you'd be first to know. I don't like what's happening to me, either. I have to live through it."

Consent flashed a smile. "We're making progress already. You admit there's a problem."

The trouble was, even with his mind focused Hecht could make no sense of what was happening. "Track everything I eat and drink and anyone who gets close enough to touch me."

"You think it might be poison?"

"They tried it on Katrin. But, no. Poison would be the hard way with me. I think it's sorcery."

He wished Cloven Februaren would turn up. That old man could break this open.

Titus said, "We need you sharp for your confabs with the Empress. Helspeth won't be as tractable as Katrin."

JUST CONCENTRATING ON THE FACT THAT HE HAD MENTAL PROBLEMS helped Hecht manage them. He drank clean water from snow brought down from the Jagos. He ate vegetables boiled in that water. He ate boiled or roasted meats from freshly slaughtered carcasses, without spices. Only the most trusted cooks prepared his meals. He exercised every morning, usually by running with his staff.

The itching persisted.

Frequent anti-itching poultices helped only a little.

Hecht told Consent, "I'm determined to whip it."

"Well, you have begun to make useful contributions to the process again."

"When I don't itch I can think."

HECHT WAS IN ANOTHER BLEAK MOOD WHEN A CLERK REPORTED, "A Grimmsson wants to see you, my Lord. He looks disreputable but his name is on the List."

Twelve people were allowed access whenever they wanted. He had not informed most of them of that.

"Bring him," his mood improving.

Grimmsson arrived. The clerk was right. He had not maintained his civilized look.

"So where the hell have you been?" Hecht demanded. "I have work for you to do."

"I didn't want Heris to go out there alone."

"To take on Vrislakis and Zambakli?"

"Yes."

"Did the old man, the Shining Ones, and my daughters abandon her?"

"No."

"You had to be underfoot, too, to make it all work out?"

Grimmsson reddened. Nothing he said could make him look less silly than he did already. "Harsh, Commander, but emotionally true. That campaign will be over soon. Zambakli Souleater is no more. Vrislakis will be nothing but a foul recollection before long."

"Excellent. I've had no help from any of you people for months."

"You had help enough in Hovacol."

"I admit I'm spoiled. But I do have real problems that only the Ninth Unknown can fix."

"I should be available from now on," clearly disappointed by Hecht's lack of excitement about Zambakli.

Another major god was dead. Not just banished or imprisoned, extinguished. Forever. And the Commander of the Righteous had shown the world how that could be done.

Hecht asked, "You spent all that time away dealing with the Great Old Ones?"

Puzzled, "Pretty much, yes."

"No side trips to the Connec? Say to Antieux?"

"You've lost me. I'm not sure I know where Antieux is."

"You do know the name?"

"Of course. A lot of recent history involved that town."

"A giant bird has been seen there recently."

"I understand you asking, then. I plead not guilty."

"Interesting. Another giant bird. Well. Not our problem. We have our own mission, coming on too fast."

Grimmsson said, "You should have everyone back before long. You can go balls to the wall, then."

That brightened Hecht's mood a lot.

HERIS TURNED UP AT MIDNIGHT, TWO NIGHTS AFTER THE ASCENDANT. She woke Hecht out of a dream about men hunting their traitor brother. She was excited and full of brags. Not only had she destroyed Kharoulke the Windwalker, eldest and ugliest of the Great Old Ones, she had been instrumental in exterminating Kharoulke's whole pantheon. "Those horrible Instrumentalities are now extinct, by grace of the Twelfth Unknown."

"They talked you into taking over for Delari?"

"Not yet. I've still got a lot to learn."

"You aren't exactly the priestly type."

"But you are a smart-ass."

"I blame my formative years." He started scratching.

Heris frowned. "I can't imagine a Sha-lug with a sense of humor."

"In that you are correct, madam. They whip it out of you early, along with all the clutter of your prior life. I meant Piper Hecht's formative years. Before the powers that be turned him into a dynamic engine of conquest."

They were alone in his sleeping quarters. They could be as silly or pompous as they liked. Heris said, "I'm not sure about you right now, little brother. Asgrimmur says your soul is in a grim place. You've been doing weird stuff. But you're maiden silly tonight."

"Yes. I'm starting to get my family back."

"Want to jump down to Brothe?"

"No." Grimly. "But the offer is comforting. Plus, I had a long, rambling, sometimes incoherent letter from Pinkus today. I think his drinking is getting worse."

"And what did that Grolsacher fraud really want?"

"I'm not sure. Maybe just a friend. He's not happy about being a glorified city watchman."

"He could be back in Grolsach trying to mill rocks into flour."

"He knows that. In one of his more coherent passages he said that. But we get spoiled. We always want more than what we've got."

"Little brother, you have been hanging out with the wrong crowd.

Plenty of people, like me, are ecstatic with what they've got. We wake up every morning thanking God for our lives and the good days we're having."

Hecht grunted. He had not had many bad days once he grew up. Heris had had several dark decades. Maybe those times made her appreciate today more.

"I get it, Heris. I think. Pinkus, though . . . He'll be a malcontent even if he gets into heaven."

"I'll buy that."

"I think what he really wanted to know was, could I find a place for him in the Enterprise."

"The Enterprise?"

"Churchspeak. Wordplaying. We don't call crusades crusades any-more. Officially, it's 'an Enterprise of Peace and Faith.'"

Heris snickered.

"What?"

"You sounded like one of those pompous clowns from the Colle-gium."

"Jobs do shape the man."

"Right again. But I didn't come to help you handle your worries. I need a little family reinforcement myself. I've just killed three of the worst old-time gods, for Aaron's sake! *Killed* them! Nobody else in the entire history of the world ever did anything like that. And I can't even get my own brother to tell me I did good."

"Sorry. You did good. Really. But people aren't made to build up, we're made to tear down."

"The Designer might not want to find Himself on the business end of my falcons, then."

Hecht had been outside of everything while Heris finished the Great Old Ones. "How many falcons did I lose, darling sister? How much godshot did I spend? My troops will be whining for godshot in the Holy Lands."

"Piper, we'll get them back. All but three or four. Six at the most."

"Six?"

"There were failures. Some turned themselves into scrap."

"Krulik and Sneigon falcons? That's hard to credit."

"Credit as you will. You weren't there. You have no idea what it took to kill those things."

"I don't. The cost is, plainly, acceptable. You're here."

"But?"

"One has a wish to hear details so one can assess and apprehend the full cost and product of one's investment."

Heris laughed. "Wishful thinking, little brother. It cost you some obsolete falcons that your Deves already replaced with better weapons. Right? So take it up with those goons Rhuk and Prosek. You told them to give me what I needed. They picked the weapons and powder. Some of which did nothing but sputter."

Rhuk and Prosek must have cleared their inventories of the powder and weapons they trusted least. His fault. He had not given them any good reasons why powder and falcons had to be turned over to people they did not know.

"Was anybody hurt?"

"Some of the Shining Ones got their fingers burned. They aren't made to handle high-density godshot. I'm going home now, Piper. I'm tired. I want to lay down in a real bed, in a place where I don't have to sleep with one eye open, and not move for a week. Grandfather should have some of the townhouse restored by now."

"Wait! Let me send a letter to Anna."

"Don't dawdle." She read over his shoulder as he wrote. "She won't go for that, no matter how much she misses you. She won't come out of her house for love nor money."

"Just deliver the letter. You never know."

"I will. No problem." She turned sideways and disappeared.

In a moment Hecht was back in bed, drifting off, but expecting a daughter or Cloven Februaren to burn his chance to get any sleep.

That did not happen.

THE PEOPLE OF ALTEN WEINBERG OFTEN COMPLAINED ABOUT THE length and harshness of their winters. To an outsider from a warmer clime the cold and gloom did seem a persistent divine punishment. A man from Duarnenia, however, dared not see them as anything but blustery and refreshingly brief.

Being Commander of the Righteous meant there was always a need to go out on Enterprise business. Hecht resented those demands on his time. There were things he *wanted* to do, things he *needed* to do, before spring arrived. Time wasted cajoling and schmoozing was time not spent preparing.

Heavy snows suggested the chance of a late spring and heavier spring melt, which would mean bad floods. The Bleune could turn particularly unfriendly. Hochwasser might be affected. Downstream, the river could carve new channels and create new navigational hazards. He meant to barge his heavy stores and equipment down the Bleune to the Negrine Sea, where it would be put aboard deepwater ships for transport south to coastal ports still in Chaldarean hands.

*   *   *

A MESSAGE CAME WITH HECHT'S BREAKFAST. THE EMPRESS WANTED A word. Time stated. He should bring his associate Hourli.

Rivademar Vircondelet reported immediately when summoned. Hecht asked, "You saw this note from the Empress?"

"Yes, sir. Until there is no one left who wants to kill you we'll vet everything."

"There are still some of those?"

"We can't get them all. You have a knack for making more." There was a wistful edge to Vircondelet's voice.

"You're easier to get along with than Madouc was. But never mind that. Have you seen Hourli?"

"Not for five days, at least."

"Really? That recently? Because I never see her. Or any of them."

"They wander in and out all the time, usually with something interesting."

"Like what? I haven't seen anything in the dailies."

"When I said interesting I meant it's always some fairy tale. Something they couldn't possibly know because it happened last night in Camaghara, Direcia, or Salpeno."

Hecht invested in a long, deep breath, which he held for a count of eight. He repeated the process. "From now on the fairy tales will head the briefings. They will be treated like words fallen from the lips of Aaron. Go back to your section. Resurrect every detail of those reports. I want them waiting when I get back from the palace. Understood? Is anything I said unclear?"

Face colorless, Vircondelet replied, "You are crystalline, sir."

Hecht waited for a caveat, a condition, or a question. Vircondelet restrained himself. "Good. Pass the word to the lifeguards. They'll need to walk me over."

HECHT JOINED LADY HILDA AND THE EMPRESS INSIDE THE LATTER'S newly expanded, reengineered, and again refurbished quiet room. There was space, now, for thirty people. Lady Hilda poured coffee, flirted mildly. He asked Helspeth, "Am I the first one here?"

"You are. That's deliberate. I want you to know that the Throne has acquired the Chapel of Saint Miniver, Martyr."

Hecht could not help looking baffled. "Congratulations? But . . . I don't know the place. Or the saint."

"Miniver was the first Chaldarean missionary to the pagans in these parts. The chapel is behind the palace, on the site where Miniver was martyred."

Lady Hilda said, "There was a famine. He was the most useless body around. They sacrificed him to appease their gods."

"Did it work?"

Shrug. "We still know Miniver. Nobody remembers them."

"All right. But I'm still not illuminated."

"The chapel can be accessed from the back of the palace by means of a postern. One of the early Johanneses was a devotee of Miniver. He liked to visit the chapel secretly, probably for more than religious reasons. Lady Hilda has started performing her night devotions there."

A flirty look from Daedel followed.

Piper Hecht, less schooled in romantic intrigue than the virgin Empress, never had a clue. He sipped coffee, frowned, asked, "And?"

Lady Hilda swatted him across the back of the head. "Aaron's eyes! Are you really that dense?"

Yes. He was. Because once he completed the calculations that led him to conclude that a place of assignation had been developed he assumed that Lady Hilda was the wanton who hoped to meet him there.

She freshened his coffee, asked, "You still think he's a genius?"

"Possibly an idiot savant. I do confess, Hilda, that I've seen boulders catch on quicker. Draw him a picture."

The Daedel woman did so using words of one syllable and flagrant hand gestures. Hecht had figured it out but said nothing. He was embarrassed both by the proposition and by his own inability to pick up on the situation. He sat there and glowed red.

Lady Hilda observed, "He's got it. It won't be necessary to summon the beadles from the madhouse . . . yet."

Not trusting himself to keep his feet out of his mouth, Hecht kept that mouth shut. He did not state the obvious, that no good could come of this.

The Empress said, "Ten of the clock, most nights, Hilda will be praying over the relicts of Saint Miniver. And now, because it took us so long to get this far, we're out of time to talk any more."

Hilda opened the door, began to hustle about. Hecht ignored her, focused on calming himself and wondering if he had the strength to stay away from St. Miniver, Martyr.

The expanded quiet room went to waste. Few of the usual conferees appeared. Helspeth observed, "This is a disaster. Lord Arnmigal, where is your intelligence specialist?"

"Hard at work somewhere, I hope. I couldn't find her."

The unannounced object of the meeting, Anselin of Menand, turned up right on time, accompanied by his newly found friend Armand.

Hecht marveled but wondered why he was surprised. There had been ample clues.

The Empress said, "Prince Anselin, we would prefer you to have brought the Compte de Longé."

"Apologies, Majesty. The man was not at his residence. No one knew his whereabouts."

Hecht said, "Forget him. He's a dedicated snoop. He heard I'd be tied up here so he's out sneaking around the edges of the Righteous, looking for something Anne might find interesting."

Helspeth said, "He should be here. This concerns him, too. But we'll go forward without." She glared holes through Armand.

Hecht said, "Armand will not be a problem. I've known him a long time. He's trustworthy. He brought my son here from Brothe."

Now Helspeth was unhappy with him. He ought not to be mentioning his family after the offer so recently presented.

Helspeth ordered, "Everyone sit. Hilda. Coffee."

Hecht passed. He had drunk too much already.

The Empress said, "Straight to it. And let the others whine about missing out. Prince Anselin, your mother has agreed to ransom you. You'll be headed home soon."

Anselin said, "Get it in writing and have it witnessed by the Patriarch. Otherwise you'll see nothing once I'm over the frontier."

Hecht remarked, "She did short Sublime V on a deal they had."

Anselin nodded. "True. But that was more his fault than hers. The shipments were taken by bandits or enemies, en route."

Hecht said no more. He had engineered the disappearance of most of that specie.

Helspeth said, "We do understand that you don't get on with your mother. That comes up whenever we dine or walk the Winter Garden together."

Hecht frowned. She wanted to make him jealous with Armand right there?

Helspeth went on, "You seem obsessed with her bad behavior. You threatened to send her into a cloister. We would like to hear your thinking now that you know you will, in fact, be in a position to do something of that sort."

Anselin had no ready reply.

Hecht said, "She does have talents any ruler would find useful—if her more wicked habits could be curbed."

Hecht meant Anne's talent for intrigue. Anselin thought he meant her appetite for adventures of the flesh. "Another reason to put her into orders."

Helspeth said, "She has powerful allies."

"She has allies but no friends. There will be dramatic changes once I'm crowned. The landscape of the court will shift immediately."

"Good luck with that. Hilda heard an interesting story recently. Hilda, share that with these gentlemen."

"It was in a letter from my brother Ewald, who writes dutifully whether he has anything to say or not. Being the youngest, management of the family holding in the Roessen devolved on him. The Roessen is in Arnhand, on the north bank of the . . ."

"Hilda. To the point."

"Mestlé, Anne's estate in the Roessen, isn't far from Oferin Bostal, Ewald's estate. Henri of Mariscot visits Mestlé whenever Anne is there. That started after Regard's death. Ewald thinks that could be important."

Hecht did not know Henri of Mariscot. Anselin, obviously, did and was not happy to hear the name.

Lady Hilda said, "Ewald also says Anne has installed Serenity at Mestlé. That has caused a lot of traffic past Oferin Bostal."

Hecht smelled intrigue. Its nature became clear when Anselin said, "Henri d'Mariscot is my father's cousin. Till I provide an heir he stands next in succession. He suffers the same weaknesses for which my father was famous. Thank you, Empress, for this conversation. It has been illuminating. I must find the Compte de Longé and hear his tall tales. If I may be so bold as to withdraw immediately."

"You have our leave. Hold yourself ready for further consultation."

Anselin agreed and departed quickly. Armand trotted to keep up. Hecht asked, "How much of that was true?"

"All of it," Lady Hilda replied.

"So. Anne agrees to ransom Anselin but at the same time she's scheming to replace him with a more tractable candidate."

"She's a hard woman," Helspeth said. "Who, for reasons known only to herself, has never entertained a motherly emotion toward Anselin. I think she'll ransom him just so she can lay hands on him."

Hecht said, "Then his advice about financial arrangements would be sound."

"Yes. What should our position be? Lord Arnmigal. You got to know him during your return from Cholate?"

"No, Majesty. He was *not* sociable."

"Nor has he been since his arrival here." Helspeth sloughed her imperial mask. "What we just saw, in the person of that foul boy, makes me think that Anselin might be my ideal husband."

Lady Hilda remarked, "Lord Arnmigal appears to be disconcerted." He was, indeed.

Helspeth said, "That would ally the Empire with a rich kingdom and would silence those Electors who keep barking about a marriage."

There would be succession complications, of course, if Helspeth married Anselin and produced a child. Hecht ignored that. He thought he knew what was going on. "That's ingenious. We'd have to protect him from his mother till he was soundly established in Salpeno, though. We'd have to send an escort. Clej Sedlakova or Hagen Brokke? Brokke, I suppose. How many men? We don't want to short ourselves for the Enterprise. Rhuk or Prosek, one of them would have to go . . ." Both women looked at him like he had sprouted antlers.

He shut up, sipped cold coffee.

Helspeth said, "We are pleased by your enthusiasm, Lord Arnmigal." She did not look pleased, however.

"My apologies, Majesty. I got carried away by facetious notions."

"Facetious? I wonder." Then, "Give us a status report on the Righteous, then on plans for assimilation of the broader host."

Each day requests arrived from men of substance who wanted to join in the Enterprise. A wind of religious passion was sweeping the west, though its reality was not evident in Alten Weinberg.

The Chaldarean world had become convinced that the mission would be successful this time. Those who considered themselves great men wanted their legacies to include participation in a great holy work.

Helspeth had gone very cold and remote, suddenly.

And Lady Hilda considered him almost with pity.

He had stepped in it somehow.

22. Tel Moussa: The Slide

It had grown too cold for the Mountain to spend his nights beneath the stars. His old bones could not take the chill. He would spend a few minutes studying the winter sky, then would fling a silent curse toward Shamramdi, then toward the Idiam, and then, finally, toward Gherig. Frustration lay in all directions.

Worst cursed first. The functionaries in the Lucidian capital were not providing adequate reinforcements, whatever Indala promised. The Great Shake had his health problems. Every underling wanted to take advantage of weakened oversight.

Little was heard about the monster in the Idiam. Nassim could not do much to help the tribes—who did keep the Rascal under observation.

The Master of the Commandery in Gherig continued to be more competent than Black Rogert. Nassim now doubted that he could hang on to Tel Moussa and be a strategic nuisance in the time of the new crusade.

When full dark fell the Mountain could see the lights of Gherig. The new people were repairing and upgrading, day and night. They kept patrols out all the time. They considered any contact productive.

The Mountain found himself confused by an enemy determined to fight a war of attrition far from the wellspring of his strength.

Every man Gherig lost had to be replaced by someone from overseas. Alizarin's replacements needed only travel a few days. But Nassim lost two men for each replacement received and those were green boys. Few lived long enough to become seasoned.

The Mountain considered his days to be numbered. Unless the God whose mercy he had begun to doubt stirred the hearts of the warlords of Qasr al-Zed, Tel Moussa would fall.

IT WAS THE COLDEST WINTER EVER. THERE WAS NO FUEL TO WASTE ON heat. What could be brought in had to be conserved for the cooks.

Nassim did not handle cold well. He could not get warm even buried in rugs, blankets, and furs. His men worried. They wanted to install charcoal braziers in his quarters. He refused. He did not believe a commander should enjoy perquisites not available to his followers. Commanders who believed they deserved every comfort denied to those who did the bleeding became Gordimers and Abads, lost in luxury and pleasure.

In the end, though, he surrendered. He let them bring the braziers. Some nights the chill came so badly his shivering left him exhausted. Next day he would be too weak to do anything useful.

Sitting with Az one evening, he said, "We never get too old to learn surprising things about our fellows."

"Good to hear that, General. Will you take the lesson to heart?"

"The lesson?"

"Yes. That being that, while the men find it admirable that you won't demand what you won't give yourself, they also know you've been that way longer than most of them have been alive. What they want from you is leadership and guidance, not an example. They want you healthy in body and mind because it's your genius and experience that give them a chance to get through the bleak season alive."

Nassim grunted. Old habits. His flesh had become enamored of warmth.

One Moufaq Hali al-Aliki, a recently arrived captain who had managed to slide twenty-eight recruits through the Brotherhood blockade, interrupted. Nassim did not like Moufaq. Hali combined all the worst characteristics of the Qasr al-Zed aristocracy in one young, handsome, supercilious package. Hali said, "General, pardon the intrusion, I pray. Officer of the watch begs to inform you that the man Bone has returned. I don't know what that means."

Alizarin wanted to kick the man for his tone. Why, he was not exactly sure. Some relationships were poisoned from the beginning.

"Thank you, Moufaq Hali. That could be important." He allowed er-Selim to help him up. He told himself he needed endure Hali only till the fools at Shamramdi moved him to another theater. "I'll be there shortly."

Once Hali was gone, Alizarin asked, "Az, how likely is it that Shamramdi makes personnel decisions with an eye toward maximizing casualties?"

"I can imagine those people being capable. I don't think they are, however. I can't conceive of a motive."

Neither could the Mountain. All Qasr al-Zed must, by now, understand that he had no ambitions.

"Let's see Bone."

"Promise you won't send that old man out again, General."

"Promised, and sworn on God's Name."

He had not expected Bone to complete his assignment. He had entertained a secret hope that the old man would just settle in al-Qarn.

Nassim had Bone brought to a place where they both could be warm. Food and drink were waiting.

It was clear that Bone did not bring good news. Nor was he interested in extended palaver. He was old and tired. He wanted to go lie down forever. Straining to remain awake, he said, "The mission was both a success and a failure, General."

"I see. How so?"

"Begging your indulgence, I did locate your wife. She does not wish to see you again. I'm sorry, sir. That is the gentlest way of putting her words. She blames you for the death of your son and considers you a traitor. She has returned to her father's house."

"Her father is dead."

Bone scowled, one eyelid drooping. "Then will it satisfy you better if I say she has returned to the house of her brother, which belonged to her father when your marriage was negotiated?"

"Ignore me. I'll try to avoid interjecting irrelevancies."

"Excellent. I'll hold you to that."

Nassim reddened slightly.

"I located Captain Tage's family as well. A surprise since that had proven difficult before. The wife and daughters are alive, well, and convinced that Else Tage has been dead for years. His return would not be welcome."

"What do you mean?"

"The Lion was entirely proper where the Captain's family was concerned. Once the Rascal told him the Captain was dead, Gordimer found a new husband for the widow. He added a pension to make her more attractive. Today they live much better than they did as the Captain's family. I did nothing to destabilize that."

Nassim considered his folded hands.

God inscribed one's destiny upon one's forehead at the moment of birth. All this had been Willed long ago. God was a jerk. God insisted that the harshest sacrifices be endured by those who loved Him most.

Nassim could no longer raise the full fatalism of the stout-hearted Faithful. "Did you speak to them?"

"To your wife only by exchange of letters. I was permitted to speak to Captain Tage's wife, through a screen. Her new husband is forward-thinking. He was also terrified of how the Sha-lug might respond if he refused. Many of our brethren melted into the population and have been wreaking miseries on the Lucidians and their collaborators—even though the most senior Sha-lug at least pretend to be cooperating."

"Sum total, Bone. You could not get anyone to join an effort to remind Else Tage of his Sha-lug roots. Correct?"

"Exactly. He was reported dead. They have moved on. Best for all concerned if he remains dead."

"If I knew somewhere to go I think I'd pack it in and move along to the next level of exile."

"Can I get some sleep, now?"

"Of course. Sweet dreams. We'll mine your tidings of despair more deeply later on."

Bone, Nassim noted, was not filled with despair. Bone did not care, one way or another, about choices made and changes pursued by the women he had been sent to find. He had done his job. He had reported the results. He was content. Time to nap.

* * *

MASTER OF THE COMMANDERY MADOUC OF HOELES WAS RELENT-less. He strengthened and contracted his blockade round Tel Moussa. Nassim fought back, brilliantly. He won most of their skirmishes, but every triumph cost. He could not afford losses.

Somebody loved Madouc of Hoeles. New fighters reached Gherig regularly, always men who knew their trade.

The quality of Nassim's replacements kept falling. Az remarked that by next year only those already missing eyes and limbs would be sent out.

The Mountain began to suspect the existence of a conspiracy to ruin his reputation. His men demurred. They believed an even more sinister hoax was afoot. They thought the Great Shake's family was using Tel Moussa to winnow the manhood of Qasr al-Zed. The stupid, the weak, the lame, and the dangerously self-destructive fanatics were being eliminated so they would not cause problems later. Only the clever, the swift, the strong, and the skilled would survive to resist the new crusade. Only they would be there to face the sons of Tsis-timed the Golden when that half-Instrumentality resumed his east-ern predations.

Nassim refused to see his world through that dark a glass. Only one man living was capable of a wickedness that foul. He was holed up in the heart of the Idiam.

No strongman was so strong that he could hang on if he deliber-ately wasted the lives of his subjects' sons.

The tribes would rebel.

Az demanded, "What do we do? Plot or no plot, our situation is real. We're at the tip of the spear, nose to nose with Gherig."

"You have been preparing to deal with Gherig since last summer."

Az's eyes widened. "You think it's time? So soon?"

"I had hoped to hold off till the crusaders come. But they've been pushing us too hard. If we do nothing we'll be dead before summer."

"That's true, General. And our smugglers might give themselves away. Or they might figure out what we're really having them do."

Nassim grunted. That had worried him from the beginning.

His knees had begun to ache more than usual. "You do have a true agent inside there, now, don't you?"

"I have two. Neither knows about the other. One is responsible for our plot. The other just spies. The new order did bring a weakness with it. They aren't as clever as Black Rogert at protecting themselves from spies. They disdain Rogert's obvious paranoia."

"Could it be that they don't care?"

"They're righteously sure of themselves."

"Where does the plan stand?"

"I found an educated local, dedicated to God. A carpenter. They know him up there. He worked there when Black Rogert was there before. He isn't allowed to come and go as freely as I'd like but he has recruited several people who do commute daily."

"The plan of execution is in place?"

"My carpenter receives regular meals from his mother. The crusaders won't prepare meals that fit our dietary laws. When the right meal reaches our man he'll know it's time. It's up to him to execute in the manner he expects will be most effective."

One of Az's pet peeves was management from a distance, by people who had no clue about local conditions.

The Mountain said, "See that he gets his special meal. Then have everyone here get ready to exploit the confusion." Pain shot through his flesh, more irksome than anything. "I miss having Black Rogert in charge."

"He was wicked and lucky but he wasn't that competent, was he?"

THE BROTHERHOOD OF WAR FIGHTERS PUSHED UP CLOSE TO THE tower gate, daring the Mountain's falconeers to waste powder and shot. Alizarin undertook experiments to determine whether the crusaders were getting supernatural help.

Az thought they might be, at some trivial level, but did not know it. "The Special Office operators haven't noticed, but they're here to winkle out the Night's friends in Rogert's gang and to handle us if we unleash any foul eastern sorcery."

Nassim said, "Let them come. Fire the lightest falcon first. If you hit someone, touch off the big one. Then scream and yell about idiots wasting firepowder when we're almost out."

Done.

Next morning saw the final test, when infidels sneaking toward Tel Moussa ran into three falcons that had been slipped out and positioned during the night.

Gherig suffered a dozen casualties. Elated, the Mountain sent his horsemen to harass the foreigners the rest of that day.

He now knew his enemies understood his language and knew they were not using the Night to scout. And he knew they did not expect him to risk his precious falcons.

He had grown fond of those. He meant to use them any chance he had.

*   *   *

AZ'S EFFORTS AS A SPYMASTER CAME TO FRUITION THAT NIGHT.

Nassim had fallen asleep watching the stars. Thunder in the west wakened him. He was confused for a moment, able to think only of his cold-sensitive joints. Two more rumbles sounded. Tel Moussa shivered.

There were no clouds in the direction of the White Sea—except where Gherig stood.

Alizarin got his aching knees beneath him, stood up just in time to see a flash backlight Gherig's battlements.

"Oh." This was what he had asked for. He had not expected the explosions at night. Maybe more damage would be done at night. Most of the garrison would be in their quarters. Casualties might be brutal.

A rumble reached Tel Moussa. The earth trembled slightly.

Then came another explosion. The fifth. Amazing! How much firepowder had Az gotten in there?

He got the chance to ask as a sleepy, boggled Master of Ghosts joined him. Several fires burned in the crusader fortress.

Az said, "I don't know. Between six hundred and a thousand pounds."

"You're kidding. I was hoping for twenty-five, critically placed."

"It was all in Abu's hands. I don't know his methods."

"Abu? You're kidding."

"Suitable, eh?"

The sound and shock of the fifth explosion arrived.

Abu meant servant. Or slave. And Nassim suspected the agent's full name would be Servant of God. "That much powder, properly placed and packed . . ."

A sixth explosion dwarfed the others. Flames flew up a hundred feet, illuminating roiling smoke that climbed a thousand more. Flaming wreckage arced a half mile into the desert.

The sound arrived. The long, fierce roll staggered Nassim. He had troubled breathing for a moment.

The shock wave came right behind. It shook Tel Moussa to its foundations. Nassim felt rather than heard the creaks and groans of stones moving on stones. Over there, in Gherig, little explosions popped off in the aftermath of the big one.

The footing shifted slightly beneath the Mountain. "What the hell was that? No way you got that much powder into Gherig."

Bug-eyed, Az shook his head. "That went better than in my wildest fantasy."

There was a seventh explosion, out in the barbican of Gherig. It seemed puny.

Nasty fires burned over there, now. The Brotherhood of War was suffering tonight.

Nassim wanted to wave his arms and shout God's praises. This should be a time of jubilation.

Unfortunately, the squeak, creak, and groan in the masonry had not subsided after the last shock.

"Az, we may have a problem."

"General, you may be right."

"Get everybody out, carrying whatever they can. Just in case." He could not imagine the fortress collapsing but did not want to lose anyone if it did. "Horses and tack, first priority. Then falcons and powder. Then whatever else you can save. Move it."

There was every chance he would be embarrassed when the sun came up on a tower still standing. But his people would be alive to sneer.

The Mountain was at the assembly point beside the Shamramdi road when Tel Moussa surrendered to the blandishments of gravity.

Nassim was pleased that neither man nor animal had been caught in the collapse. Nor had any falcon, keg of firepowder, or favored possession of any man.

Only Nassim's pride and too much food and water failed to survive.

There were no flames over Gherig, now, but smoke continued to roll up.

It took Nassim a long time to collect his men and get them moving. They had been numbed by the collapse of Tel Moussa. Now they just wanted to mill around and waste time speculating.

They did not know that there had been a disaster at Gherig, too.

Az said, "General, I have a bad feeling." He was staring at Gherig. False dawn was gathering behind him. Smoke obscured much of the western sky. "And it's headed our way."

"What?" Then, "That would be crazy. With all the rescue and salvage work they need to do? No." He had considered a mass raid to hurt the crusaders one more time before he ran for Shamramdi.

"Crazy or not, General, they're coming."

Nassim felt it in the earth, now. Many horses were coming.

There would be no time to get away.

The Mountain slapped together a hasty plan, got his men into place barely in time.

The falcons he lined up across the road, in plain sight, with mounted men behind them. The falcons roared when the crusaders were close enough. Archers flung missiles in from both flanks, as did the horsemen from in front. Then Nassim led the latter in a charge. That struck but did not persist. Nassim drew back. His reloaded falcons spoke again. One, overcharged, exploded. Nassim then tried to repeat his charge but had no success. The enemy was too close in. The contest devolved into a melee.

The matter did not go well for the Mountain. The superior armor and training of the crusaders told. And all Nassim's men ever wanted from the start was to get away to somewhere safe.

Nassim thought he would choke on the irony. Once the bodies were counted he would have dealt the foreigners their worst loss since the Battle of the Well of Days, but they would have won and he had lost Tel Moussa. And he was unable, even, to save himself to fight another day. For a number of crusaders got behind him and stole his chance to fly to Shamramdi.

His little knot of survivors, with two falcons, took the only remaining option.

They fled into the Idiam.

23. Antieux: The Widows

Socia shuffled in to join Bernardin and Brother Candle for the isolated breakfast that had become a morning custom. They would consider the demands of the coming day. Come evening they would share supper and assess the day just past.

Brother Candle liked the arrangement. It allowed him to temper the natural ferocity and impulsiveness of the others.

Escamerole bustled around, making sure there was tea and wine and breakfast ale. Socia slumped into her customary seat. The old man asked, "Out again last night?" He wished he could separate her from that crystal.

"No. Lumiere has the colic. I stayed up with him."

"And you have the assizes today."

She frowned his way.

"Only two cases," Bernardin said. "One is Bishop LaVelle with the usual complaints."

Socia forced a weary smile. "Thank the Good God for that."

Brother Candle asked, "You didn't go out? In any shape?"

"Master." Socia jerked her head at Escamerole, delivering a basket of rolls so fresh they steamed.

Bernardin said, "I'm interested in the answer myself."

The old man and Countess harkened to Bernardin's tone. Socia said, "No. What's happened?"

"The overnight watch reports include multiple sightings of a giant eagle."

"It wasn't me. I promise. I wish it was. I haven't seen Kedle in ages. I don't even know where she is anymore."

"Deep in Arnhand, making a screaming nuisance of herself. So what could that have been last night?"

Socia and the old man shrugged. Brother Candle was troubled. "More attention from the Night."

"No doubt," Amberchelle said. "Why? I'll find out what I can while you entertain the Bishop." Then he snorted and reddened. "Sorry. Unintentional." With apology wasted. Neither companion recognized the lower-class slang for male masturbation.

AT THE EVENING MEAL, BERNARDIN SAID, "I TALKED TO EVERYBODY who saw the eagle. They did see it. Most didn't know each other. They didn't discuss it. Their descriptions were pretty much all the same and they all said that this bird was bigger than the one sometimes seen around the citadel. Several witnesses said its right wing tip was deformed."

Brother Candle said, "I saw a mule today with a deformed right fore hoof. I've never seen a crippled horse or mule before."

"An omen?" Socia asked.

Bernardin, smiling weakly, said, "No. A shape-changing Instrumentality with a deformed right hand."

Brother Candle said, "That's a wild leap."

"I wasn't serious. But . . . it could be. We've been up to our ears in strange stuff lately."

"Scary," Socia said. "But he's right."

"I don't want him to be right. I'm supposed to have achieved Perfection. I can't believe in . . ."

Bernardin said, "You know the saying, Master. All things are true inside the Night."

While Socia said, "They're minions of the Adversary."

"Indeed. Are we become minions of minions?" He rolled back his left sleeve. The deadly tattoo had gained color. "It won't pay off but I'll see Radeus Pickleu again."

"You never know," Bernardin said. "You wouldn't want to miss something because you didn't think you'd find it. I'll put out word to keep an eye out for critters with a deformed right front whatever."

Socia shivered. "It's cold."

"It's winter," Brother Candle reminded her.

"I'm going to bed early. I'll have Guillemette build me a nice fire, then I'll get under the eiderdown and toast. And I'll drown Lumiere if he keeps me up again."

SOCIA DID SLIDE UNDER HER COVERS EARLY AND FELL ASLEEP IN-stantly. She wakened around midnight, used the chamber pot, then could not get back to sleep. She could not stop worrying about Kedle.

The world had begun to call Kedle "The Widow." She and Socia were, collectively, "Death's Brides," or "The Deathwives," depending on the region.

Socia worried because Kedle was unacquainted with failure. Each success lured her on toward something bigger and bloodier. Her luck could not last.

Socia climbed out of bed, went to her window. It was cloudy out but not so much so that she did not catch glimpses of a brilliant moon.

Concealed in a chest close by was a packet of lightweight clothing kept for those nights when she could not resist the need to see Kedle. She could carry it easily in her other form.

She had to have something to wear on the far end. Kedle's killers were troubled enough by the unexplained appearances of their Count-ess. Her roaming around naked would be too much.

Socia took the packet out and set it by, ready, before ordering her-self not to make the flight. It would take six hours to reach Kedle's last known location, then she would have to work out where the Widow was now. That might be another hundred miles. It would be tomor-row afternoon before she could catch up.

No. Not practical. This Deathwife had to stay home and do work that needed doing here.

To soar where the clouds lay in fluffed and silvery drifts below her would be wonderful, though.

That Instrumentality had given her a unique and marvelous gift. Had any other human being ever been so blessed?

She did not think so. Not outside the legendary beings of antiq-uity.

She suspected that flight was not a wonder to creatures of the Night.

Socia stripped to the raw, positioned her crystal. That she would not take. She would be right back. She opened the window, swinging

its two panes outward, sideways. Winter wasted not one instant before tasting her bare skin.

Shivering, Socia changed, then launched herself. Her feathers held
the heat generated by her exertions.

She flapped lazily, let the wind carry her to one side. She banked
right, looked for an updraft. How marvelous! How liberating! She
could forget a thousand cares as the things of the earth dwindled below. How she wished she could show this to Brother Candle. But he
was down there in the darkness, trapped in flesh that could never be
anything but an old man tangled in a restless, sweating dream of a
delicious devil.

The moon jabbed rays through a gap in scooting clouds, sweeping
Antieux with patches of racing light that rippled across the rooftops
and the gullies of alleys and streets . . .

Socia's heart leapt into her throat.

She was a thousand feet up. Between her and the rooftops below a
vast eagle was rising.

The moonlight swept onward. In the instant the eagle's eyes would
be adjusting Socia tipped over into a strike dive.

She closed most of the separation before the eagle discovered her.
It thrashed out of her way, evading attack. But a strike was never her
intent. She continued her plunge. The eagle lost track.

Socia changed into a naked young woman as fast as she could. She
dressed, clumsily, shaking badly.

She watched the eagle from the darkness behind her window as it
searched for her.

She squealed when Guillemette asked, "Are you all right, Countess?"

"Oh. I'm sorry. I didn't hear you come in. What are you doing
here?"

"I came to build up the fire. I do that every night. I've never found
you awake before." Nor with the window open, her curious glance
said.

"I had a bad dream. Then I couldn't get back to sleep."

"Yes, ma'am." Once Guillemette finished building the fire, she shut
and latched the window. "Good night, ma'am."

"She would have caught me if she'd walked in five minutes
earlier," Socia said.

Brother Candle nodded. "A cautionary event, then."

"For sure. It was looking for me, Master."

"You thought fast and did what you had to do. Another caution-ary event."

Socia scowled. "Always lessons. Always learning."

"And when you don't pay attention you end up suffering through the same lessons again."

"Stuff all that. I want to know what the hell was chasing me."

Brother Candle said, "I'll visit Radeus Pickleu again."

"As soon as you finish stuffing your face."

Brother Candle told Bernardin, "You would think that, after all my years educating her, I would have drummed *some* manners into the girl."

Socia chose her response from the vocabulary of a day laborer, and added, "I'm as civilized as the world lets me be."

"Or, we could say, the world is as civilized as you let it be."

Socia stared, glared, growled, "There's no winning with you, is there?"

"There won't be breaking even if you observe normalcy's rules."

BERNARDIN HAD A SOLDIER TRAIL BROTHER CANDLE. THE PROTEC-tion proved unnecessary. The Perfect found Pickleu's home by asking. The physician welcomed him as an honored guest. "Come in, Master. Come in."

"I hope I'm not intruding . . ."

"Not today. No patients. Somebody might break an arm later. We all thank you deeply for speaking to the Champion. It's been peaceful since. How may we honor you?"

Brother Candle vaguely recalled having heard Bernardin called Champion at some point. "I've got another mysterious Instrumentality to identify. I hope to have better luck with this one."

"Yet here you are at last resort. I hope I'm more use this time."

"Yes. Well. So. Last time here I was not entirely forthcoming. As you no doubt realized."

"My feelings suffered no permanent damage. It must be hard to trust the discretion of a man who never stops talking."

"Indeed. I'll be more honest this time."

"Something has happened."

"Yes indeed. Something entirely unexpected. The Countess may be in danger from this Instrumentality."

Pickleu frowned, pursed his lips, made a little sweeping, bouncing hand gesture. "And this is a different one?"

"For certain."

"All right. You have my word. Short of torture no one will hear any of this from me. But let me make sure the wife and the boy don't hear something they should not."

Pickleu gone, Brother Candle considered the small room. It was perfectly comfortable and reflected Pickleu's personality. It was busy and cluttered.

Pickleu returned with two pieces of Firaldian glassware, probably blown in Clearenza, simple cylinders in glass of mixed colors. "Rhaita was just making lemon water. She'll do her marketing while we talk. The boy is out working somewhere. So say on."

Brother Candle provided a more detailed report on the visit from the girl, to which a dreamy-eyed Pickleu said, "I wish she would come see me. So. She blessed you with deadly tattoos. And put strange fish into Amberchelle's flesh."

"Yes."

"What do they do?"

"We have no idea."

"And the Countess? It stands to reason the demon's gift to her stands behind this visit."

"In a way." Brother Candle explained the power of the crystal and Socia's use of it.

"Ah," Pickleu said. "I do believe I'd like that even more than seeing my little friend learn to stand up all over again."

Brother Candle had not withheld the fact that his own little friend retained its renewed vigor—when he thought about the demon girl.

"A marvelous gift," Pickleu said. "The crystal."

"You said before that you might have heard of something like it."

"I was wrong. I don't know of anything that bestows the ability to change shape. The Countess hasn't shown much imagination using it, has she? She's treating it like a toy."

Brother Candle nodded.

"I understand that she is an impulsive sort. That she still has little feel for the weight of station that came with her marriage."

"She is trying."

"So. What has you so excited? A new Instrumentality in the mix?"

Brother Candle related the facts as they had been given to him.

"She was chased by an eagle several times her own size."

"With a deformed wing." The Perfect was sure that was important.

"Right wing tip. Yes. Uhm. Not many Instrumentalities are known for their deformities. Some pantheons have a smith figure with a bad leg. Said to harken to a time when a tribe's smith was so important its people broke his leg, then let it knit badly, so he couldn't run away. The Devedian experience makes me suspect that those smiths were outsider slaves. Otherwise, most gods and goddesses resemble your visitor. Young and ferociously beautiful. Or middle-aged and endlessly randy."

Brother Candle sighed. He sipped lemon water. Pickleu's spouse had garnished that with a touch of honey.

Pickleu said, "The northern pantheon has several handicapped gods. A Beyish, Bayish, Boyish, something like that, was blind because of a cruel practical joke. Zaw, or Zer, the god of war, was missing a hand that got bitten off by a monster. Which he killed with the mystic spear, Heartsplitter, using his off hand. And the top god only had one eye. Sacrifice was big with the Shining Ones. He traded the eye for . . ."

"Which hand?"

Pickleu shrugged. "I don't know. Right hand sounds logical, doesn't it?"

"It does. Is that the extent of it, then?"

"My expertise is entirely relative. As you should know by now."

"And you know no better source?"

"Certainly. But I don't think you can tap it."

"That would be?"

"The Collegium. In Brothe. Several Principatés are as conversant with the old religions as they are with their own."

"I see. So, once again I return to the Countess no wiser."

"Here's a thought. Have her fly to Brothe and take the shape of a member of the Collegium. She could ask those who have access to the right information."

"Take someone's else's shape?" Socia asked. "He actually suggested that?"

"He did. And he was dead serious."

"Can I do that?"

"I don't know. I never thought of it."

"Nor did I," Bernardin said. "I expect on account of the old stories. Shape-shifters turn into animals. Especially wolves. Not into other people. An evil sorcerer who wants to disguise himself as somebody else always uses a glamour."

"A glamour would be easier for your garden-variety sorcerer. He'd only need to make somebody think he sees who he wants them to see. In real life you would need to mimic mannerisms and speech patterns."

"I get it," Socia said. "And, suddenly, I realize that we haven't put any serious thought into what we've been given. Or to what she thought we should do with it."

Brother Candle chuckled darkly. "So the next stage in my life is, I become a sixty-nine-year-old professional assassin."

Bernardin cocked his head. "Something is going on. I'll be back as soon as I find out."

Socia and the Perfect exchanged looks. The old man said, "I didn't hear anything."

"Nor did I."

Neither mentioned it but both had noticed. Bernardin was growing brighter and more alert, quicker, and sharper in his senses. And Brother Candle felt younger. Not a day over sixty-one.

BERNARDIN RETURNED ACCOMPANIED BY AN EXHAUSTED, FILTHY SOL-dier no more than sixteen years old. "And here she is herself, lad. Tell her what you told me."

The boy tried to make his obeisance. Brother Candle feared he would collapse and be unable to get back up. Socia said, "Never mind all that foolishness. Talk to me, Aaron d'Fitac."

The boy glowed. His Countess knew him. "I ride with the Widow. We were in a big fight. The biggest yet, near the ruins of old Vetercus. We were up against Anne of Menand's best."

Brother Candle's spirit sank. The way the boy approached his story hinted that Kedle had found the end of her string.

"And?" Socia croaked.

"We killed most of them. The Widow told us to take no prisoners because it might be the fight that broke them. We took none amongst the nobles and knights."

Bernardin settled the boy in his chair, then, as his story unfolded, had Escamerole bring food and drink.

The boy attacked food and drink alike, but between mouthfuls he named Arnhanders known to have fallen. The list sounded like a roll call of Arnhand's peerage.

"No prisoners," the boy said again. And, "The Widow's ambush was ingenious. They didn't suspect anything till we started killing them. They were all piled up at the ford. They were following a game trail, trying to get behind us so they could cut us off from the Connec. But the Widow knew their plan. She always knows what they'll try to do. So she had us there waiting, hiding. We discharged four falcons into their horses. They probably lost three hundred men just in the stampede.

Meantime, every man who could bend a bow or span an arbalest laid missiles into the confusion. Even the proudest knights. There isn't a man amongst the Vindicated who will do aught but what the Widow orders."

Brother Candle asked, "How large was this Arnhander force?" It would have grown in the boy's mind, he was sure, but he knew it would have been sizable if it had included that many important men.

"You will think me a liar but at least a thousand by actual count."

Bernardin said, "The Commander of the Righteous slaughtered a vastly superior force at the Shades without the advantages the boy mentions, using falcons."

Socia asked, "How many were you? How many falcons did you have? And where did you get them?"

"There were three hundred eighty-six of us. We had four falcons taken from the castle at Artridge."

Brother Candle said, "I'm lost. Where is Artridge? When did Kedle capture it?"

Socia shrugged. "I don't know. I'm not allowed to go see her anymore."

Bernardin said, "There is more. The critical more."

Brother Candle realized that this was the point where the boy would pass on the dread word that he had ridden so long and hard to deliver.

Socia said, "Aaron, you came to tell us what else?"

"We killed more than a thousand. By honest, actual count. We lost only thirty-seven of our own."

"Aaron!"

"They captured the Widow, Countess!" The boy burst into tears. "There was snow on the ground. All the blood and trampling around turned the earth to mud. She led the attack on the last Arnhanders. There weren't a hundred who hadn't fallen or fled. Her horse slipped in the mud. She didn't jump free. The horse fell on her. It crushed her leg. The man leading the Arnhanders then was Stephan of Bley, a really big man. He grabbed the Widow and threw her across the neck of his horse, then galloped off. He outran us. He's holed up in the castle at Arngrere with survivors from the battle. He's threatening to have his revenge on her."

Bernardin grumbled, "The Society must be salivating over the opportunity to put her on trial."

Brother Candle nodded. That would make a great show.

Aaron went on. "He has been warned that if he harms her, not just he will pay a cruel price but all those of his blood will as well."

Brother Candle could not speak. He had been expecting this forever. He had schooled himself to bear it. But the shock was still fierce, as it was when a long-suffering parent finally surrendered to the Will of the Night.

Socia said, "Bernardin, start putting together an expedition . . ."

"No."

"Excuse me?"

"That would be pointless. This drama will play out long before we can influence it. It may have done so already. Aaron d'Fitac, how long did it take you to get here?"

"Six days, and some. I came as fast as I could."

"You see, Countess? A week already. How long to assemble a force, arm and victual it, and get it to Arngrere? How long for the witch of Menand to put together a force to welcome us? Kedle's whole campaign has depended on her not being where she was expected."

After her initial emotional response subsided, Socia saw the truth in what Bernardin said. Still, "But I can't sit here and do nothing."

"Not only can you, you must. For the sake of Antieux and the Connec."

"What?"

That was an odd thing to say. Brother Candle heard it but was too focused on Kedle's predicament to concern himself.

The old man felt a fierce, shooting pain in his right temple. For a moment he feared this was the end. That his allotted time had run out. That the Good God had chosen to spin his ever-lapsing Perfect round the Wheel of Life again. He gasped out, "Socia, this is exactly where I've been warning you that we were headed."

"Yes. Enjoy your vindication. Aaron, is there anything more? Can you break my heart one more time? No? Then go somewhere. Sleep. For a week if that's what you need. Escamerole. Come out of there. Have you been spying?"

"No, Countess." Face red, Kedle's cousin slipped into the room. "And it please you, I just wanted word of my kin." She was shaking. She did not like being the center of attention.

"So now you've had word. Grim as it is. Show Aaron somewhere to lie down, then come to my apartment. Bring Guillemette. And don't breathe a word about what you've heard. Understand?"

"I do, Lady."

"Master? The same for you. If you go jogging off to tell the Archimbaults I'll have Bernardin cut your tongue out. Clear?"

"Clear." He exchanged glances with Amberchelle. Bernardin shrugged.

Socia said, "You two go get some sleep, too. You'll need to be rested, clear of eye and mind, and ready for war in the morning." She rose and stalked off, pulling an emotional vacuum along with her.

Brother Candle considered Bernardin momentarily. "There was something else we needed to hear about, wasn't there?"

"She didn't give me a chance to bring it up. It won't be official till the Queen's deputies get here from Khaurene but I had a secret warning from one of Isabeth's agents. So we would be ready when the delegation arrives."

Brother Candle said, "What?" He had no idea.

"Isabeth is going to do what we thought she never would. She's going to confirm Count Raymone as her brother's heir as Duke of Khaurene."

"But he's dead."

"Despite the fact that he's dead."

"Meaning Lumiere . . ."

"Exactly. Because Lumiere has a strong mother. Because his strong mother has a terrible friend. The Connec is unlikely to become subservient to Arnhand with those two guarding Lumiere's interests."

"But . . ."

"I've known since yesterday. I was sworn not to tell Socia. The Navayans want to tell her themselves. But then that boy rode in."

"Interesting times," Brother Candle said. "Better go tell the lad not to spread his news. The Navayans could change their minds."

"Terrible times. Cruel times. I'll talk to the boy right now."

SOCIA EXPLAINED THE ENTIRE SITUATION TO GUILLEMETTE AND EScamerole, including her entanglement with the Night. She was in a rush. "This is what we're going to do." She answered questions while they proceeded.

Socia meant to sneak out of Antieux, avoiding the eagle demon. She and Guillemette were of a size and coloring. Guillemette would pretend to be Socia. She needed only lay low, being seen only from a distance, while the actual Socia was away.

The hard part was getting Escamerole fully engaged. Escamerole grew more timid by the day. She was afraid to leave the citadel. "If you can change shape you don't need me. You can be me."

"I need you to manage Kedle's family, Escamerole. They have to be part of this. And I need them to keep quiet. If I tried to be you they'd know better first time I opened my mouth. So I'll be Guillemette and you'll do all the talking. By the time they realize that I'm not really Guillemette, they'll be caught up in the plan."

"It'll do you good to get out of here," Guillemette told Escamerole.

Escamerole sulked but gave in. "Tomorrow. I don't want to go out there tonight."

"It's perfectly safe," Socia said. "But I could have Willing Davids escort us." Willing Davids was a handsome young man-at-arms related to Bernardin Amberchelle. Socia had noted that Escamerole became misty and even more timid when Willing was around.

Guillemette said, "Not fair, Countess."

"No. You're right. I'm sorry, Escamerole. That was almost cruel."

The shy girl said, "We weren't all brought up amongst teams of brawling brothers out at the edge of beyond."

"Well said. Well done. Only one thing left to do. Guillemette, get undressed."

Socia was shaky before that part was over but once it was she had become Guillemette's mirror twin, wearing the girl's clothing.

SOCIA STOPPED ESCAMEROLE OUTSIDE THE ENTRANCE TO THE HOUSE occupied by the Archimbaults and other refugees from Khaurene. "Now is when you need to be strongest. Stand up to their bullying. For Kedle's sake."

"For Kedle's sake." Said with quavering voice.

Socia rolled her eyes and hoped the mouse would hold out at least until she made her getaway.

Maybe she should do it right here, in the street, by the light of the moon, and let Escamerole collect her clothing. That would be easier than dealing with Kedle's parents.

Maybe. But Socia had to come back once she had done this. Whatever this turned out to be. She was not sure. Something told her she had to help Kedle and had to do it without attracting the attention of that demon out there.

Escamerole found her courage first. "We'd best get on with it. If you're going to get there before it gets light out."

"We had best, hadn't we?"

Kedle's family surprised Socia. Her worries were all for naught. Escamerole did not hold up but neither did Kedle's mother or father waste time on argument or recrimination. They remained true Seekers. They loved their only surviving child. They were prepared to play their part with few questions and no disputation.

The Archimbault home had a hatch accessing its roof, a common feature in the Connec. During summer people slept on the cooler roofs.

Roofs were not much visited during the winter, however.

The Archimbaults wanted to see Socia off. Escamerole discouraged them. "She has to undress before she changes."

To which Madame Archimbault said, "Oh, my!" while Raulet said nothing—though there might have been a mischievous twinkle in his eye.

Socia said, "I won't waste time. I'll be back before things fall apart." She was confident she could make everything right.

The Archimbaults offered blessings on her, then withdrew. Socia readied herself. Her bag included not only clothing but the changing crystal. She anticipated having to make several shifts at the other end. Also, she wore the demon's forgotten necklace. She had no reason to expect it to be useful but wearing it did seem right.

"Ready?" Escamerole asked, teeth chattering.

"Ready. And be brave, little sparrow. Whatever happens, be brave. And make sure this door doesn't get locked."

The chill felt extra bitter because a big part of Socia did not want to be out in it, in pursuit of this insanity. She quashed that timorous voice, made the change, took wing. She stayed low to avoid being silhouetted against the sky, though there was a heavy overcast. She thought it might snow. Only the timid girl marked her departure.

AARON D'FITAC'S REPORT HAD BEEN CLEAR ENOUGH TO BRING SOCIA to the site of Kedle's amazing success at Vetercus. Just follow the Dechear north to its tributary the Nar, then that into its hilly watershed southeast of Salpeno, and look for a creek . . . The last few miles were the easiest. Her bird senses picked up the stench.

She settled into a huge dead tree standing alone, overlooking the killing ground. The branch creaked but held. She kept her form. She was tired to the bone. She had flown for eight hours, often into the wind.

False dawn's light showed most of the corpses cleared away. The Vindicated had cared for their own. Fallen Arnhanders had been recovered by friends and family—excepting those who had no one who cared enough to come looking.

There were plenty of those sad ones still down there.

Socia imposed Aaron d'Fitac's report upon the field. But to what point? Those events were more than a week old. Events had moved on.

She had to find the castle Arngrere, now.

She readied herself to take wing.

"Prithee, wouldst hold a moment?"

Socia gripped her perch tightly, turned her head slowly. Behind her, seated with knees under her chin, on a branch incapable of bearing her weight, sat the Instrumentality who had given her the crystal. She wore archaic clothing. Her hair was in a single braid wrapped around her crown.

Socia changed her head to something vaguely human, baby size, and squeaked, "Why don't you talk like a normal person? And what the hell are you, anyway?"

That earned a wan smile. The Instrumentality stood up on her precarious perch, balanced on one foot, grinned, rose onto tiptoe, indulged in a pirouette. "I be the answer to what thee needs do to save thy headstrong friend." Her gaze caught on the necklace Socia wore. Her eyes grew larger and troubled, but only for a moment.

"I'm listening."

The Instrumentality smirked.

Socia revealed a neutral expression though her thoughts were not charitable.

"Thy Kedle doth be a genius at making use of what she receiveth but she doth be impulsive." The Instrumentality's pronunciations and rhythms remained odd. Her gaze kept drifting to the necklace.

Socia nodded. "That's why she's a prisoner."

"Didst thou bring a plan?"

"I can't keep talking this way. But if I change I'll freeze."

"Thou wouldst betray thy treasures as well. Follow." The girl giggled, became a raven in a wink, took wing, headed west. Socia followed. There was light enough to see the unremembered dead and a few scavengers belatedly trying to find anything else worth taking from fallen plundered for a week already.

The entire countryside would hear about the giant birds by nightfall.

The Instrumentality planed down over the western edge of the wood, landed in front of a woodcutter's shack. Socia settled beside her. The place was abandoned but had not been so for long. The tenant had chosen not to be discovered in an area where wholesale murder was being done.

Socia changed. "Oh, Aaron's Sacred Ass, it's cold."

"Clothe thyself. I will start a fire, then find thee something warmer."

"Who are you? What are you? Why must you interfere in our lives?"

"Some call me Dawn, some, Hope. I be the dawn destined to rise beyond the Twilight."

That made no sense. "What is this twilight?"

The Instrumentality got a fire blazing with magical swiftness. "Twilight is this age. The one in which thou livest. The time when the gods themselves may be slain. Old Ones have fallen in thy own land. Great Old Ones, from the time before time, are dying at the hands of my kin. I, with my brother who is lost, will be the bridge into the time that is coming."

"Now tell me a story that makes sense." Shivering despite the fire.

"As thou wist."

DAWN EXPANDED HER TALE IN SNATCHES, BETIMES SKIPPING IN AND out to steal clothing. Socia stayed close to the fire. In fits and starts the Instrumentality got Socia to explain what she hoped to accomplish.

Dawn said, "Thy ability to change is thy sharpest tool, aye, but thee needs must plan, not just charge and rely on confusion."

The Instrumentality vanished. She wanted to develop a specific inventory of clothing. She explained, "A common look, so thou may shift face whilst none do look."

Socia grunted. The child-goddess was thinking more deeply than she.

"Thou hast no mind for the cunning, methinks. Thou art infatuated with the direct. Thou preferest to assail the object of thy frustration till it dost break. Would it not confuse thy enemies more if his captains kept appearing and disappearing with confusing and contradictory orders?"

Socia shut her eyes. She wished Brother Candle were here to advise her—and to tell her what she was learning about the Instrumentality. "Better still if those captains appeared unexpectedly and stuck knives in their comrades' livers."

"Ah. Thou art truly the soul sister of the Widow."

"I'm pragmatic. I go with what works. The opinions of moral scorekeepers mean nothing. The men I may kill would send me to the stake if they could."

"Let us begin. Arngrere is four miles west. Thou shouldst consult the Widow's captains. Thou couldst end this with a single bold stroke."

"I could. But that's not the way I'm doing it."

"Pardon?"

"They'll waste time fussing over me. Then they'll waste time planning, mainly to keep me far from danger. Which will void my strength and purpose."

"But . . ."

"I'll go straight in. I'll cause chaos and confusion. I'll open a gate somehow. You will alert the Vindicated to their opportunity."

The Instrumentality stared, peeved. She did not have control. But she did not argue.

"We'll stay here, keep warm, and move after dark."

"Unless the smoke from yon fire doth attract attention."

Socia asked, "Are there more like you? Your brother is in prison?"

"He is trapped in another world. Eucereme. The Aelen Kofer have sealed the gateways between the worlds. He is a prisoner in that sense. We will find a means of opening the way."

"We? There are more like you, then."

"There are other Shining Ones. None like me."

"Would one have a crippled right hand?"

"Uh . . . ? No. Zyr lost his sword hand, long ago. But he did not escape the Realm of the Gods."

Socia understood none of that and was disinclined to find out what it meant. She wanted to talk about the giant eagle. She did note that Dawn's speech seemed slightly less archaic. For the moment.

Dawn sighed. Despite the fire her breath clouded briefly.

"You do have some idea of what I'm talking about."

"I know who that was. He must have been investigating sightings of a giant bird. No doubt he meant to deny thee thy ability to change shape."

"So, not only are there more of you, there are factions."

"Those Shining Ones dedicated to the success of the Chaldarean invasion of the Holy Lands might view what I have been doing negatively."

That was a thick slice of cautious evasion. "Old heathen gods, who aren't even supposed to exist, will help the Commander of the Righteous drive the Pramans out of the Holy Lands?"

"Yes."

Socia had trouble getting her mind around that.

Dawn said, "Once thou art established with the Widow's soldiers I shall get the story from Asgrimmur."

"Weren't you listening? I'm not going to deal directly with the Vindicated. I'm going straight into Arngrere. You'll stay outside, with the Vindicated, in whatever guise you like. You want to visit your friends, do it after Kedle is free."

The Instrumentality's irritation was intense. Socia felt it as an actual physical pressure. Dawn should not be pushed any more.

"Asgrimmur?" Socia asked. "Odd name for a god."

"Asgrimmur is no deity. He is an ascendant. A mortal who achieved

Instrumentality status. In his case, unintentionally, as a result of his part in destroying two Instrumentalities who tried to use him as a weapon against one another."

Socia remained at sea.

She continued to engage Dawn in conversation. And concluded that the Instrumentality was not as bright as she thought. Which reinforced the Countess's estimate of the Old Ones in general, based on myth and legend.

Before Socia knew half what she wanted, Dawn announced, "I am going. Do thou as it pleaseth thee."

Socia felt an immediate sense of loss, loneliness, and isolation. It might be manipulation but it was real, emotionally. She got up and followed the Instrumentality into the light of late afternoon.

Dawn stopped not far from an outpost where pickets watched for an Arnhander relief force. "They waste their time. The Arnhanders squabble amongst themselves, pointing fingers. That Stephan of Bley holds Arngrere hinders the process. Nobody likes Stephan of Bley."

"This is where we part," Socia said. "You go tell them the castle will be betrayed."

"As thou wilt."

Socia examined her companion. Dawn had become a woman with hard eyes and weather-beaten skin, like a once-handsome peasant of middle years. She strode toward the pickets with purpose. The soldiers welcomed her, chatted with her, provided her with a horse.

What Socia saw confirmed suspicions birthed when she found the Instrumentality in her tree.

Dawn explained Kedle's success. Dawn helped Kedle evade every ambush and showed her how to be perfectly positioned at the perfect time to inflict great embarrassment on Anne of Menand and those Arnhanders who had participated in the invasions of the Connec.

Socia watched till Dawn passed out of sight, headed toward Arngrere and its besiegers. In this unfriendly season the Vindicated would depend more on the Instrumentality for intelligence about food supplies than for the whereabouts of enemies.

Socia withdrew into better cover, with less wind, and awaited the night. She began to learn truths about Socia Rault.

SOCIA SOON WISHED THAT SHE HAD RETREATED TO THE WOODcutter's hut till it was time. First point of learning: Socia Rault was impatient and impatience always cost. She shivered till she feared her body would be too exhausted to make any changes.

The sky became overcast. Snow might be coming. Eventually, she ground her teeth and stripped, carefully folded each article, and stuffed it into her sack.

The chill gnawed her bare flesh like wolves with fangs of ice. The stones in the necklace felt colder still, but all that retreated to the level of annoyance once she took a winged form.

She rose a thousand feet. From that vantage she quickly discovered the unique nest of shadows that marked Arngrere, which was more imposing vertically than horizontally. It was sited badly for defense. It was one of those Arnhander castles built more to overawe the neighbors than to offer sanctuary in times of danger.

Socia drifted down, looking for sentries. She did not see a one. Stephan of Bley was not fierce enough to make men stay out in the cold when their enemies were content to starve them out. In fact, the defenders could be under orders *not* to man the walls at night. The castle had not been provisioned for a siege. Men on night duty might be tempted to climb down and run away.

Socia considered a parapet on a tower that rose twenty feet above the rest of Arngrere. Definitely no lookout. She landed there.

She changed shape. The wind was so biting bitter she nearly screamed. Her fingers would not stop shaking. She fumbled fastenings repeatedly as she dressed. She thought longingly of the cozy off-kitchen at home where she ate with Bernardin and Brother Candle. Oh! Had Guillemette been found out yet?

Dressed sloppily, the best she could manage, she took up her bag and crept down the stairway that ran round the inside wall of the tower. She could see nothing. The steps were wooden. She tested each carefully before putting her weight on it. She stayed hard against the wall. No point exploring the axis of the tower. There might be nothing there but a long fall.

The tower existed only to provide a high place from which to observe the countryside. Socia counted steps till she was sure she had descended twenty feet. No change. She descended another twenty before she heard the slow, snorting breathing of someone who, likely, was the man supposed to be in the parapet. Two steps more and she spied a hint of pumpkin-colored light.

Socia entered a small landing watch room, oozed toward a sleeping soldier. The pumpkin light leaked from a lantern turned so low its flame barely remained alive.

Maybe the proximity of human warmth made the soldier stir. Like Aaron d'Fitac, he was just a boy. He sat up straighter, groggily.

Socia's hand darted to her lips, then to her necklace. She fingered the stones. Their touch soothed her. She prayed that the boy would drift off again so she need do nothing dire.

The soldier shuddered, shifted slightly, and began to snore.

Cause and effect?

Probably not. In case, though, she set her bag down, moved the necklace from around her neck into the pocket of the peasant apron she wore. Sack over shoulder, hand in pocket gripping stone beads, willing the boy to sleep till his relief arrived, she slipped out of the watch room and continued downward.

She reached a deserted residential level. There were neither doors nor door-masking hangings there. Nor were there any people. She suspected that she could beat a drum if she wanted.

She did find people in the great hall. They were crowded around one large fireplace, sharing body heat more than the warmth coming off a dying fire. There was coal light enough to reveal two dozen crowded bodies and just a few sticks of firewood remaining.

She entered not far from that fireplace. Though disoriented she thought the main entrance should face the castle gate. She drifted that way, staying near the wall.

One of the sleepers surged up. She froze. He stepped over, around, and on his fellows to get to a tin bucket. He urinated noisily. Done, he looked around. Seeing no one watching, he chucked the last firewood onto the coals. Socia gripped her necklace and willed herself to be a shadow amongst shadows.

All the while she contemplated the probable layout of the castle. She was at ground level now. The other Arnhanders must have been elsewhere. She did hear snoring from the kitchen beyond the big fireplace. Some might be in the stables, where the horses and any livestock or poultry would generate heat.

Socia started moving again, looking for an exit. She wondered where they kept Kedle. She no longer meant to look. Those fantasies about slipping around assassinating captains and sowing chaos had perished. The cold reality was, there would be no sneaking Kedle out while the Arnhanders brawled with one another.

She was too cold. Or thought she was because of stress. Intellectually she knew the cold had been worse during the winter when she was fleeing from the Captain-General with Brother Candle. This time she was operating alone, with no margin for error. Willful choices had created a potential for catastrophe. If she failed, if she ended up in chains with Kedle, the struggle for Connecten independence would collapse.

That realization struck her immobile. For some while Brother Candle's voice muttered in the back of her mind, possibly about willful children who refused to consider possible consequences.

She found a door that would let her out the side of the great hall. She pushed out hoping the gust she admitted would not waken anyone. She shoved her right hand into her apron pocket, fondled the stone beads. Her fright and nerves receded. Winter backed off its fury.

A touch of moonlight slipped through the overcast, not enough to help her avoid a pile of frozen horse apples but sufficient to show her the shapes of general features. She was in a courtyard that crossed the front of the keep and stretched along its left side. She was in the foot of the L. The stables were to her left. She moved to her right. More moonlight came down briefly, painting the world in ghostly shades. This might fit some religion's notion of hell, a cold, dark place where you would be all alone forever.

She approached the gatehouse almost incautiously. Had the Instrumentality cast a spell to put the garrison to sleep? This was going awfully easy.

She found the gatehouse manned by two shivering youngsters, huddled for warmth in a corner, behind a single fat, smoky tallow candle. One boy was crying. He was terrified even before he saw Socia.

"Get up. There's work to do."

They clambered to their feet, stiffly. Neither glanced at their weapons, pole arms standing in a corner beside the entrance.

Socia asked, "You. What's the matter?"

She got no answer. The other boy said, "He doesn't understand your dialect. He's scared of what Stephan of Bley will do when he finds out that we let more than thirty men get out tonight."

Socia considered his open face, his wide, frightened blue eyes. She saw no guile. "Why didn't you go with them?"

She received no answer but a downcast look. And that, she supposed, told the tale. Going would have been worse than staying.

"Time to open up again."

The spokesman said something to the other boy. Socia did not follow but felt no threat. The two began a reluctant drift toward the doorway. Socia stepped in front of their weapons. "You will be protected. There will be work for you."

These days most soldiers were in the martial life because they needed some way to support themselves. Common folk suffered ever more as the ice advanced.

Arngrere's gateway was just wide enough to pass two horsemen abreast. The gates themselves were heavy oaken doors in need of replacement. They could not long resist the advances of a determined ram. They would have been broken long since had Kedle been in charge outside.

There lay the weakness of charismatic leadership. The worshipful followers were too accustomed to having the messianic one do all their thinking. They froze up once the genius was removed.

"How wide do you want them opened, ma'am?"

"Six feet should do."

The gates creaked and shrieked but no one came to investigate, evidently for the second time tonight.

"Six feet, ma'am." Voice quavering with fright and cold.

"Step through, please."

They did so.

The moat was empty, its sides caving in. A bridge spanned it. It was made of planks meant to be taken up in time of siege. That had not been done. The fugitives from Vetercus had been too hard-pressed when they arrived.

"Move to the end of the bridge."

The boys did that, too. The one who did not understand Socia said something softly, scared. His friend said something reassuring.

Socia looked out into the darkness and wondered where Kedle's people were. They were supposed to be watching.

Another minute of nothing happening. Able to come up with no alternative but a shout, she reached into her bag and fished around for her crystal. She raised that overhead while fingering her beads, willing the crystal to shine.

The crystal began to glow.

Connecten soldiers trudged out of the darkness several minutes later. They were not happy. They would rather be sleeping somewhere warm. They were not, apparently, especially concerned about the welfare of the Widow. There were just a half dozen of them, far too few to invade Arngrere.

Socia controlled her anger. "If I have to do this over I will be one unhappy Countess." Next time there would be no fast and easy—though for now Stephan of Bley ought to suspect nothing more than mass desertion.

The soldiers did not recognize Socia. They did not believe she was who she claimed. Still, they were no more rude than they had to be. Socia kept the boys close as the soldiers moved them toward the Connecten camp. Ten minutes later they were inside a warm house, where some of Kedle's officers did recognize her.

Few were willing to believe that she was the real thing—even if she was a dead ringer for Socia of Antieux and had the Countess's country accent. They saw a trick by Anne of Menand.

"Weren't you warned that I would be opening the gate?"

Humprie of Belbois shook his fat head. "The Widow's friend, Lady Hope, advised us to watch the gate. We did. A band of deserters came out. We rounded them up."

The boy who understood the Connecten dialect stirred nervously.

Socia said, "The gate is open. The Arnhanders are huddled around their fires. Go round them up. Go liberate Kedle."

"I don't think that would be wise," a man said. "It has to be a trap."

"Where is Lady Hope? Get her in here."

"She went away after she told us we should watch the gate."

Socia could think of no way to convince these men. She became angry. She grabbed her crystal. She gripped the necklace with her other hand. "You *will* listen! You *will* believe! You *will* act now or your sons are going to grow up without an inheritance!"

Eyes got large. Men looked at one another, baffled. Then, one by one, they rose and did as they had been told, albeit as though sleep-walking. But then they began to believe. Soon Kedle's captains were bustling around like this was all their idea.

And then the newcomers were alone beside the fire with no company but one grizzled veteran nursing a deep arm wound.

The boy Socia could understand asked, "How did you do that, ma'am?"

"Magic."

THE INSTRUMENTALITY ARRIVED AN HOUR LATER, NOT IN HER MAD-dening form. "Where is everyone?"

"Gone to rescue Kedle."

"I thought thou hadst reserved that mission to thyself."

"I adjusted my goals. You did a bad job telling these idiots what was going to happen."

The Instrumentality shrugged. She did not care. "It is working out. I went to visit my aunts. There was shouting involved. I learned things of interest to thee and the Widow."

Socia thought it might not be long before the Instrumentality could converse like she belonged to the present century. She now used a modern sentence structure, in the main, along with fewer archaic verb forms. Of course, she clung to the antiquated second person. That might never go. That might be customary in her mother tongue.

Socia was vaguely aware that languages were in flux. Changes had begun with the fall of the Old Empire.

"Why am I thinking about that?" she asked herself, then realized that she had dozed off. "I'm sorry. I missed most of that. Exhaustion is catching up."

"Never mind. I will tell it again when the Widow gets here. I visited the ascendant who was trying to attract thy attention."

"That eagle just wanted my *attention*?"

"Yes. He was curious. It won't happen again."

That smelled like a cartload of goat dung, but Socia was not interested in the ascendant's motives if, in fact, he did stop chasing her. "That's good." She really did need some sleep.

"There. The conquest of Arngrere is complete. The villain Stephan hath been brought low and the Widow freed. She will be with us ere long."

Socia grunted and went to sleep. The last thing she saw was the amazement of the boys. They should be all right. Kedle's officers had not demanded an explanation of who they were. They were with her. And the Widow would be back soon.

Sleep felt good, especially so close to a hearty fire.

SOMEONE SHOOK SOCIA. SHE WAKENED. A SALLOW, WASTED KEDLE lay beside her, on a litter that had begun life as a low table. Socia stirred. The chair in which she had been sleeping was miserably hard. She was rested enough to complain. "Kedle?"

"It's me. Free. Thanks to thee. What the hell are you doing here?"

"I am a clever dancer." Which made no sense but she was still trying to wake up. "We could toss you back." She concealed her worry. Kedle looked awful. She was in pain. She had received little medical attention. Stephan of Bley had seen no need. The Widow would be burned after a quick show trial presided over by the Patriarch Serenity.

Would she walk again?

"I'm here, Kedle. You're free. These handsome young men were very helpful. Find them work that doesn't require them to use weapons. And talk to Lady Hope. Make her tell you what she really is."

"I already know, Socia. She can't really keep her mouth shut—if you're clever and give her a chance to brag."

The Connectens who entered Arngrere found fewer than forty men inside, none in a mood to fight. They had lost hope of seeing help from Anne of Menand.

Socia asked, "What now?"

"Now I eat. I sleep. I get used to the idea that I'm free again. Hope helps me heal. When I can I'll go after Anne's dogs again."

"You could end up dead, dear heart. Look at you now."

"I'll fight them till they put me down, Socia."

"Suppose you win?"

"Win?" That possibility, apparently, had not entered Kedle's mind.

"Talk to our supernatural friend. She has an interesting suggestion. Meantime, I need more sleep. Then I need to get back to Antieux. Guillemette could start thinking she's the real Countess."

SOCIA SETTLED ON THE ROOF OF THE ARCHIMBAULT ESTABLISHMENT. She found Kedle's father standing vigil. Raulet was vague, confused, and exhausted by anxiety. His grandson, little Raulet, had just brought him a light repast and heavy, bitter tea. The child was not awed by her shape change but was very interested in what he got to see before she clothed herself.

She impressed the elder Raulet as well.

The boy asked, "Did you see my mother?"

"I did. We got her away from the bad people. She's all right." Over his head she said, "She had a hard time. One leg was crushed when a horse fell on her. But she'll recover."

The old man's relief was palpable. He looked like he could die happy. Then he pulled himself together. "We need to get you back to the citadel. Guillemette and Escamerole can't go on pretending that you're sick."

"True. I need to get back into the fray. But not till I sleep for a couple of days."

"That won't happen. We were scared that you would be gone another day and miss your meeting with Queen Isabeth's envoys. Guillemette couldn't fake her way through that, even with the Master's help."

So Brother Candle was helping cover her absence. That crafty old busybody.

Socia wondered what that business about envoys meant but was too exhausted to pursue it. All she wanted was a swift transit to the comfort of her own bed.

She did spend a moment cautioning Archimbault. "The boy saw things he doesn't need to share with anyone. Can you control his tongue?"

"Of course, my Lady. Absolutely."

"You might do some forgetting of your own while you're at it."

"I'll never say a word. But I will cherish the memory." His smile was mischievous.

Socia snorted.

DESPITE HER DETERMINATION AND THAT OF ESCAMEROLE AND GUIL-lemette, Socia overslept. She was late to her audience with the Navay-ans. Neither Bernardin nor Brother Candle was able to stall the Queen's men.

The entire delegation was waiting, irritated, when Socia hustled in to join them. She had dressed in haste. Her toilet had been sketchy. She had not eaten. She looked like a woman who had clambered out of a sickbed to meet her obligations.

She halted several steps short of her formal audience seat. She had recognized one of the Queen's men, Hercule Jaume de Sedulla, Count of Arun Tetear, one of the most important Navayans and one of the Queen's favored generals.

The Count was not in charge, despite his exalted standing. The man who held that honor was Count Diagres Aplicova, Isabeth's clos-est confidant, advisor, and operative. Rumor suggested that he might have become more since King Peter's death. It was no secret that Apli-cova worshipped his Queen.

Isabeth's feelings were less well known. There had been no scandal while Peter lived.

Socia began to shiver. The presence of those men guaranteed that this would not be some pro forma scolding about provocative behav-ior. This was serious.

Though this was her court Socia was junior to both Direcian counts. She strained hard to avoid giving offense.

In particular, she prayed that she had done nothing to rouse the ire of the Queen, whose will was about to change her world. Her per-sonal war with Arnhand should not trouble Isabeth, though. Isabeth's Peter had yet to be avenged.

Brother Candle stayed close. He helped her seat herself once cere-mony allowed her to do so. His presence kept her focused. He whis-pered, "Stay calm. The news isn't bad."

Once everyone was in place Count Aplicova beckoned the Count of Tetear. Count Hercule stepped up, bent a knee, astonishing Socia. His outstretched palms presented a roll of fine parchment tied with a scarlet ribbon and sealed with wine-colored wax bearing the impress of the Navayan royal signet.

This would be something from the Queen herself. It might be written in her own hand. Isabeth was known for her penmanship and her willingness to show it off.

The Count and Brother Candle alike urged, "Open it. Read it."

Socia started to slide the ribbon off the tube of parchment. Brother Candle whispered, "Untie it."

Of course. Sliding the ribbon off the wrong end could bring bad luck.

She had not had contact enough with diplomacy to know its special superstitions.

She read the rescript while everyone waited expectantly. This could not be possible.

Raymone Garete had been named Duke of Khaurene, with the title to remain in his line. The Patriarch himself had agreed. The new Patriarch, not the devoted enemy hiding somewhere in Arnhand.

Socia did not know how to respond. The parchment slipped from her hand. She had trouble breathing. Her heart raced. She tried to ask for help but could not form words that made sense.

She thought she might be dying.

Consternation swept the chamber.

The Perfect got in front of her, talked to her, soothed her, did not cease blocking all else until calm reasserted itself.

She regained her breath. "Thank you, Master. That was such a huge shock."

THE OLD MAN FACED THE NAVAYAN COUNTS. "SHE'LL BE ALL RIGHT. That was too much of a shock in her weakened state."

Aplicova said, "It might have been wiser to send an informal advisory beforehand, but Her Majesty insisted the news be closely held."

"I understand." He surveyed the party behind the counts. He knew most of those men. "So large a delegation."

"Khaurene has operated without a Duke for some time. These are the men Her Majesty wanted to explain the state of affairs there." Aplicova sounded like he did not quite approve of Isabeth's thinking.

He might not. Among those the Perfect recognized were leaders from minority religious factions, senior guild officials, and Mas Crebet, consul again despite his less than savory past.

The Perfect asked, "How pressed for time are we? The Countess has fallen behind because of her indisposition. She will need time to make arrangements. Advance notice really would have been useful."

Aplicova said, "It's winter. Nothing is pressing. But the sooner assailed the sooner Khaurene will be tamed."

Ah. An angle hitherto unconsidered. Kedle and Socia were the sort to tame that fractious polity. "Of course. Socia? My Lady? Are you back with us?"

"I am, Master. Yes. I do not believe I've ever suffered such a grand shock."

"But a positive one this once. Yes?"

"Yes. Positive."

The old man wondered what all had happened way off in Arnhand. Socia must have seen some unhappy sights there.

He would not press. She would come to him when she was ready.

24. Alten Weinberg: St. Miniver, Martyr

What is this place?" Hecht asked.

He had been tangled in a dream featuring Helspeth and himself absent all constraints, with all the time they wanted, and no one would ever know. Then he wakened, paradise gone sudden as a candle snuffed. He was in a big place where the ceiling was lost in shadow. There were limestone pillars. A rack of votive candles stood to his left.

A church. The only light came from the candles. Those had not been lighted by Chaldareans presenting special appeals. Every candle was aflame.

Hecht was surrounded by Shining Ones.

Hourli said, "Aldi will be here soon."

Hecht's mind cleared. He was seated on the marble bench occupied by the assisting priest when he had no active role during services. He asked, "What is this?"

"This is the chapel where you and your lover will meet. It should be the last place anyone will look for you. We have time to talk."

Hecht suffered an absurd urge to defend his conduct toward Helspeth. No defense was necessary. He had done the right thing.

"For the wrong reasons," Hourli said. "You aren't controlled by your conscience. You just don't want to get caught. You would be here with her every night if you believed the secret would stay safe. But you know that nothing happens in a vacuum. That someone always knows. If that someone said anything to someone else, the scandal would be loose."

Yes. That was why he did not surrender to the endless aching beat of his desire. People would be hurt. People for whom he cared.

Hourli said, "But that is incidental. For now."

The scrutiny of the Shining Ones intensified. They leaned in slightly. "You have me at a disadvantage."

"Possibly. We brought you here because it has been impossible to talk otherwise. When I do get to see you there are constant interruptions. It's irksome."

"It is frustrating. When you're in charge everyone wants some of your time. Usually, they want it right now."

"And that is why we have stolen time. We can handle our business without you missing much sleep."

That caused smirks. Must be an inside joke.

Hecht understood. It was obvious enough. Those candles were not flickering. Shadows refused to dance.

The Shining Ones had stopped time. Almost. It moved on at an imperceptible pace. An observer outside the time bubble would see nothing because those inside would be moving too fast.

Hourli nodded slightly. "Close enough. It takes a great deal of power to manage this, Commander. We can do so only a short while."

"Then talk to me."

"We have been as industrious as ants, preparing for your spring campaign. You will find the weather clement most of the time. Most of the roads will be in good shape. Princes and nobles will be well disposed and helpful, so long as you treat them well in turn. We got started too late to improve last year's harvests but the spring lambing, kidding, and calving will be the best in living memory. Most of the ewes and cows will drop twins. Mares will foal well and camels will calve better than usual but twinning won't be common."

The Commander of the Righteous tried to encompass the possibility that nature itself could be enlisted in the Enterprise of Peace and Faith.

Hourli said, "Everything we do for you will profit us twofold."

He did not see that. He did not understand how his fortunes could shape those of the divinities. He still had trouble seeing the Shining Ones as more than revenant demons.

Hourli told him, "Our rescue simply released us into the larger prison of the middle world. In that we now live under sentence of death, as mortal as you are, though over a longer span. Dear Eavijne has done her best. She found an auspicious place to plant her seeds. The rest of us brought our brightest magic to bear. But the seedlings in this orchard will be shadows of those of the Great Sky Fortress. Their fruit will help, we hope, till we can open a way into Eucereme. The trees will grow strong and true there."

Had the Aelen Kofer sealed the doorways between all the worlds, or just those to the Realm of the Gods? Evidently the former, at least for now.

Hecht considered Hourli's remark about nothing happening in a vacuum. Did that apply to the gods as well?

He intuited that the gods in Eucereme were aware of the situation in the middle world. They would want to open doorways, too. They would want to enjoy Eavijne's apples, too.

Hourli said, "We need not share details but we have discovered ways that we can prosper here, despite the weakening wells of power. Moving with you to your Holy Lands will be part of that. In time, we could return to being major gods again."

"But for that you need healthy apples."

"We do, yes, to make it last."

"And my God, or any of our gods today, don't concern you?"

"They do not. Their very nature makes them no threat."

"But! . . ."

"Your God is everywhere. He sees everything. For those things to be true he gave up the ability to be all-powerful wherever that suited. Once we left the world, and others like us did the same, he needed only be a god who listened and comforted and meddled in small ways, locally. He spread himself out so he could be in touch with every worshipper all the time. Now it would take him an age just to understand that he needed to pull himself back together, then another age to do it. So we're free to do as we like. All of our divine jeopardy comes from those great primal things that were here before our own advent. With your sister as an ally we destroyed the worst of those. But another, that we do not know, is stirring in a far place called Andesqueluz; Asher, the Mountain, who was *the* god in that land before the appearance of any of the gods of today. And those, it seems, are all aspects of a son of Asher once connected with wind, thunder, and storms, who was unpredictable and frequently unpleasant."

"None too smart, either."

"Yes. The son of Asher shared many of Red Hammer's less endearing traits. Less so, these days, diffused, of course." She went on, "Spring will come early and remain cool. You will have an extra ten days to get started. Snow melts will not be catastrophic, despite the heavy falls this winter. They will proceed slowly and steadily. The rivers you need to use or cross will never run too swiftly or too high."

A flicker where nothing changed made Hecht glance to his left.

Aldi had come straight from her day job as every lad's fantasy. He felt a stirring himself. He wondered if different men saw different Aldis.

Aldi had nothing to say. She just nodded to Hourli. Hourli told Hecht, "Things are in motion. Our endgames begin."

Which meant what?

No matter what the Shining Ones contributed, Piper Hecht was not prepared to trust them fully.

Hourli did something with her hands. Her fingers became ropes of smoke. In a moment she was holding a fat candle a foot long that appeared to be purest beeswax. "A gift for you and your Empress. Light it and time will stop for you as it has for us here. Those whose attentions you fear will not realize how long you have been missing. Employ it carefully. You will still age while it burns. It will last a long time but not forever. There won't be another." She placed the candle in his hands. It was massive. It had to weigh more than ten pounds.

Hourli smiled a small smile. Hecht thought it might be the very smile the Adversary wore when he presented an irresistible temptation.

"Enjoy, Commander of the Righteous."

HECHT WAKENED IN HIS OWN BED. HE DID NOT REMEMBER HIS TRANsition to the chapel, nor his return. He had a headache. It was dark out still but breakfast smells came from the next room. He heard Carava de Bos talking to somebody who sounded like Titus Consent. Hecht clambered out of bed, hunger driving him.

Consent and de Bos, yes, making free with breakfast foods as they chattered. Their conversation was animated but did not register. Hecht settled into a chair where the steward was already filling a platter.

"And why are you two here? Especially you, Titus. I sent you to command a line company at Hochwasser but here you are, underfoot again."

"One of your odd female friends woke me up last night. She gave me this." He tapped a stack of papers half a foot thick. "I read a few pages, decided they were crazy to bring the stuff to me, had a horse readied, and got my ass down here in time to catch Carava going on shift."

De Bos said, "Carava read a few pages and decided we should be here to share your breakfast."

"What have we got?"

De Bos said, "Based on the pages I skimmed, transcripts of meetings

between people involved in plots against you, the Empress, one another, and the Enterprise. Lots and lots of plots. The third sheet down
got me all wet. It tells us where to find Race Buchels and Willem
Schimel."

"Really?" Even the Ninth Unknown had been unable to find those
would-be Hecht killers. Schimel had masterminded the attack that had
seen Hecht die and be resurrected. "I'd like to sit down with those two."

Hecht chose a random page. He held it in his left hand while he
ate.

He had drawn the record of a conversation between Helspeth's
uncles. Clearly, they meant their pledge to give Helspeth the support
they had failed to provide Katrin. They were scheming to rid their
Empress of an Elector she and the Commander believed reliable.

"Good stuff," Hecht muttered, never questioning the facts. He did
not doubt the Shining Ones in that.

"Earthshaking stuff," de Bos said.

"Who else knows?"

Titus pointed. "But only that it's really important."

Hecht stared at the steward, who had come with the Still-Patter
house. The man froze.

The Commander said, "I think we can control this potential leak."

De Bos nodded. "I'll make sure." At which point the steward began to protest.

"Of course it's unreasonable," Hecht told him. "But something is
going on and I don't want you talking about it to your wife, your
brother, your best friend, your confessor, or anybody else."

The steward protested that he would do no such thing, that he
knew better, that he never talked about work when he left the house.

"I don't believe you. You talk to somebody about things you
shouldn't. You all do."

Titus presented a couple of sheets from high in the pile, chapter
and verse about the household staff, including the steward. None of
the staffers were spies. But they all had talked to somebody about
something, never thinking of that as a violation of security.

Hecht read briefly, aloud. The steward's eyes widened. "Now, who
do you suppose she told?" He did not have that information. His point
had gone home. "Titus. Send word to your number one to take over
your company. I need you here. Start by talking to all these people who
don't think they're doing anything wrong. Convince them of the error
of their ways." After scanning only a random few pages he knew that
he and Helspeth had some serious housework to do. "Carava, you and

Vircondelet drop everything else and focus on this stack. Identify and number each page. Make a separate synopsis. Tell me about anything that needs immediate action. Buhle Smolens hasn't had enough to do lately. Pile your current work on him. Sedlakova, too. And Brokke, when he gets back. Have we heard from him lately?"

De Bos replied, "Not for several days. Last report had him at the Arnhander frontier being cranky because there was nobody there to meet him. The King's mother was busy with raiders out of the Connec. Brokke said he was going to go on, cautiously."

"He should probably try harder to keep us posted."

De Bos and Consent both gave him a hard stare.

"All right. I see." He had espoused the philosophy of giving a man a job, then getting out of the way, for as long as he had been less than the man who was ultimately in charge. He had waxed quite bitter about the waste of time and manpower needed to run messages to people far from the head of the spear, whose input could not possibly do anything but make things more difficult for the men doing the actual, everyday work.

"All right. Suggestion withdrawn. We have plenty to do here." But he did understand the other side now, some. "We'll need to screen my appointments more tightly. I want to push this . . ."

Consent said, "Boss, don't change anything. Let us deal. That's our job. You aren't a worker bee anymore. Your role is to be the lightning rod for everybody who thinks they should be able to use us. Just go right on having fun doing that."

Titus was right. And Hecht did not like it. "I'm wondering if it's too late to fire you."

"Probably." Consent chuckled. He beckoned the steward. "You can take this stuff away, now, Maxillan."

THE MEETING WITH THE EMPRESS AND HER ADVISORS STRETCHED INTERminably. Several councilors were blatantly obstructionist in their efforts to extort concessions. Helspeth was, after all, only a woman. She did not have that much strength behind her—though every one of those men quelled under Hecht's glare.

Hecht was patient. He contributed little. He refused the bait when challenged to offer assurances no commander could provide before a campaign. Each time someone came at him directly he responded with a knowing smile that left them uncomfortable.

The Shining Ones made it sound like the entire Chaldarean world was excited about liberating the Holy Lands. Even in the Connec commoners and nobles alike were finding money and men to contribute. In Arnhand, despite the flood of specie that had gone away since the advent of Anne of Menand, they were raising noble companies of dedicated adventurers. Inside the Grail Empire the folk seethed with eagerness. Many of the nobility remained oblivious to that. They seemed interested only in locking horns with the Grail Throne while it was occupied by a woman with no strong man coming up behind her.

Hecht stood. "I would like to request a recess, Your Majesty. And permission to approach with intelligence recently received. Intelligence I will share with the Council following the recess."

Helspeth was tired of the bickering, too. "One hour, gentlemen." She rose, ignoring all protests. "Lord Arnmigal. Follow me." She left the council chamber. Lifeguards and ladies-in-waiting scurried. Helspeth went straight to the closest quiet room. She let no one in but Hecht. She was rude to one dowager who said something about propriety.

To Hecht's consternation Helspeth threw herself against him the instant the door clicked shut. "This isn't what I had in mind."

"You did. But you didn't expect it to happen."

He extricated himself reluctantly. "We'll see about that later."

"Always business first. What is it?"

"You have been tasking me about my intelligence crew not producing."

"We never see them. They don't seem to be doing anything."

"This morning they delivered a six-hundred-page stack of reports. The detail boggles. There are minutes of scores of conspiratorial gatherings, many featuring some of those men out there. I brought a representative sample." He pulled the sheets from beneath his shirt.

She had not stepped back when he peeled her off. Now she turned away but leaned back against him while she read. He did not push her off. In fact, he discovered his arms around her, his hands clasped. He felt her anger build.

"Is this stuff credible?"

"It is."

"How could anyone get that close?"

"You know who they are."

"I didn't really believe it. I have to, now."

"I'll never tell you anything but the truth."

"That might not always be smart, love." She turned. They kissed.

ALGRES DREAR AND A DOZEN BRAUNSKNECHTS ENTERED AND LINED the walls. The councilors eyed them nervously.

Helspeth announced, "I am going to read from an intelligence report. Captain Drear, I am not to be interrupted."

Drear clicked his heels and bowed.

Helspeth read from the record of a meeting that had taken place eight days earlier. Four men now present had participated, two of whom had made a great, mocking show of firmly supporting the new Empress. Subjects discussed had included the possibility of ridding the world of the Commander of the Righteous to facilitate the subsequent deposition of "that Ege chit."

The truth was made obvious by the ghastly pallor of the conspirators.

Algres Drear kept order, though he faced no real challenge. None of those men were prepared to fight his Braunsknechts.

Hecht could almost hear the conspirators thinking the Imperial lifeguard would have to be disbanded once the Ege chit went.

Interestingly, Ferris Renfrow had come in with the returning recess crowd. He made certain his presence was noticed. Too, Hourli, in frumpy middle-aged form, blocked the main exit. Hecht was sure she was recognized as his new head spy.

Helspeth said, "Graf fon Gerilein. This conversation took place in your home. Care to comment? Without bluster or wasting time denying the facts?"

The Graf shook his head, conceding that he was well and truly caught.

Helspeth polled the other conspirators. None cared to comment.

"The Ege chit is not pleased. There are more of these transcripts. Hundreds of pages. Here is one that pleases the Ege chit even less. It is a blatant praise of treason." She read.

Then she read from several other reports. Finally, she asked, "Have I made my point? You didn't hear *your* plot mentioned? I have six hundred more pages to examine. Should you feel a need to know if your own flirtation with treason is on record, consult the intelligence arm of the Righteous." She paused, glared. Men began to shift nervously. "The answer will be yes. Your villainy is known. Now that you know that I know, we can wipe the slate. I will take no action on any of these reports, however foul the crimes contemplated. A new era begins. This is now One Empire ruled by One Will. Future bad behavior will not be tolerated."

Hecht killed a frown. She was being too dramatic. From now on the worst of them would make sure they spoke no treason outside the tightest quiet rooms.

Hecht immediately wondered what more clever and dangerous plots had been hatched by smarter conspirators, protected by quiet rooms.

Helspeth scanned the chamber. She made eye contact with the cream of the Imperial nobility. "Again. A new start. The function of this gathering is to finalize mobilization of the Empire for the Enterprise of Peace and Faith. To which I say, to you, join in or not, as it pleases you. Do not obstruct. Be part of the process or stand aside from it. If you get in the way, I will trample you."

She was in an Ege mood, now. They had best have the wit to listen.

Again, Hecht thought the villains would just be more careful. A tiger could not help being a tiger.

Helspeth called for his readiness report.

He had little to say that interested those people. It was not political. He did lock gazes with known villains while he talked.

It would be interesting, watching them squirm in Helspeth Ege's new New Brothen Empire.

LADY HILDA DAEDEL DRIFTED BETWEEN PILLARS TO HECHT'S LEFT, A wisp of white departing, pretending not to see him, pretending she was not a party to what might be about to happen. Her presence unnerved him, though it was expected. That Helspeth had managed to get out unencumbered by Algres Drear was a testament to her cleverness.

The pattern of the women coming here for prayers had been set. St. Miniver's remained a holy place. The few who visited it told no one. They did not want it swamped.

Visits by the Empress and her women were no longer a matter for speculation, though some gossips wondered if Lady Hilda might not be connecting with one of her several lovers.

Hecht was more concerned about other eyes.

How could the Shining Ones *not* be watching? Or Ferris Renfrow? Or the Ninth Unknown? Or Heris or Vali or Lila. Any of them could be on to him.

His feet refused to turn back.

Yes. Those perfidious feet.

There she was, kneeling before the altar. A few votive candles burned to either hand. Her simple white gown matched the one Lady Hilda wore. For an instant he worried that Daedel meant to lure him into her tender snare. But, no, Hilda was neither that slim, that tall, nor that blond.

He stepped up on Helspeth's left, dropped to a knee in respect to the altar, then stepped to the votive candles. Only a handful were burning tonight. He used one to fire the massive candle given him by Hourli.

Time stopped everywhere but inside a circle ten feet across. He saw dust motes, illuminated by the candles, hanging motionless. The flames of the candles and their rising smoke had gone still.

Helspeth, shaking, took his right hand in her left. He said, "This doesn't have to happen."

"Oh, yes. It does. I've waited years too long already. I knew under the walls of al-Khazen. Every day since has been wasted." She went on shaking. This was a momentous choice.

"This is treason, under the law. Even for you."

"Stop talking." She faced him. The hunger in her seemed a beast looking out of the drowning-pools of her eyes. She had been working herself up for hours.

He knew it was too late. Rational thinking would not intercede. What was about to happen between one man and one woman could impact the lives of millions. Empires might stumble because two people could not help being a man and a woman.

Helspeth asked, "What just happened?"

Hecht explained about the candle.

Her face filled with wonder. "Our God would never be so kind. And . . . oh! We have all the time we want. It doesn't have to be like vermin hastily coupling."

"No."

The cost to Hourli's candle was imperceptible when Hecht snuffed it. He stared at it like it was a magical artifact from a fairy story that would, in the end, become the bane of the lovers who had defied the natural order. He could not help thinking of Arlensul, Gedanke, and Ferris Renfrow.

He and Helspeth had said everything that needed saying, and had shared all the final tender moments, before he silenced the flame. When it went out Helspeth appeared to be praying while the Commander of the Righteous rose from a briefer stint of worship. A watcher might sense an instant of dislocation but nothing to stir suspicion.

Hecht went away, neither looking back nor turning back. He glimpsed Lady Hilda amongst the pillars, maybe sneaking back to peek.

Hecht thought he would lie awake for hours in a grim feud with his conscience. Not so. He fell asleep the instant his head hit his pillow.

HECHT WAS NOT YET DRESSED WHEN CARAVA DE BOS BROUGHT A stack of papers. He was troubled. "Can we talk, Boss?"

"Sure. What's all this?"

"More news from your spy lady. Mostly boring, but you need to know."

"So you wanted what?"

"An honest answer. Are you all right?"

"I'm fine. Why shouldn't I be?"

"You seem awfully tired lately. And your lifeguards keep complaining about you sneaking out at night."

"Carava, I don't sneak. The Empress and I meet in her chapel for evening prayers. That gives us a few minutes when nobody is clamoring for our attention. She's properly chaperoned, usually by Lady Hilda Daedel but sometimes by another lady of the court."

They had wrung special enjoyment from sinning vigorously under the nose of Lady Delta va Kelgerberg.

"Even so, you *must* stop giving your lifeguards the slip. Don't become overconfident because your strange friends are rooting out all these conspiracies. They can't read minds."

"What?"

"There must be hundreds of people who wouldn't shed a tear if an assassin nailed you. There may be dozens willing to try. What happens if a loner decides to take a crack? He could be watching you right now. When would he be most likely to strike?"

"You're right again. And you know how I hate it when any of you are right about stuff like that."

"Just you letting people look out for you is good enough for me."

Hecht grunted, pulled the new reports closer, skimmed the first. Whoever recorded it had a wonderfully readable hand.

"Sir?"

"You still here?"

"I am. There is another matter."

Hecht felt defensive immediately, for no discernable reason. De Bos said, "And here we have the further problem."

"Carava? *The* further problem?"

"You seeming to be different men at different times."

Hecht felt deep discomfort immediately. For no reason he was ready to fight de Bos. He stifled the reaction. "Explain."

"You seem tired all the time."

That would be Helspeth's fault. Every assignation stretched a little longer. How did she manage her prolonged days?

"You've started nodding off during meetings. When you wake up it's like you're a different man, determined to get things done, fast and right the first time."

"Excuse me? That's unlike me, how?"

"The you with me right now wants to figure people out. He wants to understand. He wants to talk about things. He wants to form consensus. The other you cares about none of that. The other you tells us how it's going to be, accepts no excuses, and always guesses right. The other you is a dictator who is frightfully efficient. This you wants to *convince* people that they should do things your way."

"Carava, I'm wondering what you have been drinking this morning."

"The other you wouldn't care. The other you would have tossed me out with some potent admonition about wasting time."

"This one is about to give you a whack upside the head."

"The other you would use his left hand." De Bos made his exit.

Hecht stood leaning forward, unmoving, for a dozen seconds. That remark had been a hammer blow. But why?

He stared at his left hand.

25. Lucidia: Living and Dead

Nassim Alizarin and a half-dozen hardy veterans reached Shamramdi at sunset, to no welcome. Nassim had been summoned. The Great Shake wanted to know why the crusaders no longer faced a challenge in the gap once commanded by Tel Moussa.

Nassim had an answer. Indala might not accept it but he would stand by it. He had done remarkably well with what he had been given. He had been bested by a determined enemy, nature, and the indifference of those who were supposed to support him.

Nassim Alizarin was angry. He felt that he had been betrayed.

News of his arrival ran ahead. Azim al-Adil ed-Din materialized. He told Nassim, "If Uncle's summons has you worried, don't be. It isn't your effort that he wants to review."

The Mountain was not prepared to believe that. Neither did he argue. "Good to see you again, youngster. I don't expect to be here long. I hope we can find a few moments for one another."

Young Az was as fond of the old wolf as the General was of him. They were kindred spirits looking at life from its nether ends.

The youth led Nassim to the house he had occupied before. "A messenger, probably me, will come when Indala is ready."

And so it was.

*   *   *

Nassim Alizarin and Indala al-Sul Halaladin faced one another across a low table burdened with shelled nuts, fruits, and some
spicy shredded lamb. No one else was present. Indala's own brothers
made sure that there were no eavesdroppers.

The General did not stint. "I haven't eaten this well since the last
time I visited."

Indala inclined his head in response to the implied gratitude.
"Your due, General. You haven't been afforded any opportunity to
live well, for which I apologize." He meant that in a limited and dip-
lomatic sense. The behavior of his people toward Nassim had dishon-
ored him.

"You are most gracious." Nassim understood Indala's position.

"Azer tells me you brought documents."

"The daily logs from Tel Moussa. I understand that you're impatient with such things. I ask only that you have a reliable reader report
their gist. My scribe was not Sha-lug. He wrote in the Lucidian script,
which I do not read well, so I present his record on faith. The man
came here with me should you wish to talk to him."

The Great Shake smiled. Nassim thought that might be hard work.
Indala's wounds still troubled him more than he cared to admit.

Indala said, "Present the basic argument. Be as neutral as you can."

Nassim told his story, actually downplaying the lack of support he
had received.

"These journals will say the same, in finer detail?"

"Yes."

"So. What now?"

"Me? When you're done with me I'll go back to my band of survivors. I'll release the men who don't want to roam the haunted desert
with a crazy old man. The rest of us, with the Ansa, will hunt and kill
the Dreangerean sorcerer."

Indala was startled, confused, and inclined to disbelieve.

Nassim observed, "Lately it seems that no one who is not Sha-lug
understands who we are or what we really believe. I've been away so
long that I'm no longer sure myself."

Nassim could barely admit to himself that Bone's report had produced a disappointment more painful than his wife's rejection. Bone
had not found one senior Sha-lug who wondered if the Mountain would
be interested in becoming Marshall. Bone had not asked anyone. Nassim had not asked Bone to do so. But it was clear that the idea had not
occurred to anyone in al-Qarn.

Not long ago no one but Gordimer the Lion had been more hon-ored. The Mountain was old history today.

Letting himself be imposed on the Sha-lug by Indala would have been a greater travesty than he had imagined.

Indala sipped tea. Then, "That is true. I have no idea what moves the Sha-lug. I beat them on the battlefield but still they . . ."

Nassim pretended to miss Indala's frustrated intensity. "They don't see themselves as defeated, only as betrayed."

Indala consulted his tea, then said, "I see. The desertions of the Maxtreans and Arianist Chaldareans."

"Exactly."

"I see your need to deal with the monster in the Idiam. You were faithful at Tel Moussa, beyond reasonable expectation. I had to re-strain Azer, threatening him with discipline, he was so distraught over what he perceived as deliberate sabotage. Privately, I think there is some merit to his accusations. Some who were supposed to support you behaved badly. Possibly there was corruption. If that proves to have . . . They will be sent to greet Tsistimed's sons in the land be-tween the rivers."

"You might want to reflect on that."

"Meaning?"

"Would you want such men out in front in a struggle with the Hu'n-tai At?"

Another silence. Indala did reflect. "You're right, General. I might be better served by keeping them close."

"Yes."

"So. I did not bring you here to criticize you. You did well. The damage to Gherig was extensive. You could have taken it had you had the troops I thought you had. Were I healthy enough I would hit the crusaders now, myself. They have only a few dozen able men."

"Send Azim."

That startled Indala.

"He's ready. Or, if not, this would be a good time to discover his limitations. Before the crusader flood arrives."

"You think well of the boy."

"I do. He is the man I would choose to succeed you."

The Great Shake withdrew inside himself. He came forward again to say, "You see with a clear eye. I, too, love the boy. I have kept him away from the worst dangers."

"You unleashed him during the Great Campaign."

"It may have looked that way from a distance. That was more

show than substance. Men who expected to be hammered by the Shalug pushed Azim out front to take the blame for the defeat."

Nassim sighed. How did civilization advance when so many men wasted so much time trying to embarrass one another?

"I'll think about that, General. Meantime, ask what you will for your monster hunt."

"I need food, not just for my men but for the Ansa. The tribal peoples have made common cause against the sorcerer. He has done them considerable evil, poisoning wells and savaging already meager flocks and herds. He wants the Idiam to be his. Peoples who have dwelt there since the time before time he means to drive out."

"Those are people who bring the wrath of others down upon themselves."

"He invaded their country, not they his. And he showed up behaving badly. That was my fault. I ambushed him. I killed his men and animals. I wounded him. The Ansa say he still has some paralysis on his left side."

"He's vulnerable, then."

"He is. I will exploit it."

"Food, then, will be provided. What else? More men?"

"I have the men. Unless you want to loan me those obstructionists. No. Not more men. Just a lot of what men need. Horses. Camels. Sheep. Cattle. Goats. Flour for the men and grain for the beasts. Water. Tack and equipment. A physician. Weapons for the Ansa. Ammunition for everyone. Firepowder. Lots and lots of firepowder. Only firepowder weapons can end the saga of the Rascal." And, appropriately, round full circle, for er-Rashal had been first to make those weapons work reliably enough to take into the field.

"Firepowder is more dear than silver these days, General. Half of what existed east of the White Sea went up that night at Gherig."

"God had a good laugh then."

Indeed.

Madouc of Hoeles had begun smuggling firepowder there the moment he reached Gherig. He had seen its capabilities at Arn Bedu. He had planned a similar surprise for Tel Moussa, unaware that his opponent had understood the lesson of Arn Bedu as well.

One of Abu's mines had ignited Madouc's poorly designed powder magazine. The shock wave shook Tel Moussa off its foundations.

A cosmic jest, the Unbeliever triumphing in that long contest by virtue of having suffered an incalculable disaster.

Indala said, "You will be given what you need, I promise. Water, though, will be problematic. And firepowder will be more so."

"I have a suggestion about the water. Assign us to the outpost at al-Pinea."

"I don't know that place."

"West of here, and somewhat to the south, in the foothills, is a small spring called al-Pinea. It was once an Antast Chaldarean monastery, built on the ruins of a fort from Imperial times. That guarded the eastern end of a road through the Idiam. Al-Pinea derives from a Rhûnish name."

"You embarrass me, Nassim Alizarin. I didn't know this place existed."

"You have larger issues to attend. The garrison, never more than twelve strong, is always old men meeting their annual obligations by going there to pretend to be fierce warriors. It's an easy post. The mountain road isn't much used."

Indala considered his folded hands, frowning.

"Shake, that spring would be priceless to the Ansa. And al-Pinea is a fine place to deliver my supplies. A slow caravan can get there from here in two or three days."

"How long will the hunt take?"

"The rest of my life."

"It's that sort of mission now, then? And the coming war?"

"I'm not likely to be much use there. I've failed at every task I've been given since Hagid died. But I'm determined not to fail at this. In Hagid's memory."

Indala grunted. Nassim was not sure what that meant.

A minute of silence passed. Then the Great Shake said, "It will be as you suggest. I ask again, though: can you finish before the crusaders arrive?"

"I can try. A promise will be of no value. The Rascal will have his own say."

Indala did not disagree.

"In any event, what can Nassim Alizarin do to stem that flood? *If* it does materialize?"

Many of the Faithful doubted that the Unbeliever could organize sufficiently.

"You underestimate yourself, General. Be that as it may, however, it is time to part. This old corpse has reached its limit. Go. Al-Pinea is yours, along with whatever you need to crush the sorcerer. Before the coming of the Unbeliever, please."

Nassim expressed his gratitude and got out.

THE MOUNTAIN DID NOT SEE YOUNG AZ AGAIN BEFORE HE DEPARTED Shamramdi. The Great Shake pulled the boy out of circulation.

*   *   *

NASSIM LEFT SHAMRAMDI A TIRED OLD MAN, BUT HOPEFUL. HE HAD fared better than expected with Indala, though the Great Shake had wakened no new inspiration, nor had he sparked any spiritual renewal.

Which thought left Nassim slightly embarrassed. Indala was a warrior, not a religious thinker.

The men who rode with the Mountain supposed his interview had gone badly. They gave him room to be alone with his despair.

26. Arnhand: Harsh Encounters

The Widow and three hundred fifty men who worshipped her emerged unexpectedly from a forest in the northern Roessen. The Widow rode in a litter. Counts vied for the honor of bearing her.

Dawn was breaking. The Vindicated attacked immediately. The surprise was complete. Those Vindicated who recalled the massacre of Antieux, not so many years ago, meant to murder every man, woman, child, animal, and blade of grass that constituted Mestlé. Anne of Menand had sown the whirlwind. Harvest time had come.

The Widow was outnumbered three to one. Those odds did not daunt her. She rolled across Anne's estate like a flood. She left dead everywhere, few of them Vindicated.

The Widow told her champions, "Today the world changes. Arnhand without Anne to whip it on will be just another impotent Chaldarean kingdom wracked by internal squabbling."

Lady Hope, unseen, assured success. In little more than an hour the Vindicated killed four hundred and captured as many more. A dozen structures were fired. Vindicated not in direct contact with Anne's people began systematically destroying everything. Mestlé would become a desert.

Lady Hope roamed the outskirts, making sure no one important escaped.

The Queen Mother tried treating with the Vindicated. The deposed Patriarch made an effort of his own. Neither had any luck.

Lady Hope discovered soldiers approaching from the east. She leapt to an unfortunate conclusion. They were not Vindicated so they must be friends of the besieged. Hastily collected troops rushed to meet them, intending only to scare the newcomers off while the Widow finished Anne and Serenity, now cowering in a stone watchtower from ancient times.

The newcomers did not scare. The Vindicated assailed them, and encountered something outside their experience—massed falcon fire laid down by professionals. Chastened, the survivors fell back to lick their wounds. The newcomers improved their position systematically, using their firepowder weapons to perfect advantage.

The Vindicated were using their own three falcons to hammer the watchtower, where Anne and Serenity now believed that rescue was at hand.

Hope erred by assailing the newcomers herself before determining who they were. She got a quick, sharp awakening. These men had dealt with revenant gods before.

In deep pain, stunned, she fled. Out of range, she consulted her intellect at last.

Those men yonder could not be Anne's friends. They had to be the Righteous. No other force could have bloodied the Vindicated with such composure.

Still hurting, Hope found the Widow. Kedle was in a frustrated rage because her leg left her able to do nothing but observe. "What is it, Hope? You look awful."

"I have made a huge mistake yonder. Those men haven't come to rescue Anne. They are Prince Anselin and a lifeguard from the Righteous. I may have started a war with people who weren't our enemies."

Kedle's pain made it hard to focus. "Not our enemies?"

"They weren't before, though they would not have been allies, either. Now, I don't know. It could turn ugly."

Kedle pushed her pain down into the place she had created for it, with Hope's help. It would not go away indefinitely, but it might stay there long enough to let her deal with this rationally. "Go back. Stop the fighting. Find their commander. Make our situation clear. They may be after Anne themselves."

The Instrumentality said, "I understand."

"Don't let them hurt you any more."

"Thee can count on that. I am permitted to make peace, am I not?"

Kedle nodded. "Go. Be craven if you have to. Promise them anything but get them out of the action."

Lady Hope did not appreciate that attitude. Still, "I will do what is needful. I must caution thee. Thee must do nothing to give further offense. The Righteous enjoy the protection of my aunts."

Pain helped Kedle restrain her excitement. "The Commander of the Righteous used to be Captain-General. His army razed the Connec."

"And he was there, watching, at the time of the Massacre. But now he is neither. I warn thee, even a malicious glance his way will bring my aunts down upon thee. Be content."

Kedle heard fear. "Hope?"

"They are here, Kedle. There may be others watching, too. The Bastard, almost certainly. For the next few hours thee and I must be extremely circumspect. Go root thine enemies out of their hide. I will placate the Righteous."

Kedle suspected that her obsessions had led her into something bigger than her private war. Today was not just another black pearl on the strand of incidents defining her rush toward self-destruction.

Not since leaving Antieux had she thought beyond her next chance to vent her rage. She had thought little about her children, her parents, or that maddening old Perfect who had infested her life since she was a toddler. Recollections surfaced. Being invited, at just thirteen, to speak to a gathering of Maysaleans. Her wedding. The birth of Raulet, that had taken so long and had been so painful, yet had seemed so wondrous once they laid the baby at her breast. Loosing the shaft that had killed the King of Arnhand. Putting aside the grim fury that made her the Widow, in deepest secret, to lie in the embrace of her demonic consort . . .

Should the Society for the Suppression of Sacrilege and Heresy ever catch her she would be one prisoner whose guilt they could not exaggerate.

A runner's arrival scattered her dark reverie.

"Ma'am, the Whore of Menand wants to parlay."

"Again?" There was a great deal of silence. No falcons bellowed. Trumpets had nothing to say. Nor were there cries or screams from the dying, man or animal.

Amazing.

How long could this last?

"Show me the way." Though there was no point. That woman would never recognize the truth of her situation.

LADY HOPE LACKED NO CONFIDENCE. SHE WAS WHAT SHE WAS. IN THIS instance, though, with the old women of the Shining Ones watching, she had few options. She had no room for fun. Nor did she want to make trouble for Kedle. She needed Kedle's angry Connectens.

She could not adequately credit the changes in the world. What the Shining Ones wanted to be true no longer signified. Only what middle-world mortals believed was relevant now.

The Vindicated and Righteous stopped fighting. Bruised, stunned, the Vindicated withdrew to defensive positions. The Righteous maintained contact without combat, trying to get a better understanding of the situation.

Good. Their anger did not control them.

Lady Hope became young Aldi, with the sensuality constrained, a pretty girl lost and distressed but bearing up bravely. She strode toward the Righteous, who had moved into a field disposition resembling no military formation of the Instrumentality's experience. The danger was as sharp as it had been those first few minutes out of captivity in the Great Sky Fortress. Death was a single misstep away.

She did her best to appear unthreatening.

She still hurt, when she let that impinge on her consciousness.

A man came to meet her, cautiously. Light falcons with long barrels backed him, positioned to fire past him.

They knew what she was. They were ready.

Men yelled at someone to get back to his place in the line. A boy charged forward. Aldi reached out so she could eavesdrop.

The boy told the man, "She knows me. We can talk."

"Yeah? You being the Commander's kid, I'm not even going to ask you how."

Aldi did recall the boy from the Great Sky Fortress. She would play to him, but carefully.

Man and boy halted where falcon fire would remain a serious argument. Aldi focused on what was going on behind her.

Anne of Menand's request for a parlay had failed. The Widow would accept nothing less than unconditional surrender.

The boy said, "Hello, Aldi. You look pale this morning. Why did you attack us?"

The man seemed content to let the boy talk. Ah, yes. Hagen Brokke. One of Piper Hecht's less famous captains.

"I made a grotesque mistake, Pella. I apologize profoundly. Serenity, Henri of Mariscot, Anne of Menand, and their dearest henchmen are trapped in that watchtower back there. When I heard that soldiers were coming I assumed it was a rescue attempt. I should have made sure beforehand. I hope thy casualties were few."

Brokke said, "The damage was all yours."

"We have been punished for our stupidity, then. Can we put it behind us?"

Brokke said, "We can. But we need to understand what we each would like to accomplish."

"Thy mission would be?"

"To bring Arnhand's new King safely to his throne. We hoped he could deal with his mother today."

Aldi said, "We will capture Anne of Menand and Serenity. We will end their boundless malice toward the Connec."

Pella asked, "What will you do once you have them?"

"That choice belongs to the Widow and the Countess of Antieux. I do not expect either will be overwhelmed by any urge toward mercy."

Then Serenity and Anne could expect execution. They might be caged and dragged from city to town to castle across the Connecten hinterland first. Those who had survived their evils could curse them, throw filth, make clear how much they looked forward to watching them burn.

Brokke said, "Anselin might not agree . . ." He stopped.

"Anselin has a say, how?"

"He isn't emotionally entangled with the Connec but he does have feelings about his mother. She *is* his mother. He may not be able to ignore what outsiders do to her."

"I will consult the Widow but the prospect of Anselin's enmity is unlikely to move her. She trusts in her own ferocity."

"What about the deposed Patriarch?"

"Does anyone care? I think not. Do as thou wilt."

"I care," Pella said. "Armand cares." He did not explain that. "I want Doneto to wallow in filth. I want to kick him while he's down."

Aldi tilted her head. The boy was truly bitter. "I will see the Widow. Do thou consult thy prince. But I see little hope for a triumph of reason."

KEDLE WAS THOUGHTFUL. "A DOZEN MEN-AT-ARMS LEFT THE TOWER while you were away. We disarmed them and cut them loose. Ten people are still in there, some of them wounded. They have no food or water. Anne still thinks help will come. What have you got?"

"Complications."

After listening, Kedle asked, "We can't just eliminate Anselin, too?"

"The Righteous won't let us. Nor will my family. They don't care about the Connec."

"I was looking forward to dragging Anne hither and yon, then leaving her caged outside Metrelieux till the elements claimed her."

"Thee needs might cede that dream."

"Only in absolute extremity. Go back. Convince them. Failing that, stall them. Our position will be stronger once we have Anne and Serenity."

"I shall begin by failing to hurry back. How is thy leg?"

"It hurts like hell. What do you think?"

"Take something. Thee needs be less bitchy."

Kedle growled.

"At least thee will heal aright if thee doth take care not to stress it. Doth thee take care?"

"I try. There are limits." Both true.

Headstrong and fierce though she was, Kedle Richeut would listen to experts, unlike her friend Socia.

In that, even Kedle missed Count Raymone. Only Raymone could rein Socia in.

Lady Hope faced the Widow's nearest lifeguard. "*Hast* she behaved herself?"

That grizzled peasant, missing several front teeth, grinned. "She has, Lady. Them boys what the Countess left behind nag her all the time. They won't hear a word if'n it's somethin' agin what the Countess told them."

Kedle met Hope's gaze. "I do what I must. I want to ride again. I want to walk and run. It's frustrating but I'll wait till somebody who knows better than me says I'm ready."

"Thee be a true treasure, love. I will see our Imperial friends, now. We don't want them getting impatient."

Kedle watched the Instrumentality go. What was it like to be a god? Hope had a distinct hitch in her gait from that bit of godshot. Instrumentalities were not immortal in an absolute sense. Nor did Hope appear powerful in the thunderous, psychotically destructive style of gods spawned amongst the Wells of Ihrian.

On the other hand, she *could* be seen and touched.

Kedle blushed.

Lady Hope paused behind the artillery tormenting the watchtower. She made a hand gesture as the next missile struck. Tons of stone tumbled, exposing interiors on three levels. A shout went up. Men rushed forward.

FOUR MEN CAME OUT AS ALDI APPROACHED THE RIGHTEOUS. THE NEW two reeked of perversion. "Huh?" That boy was much older than he looked. Older than any of his companions, in fact.

He had been twisted into something wicked, yet innocence remained. He had been forged as a tool of evil but had not become evil himself. Interesting.

Aldi focused on the tall, pretty one, Anselin, the king to be. His confidence waned as she approached. He had been warned. As his contemporaries all did, he had refused to believe.

He felt the weight of her presence now.

Should she become irresistible Aldi and make Anselin over as the vigorous heterosexual his mother wanted him to be?

No. There were witnesses, mortal and divine. The latter would not approve.

Pella announced, "Anselin wishes to speak for himself."

"And the princess?"

Pella did not react.

Did he not know? Unlikely. So, he did not care.

"Never mind. The Vindicated have captured Anne of Menand and several men close to her, including Henri of Mariscot and the fallen priest, Serenity." She would deal in facts, not emotions.

Pella said, "The King wants to know your intentions toward your prisoners."

"He is no king. He is a man who would be king. I hope that he becomes king. I hear much good of him. But he is spawn of Anne. That will weigh against him."

"Madam, I am her son but I am not her."

"Then there is hope. Then thou shouldst not be troubled by how we handle our prisoners."

Anselin inclined his head slightly. "I might face uncomfortable questions if I let you treat my mother the way I expect you want."

"I care not. The Widow and the millions of the Connec who suffered because of thy mother do. No humiliation or degradation will seem sufficient to them."

"Take the deposed Patriarch."

"We shall, though he means little to anyone outside Antieux." That tickled the strange catamite. He snickered.

"Then we have a problem," said the future king.

"Thou mayest." She did not turn that into a challenge.

"Are you what they tell me you are?"

"I am that and a great deal more. Nor am I alone." The ring of swords unsheathing sounded behind her, where nothing but open ground could be seen.

So. The old women *were* out there.

"How about this?" Anselin asked. "Take Anne for a year. Use her as you will, but keep her alive. Return her after the year is over. By then she should be disinclined to leave the nunnery where I put her."

Aldi was surprised. That was an astute offer.

Anselin continued, "I would claim Henri d'Mariscot and my mother's henchmen—excepting the guerrilla Patriarch."

Pella said, "I want to entertain Bronte Doneto for a while. How about you, Armand?"

Aldi glanced at Hagen Brokke. Brokke smiled and winked.

Pella continued, "All we Righteous want from Anne of Menand is that she stop running Arnhand."

Aldi looked the boy in the eye, handed off the wink. The kid had promise, maybe because he had adopted the right father.

"This will work. I need not consult the Widow." Though Kedle would complain because she could not kill Anne.

Anselin smiled smugly.

The catamite did the same, but more so. Aldi suspected the little devil might be on his way to becoming the true master in Arnhand.

Pella looked like he had conquered the world.

These beings saw everything from briefer perspectives.

The captain of the Righteous detachment seemed satisfied, too.

Aldi said, "I will go make sure our prizes survive being captured."

Turning, she spotted the Bastard watching from hiding.

27. Alten Weinberg: Gathering

Hecht summoned his staff. "What's happened?"

De Bos asked, "What brings that on?"

"I suddenly felt like something big was shaking."

"We haven't heard of anything." Suspiciously intent.

Hecht had to face the fact that he made his men uncomfortable. "Then let's just get back to work."

Clej Sedlakova said, "I want to start rejecting petitions to join the Enterprise. We can't support any more troops traveling overland. Some could go by sea but they might get there first."

"And cause problems?"

"Probably. How about we split off a section to set up a wave for next year?"

"That won't sit well with people who want to go down in history."

"If you found a respected leader willing to take charge?"

"Got a candidate in mind?"

"Brill of Santerin."

Hecht said, "That might work."

Sedlakova asked, "Or Stain of Hovacol? The honor might ease the sting out there."

"An even better suggestion. Keckler?" A lifeguard wanted his attention.

"It's Ferris Renfrow, sir. He wants to see you."

"YESTERDAY AT DAWN," RENFROW SAID. "THE WIDOW ATTACKED ANNE of Menand at Mestlé."

"Really? Hilda Daedel's brother has an estate out there. He said Anne was scheming to keep Anselin from becoming king."

"That why you sent such a big escort?"

"I thought she might ambush him."

"That didn't happen." Renfrow reported what he had seen.

"Pella did the talking? I'll be damned."

"Then he and the catamite beat Serenity half to death."

"Osa Stile? Your special agent?"

"Not anymore. Not since he hooked up with Muniero Delari."

"And then you came back here?"

"Not directly. If you want more you'll have to ask your special sources. They were there, too."

Hecht rubbed his temples. "If I can find them." The Bastard shook his head, said nothing.

"Tell me, are the Shining Ones desanctifying the churches?"

"Probably. You could say that they're eating God."

"That's repulsive."

"Commander, they have survival imperatives, too. They're up against a doomsday deadline. Eavijne's apples aren't good enough. They have to reach Eucereme or go extinct. The Aelen Kofer won't help voluntarily. And the only power wells they can reach are weak. They can get stronger only by taking the strength of other Instrumentalities. They can't tap the Wells of Ihrian till you take them there. Meantime, the scraps of God in the churches are easily exploited."

"This Twilight and Rebirth are more complicated than the myths make them appear."

"The mythic process got fucked when Ordnan read the Godslayer thing wrong."

"Maybe it goes back to Arlensul and Gedanke."

"Not a comfortable subject, but quite possibly true. I have to go."

"Do visit Helspeth occasionally. You help keep her emotionally grounded."

Renfrow responded with a suggestion of a nod.

Hecht sent for Carava de Bos. "I need to see one of my new intelligence people. Can you find any of them?"

"The pretty, shy one."

"Who?"

"Evie. The quiet one. The garden freak with her head in the clouds."

Evie? Interesting. "She'll do."

THE COMMANDER OF THE RIGHTEOUS WAS ABOUT TO LEAVE FOR HIS prayer meeting when the Shining One walked out of a wall. He had not dealt with Eavijne before. As de Bos had noted, she was shy.

She kept her eyes downcast. "I talked to Aldi. The Bastard's report was correct."

"I see. How goes the new orchard?"

"Not well. The magic here is too weak. We must reach Eucereme."

Hecht was surprised. He felt disappointed himself.

Eavijne walked back into the wall before he could ask his next question. But he knew the answer.

Yes. "Evie" had sported with Carava de Bos. And, likely, Vircondelet, too. Toying with mortals was what Shining Ones did. Even shy girl Shining Ones.

He shuddered, though. He liked both men. He would not want either to become this century's Gedanke.

Eavijne was, for Aaron's sake, a fertility goddess!

He would chide Hourli—if she ever turned up.

HECHT GRUMBLED, "BE CAREFUL WHAT YOU WISH FOR." HE HAD JUST collected his time candle when Cloven Februaren turned sideways, dropped an inch, and began cursing a twisted ankle.

"You need to see me?"

"Your timing is abominable, but I do." He removed his coat, rolled up his left sleeve, extended his wrist. "Do something about this."

"Whoa! That's ugly. Does it itch? Never mind. Stupid question." Februaren bent, sniffed. "It hasn't gone bad, more is the wonder. How long has this been going on?"

"Since we got back from the Realm of the Gods."

"Oh. Right. Sit. Let's think."

Hecht thought about the woman who was waiting. She would not be happy, but she did know that events could keep him away. Something had kept her once.

He sat. On a hard chair. Impatiently.

The wonder of Helspeth had not worn off.

Februaren pulled another chair close, studied wrist and amulet.

"Everything looks like it's working the way it should, Piper. You're itching because an Instrumentality is close by. If that has gone on for months the Instrumentality obviously must not be malicious."

"Got to be the Choosers, then. My supernatural lifeguards. I'd ask them to back off but I don't know how to talk to them. The one time they did turn up was in Hovacol. I didn't know I was summoning them, then. That was pure instinct."

"Whatever, we have to take the amulet off so this can heal."

"Thank you." With depthless sarcasm.

"I couldn't get here sooner. My time is as full as yours is."

"Is that true for my sister and daughters, too?"

"Yes. For Heris in particular. Though the family has the impression that you're fed up with our pestering."

"The occasional pester would be nice."

"But only when it's convenient for you."

Yes. He did resent people dropping in at their convenience rather than his. Just now Februaren was keeping him from seeing Helspeth.

"Let's take a chance on the dedication of your guardian angels. Have Asgrimmur ask the Shining Ones how they can protect you without driving you crazy."

"I used to worry that I'd have them underfoot all the time. Now I'm irked because I don't. I have no idea what they're up to, except that one is in Arnhand with that Connecten madwoman called the Widow."

"Must be hell to work with beings whose attitudes are so much like your own." The old man grinned.

"You think there's a life lesson to be learned?"

"Lesson or no, you see the point."

"I'll keep it in mind. But I really would like to be kept informed."

"You want to send a message to Anna or the girls?" The old man tinkered with Hecht's amulet as he talked. "You don't see Vali or Lila because Muno has them on a crash education course. They're too damned tired to come aggravate their daddy."

"So it's not about me being surly because they come whenever they feel like it?"

"Oh, it's that, too, of course. You do put on the attitude. About Muno, though. He's determined to include them in the deal when Heris takes over as the Twelfth Unknown."

The itching in Hecht's wrist went away. "Damn! That feels so good."

"Maybe you won't be so nasty, now. Anything for Anna?"

"Let me write a note. How is she?"

"Well enough. Forted up in her house. Comes out for the occasional command performance at Muno's townhouse. She's happy, considering her circumstances."

"Circumstances?"

"Her man is hundreds of miles away and not particularly interested in visiting. How is the wrist, now? All right?"

"It's wonderful."

"Keep using the ointment. I'll take that." He snagged the note to Anna, turned sideways, and was gone.

The Commander of the Righteous did not get to St. Miniver, Martyr, chapel that night.

Hecht was studying maps prepared by the Shining Ones. They were wondrously detailed and generously annotated. Any commander would have been thrilled. He was unhappy only because the Instrumentalities continued to duck him.

Asgrimmur arrived. "You want to see me?"

"Occasionally, yes." Hecht glanced at his wrist. It was healing nicely. "In fact, frequently, lately. You've let your personal appearance slide."

"Indeed?"

"Why is whatever is happening in Antieux more important than our preparations here? Why is a skirmish in the Roessen more important?"

"The old girls have been carrying tales."

"No. I can't find them, either. They do, however, generate the occasional useful report. In your case I've started to think our arrangement is a waste. There's been no payoff for me."

"I follow my conscience."

Odd answer. "What does it say about keeping your word?"

Grimmsson shrugged.

"Come with me. We can't talk here."

A half minute later Hecht shut the door of a quiet room.

"I know about your travels from the Bastard. I see the Shining Ones less than I see you. I can't get hold of them."

Grimmsson looked baffled. "Why not? You could see Fastthal or Sprenghul any time you want and a summons to Hourli will get her here in less than an hour." Grimmsson stopped. He stared. "Are you having memory problems?"

"Sometimes. What do you know about that?"

"I'm marveling that you would handicap yourself by forgetting that you can summon any Shining One you want any time you want, Hourlr excepted."

"All right. I'm a virgin. I have no clue. I'm worse than a virgin. I'm a dimwit four-year-old. Tell me what to do."

"Commander, just say, 'Hourli, it is necessary that I speak with you.' Using that formula. Add the time and place and what guise she should wear if you think that's necessary."

That seemed awfully simple.

"Write it down. Right now. Make notes of where you put the information. You've been told all this before. The formula will work for your guardians, too, though you might not like what you see when they arrive. They're slower to manage their aspects."

"And you?"

"I'll respond to the formula, too, though almost certainly not as fast as the Lord High Duke of Arnmigal might like."

"I'm a Grand Duke, not a Lord High Duke. So. Sprenghul. I need to see you. Right here, right now. No excuses."

"You messed it up already. Write it down! It has to be exact, and by will, so impossible things don't turn up during a casual conversation. And you can't summon the Shining Ones from inside a quiet room."

"Yeah. Stupid me." He had paper and quill, now. "The exact formula, then." He wrote.

Asgrimmur said, "There have been unconscionable oversights in your supernatural education."

"What supernatural education?"

"With the Unknowns in your family? You may have the talent of a stone yourself but you should have some idea how things work."

"They never took time to teach me."

"You sure it was them who didn't take time?"

"You're right. I always found an excuse."

"Suppose Sprenghul heard your summons? If you'd gotten it right? When this isn't your house to destroy?"

"She'd really . . ."

"She would. The Choosers aren't smart. Arlensul was brighter than the other two put together but she was still dim enough to get herself knocked up by a mortal."

Hecht turned toward the door.

"Hold up. Sprenghul did stir some. You named her name. You may hear about apparitions and unusual activities out there."

"Conjuring plausible explanations seems to be where I excel. Poor Destiny. She rode the wrong chariot this time."

"What?"

"Nothing goes the way it should around me. My story is all about things that don't work out according to someone else's plan."

"In which case the Enterprise of Peace and Faith is doomed."

That was not what Hecht meant. "Possibly. But it will be an interesting venture, even so."

"Even so. Are you done with me, Commander?"

"For the moment. But I want to make my point again. I want to be able to ask questions."

"No problem. Just ask the right questions, in the right place, at the right time."

"Meaning?"

"Don't demand trivia or information you could develop yourself if you weren't lazy. Or that has nothing to do with the Great Work. Don't call the Shining Ones out in public. A meeting should be necessary, not just because you're feeling left out or because you want to remind everybody that you're the guy in charge. The Shining Ones are giving you the information you need to make your crusade work. They do so in a timely manner. Where they are or what they're doing otherwise is of no import to you or to the Enterprise. The fact that you want to know something has little bearing on your need to know it."

"I don't get to decide my needs?"

"No. All the stamping and roaring in the world won't change that, though I do think that you could make yourself obnoxious enough to chase Hourli away altogether, despite her crush."

Hecht heard that as a cautionary suggestion, not a real threat. "I have no problem with their work. I just want to know what they're doing. And why."

"Are your ears full of shit? What did I just tell you? How will knowing those things help you with the Enterprise?"

They would not. Of course.

"Go, Asgrimmur. And, please, when you come round again, try to be clean and neat. I demand that from everyone."

"As you will."

Hecht went back to his maps. He had wasted the interview. It was true, though, that what he wanted to know was not material to the success of the Enterprise.

He still wanted to know. He wanted control. He wanted no loose ends. No unpredictable variables. No surprises.

He rubbed his left wrist. That was so much better now.

THE EMPRESS AND LORD ARNMIGAL WERE REVIEWING THE VAN OF the Enterprise: favored champions the Commander of the Righteous considered least likely to generate enmity toward the crusaders coming along behind.

The spring melt had begun early, as Hourli had predicated. The van would move out in four more days.

Meantime, captains studied maps and the intricate supply system the quartermaster staff had developed. And they paraded.

Lord Arnmigal wished he could ride with the van. His place would be with the main host, wrangling the willful, the selfish, the stubborn, and the stupid.

The Empress, as titular monarch of the western world, had taken an oath from each member of the host. It required obedience to the precepts of a charter from the current Patriarch, and to Lord Arnmigal as Commander of the Righteous. With Church and Grail Throne behind him Hecht had the legal power he needed.

Those who would not take oaths had been sent home under obligation to make fiscal contributions. Nothing was required of anyone who did not ask to participate.

Many wished for a different order but few challenged it. Lord Arnmigal and the daughter of Johannes Blackboots recognized challenges before they developed. Their intelligence was golden. Further, they controlled the artisans of Krulik and Sneigon, who provided tools that made argument a very bad idea.

Since the Shades only blind tortoises refused to admit the power of the new weapons. The Righteous had the best of those and the most talented and innovative falconeers.

Some tried to resist, even so. They came up wriggling in Hourli's nets. But the gods themselves fail to notice what makes no noise.

Neither the gods nor the most skilled spy can thwart an assassin who shares his thinking with no one, makes no threat, never complains, never seeks allies, and cares nothing about his own continued existence once the needful is done.

Franz-Benneroust Plaza was a sea of glamorous champions honoring a woman whose decisions would shape the next thousand years. Batteries of falcons passed in review. The bird and the weapon had become tutelary emblems of the Enterprise. The crusaders would carry more firepowder than flour to the Holy Lands.

An ammunition wagon drawn by a four-mule team rumbled along near the end of the column. It exploded as it neared the reviewing stand.

It carried a half ton of firepowder made at home by a madman who was not entirely sure of his formula. Most did not explode at all but just flung out in gouts of smoke and gobbets of burning sulfur.

The villain was one Rolf fon Utmeg, bachelor baronet. He had avoided detection by the Shining Ones by relying entirely on himself. He got what he paid for.

He got dead. His mules got dead. Scores of onlookers got burned. Hundreds suffered lung damage. Among the burned was the Empress Helspeth. Likewise, Lord Arnmigal and others on the reviewing stand. But the disaster touched them only for an instant, though shock, shrapnel, and poisonous air should have claimed them all. But a dark curtain fell an instant after the first gust of fire rolled out of the wagon.

Hecht had a fraction of a second to register the appearance of something all fang, claw, and stench of corruption, interposing itself between the explosion and the reviewing stand.

A second horror materialized between the wagon and the parade.

Long screams ripped through Hecht's mind. Bits of iron from the wagon tormented Fastthal and Sprenghul. Then they vanished.

Poorly made firepowder, burning and bubbling still, fell.

Few in the square failed to see the Choosers. Few failed to understand that they had saved the Empress, Lord Arnmigal, and senior leaders of the Enterprise, as well as the men on parade.

Hacking sulfur smoke, Hecht ordered, "Wrap this up. Captain Drear, get the Empress to her physician."

Helspeth wept with pain. She had suffered several burns, small but fierce. A blob of sulfur had landed in her hair. Drear had gotten it out before it reached her scalp, getting burnt himself in the process. "Will do, my lord."

Hecht mentioned guardian angels repeatedly. Unfortunately, those inclined to believe in angels wanted them to be beautiful creatures of light.

Hecht overheard veterans of the Hovacol incursion claim to have seen these same dread angels before.

HECHT AND HELSPETH, FERRIS RENFROW, ARCHBISHOP BRION, ORMO va Still-Patter, the Lord Admiral fon Tyre, and others the Empress had drawn into her circle shared a table in the palace's biggest quiet room. Hourli and Hourlr accompanied the Grand Duke of Arnmigal. Others could see that those two were siblings but not that they were Instrumentalities.

Renfrow said, "I fail to see any excuse for further excitement. A lone madman tried to . . . All right. We don't know what he wanted. To kill the Empress? The Commander of the Righteous? Or did he just think a nasty big bang would scuttle the Enterprise? It doesn't matter. We survived. He did not. Let's get on with our work."

Hecht sipped coffee, flirted with Lady Hilda, and stayed small while Renfrow took the heat—though there was little enough of that. That was all out in the city, where rumors had grown so crazy that only crazy people listened. But Hecht worried that superstitious soldiers would abandon the Enterprise if they decided it was connected with evil Night.

Helspeth said, "There will be no change in plans. The vanguard marches on time. Rolf fon Utmeg was a fever dream. Forget him. Don't mention him again. We do not have to apologize for surviving. Disdain the distractions. Let the Enterprise unfold. You in particular, Archbishop. The Holy Lands await."

Archbishop Brion had learned some sharp lessons lately. Foremost was that he could serve his Church best by not irritating his Empress. And he did want to experience the Holy Lands for himself.

Lord Arnmigal smiled across the table, rested a finger familiarly on the back of Daedel's hand as she poured him an extra coffee.

Most attendees left the meeting puzzled. What had been discussed? What had been decided? Nobody could say for sure.

Again, the Enterprise went forward as the Commander of the Righteous desired.

Or such was the rumor spread by someone who wanted to undermine the baseborn foreign upstart with unholy control over the Empress.

During a hectic four days scribes and secretaries transcribed hundreds of letters. The Empress signed them all. Each was tailored to its addressee. Each listed sins and suggested that Helspeth would not be in a forgiving mind should such behavior persist.

Battle group after battle group headed down the roads and rivers toward the Holy Lands. The Enterprise could no longer be stopped. It was like nothing gone before, in weaponry, planning, or organization. The Righteous staff had determined the optimum means of accomplishing the mission, then had mapped out how best to make it happen.

Lord Arnmigal believed that the worst peril the Enterprise faced was the potential bad behavior of its members. The last crusade, grand as its successes had been, had done more damage to fellow Chaldareans than to Unbelievers. That Enterprise had wasted strength, power, and moral credibility by oppressing those who had cheered its coming.

Hecht was determined that there be no repetition. Unambiguous articles of behavior had been read out to each contingent, in its own language. Hecht knew some would have listened with their fingers crossed. Lords who came with black reputations would have a Righteous liaison close by. The Commander reiterated his attitude daily.

Despite every effort, the Enterprise had serious flaws. Most dangerous of those was the fact that command was not monolithic. The Enterprise was a hosting, not an integrated army. It was a collection of mobs following numerous princes and nobles, each with an inflated opinion of his own worth. For the moment they were headed the same direction, professing the same ambitions.

Hecht could not be everywhere, heading off trouble. He had to count on the Shining Ones.

Titus Consent reminded him, "You have better control than the lords of the last crusade. You did think about what needs to be done. You studied their mistakes. You laid out . . . Never mind. Relax. Get wasted. Turn it off for a few days."

"A bit late, isn't it? The Enterprise is under way."

"Sure. But we won't move out, yet."

Yes. But . . . Hecht had an idea. It terrified him. But once it occurred he had to pursue it. "Titus. Have breakfast with me tomorrow."

Consent looked puzzled. "All right. Can I get a hint?"

"No. Now scoot. I need to think." He retreated to his private quarters, he executed the summons for Hourli. The Shining One was not pleased when she materialized.

"Did I drag you away from something important?"

"From scouting for hazards ahead of the Enterprise."

"I'll try not to waste your time. I need messages delivered."

Hourli seemed mildly impressed. "It's not much yet, but here you go, starting to act like the man in charge."

"You'll handle it?"

"Of course. It's what we're here for." She vanished. She had not smiled once.

Hecht collected his time candle and slipped away to the church of St. Miniver, Martyr.

HELSPETH ARRIVED ACTING MOPEY. SHE WAS NOT INTERESTED IN A passionate encounter. Nor was Hecht. She observed, "You're glum tonight."

"I haven't recovered from the blast." No one had asked about the miracle of their survival but a lot of speculation was afoot. Good thing the Choosers had gone away fast.

"That and the fact that we're jumping off into history?"

"There is that, darling. I'm overwhelmed by the magnitude. God Himself may think we're overreaching."

"You're overthinking. You should be stripping me naked, but I'm having the same thoughts. I'm terrified that we'll stumble into a disaster so huge they'll mock us till the end of time. I'm scared that my name will become the punch line to a thousand jokes."

"Helspeth Ege, possibly with her identity slightly disguised, is much more likely to become the subject of a cycle of love songs."

This relationship was the sort that jongleurs lauded.

The suggestion pleased Helspeth. He snuggled close. Neither spoke for a while. Then Helspeth said, "Hilda says that some courtiers are starting to ask questions."

"About us?"

"About you and her."

"Oh."

"Is that disappointment? It was the impression we were trying to give."

He laughed without humor. "No. Though that liaison would be easier."

"Don't start that stuff."

"It's human nature, lover. God made us all want more than we have, no matter what we have or how much of it."

"God? Or the Adversary?"

"That could be. With all the other devils around, why not the biggest one of all? You're not the Tempter, are you?" He failed to make that sound like he was joking.

"Why don't we do what we're supposed to be doing?"

"Pray?"

"Yes. But let's not waste our magic candle on it."

Hecht did pray for the first time in a long time. He felt self-conscious. As luck or a clever Shining One would have it, Archbishop Brion and several ecclesiastical henchmen caught them in the act of the chaste nonevent. And were disappointed. Could it be that Lord Arnmigal and the Empress were more devout when they did not know they had an audience?

The Grand Duke of Arnmigal won a serious victory because of an impulse and a bad mood but never knew it.

TITUS OBSERVED, "YOU'RE NOT YOURSELF THIS MORNING."

Puzzled, Hecht asked, "How so?"

"You look like you got a good night's sleep."

"I did. I prayed last night and it seemed the Lord lifted a huge weight off me."

"What?"

"It came to me while I was in front of the altar. I haven't been trusting God. I've driven myself, and you all, to our limits because I couldn't trust in Him. He touched me last night. He reminded me that we can't do this without Him. I built the machine in His name. I should put the machine into His hands."

Consent stood there with jaw dropped. "You really mean that."

"Yes."

"If prayer at Saint Miniver, Martyr, can relax you this much, I need to get over there myself."

"Too late. You'll be doing something else. I told de Bos and Vircondelet to cover for you for two days."

"Two days? Why? Especially now?"

"You and I are going on a wonderful and terrifying journey."

Cloven Februaren turned sideways and materialized. Consent gaped as the old man hustled away from the center of the room.

Lila and Vali twisted into being where Februaren had been, holding hands. Giggling, they scattered.

Heris appeared. She dropped several inches, cursing. She was not in a good mood. "This better be worth my trouble, little brother."

Hecht told Consent, "Come over here, Titus. Stand back to back with me. Family?"

Heris asked, "Sure you want to do this, Piper?"

"Want to, no. Need to, yes. Titus needs to. In a few days we'll be off on a quest that isn't likely to forgive us. I need to . . . Titus . . ."

"You're so full of shit. Let's do this, family."

Heris, the girls, and Cloven Februaren crushed in. Hecht's last frightened thought was, *Darkness always comes,* as darkness descended.

28. Khaurene: New Blood

The journey took longer than expected. Brother Candle proved less able to endure the hardships than he had foreseen, though mostly he rode in a wagon. Too, there were delays because people everywhere wanted to see the Countess who was one of the saviors of the province.

The adulation troubled Socia. "The more they applaud me now the more they'll be disappointed later."

Brother Candle said, "You will have a hard time being the legend they need."

"I don't want to be a legend." She met his gaze briefly. "All right. I don't mind being a legend. I just don't want to put in the work."

"Those who take the easy road become the legendary bad lords."

"You can be so frustrating."

"I know. I frustrate myself sometimes. But look on the bright side. I won't be a plague on your house much longer."

"What? You'll outlive me. You're too righteous to die."

"I did not mention dying. Though even a Perfect must someday stand before the Good God and make his accounting."

"I don't understand."

"It's possible that I don't, either. With this journey beating me down this way, a worse journey would be insane. But I begin to feel the call."

"What are you talking about?"

"That's enough for now, darling girl. Before anything else I have to see you through this, then safely through the travails of becoming the guardian of the new Duke. Only after that can I consider what to do to benefit my soul and the Light."

The company reached Castreresone while the light splashed its walls to the most flattering effect. It was obvious why it was called the White City.

Scaffolding clung to those walls in a dozen places. The Berg and Inconje were being rebuilt. The magnates, encouraged by Queen Isabeth, were being particularly energetic.

The White City was filled with talk about being ready next time Arnhand came.

There was a despairing confidence that the Arnhander threat would never fade.

Thousands came out. Lumiere slept most of the time. Escamerole and Guillemette took turns carrying him so people could see. There was much shouting of blessings and offering of gifts. Brother Candle insisted that Socia accept the latter. They meant a great deal to the givers. She saw innumerable faces excited about the future. Their blessings made it clear that the Widows had the people believing that they no longer must despair over the certain evil in the north.

"That was what I meant about terrible expectations," Socia told Brother Candle as Castreresone fell behind. "They don't just want a champion, they want a redeemer. In real life Kedle and I are thugs in skirts."

"Thugs in skirts who have gained the favor of the Night."

A man had come to Socia, last night, unnoticed by her lifeguards. He had explained the situation in Arnhand: Kedle had captured Anne of Menand and Serenity. The new Arnhander king was there, making peace. That would be enforced by the Righteous. The Righteous had had a scrimmage with the Vindicated. That had left the latter stunned and disinclined toward further argument.

The man walked out when she started to ask questions. She mentioned him to no one but Brother Candle.

"Was his right hand damaged?"

"You think . . . ? Let me think. I don't know. I don't remember anything but his eyes. They were hypnotic."

"I don't suppose his identity matters. His message does, however. Let's keep that to ourselves. Travel will be difficult enough without having to manage seven score drunken celebrants."

Progress did remain slow. Their best day, after departing Castreresone, saw nine miles put behind. Two days of no travel followed when rain made the roads impassable. Rain came frequently. That season had arrived. It made up for the more clement weather farther east.

A drizzle was in progress when Socia and the Perfect finally sighted Khaurene's northern and eastern faces. It was just past noon. No rain was falling on the city, which sat in an island of sunlight, glistening, surrounded by the thousand greens of spring.

Socia said, "Let us hope that is an omen."

News of their approach had run ahead. People began to come out while the travelers were still hours away. Socia whispered, "I'm spoiled. I can't help thinking that I could be there in ten minutes if I flew."

"That must stay secret. *Never* give in to the urge to brag or show off."

"I know. I know."

"People will be afraid, not impressed."

"I know. I'll burn if I can't tame my flamboyant side." The old man chuckled.

The company entered Khaurene as day faded. The streets were bright with torchlight. People wanted to see the new rulers. Lumiere obliged by being awake and fussing.

Brother Candle noted some sullen faces. Despite all, a few Episcopal Chaldareans remained, of the sort who believed that the Society for Suppression of Sacrilege and Heresy, and burning people, were good ideas.

He might actually pine for Bernardin's no-nonsense justice.

The Archimbault family, less Guillemette and Escamerole, and those Maysaleans who had come back to Khaurene, left the company to reclaim their homes. Socia sent mounted soldiers to help evict squatters. She meant to make clear from the onset that she would be partisan. Her friends would be well treated. She would rule fairly but those who did not offer friendship should not expect kindness in return.

Brother Candle stayed with Socia. He would do so till she settled in. He would introduce her to the influential men of Khaurene and would lend moral support in her dealings with the Direcians. He feared the Direcian nobility would be disinclined to surrender the power they had acquired.

Soon, though, he told Socia, "This may be easier than you expect. Isabeth is here. The Navayans love her as much as the Khaurenese do."

"How do you know she's here?"

"The troops at the intersections are wearing Navayan livery."

The remnants of the company entered Metrelieux after nightfall, in a drizzling rain, with Lumiere vocalizing prodigiously. The situation was outside normal protocol. The new Duke should have made his entrance in the morning, on a sunny day, to the blare of trumpets, amidst great pomp and ceremony.

The travelers dismounted in the bailey court. Servants hustled everyone off to appropriate quarters, where meals, baths, and other luxuries awaited, including real beds. The pomp and ceremony could wait.

"Very practical, usually, Isabeth," Brother Candle told Bicot Hodier. The ducal herald had insisted on visiting while the Perfect lay back in warm water in a hammered copper tub. Brother Candle asked, "Why aren't the public baths used anymore?"

Hodier said, "True religion came to the Connec. Good Chaldareans don't expose their flesh to the eyes of strangers."

"And most shouldn't."

Hodier got the jest. "Speak for yourself."

"I am. What do you want?"

"I am terrified by this savage woman from Antieux. But, first, where did you get those bizarre tattoos? And why?"

"Where would be Antieux. I wasn't given a choice. A thing of the Night took hold of me. When she turned loose I had the snakes. You didn't come to gawk at my bony old corpse. Get to the point."

"Seeing that, it's a bit hard to remember."

Brother Candle was inclined to be sharp but the servants remained within earshot. The city would simmer with rumors because of what he had said already.

"Please, Bicot. We're too old to waste time."

"Of course. I have no actual agenda, other than to tell you what's happened since last you were here."

"Do, then. Without trying to enlist me in anyone's fantasy. I'm a Seeker After Light. The things of this world . . ."

"All right! Listen!" The old herald described social adjustments
that had taken place. "You fled east because you thought Anne would
throw the full might of Arnhand at Khaurene."

"She would have if she could have."

"Yes. But her support was evaporating. And the Vindicated forced
her onto the defensive." Then Hodier described a resurgence of the local Brothen Episcopal party, which he applauded.

Brother Candle warned, "Don't expect another reign like Tormond's.
Socia will make mistakes but she won't be indecisive. She won't tolerate
the usual squabbling."

"She may be in for some surprises, Master."

"As may be Khaurene, Bicot. I'll let you in on a secret. The Vindi-
cated are coming. You'll hear the full story soon. The salient point is,
Kedle Richeut, the Kingslayer, is on her way. Those who irritate the
Countess won't do so for long."

Brother Candle had ignored his own advice. He excoriated himself
silently. He rationalized by telling himself that Khaurene would make
a more peaceful transition under threat of the Vindicated.

Bicot Hodier was at sea now. His mission, whatever it had been,
was dead. As seconds passed he looked ever more like a cornered ro-
dent.

He blurted, "Where are the tokens Tormond gave you? There can't
be a new Duke . . ."

"Bicot, calm yourself. Why are you so upset?"

"The tokens! The seal! Where are they, heretic?"

"Where they belong. With the Duke. What wickedness have you
fallen into, Bicot? Confession is good for the soul." Brother Candle
extended his left hand.

Hodier blurted, "Extinguishing heresy is food for the soul!" He
pulled a knife.

The Perfect's serpent tattoo wriggled, slithered forth, poised to strike.
Hodier moaned.

The snake faced the servants. They went rigid.

The herald could not move but he kept babbling. "It's true. You
Perfect are marked by the Adversary."

"Not at all. But this Perfect has been touched by the Night. And
I want to know why Bicot Hodier, herald, is determined to thwart his
sovereign. Are you an agent of Anne of Menand?" The servants heard
him.

Just suspicion could become a death sentence.

Hodier was horrified. "No!"

"Then you must be an agent of the Society, which amounts to the same thing. Or is your allegiance to some other force determined to rape the Connec of its independence, wealth, security, and genius?"

"No! No! I'm my own man! I am no man's pawn! Can't you pull that thing in?"

"I have no control over the snakes, Bicot. I don't know why they do what they do. I'm their tool, not the other way around."

Brother Candle had known this man since they were boys. They were never close but neither had they ever been enemies.

"Bicot, you had some hope when you interrupted my bath. Which is getting cold, boys. One of you bring another pot of hot water."

Seldom did life afford an opportunity to wallow in luxury. Tonight he would indulge. Tonight would offset, feebly, the winter spent on the Reindau Spine, or the winter spent on the run from the Captain-General.

The serpent threatening Hodier collapsed back into an incredibly detailed tattoo, with color showing in its mouth, extended tongue, and eyes.

Brother Candle had to tear his attention away.

There had been no color and fewer details before.

He needed a mirror. He needed to see the snake on his neck. That one had killed.

"Talk to me, Bicot."

SOCIA AND LUMIERE MANAGED MORNING AND AFTERNOON CEREMO-nies without the Perfect. Nothing remarkable happened. Brother Candle watched from the gallery, studying the witnesses, seeing little emotion.

Rumors about his encounter with Hodier were out there, now. Hodier and friends had been intimidated. Their motivating force had been trivial: the fear of losing their sinecures.

Brother Candle did not understand. As long as he did nothing stupid, Hodier had been fixed for life. But he *had* done something stupid, now. Socia might make an example.

"I DON'T CARE WHAT YOU SAY, MASTER," SOCIA SAID. SHE WAS HOLD-ing Lumiere. The boy had gotten a lot of maternal attention lately. "I have certain advantages. I mean to exploit them. Khaurene won't keep secrets from me. I want it tamed before Isabeth leaves."

"Take care. Don't hand the extremists any ammunition."

"I'll give them ammunition. With them standing against a wall."

"Socia!"

"You are a wonder, Master. Like a father and a husband at the same time, only more so, with none of the fun. A treasure of an old fusspot. Let me say this: I really have learned most of the lessons you tried to teach me."

That could be. But there was another level . . .

"I do wish we could have brought Bernardin. I'd feel so much better if I had him sorting out the local villains."

"Socia, this isn't Antieux. There are ten times as many people and five times as many factions."

"And I'll tame them. If not before Isabeth leaves, then after Kedle gets here." Socia wanted to go see Kedle but was too busy. "I won't use the Queen's men unless I have to."

"You need someone. The Navayans are what you have."

"That's where you come in."

"Please!"

"You know the important people."

"I thought I did till Bicot Hodier . . ."

"He was confused. I talked to him. He won't be a problem again."

"But . . . how did you . . . ?"

"I threatened him with you."

"What?"

"In a manner of speaking. Make a list of the most influential men. I'll get them here for an old-fashioned come-to-Aaron meeting. I'll show them I'm not a girl and that making me unhappy won't be smart. You'll roam around scowling and threatening to roll up your sleeves."

The whole city knew about his tattoos. "You'd think, considering what Khaurene has suffered, that people would be worn out and ready for peace. But the conspiracy and backstabbing never end. Greed and ambition never let up."

"Evil never sleeps."

"Damn me. The girl has begun to think at last."

"It had to happen someday. You wore me down."

RUMORS OF EVENTS IN ARNHAND REACHED KHAURENE SEVEN DAYS after the new Duke. More news arrived over the following days, some factual, some exaggerated, all meeting resolute disbelief. It was not possible that a woman, even the Kingslayer, could have beaten Arnhand to its knees.

While visiting the Archimbaults Brother Candle learned that Brothen Episcopals were abandoning the city. They believed that disaster had claimed the last great champion of their Church, Anne of Menand. Their faction, already decimated, could not survive another pogrom.

They would migrate to friendlier climes and abide there till God saw fit to extirpate the apostates and heretics.

Brother Candle was happy to see them go, both because he wished no one harm and because their absence would leave Khaurene more peaceful.

"We need to exploit this time while they're still numb," Socia said.

Brother Candle agreed but was not pleased with her constant use of a non-royal "we." He was, in effect, her grand vizier. He did not want the job. There was no one else to do it. His most difficult task would be to find trustworthy people to do the work of the duchy. Socia had brought only a handful of functionaries. They knew little about Khaurene.

Isabeth meant to leave for Navaya as soon as the rains eased up. She had an empire to wrangle.

Socia wasted no time making herself the hard face of the new regime. Isabeth, urged by a Maysalean Perfect who was an old family friend, stayed out of sight and let the Garete graft take.

Navayan soldiers were never invisible, however. They enforced the peace whenever sectarian violence flared. Socia played no favorites when dealing with that.

Brother Candle knew she was shifting shape and running the Khaurenese nights. That was obvious to him, and it was effective. Three executions, a dozen imprisonments, several confiscations, and some heavy fines, in the space of a week, definitely taught the lesson of caution.

THERE WERE NIGHTS WHEN THE PERFECT LAY AWAKE CONTEMPLATING the fact that Sant Peyre de Mileage lay only slightly farther to the southwest than did Antieux to the east, and the journey thither would be no more difficult. If he joined Isabeth's party he would be safe for all but the last twelve miles. Even a man his age could cover that in a day.

Socia cornered him. "Where are you at lately, Master? What's on your mind?"

"I'm thinking about moving to the tranquility of a monastery."

"I can't let you do that."

"As ever, your last concern is for the welfare of my soul."

Socia wasted no breath on a guilt-edged response.

When next he lay down for a nap the Perfect found himself thinking not of Sant Peyre de Mileage but about the pilgrimage notion that had wormed its way into his mind a few months ago. Before that it had been just one in a clutch of trivial wishes and regrets.

It had to be a sign of the times. The possibility of making the journey began to take on substance.

29. Lucidia: Al-Pinea, in the Idiam

Nassim Alizarin was a weary man particularly tired of failing. The move to al-Pinea had gone well. Since then, though, he and the Ansa had pursued the Rascal to little effect. Cynical Bone insisted that there could be no final solution while Indala subsidized the Ansa.

The Dreangerean sorcerer suffered no success, either. His powers were leaking away. He remained formidable but each attack he fended off cost him some of what he had left.

Mowfik approached. "Message from the Ansa, General. There are riders coming on the Shamramdi trace."

"Not likely to be trouble, are they?"

"No, us being back here so far we have to get our sunlight hauled in on camelback."

"Make sure Ginter gets a gift and a thank you for the warning. And tell Az that I need him."

Riders coming did not feel right. He was not expecting anyone and had not asked for reinforcements.

Al-Azer er-Selim materialized moments before a dozen horsemen and three pack camels entered the decrepit village. "It's the boy, General. Azim. His bunch don't look like they're back from a thundering victory."

"They're on the run? Impossible. Not with the numbers they had."

"They don't look whipped, either. Just worn down and disappointed. See for yourself."

Nassim sat in the shade of a wall built by Imperial legionnaires a thousand years earlier. Young Az and some regular companions crossed what passed for a village square. On the far side, away from the water pool so their wastes would not make the liquid any nastier than it was, a mixed flock of sheep and goats bleated incessantly in makeshift pens. A brace of wagons and three animal-hide tents stood close by. The tents housed several Ansa, one of whom was the elderly and vain sub-chief, Ginter.

The Mountain hoisted himself to his feet. His years did not bother him so much at al-Pinea. Er-Selim thought that might be because of the minerals in the water. He soaked regularly.

Alizarin was thrilled to see Azim but restrained his joy. The boy was grimly unhappy. His first independent assignment had not gone well.

Someone brought cool water. Others helped with the animals, who wanted water more than did their riders. Their refreshment took place away from the spring and pool.

Nassim said, "You're exhausted. You have a reason for riding hard?"

Young Az joined the Mountain in his patch of shade. "Not really. No one is chasing us. We were working off our anger."

"I see." The Mountain awaited illumination.

"My uncle waited too long before sending us in. Gherig used the time to make repairs."

"They couldn't have had that many men left."

"New crusaders arrive every day, Uncle. They're coming by sea from Firaldia and kingdoms farther west. The ones at Gherig were Brotherhood of War. My foragers ran into them on the plain below Megaeda. The results were not pleasant for the Believers."

"How many?"

"Fewer than a hundred, but all veterans of the Calziran Crusade. They compelled us to leave off harassing Gherig."

Nassim observed, "I'm disappointed for you but I don't know what else to say."

"I didn't come for comfort, Uncle." The boy used the honorific for the second time. Nassim strained not to puff up with pride. "I'm here to pick your brain."

"Flattering but unrealistic. My few successes came a long time ago."

Young Az shrugged. "I'm afraid, Uncle. Those fighters hammered us. They didn't fall into our traps. They were workmanlike about the whole business." He flashed a quirk of a smile. "I'm afraid because the Commander of the Righteous is supposed to be more disciplined than any Arnhander we've seen before. And he will bring sixty thousand fighters."

The Mountain answered with a smile. "Be confident. Be sure God has surprises in store." But he had reservations himself.

What did Captain Tage owe the Sha-lug? Did he even recall that he was a warrior of the God Who Is God? The man had become so much more than what he had been sent out to be.

Young Az said, "Faithful who had been to the coast told us the forerunners of the overland invasion have reached the Antal Land Bridges."

Nassim had no trouble understanding the boy's despair. Indala had done what he could by unifying the kaifates—too late to do any good. The unification process was incomplete and might never be completed, so stubborn were Dreanger and the Sha-lug.

"Trust in God," Nassim said, afraid he did not sound confident himself.

In a voice that carried no farther than the Mountain, Azer said, "I do. But will He trust in me?"

"I won't speak to that. I don't want to make anyone unhappy."

The boy got the message. Too many Believers lacked any sense of humor whatsoever.

The Mountain was not sure a man ought to worship a God who would not laugh.

Never had Nassim seen or heard anything to suggest that his God had the least idea what laughter might be.

Young Az said, "Now you know my travails. Tell me yours."

"Mine? Ah! Of course. If I had been successful I wouldn't be here."

The boy listened while he explained, then said, "You need to besiege him."

"Yes?"

"There is only one of him. He has no helpers. And he hasn't gained control of the ghosts and demons he came to recruit. Right?"

"That's true."

"Then draw a cordon around Andesqueluz, as close as you can, and tighten it whenever you can. Badger him with nuisance attacks. Ambush him when he comes out to steal food. The terrain will force him to follow certain paths, right? Cover those with your firepowder weapons. Rig booby traps that make him waste power. Drain his blood one cut at a time."

"I'll think about that." Azim had described Nassim's current strategy exactly, except for committing the falcons.

"Excellent. So, before we settle down to dine on peacock tongues while virgins tempt us with lascivious dances, what can I do for you when I get to Shamramdi? Is there anything I can have my uncle send you?"

"No. He has been generous beyond my expectations and hopes."

"There's nothing you want?"

"Of course there is. Firepowder. I'll always want firepowder. But I can't demand something that can't be had."

"I see. And I am sorry, Uncle. You're right. There is none to be had anymore. The best manufacturers are outside the Realm of Peace. They no longer sell to Believers."

True. Nassim's former suppliers refused to receive his emissaries. They did not want their names remembered to the new crusaders.

Alizarin left his slice of shade. He looked up into the mountains, toward the Mountain, Asher. Was there some divine purpose to his having come to be known as the Mountain? Had Asher been scribbled on his forehead as he left the womb?

30. The Connec: Antieux: The Widow Returned

Bernardin Amberchelle strained to control his excitement when Kedle Richeut and the Vindicated returned. This was Antieux's greatest day. The Massacre had been requited. The man responsible was in chains, headed for the cathedral where so many innocents had burned to death.

People howled and threw filth. Neither Bronte Doneto nor Anne of Menand noticed but they were used least ill by those they had persecuted most vigorously, the Seekers After Light. Their most vicious assailants were Brothen Episcopals intent on demonstrating a civic loyalty overshadowing any allegiance to a fallen Patriarch. And their families had suffered in the Massacre, too.

The Vindicated began to evaporate. No discipline could hold them together now. Fewer than two score remained by the time the Widow reached the citadel.

Bernardin met her at the gate. He could not stifle his grin. Still, he did note that Kedle was neither comfortable nor happy herself. Having seen the key prisoners installed in cages where the populace could torment them, he took the Widow inside. He had her ranking bachelor followers given quarters, too, but separated her from everyone but a nervous pair of boys she would not put aside.

"As you will. Come." He led her to the kitchen, to the little room where he, Socia, and the Perfect had spent so many productive hours. She would want a decent meal. Then she would want a long soak in a hot tub, where she could fall asleep if she liked. She would want to spend a week burrowed into a feather bed.

She would want to see her children, too, but that could not be managed. Raulet and Chardén had gone to Khaurene with their grandparents.

*   *   *

KEDLE TRIED TO EAT LIKE A WOLF BUT HER SHRUNKEN STOMACH would not accommodate her. Bernardin tried several conversational sallies. She did not respond. He told her, "You're no longer a free agent, woman. You're back in the real world. It has no room for routiers. Here you are a subject of the Countess of Antieux. Here you answer questions when they're asked."

Kedle was ready to explode instantly.

Her independent assault on Arnhand, prolonged and unexpectedly successful, had convinced her that *she* was the law, with no need to answer to anyone.

The flesh of Bernardin's arms began to wriggle and knot. The fish things surfaced. Their flat eyes fixed on the Widow. And Kedle understood she had come into a narrow place.

She knew who had gifted Bernardin with those deadly fetches. She understood that their coming to life meant that Hope was not pleased. She could expect a visit from the Instrumentality, to remind her that she was a lesser mover in the Night's great schemes.

She was not ready to reject the love of the Night.

THE WIDOW SPENT THREE DAYS IN ANTIEUX, RECUPERATING. SHE should have stayed longer. Her bones still ached. She, the Vindicated, and their animals had been stressed for a long time. The fighters needed to rediscover their human side. But the Widow remained driven. She could not stay still.

The column that left for Khaurene was a third of what had come home from Arnhand. Kedle fumed but those standing down had the right.

Some rest came at Castreresone, where the entire population wanted to see the captives. The Castreresonese were less cruel than the folk of Antieux but their attitudes were hostile, especially toward Anne of Menand.

That woman no longer maintained her proud defiance. The abuse, the overwhelming hatred, had broken her. Serenity endured his captivity more successfully. He gave himself up completely to his hatred. He shouted threats. He spewed excommunications. Those who heard mocked him. He would die as cruelly as any Seeker whom he had sent ahead of him.

The Widow passed six days camped below the White City. Then, able to endure the pain again, she moved on. Near Homodel, where a battle had taken place during the Captain-General's incursion into the Connec, the Vindicated encountered a mob determined to rescue

Serenity. They outnumbered the Vindicated substantially but the Widow knew that they were waiting.

She could have avoided the fight. She chose extermination instead.

Serenity's friends did reach the cages. They did release him and his sponsor but Kedle kept them contained. The fire of four falcons eventually convinced the rest to surrender. Afterward, Anne and Serenity were forced to watch their executions.

Kedle rested a day, upwind of the carnage, then resumed travel.

Serenity abandoned threats in favor of prayer.

Kedle's bones continued to ache but she would not stop moving.

Lady Hope came in the night, with the Vindicated camped a day from Khaurene. She soothed the Widow's pains. "Darling Kedle, once thee reacheth this city thee *must* surrender to thy flesh. Thee *must* allow thyself to heal."

As ever, Kedle felt argumentative. But she could find no point from which to start.

Hope said, "There is naught more thee needs must do. The Connec is safe. Its enemies have been brought low. Kedle Richeut can go back to being the mother of her children."

Kedle nodded reluctantly. She had known that since Mestlé. The Widow and Kingslayer were needed no more. There were no more enemies. Anselin would make no claims on the Connec. He had his own kingdom to tame and, in the longer term, his ambition was to lead another army into the Holy Lands. He remained nostalgic for those bitter reaches.

"I'll be the Kedle Richeut that I have to be. I'm not sure God made me to be a mother, though."

"Yet thee hath children."

"I confess to being extremely fond of the act which occasionally results in children."

"Though thee hated thy husband?"

"He had one saving grace."

They stared at one another briefly. The Instrumentality said, "Permit thyself to heal, Kedle Richeut. If necessary, I will put thee into a coma for the time it takes."

"Thou art too cruel." Teasing.

"I am. I love thee too well to let thee harm thyself."

"I surrender." She paused a moment. "Tonight is the last night I'll have before I have to go back to being plain old Kedle Richeut."

Hope considered briefly. "I dare not, love. I have to be seen elsewhere tonight. I'm late already." She kissed the Widow on the forehead, then vanished. Normal night noises returned. Kedle had not noted their absence.

She did not fall asleep quickly. She brooded. Why could she not be excited? Her children and parents awaited, just miles away, but only the chance to see Socia again really moved her.

31. Brothe: Domestica

The six materialized in Anna Mozilla's drawing room. Red-faced, Titus broke away from the pack. Hecht was too distracted to notice. He felt as though he had visited several new realities while cutting the chord. He did not know why. All memory of the transition fled the moment he returned to the middle world.

Neither Heris nor Cloven Februaren were distracted, though. Heris snapped, "Girls!"

Vali asked, "What?" Lila just frowned.

The old man snapped, "You know better!"

Titus gasped, "It wasn't them. It was me. I was thinking about Noë." Consent's erection was blatantly obvious, though he tried to conceal it. He had been pressed against Lila during the transition.

Hecht growled, "Enough. Forget it. Anna! Where is Anna? Shouldn't she be here?"

Lila said, "She's probably at Noë's house. She helps Noë wrangle the boys. Noë can't always control them."

Titus had his composure back. "I'd better go." He gave Lila an uncertain look, like he ought to apologize for something, decided it was best to let it go.

Hecht said, "Yes. If she's there, tell her I'm here. If she cares."

Titus left like he was fleeing from rather than running to.

Hecht eyed Vali and Lila. Both were having trouble keeping straight faces. "Double Great, I'm thinking you and Grandfather have failed to apply the switch to these two often enough. Girls, don't do that to Titus."

"We didn't do anything!" Lila protested.

"I know. But you didn't let it go once it happened. Let's forget it, now. All of us." Because Heris was puffing up, getting ready to preach about taunting the weaker sex.

"All right," Heris said. "Double Great, it's time you and me got back to work."

Blink. Blink.

Hecht was alone with his daughters. He had no idea what to say.

Lila said, "I'm sorry. I didn't . . . Titus was . . . I don't know!" She blushed ferociously.

"I said leave it. It happens."

ANNA ARRIVED SO FAST SHE MUST HAVE RUN. "WHAT THE HELL ARE you doing here, Piper?"

He looked at the girls. "You didn't tell her?"

Vali said, "We thought it would be a neat surprise."

"I was about to start off for the Holy Lands. I wanted to see you before I left. Misfortune might be waiting out there. I could fall off my horse and drown crossing a river. A fever could get me. You're important to me. I couldn't let fate have its way before I saw you again. I can go away if that's what you want."

"Don't be an idiot. You girls will be sorry you didn't warn me. Piper, you know . . ."

"I know. I can't help it. I spend all my time being the Grand Duke of Arnmigal and Commander of the Righteous. It's hard to be Piper Hecht when I'm not on stage."

"How about that, girls? I'm the mistress of a duke."

Hecht felt a twinge of guilt. He was the leman of an empress.

The dalliance with Helspeth gnawed at him, though Anna never expected him to be faithful. Nor did he expect that of her, really, though his expectation was founded on a certainty that Anna Mozilla would not let herself be driven by her appetites.

Why did he feel guilty? He was doing nothing not done by a million other men, every single day.

Anna said, "I'll deal with these girls later. You're here now. We'll do what we always do and enjoy the time we have." She chuckled. "No doubt Titus has Noë pregnant again by now."

Cheeks slightly red, Vali asked, "Should we pop over to Grandfather's townhouse, or go visit the Construct, or something? So you can have some privacy?"

"No need," Anna said. "We're much too old for that sort of foolishness, aren't we, Piper?"

"Speak for yourself, old woman." He noted that Anna had aged some since last he saw her. She looked a touch more fleshy, too.

She asked, "Where is Pella? You didn't bring him?"

"He's with Hagen Brokke in Arnhand, lifeguarding the new king. I've had good reports. He arranged a peace agreement with that Connecten madwoman they call the Widow." He let his pride show but not his concern. Brokke should have returned to Alten Weinberg by now. He and Buhle Smolens would have to represent the Righteous while the Enterprise was operational. Brokke and Smolens would stand shoulder to shoulder with Ferris Renfrow and Algres Drear to shield Helspeth from her fractious stay-behind nobility.

Not something he needed to worry about, now. This was a holiday from being Lord Arnmigal. He told the girls, "Do go see Muniero. He's probably browned off because you're missing your studies, anyway. And let the old fraud know I'm home."

Both girls made faces, then turned sideways.

Anna said, "You really do presume."

"Not at all. Let's go into the kitchen. I'll show you how they prepare roast chicken in Alten Weinberg."

"I don't have a chicken to roast."

"Damn! And the kids aren't home. Whatever will we do?"

"HOW MANY PEOPLE KNEW I WAS HERE?" HECHT DEMANDED OF TITUS Consent. "How is it possible that, the morning after we arrive, I have a request from Addam Hauf for an interview?"

Titus was pale, frightened by Hecht's rage. "I don't know! But lots of people would know as soon as we turned up. Noë and the boys. Anna. Your girls. Muniero Delari and the people at his house. And anyone watching any of our houses."

"Enough. You're right. It doesn't have to be malice." He suppressed his anger. "Definitely not your fault. The Brotherhood didn't send the invitation to you."

"What will you do?"

"Ignore it. I don't have time. Even though I do owe Hauf for looking after Anna during the troubles."

"You might put your ear to the ground for a few minutes."

"What's happened?" Instantly sure that something bad must have.

"Not what you're thinking. Mostly foolishness. Like Pinkus Ghort talking Charity into sending an all-Brothen battalion to the Holy Lands."

"He did that? And, Charity?"

"Your friend Saluda finally picked a reign name. The news from Arnhand tipped him."

"That silly ass Pinkus. He didn't want to be left out so he worked his way around me."

"I expect he'll be waiting when we get there. Him and a clutter of others who took the sea route because you wouldn't let them come with you."

"He's gone already?"

"Four days ago. With three hundred forty veteran infantrymen, fifty-four horses, plus carts, wagons, and five falcons." Titus named Ghort's leading lieutenants. They were men Hecht knew.

"How can you know all this? I'd bet you haven't been out of bed twenty minutes since we got here."

"Your opinion of my prowess is welcome but too generous. You're right. I haven't been out of the house. But I was your spymaster for a while. Mrs. Spymaster doesn't get noticed when she's out. She hears a lot."

"I understand." He could not picture timid Noë deliberately eavesdropping. Nor was he comfortable with Noë knowing so much about her husband's business.

"Change of subject, Titus. Am I arrogant? Am I a controlling know-it-all?"

"You want an honest answer, Boss? Or the one you're going to like?"

"I think that says it all, right there."

"Not entirely. You're on your way but you aren't there yet. You still listen. You take advice occasionally. But are you controlling? Absolutely. In a huge way, and getting worse every day."

Hecht stifled his emotional response. "Go on."

"When we started out you picked people you thought could do jobs, gave them those jobs, then got out of the way and let them do their jobs. You don't do that anymore. You're always leaning over somebody's shoulder."

There was a reason for . . .

Exactly the reason he had heard from every out-of-touch senior officer who ever annoyed him by butting in to micromanage.

"Boss?"

"Give me a minute, Titus. I just suffered a bleak epiphany." He reflected for another fifteen seconds. "I've turned into what I loathed when I was a junior officer."

"The old veterans say you're not that bad. Yet. If that's any consolation."

"It's not, but it's noted. Could it just naturally evolve as we advance and get older? A squad is a team. The squad leader is first among equals, the experienced guy who makes good decisions fast. The next level is like that but four or five times bigger. Once you scale it up a couple more steps, though, you're where you don't know everybody. The mutual trusts begin to break down."

"Boss?"

"Musing out loud. Working out why these problems are inevitable. There's a tipping point somewhere. On the down-below side you trust nobody in charge because they obviously have no idea what the man at the point of the sword is facing. On the up side you can't trust any of those lazy fools down there to do what you need to get done."

"Interesting," Consent said. "I would think that a thoughtful man who didn't start at the top by right of birth would reach that tipping point later."

Hecht grunted, alarmed that he was not the ideal commander that he knew he would become back when he led the band that brought the mummies out of Andesqueluz.

Consent said, "Unlike any commander before you, you have the added ego-feeding burden of the Shining Ones."

That took time to sink in. He was not taking full advantage of the Old Ones? No. Of course he was not.

Hecht told Consent, "Titus, I'm slipping but I haven't surrendered to the Will of the Night. Not yet." He thought for twenty seconds. "I could be so much more—of what I'm not sure—if I made better use of the Shining Ones. I bet they mock me when they're with each other."

"Boss, they don't think that way. They're eternals. That kind of thinking is petty. Meaning mortal."

"All right." Hecht thought the Old Ones could be more petty than most humans, considering the myths and folklore surrounding them.

He and Titus were in Anna's drawing room. Anna was in the kitchen. Otherwise, they were alone. Unless . . . Hecht was tempted to summon the Choosers, just to see if they would come.

Titus said, "Much as I have enjoyed it, this visit wasn't a good idea."

"Titus?"

"The Master of the Commandery knows you're here. He knows you didn't ride in or sneak in on foot. He'll have Special Office help to pry."

Possibly. But Titus was not taking into account a mundane person's disinclination to believe in the things of the Night, in any practical sense.

Hecht said, "The Special Office has kept a low profile for years."

"Had to after they got caught doing what they were doing."

"Those were rogue Brothers."

Titus nodded. "Of course. Only a handful understood that they were doing the Adversary's work. The rest just did what they were told."

Hecht had fallen out of touch with all that. The Brotherhood of War and Special Office had been only marginally involved in his campaigns as Captain-General. They had only a small presence in the Grail Empire. God's warriors there belonged to the Knights of the Grail Order. The Grail Order carried God's wrath to the pagans of the east.

"Why are we worrying about this, Titus?"

"*We* aren't. You are, because Addam Hauf has shown that he may have supernatural resources."

"Right."

Hecht had options. He could send one of the girls to spy. Or he could send the Choosers. He would do that only in extremity. Hauf was not his enemy.

"You look nostalgic."

Hecht started. His thoughts had drifted to Helspeth.

"Now you look like you got caught with your pants down."

"Titus!"

"Just reporting what I see, Boss."

"Addam Hauf. Advise me. Should I see him?"

"He thinks his reason for seeing you is important enough to give away the fact that he has a supernatural connection."

"I wonder what that could be."

"He's sure to let you know. Isn't he?"

"Titus, you are, truly, a pain in the ass at times."

"We don't have a slave to whisper in your ear so I have to remind you that you're only a man. So far."

"So far?"

"That dimwit Asgrimmur managed to ascend. In a non-pagan land, in a non-pagan time. Look at the connections you have."

That was not a fate that appealed to Piper Hecht, Else Tage, or Lord Arnmigal. He was no pagan, however much he consorted with pagan Instrumentalities. Right now he owned no god at all, saving Helspeth Ege.

Anna broke his reverie by appearing with tea and a light lunch. She was so cheerful Hecht's guilt became self-loathing. "Principaté Delari is hosting a reception for us tonight. Titus, bring Noë and your children. The girls will be there. They dote on your boys. Piper, you can see Addam Hauf there. He can visit Principaté Delari without causing comment."

"Anna, once again you show me why I count on you. You think and create while I fuss, worry, and waste time."

"I do what I can."

Her response surprised him. Her tone was just short of sullen.

Titus felt it, too. He finished his tea. "Will the Principaté send a coach?"

Anna brightened slightly. "He will. Be here before the seventh hour. We'll ride over together." She gave Hecht a hard look.

Did she know about Helspeth?

No. Her attitude had to be a reflection of his own. "Titus, we'll see you then."

"All right. How will you get your invitation to the Master of the Commandery?"

"I'll think of something."

TITUS WAS GONE. HECHT FELT ODDLY DISTRAUGHT. HE COULD NOT articulate his malaise.

His loathing for Piper Hecht grew.

As Anna cleared lunch's leavings, he said, "I get the feeling you aren't happy with me. What did I do? Or not do? And what can I do about it?"

She startled him by stepping close and pulling him into a gentle embrace. "There isn't anything you can do, Piper. The problem is mine. My wishes have outstripped my expectations, and those exceed the most generous whims of reality."

Hecht had to admit, secretly, that he had no idea how the female mind worked.

Titus might be right. This visit might have been a mistake. Maybe he was supposed to leave this part of his life behind.

He could not. Abandoning Anna would mean abandoning Lila and Vali, too. It would mean turning his back on the Ninth and Eleventh Unknowns. It would mean leaving Heris behind. It would mean giving up the only family he ever had.

Heris, surely, would tell him to go to hell, even if the others tried to be understanding.

"Piper?"

"Anna, coming here may not have been the best thing to do."

"Piper!"

"I was almost at peace with being separated. Now I'll be in torment all over again." He *would* miss Anna. Anna Mozilla was the personification of home and hearth, always back there behind him, wherever he went. Anna Mozilla was the sure retreat, always waiting.

He was a selfish man. "But I'll get through it again. It's only one more year. Then there'll be no more crusades."

"So you'll just walk away from being a Grand Duke?"

"It isn't a real title. Well, it is, but without the powers and responsibilities. I get to use the revenues to pay for the Enterprise. If I don't walk away afterward Katrin's family will probably kill me."

"People haven't had much luck doing that, have they?"

"It only takes once. What do you think of Addam Hauf?"

"A true gentleman. That's unusual in a member of the Brotherhood. But he is merciless toward God's enemies."

MUNIERO DELARI'S COACH WAS CROWDED BY TWO COUPLES AND THREE children. Only three? The Consent spawn seemed like several more.

Noë Consent was radiant. Quiet and shy, she never called attention to herself. Hecht was surprised that she had become such a beauty. He told Anna, "Coming back was definitely right for Titus."

"It was right for us, too. Whatever you think."

That was wise old earth goddess Anna Mozilla talking. She was an Instrumentality in her own right, to Piper Hecht.

"I bow to your feminine wisdom."

"There is no need for ridicule."

He turned on Titus. "Mr. Consent. You're an old married man. Can't you keep your hands to yourself?"

Noë turned beet red but Titus said, "I could, but why waste time? I have to compress a year's worth into a two-day window." Unrepentant. And far from being as publicly demonstrative as Hecht's challenge suggested. Three children were underfoot, after all.

Actually, they were more present than underfoot. Only the infant was not hanging out a window, awed by the city as seen from a carriage.

Anna said, "I believe that was, in the lexicon of the soldiering trade, a diversion. Worry not, Piper. It worked. We're here, now."

True. Muniero Delari's man Turking opened the door. He put a portable step in place, then began handing the ladies down.

Anna went first. She left Hecht with a look that told him he was not as clever as he thought.

Principaté Delari himself came out to greet his guests. Hecht got the feeling his grandfather was putting on a show. He looked around for the target audience. Was Delari using him in some political scheme?

Heris and Cloven Februaren came outside, too.

Hecht felt a sudden chill. He turned. The light of an almost full moon revealed a dark silhouette atop one of the Old Empire triumphal columns that dotted Brothe. Most of those had lost the figures that topped them. This was one such.

The figure there now spread fifteen-foot wings.

"Message received." His dire guardians were with him.

The Ninth Unknown, he noted, had missed nothing.

Muniero Delari enveloped Anna in a huge hug. "So wonderful to see you, dear woman. You have become a stranger."

"An anchorite, of sorts," Anna admitted. "It's age, I think. Most days it doesn't seem worth the trouble to leave the house."

Hecht detected a note of melancholy.

He started to shake the Principaté's hand but the old man swept him into an embrace. He held that for a moment, then turned to the house with Hecht and Anna to either side. "I'm hearing amazing things about you, Piper. Amazing things. Let's get inside, away from the bugs."

Vali and Lila waited inside. So did Hourli and Ferris Renfrow, engaged in idle chatter.

Hourli was Raneul. Maybe that meant her prejudice against the Bastard was less virulent. Maybe it was just the times.

Hecht said, "You've gotten the place completely restored."

Delari said, "It's better than ever. And I'll be in hock to the money-lenders for two hundred years."

The girls came to greet Hecht. He said, "Don't you two look marvelous? Grandfather, I hope you're riding close herd on these two."

Anna said, "Really, Piper! Is that appropriate?"

"Look at them! Every randy moron over the age of eleven . . ."

"Use your head. They're women. And they're beyond any control but their own because they can go anywhere they want any time they want."

Whereupon Lila gave him an arch look that, in essence, dared him to trump that.

Februaren chimed in, "They're old maids already."

Vali said, "I see no point to getting married. Or even involved with a man. We have too much fun doing the stuff we're doing."

Hecht nodded. Considering the circumstances in which he had found the girls they were sure to have distorted attitudes about man-woman relationships.

Lila said, "I wish Pella were here. I miss that obnoxious little peckerwood."

Everyone stopped moving. Anna snapped, "Lila! Where did? . . ." She turned on Cloven Februaren, whose radiant innocence could have redeemed nations.

"As noted, the girls can go where they want, when they want. She may have been hanging out with low characters."

"There's no doubt about that."

Delari's woman Felske announced dinner, which would be served buffet style despite the status of the guests. The Principaté did not have the staff to serve a formal dinner and refused to bring temporary staff into his home.

Hecht sighed as he began choosing foods. Posted near the long sideboard, Turking seated each guest. Though not consigned to a separate table or room, the Consent dependents ended up as remote from their host as could be managed.

It took everyone a quarter hour to settle, Titus last because he helped Noë. Vali and Lila were down at the foot with Noë so they could help wrangle the little people. Muniero Delari sat at the head of the table, the end, with Hourli to his immediate right and Hecht to his left, next to an empty chair. Anna sat beyond that. Heris ended up next to Hourli with an empty seat beyond her. Titus and Ferris Renfrow each had a seat beside one of the girls. Titus was content but Renfrow seemed a little put out. A third open place lay opposite Cloven Februaren. It featured a place setting but no chair.

Even the little ones looked to the head of the table.

Delari was amused. "Considering this eclectic gathering, the traditional prayer would seem misplaced. Take a moment to commune privately with your own concept of the divine. I'll use my moment to heap curses on those who didn't have the courtesy to show up on time. Well. Here is one of them now. Him I'll only consign to Purgatory."

Asgrimmur Grimmsson came in from the same side room Februaren, Heris, and the girls used when they transitioned into the townhouse. He had a feather in his hair and was straightening clothing that looked like it had been dragged from a sack. Turking intercepted him, spoke softly, led him past the buffet, seated him next to Heris.

No one said much during the process. Renfrow's scowl deepened because he had been seated below the ascendant. Hecht watched suspiciously. Grimmsson muttered something to Heris about bad weather over the Jagos.

By then Turking had gone to greet the next tardy guest.

There was almost no talk at the table and little eating, except amongst Titus's brood.

Hecht focused on his sister and the ascendant. Something was going on there. He would have a hard time minding his own business.

Belatedly, he realized that the evening would betray his real relationship with Delari, Februaren, and Grade Drocker—if those not in the know paid the least attention.

Hecht met Hourli's gaze. She arched her right eyebrow. She needed do nothing more to communicate an admonition regarding Heris and Asgrimmur. Just a little reminder about hypocrisy and double standards.

He winced.

Hourli knew things he would rather she did not. That gave her a minor lever.

The Ninth Unknown watched from down the table. That old fox probably knew . . .

Turking returned accompanied by Master of the Commandery Addam Hauf and the head of the Bruglioni family, Paludan Bruglioni. Paludan was in a wheelchair, still.

Hecht had had little contact with the Bruglioni the past few years—though he had made Paludan's lifelong best friend Gervase Saluda Patriarch by fiat.

Paludan must be here on Charity's behalf.

Hecht left his seat, met Paludan at the sideboard. "Let me help." Turking was behind the man's wheelchair.

"All right." Bruglioni told Hauf, "You first, Master."

Hecht said, "I didn't expect to see you."

"Nor I you. I expected a quiet chat with a powerful member of the Collegium who hasn't been especially supportive of Charity. Imagine my consternation when Hauf arrived as I was getting down from my coach. Now I'm entirely at sea."

"You're not unique."

Bruglioni betrayed a ghost of a frown when looking at the girls and the Consent brood. He then concentrated on choosing foods, mainly rich dishes in heavy sauces. "They won't let me enjoy myself at home. If I eat nothing but what they let me, instead of what I want, will I live forever? I don't think so. Do you have any idea what's going on?"

"No. Though I thought I did before I got here. Same as you."

"Blindsided, eh?"

"Exactly. Isn't that enough food?"

"More than. But Delari is paying for it. So. I *am* here because of my connection with Charity?"

"I imagine."

"Why are you here? How can you be here? You should be hundreds of miles away, on the road to the Holy Lands. Gervase produced a clever bull proclaiming your Enterprise of Peace and Faith."

"For which the Empress is grateful. She thinks it appropriate to respond by backing off of some of her father's more outrageous territorial claims."

"Really? A little of that would do a lot to solidify Gervase's seat."

"I suggested she wait till I get back from the Holy Lands."

"Too bad. Gervase hasn't made many friends. Principaté Delari's threatened displeasure is the main force keeping the Collegium from trying to remove him."

"Really?"

"I'm sure there are several plots afoot."

Hecht looked past Bruglioni to Hourli, who met his eye. She nodded slightly. She would do what needed to be done.

She nodded again seconds later. What needed doing had begun.

Hecht said, "Gervase is in a less precarious place than you fear."

Bruglioni looked up with troubled eyes. "I worry about you. There's always something askew."

"If you say so. I've always done my best for the people I represent." Bruglioni grunted.

Muniero Delari asked, "Will you boys stop gossiping and join us? I'm hungry."

Hecht had been heads-together with the master of the Bruglioni family longer than could possibly be considered casual. "Of course." He carried Paludan's food choices while the man rolled his chair.

Hecht slid back into his own seat. Only Bruglioni was not eying him.

Muniero Delari said, "Everyone. Eat."

ADDAM HAUF DID NOT PRESS DURING THE MEAL, NOR EVEN DURING coffee and brandy afterward. The lower half of the table cleared away. Hecht used that time to state his appreciation for Hauf having sheltered Anna and the children during the troubles.

Delari, though, was intrigued. He asked Hauf, "Will you need my quiet room?"

"No. My news isn't confidential."

"But forewarned is forearmed?"

"Yes. Commander, most of this is from Madouc of Hoeles, who used to work for you. He's in the Holy Lands, now. I think he expected his reports to reach you via Cloven Februaren, whom he seems to think is a sort of supernatural entity."

"He's a super something," Heris interjected. "The common variety of which is found on the road behind a cattle drive."

Whereupon Februaren suggested, "Asgrimmur, you need to put a smile on that woman's face."

"Please!" Hecht snapped. "No vulgarity. Master Hauf, if you will?"

"Madouc is now Master of the Commandery at a fortress called Gherig. You know it?"

"The name came up during planning. A stout fortress, from all reports."

"It is. But less so in the age of the falcon and firepowder. A renegade Sha-lug named Nassim Alizarin wrecked part of it by igniting smuggled firepowder that set off Gherig's own secret store."

Nassim Alizarin. There was a name out of yesteryear.

"The point is, the Dreangerean sorcerer er-Rashal al-Dhulquarnen fled north through the Holy Lands after Indala defeated Gordimer. He's hiding in the Idiam, in the haunted city Andesqueluz, and is trying to resurrect an Instrumentality known as Asher."

Hecht said, "I don't know the geography or mythology but it sounds like he's up to the same mischief he was into in the Connec and on Artecipea." He glanced at Hourli. She shrugged.

Hauf said, "Asher was a primal Instrumentality of the region. Typically, all blood and thunder. He could be the father of the God of the Dainshaukin."

"Wow. That's scary."

"Madouc is concerned. So am I. You may have to deal with other players once you get there."

Hecht glanced at Hourli again. "It's always that way. Nothing is ever straightforward and simple." The Shining One had nothing to contribute. "Is that really what you wanted to see me about?"

"Mostly."

Hecht wanted to find out how Hauf had been alerted to his presence in Brothe. But that was a task better left to the Shining Ones.

"So. I'm glad Madouc is doing well. Master of the Commandery? Who died?"

"The Brotherhood created a new commandery in order to keep a villain named Rogert du Tancret from having the final say at Gherig."

"We squabbled all the time when Madouc was my chief lifeguard. He took his work dead serious and there was no flex in him."

"I wish the Brotherhood had a thousand more like him."

"Pity the world."

Hauf smiled weakly. "One thing further. In the nature of a personal favor. Take Redfearn Bechter's effects with you. They're yours, by bequest, but the Brotherhood hopes you will honor one of its greatest by allowing his few things to be laid down in the soil of the lands to which he dedicated his early life."

"That seems reasonable." Hecht flushed slightly. Bechter's little chest was somewhere in the baggage that followed him around but he had not thought of it in months. He had given up trying to solve the puzzle or message the chest represented.

Hauf flashed a squinty look of appraisal, suspecting that Hecht had forgotten. "Thank you. In time, success permitting, we'll move his bones to the Holy Lands, too."

The exchange baffled the others. Hecht said, "I wish we could talk more. Bechter was dear to me but I never got to know him well."

"He was one of the few who survived the Well of Days. That was so harsh the Brotherhood sent the survivors west. They were oppressed by guilt because they had survived. They were unlikely to stand up to another hard fight."

Redfearn Bechter never showed any weakness while serving the Captain-General. But he had not been called on to face Indala al-Sul Halaladin, either.

Hecht said, "We need to be sociable." He announced, "We're discussing a mutual friend, Redfearn Bechter, who was with me during the Connecten campaigns."

That helped. Some. Some recalled the sergeant.

Hecht told Hauf, "I hope I run into Madouc early. He should be able to tell me everything I need . . ."

Hourli's expression shifted almost imperceptibly. Hecht understood that she wanted a private moment. "I need to step out for some air. I'll be right back." He followed Hourli.

A breeze had come up. It had turned cold. Dust and trash hurtled around. "Going to rain," the Instrumentality said. "Maybe hard."

"Maybe. What is it?"

"The soldier priest knew you were here because he has a brace of sorcerers hidden in his fortress. They couldn't tell how you arrived but they knew you had, within minutes."

"Sorcerers? Not good for a man in his position."

"His intentions are pure."

"Aren't they always?"

"The Night twists men who use it to their own ends."

"Personal warning?"

"If it fits. There is another matter. The eternal monster beneath the city has arisen again. We annihilated it but it won't stay annihilated. The people of Brothe must have their diabolical duke of darkness."

"That's good. Thank you."

"You're wasting time here. Go back to Alten Weinberg."

Hecht glared, yet saw nothing to suggest that she meant more than what she said.

"You're right. This was an emotional pilgrimage. It may not have been necessary."

"We should get back inside."

"Right again."

"I'm a goddess. I'm always right."

"In your own mind." He rejoined the company thinking he was sadly underutilizing his supernatural allies.

He announced, "People, this has been as much a farewell as a celebration for me. I don't feel good about my prospects. I do expect the Enterprise to achieve great things. It will shape the world in countless ways, some of them unexpected. But . . . I do have that bad feeling. Now . . . it's time to say good-bye. Noë, don't cry. Titus will come through fine, probably sainted."

Hecht gathered his flock. Consent did the same, though baffled. He whispered, "What's going on?"

"I'm not sure. It's a feeling. We may have committed more than the obvious error by making a sentimental visit."

Paludan Bruglioni and Addam Hauf seemed thoroughly confused.

Hourli closed in on Bruglioni. She did not identify herself. She spoke softly and quickly, delivering information the Patriarch could use to consolidate his hold on the Church.

Then she told Hauf, "So long as you keep your hidden sorcerers the darkness beneath Brothe will return to life again and again."

The Master of the Commandery wanted to ask questions. He chewed on air. Hourli walked out. Hauf went after her. He found no sign outside that she had been anything but a shard of imagination.

He did glimpse a winged thing atop a triumphal column where no figure ought to be.

THE DRAMA HAD ANNA IN TEARS. NOË AND HER BROOD HAD BEEN taken home. Heris and the girls, and Cloven Februaren, crowded around Piper and Titus. Those two faced one another, by Titus's choice. Piper tried to break the tension with an uncharacteristic wisecrack.

The human ball rotated out of existence. Air whooshed in to replace it.

Anna wondered if she would ever see Piper again.

HECHT WAKENED CONFUSED AND GROGGY. HE DID NOT KNOW WHERE he was and was not entirely sure who. He was alone but that lasted only moments.

Rivademar Vircondelet shoved into the room. A team followed. One man carried a tray with bread, tea, and soup. A barber and a tailor followed. Two boys lugged a big copper tub. Other boys carried a carpet for the tub to stand on. Yet another carried towels, soap, and fragrances.

Vircondelet said, "Lieutenant Consent said you were ill."

Hecht heard an unspoken, wary, "Again."

"Bathwater should get here about the time you finish eating."

Hecht punched himself on the side of the head. "I had the most bizarre dream. It seemed so real."

"Yes?" With genuine interest.

"It was one of those ones that you know can't be true but is still so strong you can't ever quite convince yourself that it wasn't."

"Never had one of those. Except when I was four or five I dreamed there were two moons. I argued with my parents about it for days."

"How long?" Hecht asked. "I mean, this."

"Six hours since Consent said there was something wrong. You were running a fever. You talked but you didn't make sense."

"Where is Titus?"

"Getting ready to travel. It'll be sunrise in an hour. You wanted to hit the road today."

"Don't look like that's going to happen." He felt drained. The confusion would not go away. He rubbed his forehead and scalp with his left hand. "Titus makes mountains out of molehills."

"You're not sick?"

"I'm just bone tired. Let's get on with this. Maybe we *can* move out today."

"The Empress wants to see you."

"Oh. Sure. So much for heading out today."

Helspeth was not pleased. "Have I grown tedious already, Lord Arnmigal?"

Lady Hilda's expression was strained. She did not flirt when she brought coffee.

They three were alone in the quiet room.

"Your Grace?"

"You haven't been to evening prayers since you came back."

He had not. And had not thought of it, either. "I was unconscious." Would she be unreasonable?

"I know. You went off somewhere with Titus Consent and those . . . *beings*. Did they turn you into a eunuch?"

"I was sick."

Daedel tried to help. "Lord Arnmigal must be dreadfully tired, Helspeth."

"But able to consort with devils."

Logic would be wasted. Helspeth felt neglected. That was that.

Lady Hilda topped Helspeth's cup. From behind the Empress she moved her lips exaggeratedly, warning him against defending himself.

He did not. He was interested only in sleep.

That concerned him. Being ready to nap at any moment was out-side his experience. Nor could he get useful advice from his people. Nobody had any idea what was happening.

Hourli said bear with it, sleep when he felt like it, and time would cure it.

Helspeth fixed him with a fierce gaze. "I won't be discarded like some camp-following trollop."

Again Daedel signed for silent suffering. She tipped a hand, sug-gesting he sip his coffee.

It was a way to temporize.

He worked it out. Helspeth was scared. Change was in the wind. He would be gone a long time. She would be without the shield of the Righteous. Maybe she tasted his premonition, too. And he was doing nothing to still her fears. His excuses, however valid, carried little emotional weight.

"I have delayed departure a day already. I will join you tonight."

That, of course, threatened to set her off again. If he was going to show up only because she nagged him . . .

Lady Hilda whispered something Hecht could not hear. Helspeth stopped being contrary.

"What did she want?" Titus asked, worried about last-minute meddling.

"She was upset because I didn't report in and didn't go to chapel. She knew we'd been away."

"Then somebody has been talking about things he shouldn't."

"Maybe. It doesn't matter, now. We'll be on the road. We won't have to answer to anyone but ourselves."

"God might quibble. Otherwise, I'm looking forward. Tomorrow for sure, right? The baggage is already moving."

"As soon as there's light."

Helspeth was especially demanding. And she wanted to pray, too. Hecht suspected she was moved more by despair than desire.

Titus said, "That took a while."

Hecht hid the time candle. "She wouldn't stop talking. I couldn't just walk away."

"I'll find you a ride so you can sleep as we go. Oh. Pella and Brokke showed up."

"Really? They're finally done out there?"

"Anselin finally felt comfortable. And neither Hagen nor the boy want to be left behind." Brokke was scheduled to stay in Alten Weinberg, though.

"Anna will cut me if I let Pella come." Hecht headed for his quarters, eager to see the boy and hear his stories.

Anna would have to deal. The boy was old enough.

HELSPETH AND HER LADIES CAME OUT TO WATCH THE COMMANDER of the Righteous depart. It was a cold, damp day, not unusual this spring. Some less venturesome staffers whined about the possibility of snow.

Once the party left Franz-Benneroust Plaza Lord Arnmigal deserted his mount for a place in the vehicle Titus had prepared. Consent called it a coach but the level of luxury was substantially lower. The vehicle was actually a wagon with a mattress tucked in amongst onion sacks and wooden boxes.

Hecht did not care. It took only moments to fall asleep. He slept all day and still had no trouble sleeping that night.

Some staffers were not happy about having to camp out. They wanted to hop from inn to inn. Lord Arnmigal wanted everyone hardened now. Neither the Pramans nor the Holy Lands would be considerate of their comfort.

There were no serious problems. His staff handled routine well. They needed no close direction. And just as well. Ten days out of Alten Weinberg Hecht was sleeping twenty hours a day.

Which suited his people fine. They never knew which Lord Arnmigal they would get when he was awake.

Sometimes he was the Piper Hecht they had known for years. Often, though, he was cold, remote, intolerant of error or imperfection. In that character he seemed clairvoyant, too. He knew what had to be done before it needed doing. That created efficiencies but also worried men already troubled by the oddities of their commander.

After those ten days, though, Piper Hecht began sleeping less.

He met the King of Hovacol on the bridge that had featured in their first encounter. He told Stain, "You've had it all from the Empress already but I wanted to deliver my own appeal. Helspeth and I want you to lead the next wave into the Holy Lands. We had to turn away thousands this time."

Stain was no longer belligerent. He was not looking for a fight, even sanctioned by the Church. He accepted the role reluctantly.

"Hourli, I want to see you," Hecht told the air once he returned to his wagon, exhausted. Stain had kept him up for hours.

The Instrumentality materialized. She planted her behind on a box. "Yes?"

"Stain was different today. Why?"

"The supernatural wasn't involved anymore."

"I like your style. You're straightforward."

"All salesmanship, Commander of the Righteous. Most mortals hate the gods because of our disdain for clarity. We will avoid ambiguity where we can—though that will irk some clients, too."

She might be trying to irk him now, on some level.

She continued, "Stain was possessed by a regional Instrumentality that might have been a deity in pagan times."

"One that took off after mixing it up with me?"

"Apparently, Godslayer."

"My life keeps getting stranger."

"Should I resent that?"

"See things from my perspective."

"I do try. And I do so, better than you suspect."

"Is it likely to be a nuisance?"

"It's damaged, hiding, hoping to be forgotten."

"No longer a threat, then." Hecht found himself not caring already.

"No."

He was done, then. He was ready to sleep. But Hourli had something on her mind and wanted to be coaxed.

He asked, "Is it important?"

"Judge for yourself."

"So?"

"Despite observing your rules of the march your advance columns are meeting resistance in the Antal hinterland, not just from Pramans. Eastern Rite and Antast Chaldareans have been belligerent without genuine provocation. That has not served them well. Your lieutenants smash resistance where they meet it because of the remarkable intelligence they enjoy."

"Attempt to elicit a compliment duly noted."

"Thank you, Commander of the Righteous. The work is more difficult than you think. We are now operating at our extreme limits, well beyond our range in olden times."

"Really? I thought you were feasting at the Wells of Ihrian."

"You did?" Her expression betrayed real disbelief. "Where did you get that idea? No. Of course not. Much as we would love to streak in and feed till we're too fat to move, we can range only so far ahead of our nearest believers, with that distance dwindling as we as we get farther from the Realm of the Gods. To actually reach one of the Wells we may require the assistance of the Bastard, the ascendant, and your whole family. Once we do get to a Well, though, we'll get healthy fast."

Hecht questioned none of that. It made sense despite confusing him when he considered specifics.

Almost sad, though, that the Old Ones were dependent on the belief of people who followed other religions.

"Your situation will improve as I get closer myself?"

"You in particular, yes. In a reverse exponential sort of way."

"Which means?"

"Each ten miles closer you move will advance our reach by two or three miles."

"I see." No wonder the Old Ones made themselves useful. "I should be traveling faster, then." Though he was gaining on the big mobs quickly. His group had more flexibility.

"That would be good. A situation is developing on the eastern route."

Once across the Antal Land Bridges the Enterprise main body split to follow three separate routes through the central mountains, easing the strain on local populations. The easternmost route passed through small Praman states nomad tribes had hacked out of the Eastern Empire. That force would emerge from the mountains to threaten northern Qasr al-Zed and Shamramdi.

"What is it?"

"There's the rub. We don't know, exactly. We can't quite get that far. We think the regional princes are gathering a host. They might outnumber us substantially. The ground is not well suited to western-style warfare, nor can the Shining Ones get there to help."

Hecht knew that country only through travelers' tales. Nevertheless, he could picture it. And he knew the tribal style of warfare. The allied princes would deploy their horse archers first, hoping the heavier western cavalry would chase them and wear themselves out.

"Kait Rhuk is out there. Here is what he should do—though I expect that he has seen to it already. First, he must make sure that he is in complete control, in my name."

Hourli listened. "As you wish. Though getting your orders through will mean walking the last twenty miles."

32. Khaurene, the End of the Connec

Brother Candle wakened in the wee hours, suddenly, not because of pressure in his pitiful old bladder. His tattoos itched terribly.

He was not alone. Had Bicot Hodier suffered a moral relapse?

The candle on his nightstand, beside his washbasin, strove valiantly against the darkness.

Imagination? Or the shredded remnants of a too-real nightmare?

He considered that candle. Why was it burning? A night light was too costly an indulgence, though it was not *his* indulgence.

He blurted, "Devil woman?"

Shreds of black swirled round the candle like moths. The Instrumentality appeared in the guise she had worn the night he had acquired his tattoos. His flesh responded again.

He was mortified, but filled with wonder. What sorcery was this? Mankind would embrace and venerate it if it could be made available.

The itching worsened. His snakes were restless.

The woman grinned wickedly. "I am sorry. I should not be so immature. I should not have to reassure myself all the time."

Her speech was contemporary but with an odd rhythm.

Brother Candle was confused. An Instrumentality was trying to treat him with respect. He, a mere human, who considered her an agent of evil.

She flashed a spine-melting, manhood-stiffening smile. "Thee thinketh too much. Thee giveth too much import to our differences. All middle-worlders do. See me the way thee seeth Kedle and Socia. As thee would look upon thy daughter."

"Now you mock me. You cloak yourself in that aspect of carnality . . ."

"Oh! I am flattered. And I do enjoy a sporting night." The air shimmered. Moths no larger than fleas fluttered briefly. The Instrumentality stepped out of the dusky cloud an older woman, dumpy, missing an upper front tooth, wearing dark hair on her upper lip. "Better?"

"Some. My mind remains afflicted by memory."

Had he really said that? He had not been that candid with his own wife when they were young enough to be tormented by fevers of the flesh.

"Ah, thee beeth too sweet."

"Can you make these snakes lie still? And stop itching?" Then he groaned. What a thing to say to this sort of temptress!

She ignored the opportunity. "I come to warn thee that Kedle arrives tomorrow. She brings the captives from Arnhand. Thee will find her changed. She will be harder. She will be less patient. She is injured, too. She refuses to take time to let herself heal. I would see thee compel her to take the time."

Brother Candle shook the erotic fog, some, though his memories would not go away.

The Instrumentality added, "She has been known to listen to thee," and, "She is precious to me."

"Oh?" The Perfect wondered if that meant what it sounded like. That sort of romance was uncommon in the Connec, where romantic love was the ideal but happened between men and women who worshipped one another from afar.

"She reminds me of my father."

So. This Instrumentality might be capable of pursuing a dozen romances at once, with boys, girls, and goats.

She nodded slightly, with a thin smile.

"That is what I came to tell thee, Master."

"Why must you use the dialect? You don't do it very well."

"Modern speech is confusing. Too formally informal. I am trying. I do not want to stand out when I would rather go unnoticed."

Brother Candle forbore observing that her going unnoticed was highly unlikely.

She said, "Just make Kedle take care of herself. Make her stay with her family. She does love her children despite not knowing how to show it in ways thee find appropriate."

He replied, "It may take a while to wean her off her taste for blood."

"Thee hath no hope of that. She has drunk too much and found it too sweet. I must leave thee, now. I am needed in the east." The moths stirred. The intensely desirable girl reappeared. She stepped closer, laughing throatily. "Would thee like a sweet memory to take to thy pallet?"

He could not make his voice work.

She said, "Sorry, Master. I cannot help it. It is my nature."

She faded, but touched his cheek just before she vanished.

The serpent there extended its tongue to taste the back of her hand.

The shock was electric. Brother Candle did not sleep well afterward.

He needed to find another Perfect, to confess, and to be shown the way back to the Path.

But the only Perfect available was the loathsome Brother Purify.

*   *   *

BROTHER CANDLE, WITH THE ARCHIMBAULTS, WAS IN THE MOB MAK-
ing it difficult for the Widow, the Vindicated, and their trophies to enter Khaurene.

Navayan soldiers helped make way. Their eyes hardened when they
considered Anne of Menand. The caged woman did not understand
that she had caused the death of their near-sainted King. She was a
broken beast.

Brother Candle thought that he ought to stop the abuse, but he
could not. The Khaurenese needed the emotional release. He told Archimbault, "I have to leave. I shouldn't have come. I'll beg the Countess to allow you to enter Metreliux. Or I'll drag Kedle down to your
house."

Archimbault nodded grimly. He was a good Seeker. He would become an excellent Perfect one day. He should not condone his daughter's actions. But he was a father and citizen of Khaurene and the
Connec, too. He could not still his pride and gratitude.

The Widow and the Vindicated had worked wonders. They had
ended a persistent, pervasive, relentless threat to the liberties and fortunes of the people of the Connec—for this generation, at least.

BROTHER CANDLE WAS THERE WHEN KEDLE PRESENTED HERSELF TO
Socia and the new Duke. Lumiere was in a fine mood, gurgling and
wiggling while his mother handled ducal business. He charmed the
courtiers with his ready smile and flirty eyes. Only a handful thought
his presence unseemly. The Countess was no day-laborer's common-
law wife.

Kedle, the Perfect noted, had clambered down the long slope to
the mundane world of courtesies and courtly politics. She dressed as a
woman and was appropriately respectful.

This was her first formal appearance before her Countess. Socia
had trouble remaining formal when she would rather be hugging.

Both had been cautioned. The invisible observer, Queen Isabeth,
would judge their behavior. If she found the Widow too disquieting
she might leave a viceroy with troops sufficient to enforce his views.

The grand formalities, and the presentation of trophies, passed.
Socia dismissed the court. She led Kedle and Brother Candle to a private room where bread, mutton, and pickled onions waited. "I wanted
to make us a den like the one we had in Antieux."

Brother Candle did not remind her that Kedle had spent little time
with them in that room.

Socia said, "I wish Bernardin were here. But someone has to crack the whip in Antieux. So. Darling Kedle. Tell me everything. And don't leave anything out, even if I already know."

Brother Candle found the Widow's tale uncomfortably candid. The woman knew neither shame nor remorse.

BICOT HODIER VISITED BROTHER CANDLE IN HIS METRELIEUX CELL.

The Countess would not allow the Perfect to move in with the Archimbaults. She was ardent about keeping him close.

The old herald announced, "I'll be leaving Khaurene. I thought the news might interest you."

"At your age? Because of what happened before?"

"Not that. Not so much. But I do have religious motives."

"I'll miss you, truly. You're a fixture of my Metrelieux."

"I'm joining the Connecten contingent headed for the Holy Lands."

Connecten contingent? Brother Candle could not imagine Connectens heading off to participate in a religious war after all that had gone on here for so long.

"I didn't think you were the crusading type, Bicot."

"I'm not. I'm the pilgrim type."

"I see." That made sense.

Brother Candle kept toying with the idea of a pilgrimage himself.

Hodier declared, "I have nothing here. The Countess will be better served by someone younger whose thinking approximates her own, so I'll drag this old carcass east and lay it down in the land where God was born."

"Who all is going? I might tag along."

Hodier's eyes waxed huge. The suggestion did not please him. "They'll all be Brothen Episcopal. You'd have trouble fitting in. Why would *you* want to visit the Holy Lands, anyway?"

"You said it. That's where God was born. We agree on that, whatever differences we have on what he said or meant." And there was a huge one right there, the Perfect realized. Aaron was not God in flesh to any but a small cult of Episcopals whose heresies the Church suppressed as enthusiastically as it did that of the Maysalean Good Men.

"You're teasing. You wouldn't try that at your age."

"No doubt. I don't handle sea travel well. I still marvel that seasickness didn't kill me during the Calziran Crusade."

"I've heard tell." Big, friendly grin.

"So, all best, from your God and mine, Hodier. Fair winds at sea and cool breezes after you arrive."

One well-known fact about the Holy Lands was that the heat there was unbelievable. And the region swarmed with countless biting, stinging insects, some of which caused deadly fevers.

Thoughts of heat and insect miseries, preceded by deadly pitiless seasickness, as the price of admission to a cauldron of bloodshed, left the Perfect reconsidering even thinking about a pilgrimage to the Holy Lands.

BROTHER CANDLE DID GET AWAY TO SEEKER SERVICES AT KEDLE'S home. She had inherited a sizable establishment from Soames, who had left no family to dispute possession. Archimbault-related Seekers had occupied, protected, and maintained the place while she was away.

Some had ambitions involving the property but lacked the courage to argue with the Widow. She installed a dozen Vindicated, then defied the world to challenge the propriety of the arrangement.

The Perfect did not know the full facts but believed that impropriety existed more in the minds of observers than in what happened in private.

The meeting was nostalgic. The local Seekers agreed that it had the comfortable feel of sessions in the old days. Brother Candle eyed Kedle, remembering her as a shy child who nonetheless worked up the courage to express her opinions to adults. She was more reticent now though the others showed more willingness to defer.

Her father suggested she speak. She replied, "After going the places I have, seeing the things I have, sinning as I have, I have no business speaking to the Seekers. I must find my way back to the Path first."

Brother Candle clapped his hands gently. "Well said, Kedle. I, too, will defer to those who haven't strayed."

Someone accused him of attempted poesy.

"Think as you will. Right now this Seeker is far from Perfection. The rest of you go ahead. I will referee should the exchange become heated."

Kedle told him, "You come help me in the kitchen."

She began by busying herself with the teakettle. Little Raulet, having sneaked out of bed, joined them. He stood eight feet away and stared at his mother, not the least sure about her.

That saddened the old man. It said so much. It declared the rapidity of change. Kedle's babes already felt closer to their grandparents, and to Escamerole and Guillemette, than they did to their mother. And Kedle seemed both ignorant of how to correct that and possibly disinclined.

Brother Candle wondered if it might not be possible to have her boys raised with Lumiere.

"Master, I am a bad woman."

"Kedle? How can you say that?"

"I am a devil. A waste of flesh as a woman. It tears me apart but I can't stand this." She gestured, indicating her surroundings.

"Uhm?"

"The guilt. It hurts so much. But I can't live this life anymore. If I stay here I'll go mad. I'll hurt somebody."

"You'll settle in. All soldiers have to adjust."

"I'm headed for the block. I can't stop thinking evil thoughts."

"The war is over, child. You won."

"The war with the monster inside me has only just begun, Master. This morning I caught myself trying to work out how to kill Raulet and Chardén so I wouldn't have that responsibility anymore."

Brother Candle was appalled. Was speechless, as she expected him to be.

She had confessed because she did love her boys enough to want them protected.

The Perfect felt the reality behind her fear. "The Instrumentality. Can you summon her? Can she help?"

"Hope? She never showed me a way."

"Too bad, that." Should he believe her? "I can't call her, either."

Kedle eyed what could be seen of his tattoos. "What is she up to with you, anyway?"

"I don't know. Bernardin and I . . . I think her original scheme has passed her by. Things didn't work out the way she expected. These snakes, and Socia's ability to change shape, may just be useless afflictions, now." He hoped they no longer fit the Instrumentality's plan. "Hope is ancient compared to us but she's really just a spoiled, willful, not very bright child enamored of the power of a woman's body."

Kedle nodded. "Willful, selfish, and self-important because she's destined to survive beyond the Twilight. Though that whole mythology must have totally unraveled by now."

Brother Candle did not understand so Kedle passed along Lady Hope's explanation.

"I see," the Perfect said, though the northern beliefs were no less confusing for having been explained by an insider.

"Hope had to go join up with the other Shining Ones. Something to do with the crusade. She never clarified what."

The Perfect said only, "We should get back before the gossip starts."

Kedle's eyes widened. Then she laughed, but the mood fled quickly. "Master, I am truly afraid that I might hurt my sons."

This was not the girl Brother Candle had known as a child. She could now be considered a minor Instrumentality, personifying the darkness at the heart of Connecten nationalism. "We can't have that."

"That's why I brought it up, old man!"

Brother Candle sighed. Now she was angry. He did not understand. Something had warped her root nature. The twist had been slow, beginning long before it became evident, possibly even before her marriage and the time of exile on the Reindau Spine.

"I'll talk to the Countess and your father. He may never understand. He only sees his little girl even when she shows up in bloody armor."

He paused. Kedle did not need her father explained. She needed a way to come to terms with herself. The war between what she was and what she thought she was supposed to be caused pain that she expressed as rage against what might look like the source of her dilemma.

Kedle said, "Talk to Momma first. Momma understands me better."

Could be. Madame Archimbault never put herself forward but she was the backbone of the family. She had a little quiet Kedle in her. She would be more disappointed than Raulet but definitely more understanding.

The Perfect said, "Let's see what we can do for the boys right now." He had some ideas. He would run them past Socia.

QUEEN ISABETH LEFT KHAURENE QUIETLY. ONLY A FEW PEOPLE TURNED out to watch. The weather was damp and cool and Isabeth had done a good job of fading from public awareness. She left one company of sixty soldiers to defend the Duke and train local soldiers.

The flight of militant Episcopals left the city quieter than it had been for years.

The economy was recovering. The Khaurenese were hardworking people who understood that God had given them an opportunity.

Partly due to the intercession of Maysalean Perfects, Serenity and Anne of Menand went off display, to be confined in more benign circumstances. Both recovered some. Anne never did understand why she had been so maltreated.

Their God did not intercede on their behalf.

Perhaps He was testing their faith. Serenity certainly believed himself to be on divine trial.

The deposed Patriarch loudly insisted that he was still the legitimate prelate.

Two score citizens of Antieux made the pilgrimage to Khaurene to attest to the evils Bronte Doneto had inflicted upon that city.

The verdict was never in doubt. Only the severity of the sentence remained to be discovered.

Brother Candle and other Perfects argued for clemency. They won the point partially, on Anne's behalf, and that only because they argued that the judges must honor the Widow's commitment to King Anselin.

Anne went home after just five weeks of Khaurenese torment, the shine gone off her that quickly. Anselin was welcome to her.

Kedle volunteered to lead her escort.

Socia refused her.

So the Widow vanished. Like that, during the night, she and the Vindicated decamped.

Brother Candle was surprised only because Kedle said no farewells.

Evidence at the Soames house suggested that the flight had been planned and executed with military precision and little concern for family.

Socia summoned Brother Candle. "Kedle is headed for the Holy Lands. She is on the road to Terliaga. She has a ship chartered. It won't be fully fitted and provisioned for several weeks yet."

"You know all this how?"

"I went and looked."

He did not address that. She was a grown woman. She knew her own mind. Nor would he be able to change anything after the fact.

He was certain she roamed the darkness most nights, more carefully than she had done in Antieux. There were no rumors.

She was not him. She would not disdain the use of the tools the Instrumentality Dawn had given her.

He said, "She hid her intentions well."

"She wasn't happy. She couldn't be the Widow here."

"I knew that without understanding how miserable she really was."

"What are you thinking about, old man?"

"Nothing. Other than to wonder about how Raulet and Chardén will be affected." Mother preferring war to the company of her sons was sure to shape tomorrow's men.

"They're already used to her not being around."

He grunted.

"Kids are tougher than you think. I survived it. You scream and curse but ten minutes later you don't remember what your problem was." She was sad, suddenly. "Neither Raulet, nor Chardén, nor even Lumiere, will have known their fathers."

"You've been thinking about this."

"Having children makes you think."

"Unless you're Kedle."

"She thought a lot. Count on that. And she's still tormenting herself."

Probably true. "She was afraid she would hurt them. Physically."

"I know. The same hungers and dreads haunt me. But I don't have the option of running away."

"Kedle has another twist. Hope set the fire."

"I know. But Kedle wants that not to be true."

Brother Candle thought Kedle wanted it to be true with Socia, instead—the impossibility of which might have tipped her decision to run away. Choked, he said, "I know how I can help."

BROTHER CANDLE WORE THE WHITE OF A SEEKER PERFECT. THAT DREW stares in Terliaga. Terliagans seldom saw Maysaleans. Most did not realize what he was.

Though al-Prama was the majority religion in that city, most other faiths had a following. Unlike the Khaurenese, Terliagans got along.

Brother Candle was intrigued by the squawking, quarreling sea-birds overhead. He acquired an equally raucous coterie of curious youngsters. He smelled the waterfront long before it came into sight.

The vessel he sought proved to be a dismally small coastal carrier called *Darter* the way a grotesquely fat man might be called Tiny. He grew miserable just looking at it. Its aroma said it went fishing when it had no cargo or charter.

Brother Candle supposed the crew would not be above a foray into piracy, either, if the odds looked good enough.

The roguish-looking one-eyed ship's master was pleased to have another paying customer. He became obsequious once he saw the Perfect's serpent tattoos. The eyes of the one on the old man's throat tracked.

No other passengers were aboard when Brother Candle took possession of a coffin of a cabin, determined to begin gaining his sea legs while the craft was still tied up.

Raulet Archimbault and the Khaurenese Seekers had been profligately generous in their effort to succor the moral foundation of their most famous daughter. Kedle might become the face seen by the entire eastern world.

So Brother Candle could afford the ship's mess and a personal cabin.

The old man obsessed. Why must he afflict himself with the hell to come? Why was he not on the road to Sant Peyre? What hideous, insane compulsion drove him?

A Seeker pilgrimage to the Holy Lands really made no sense.

There was only one explanation.

The Good God required his presence amongst the Wells of Ihrian.

33. Lucidia: The Mountain and the Mountain

The Mountain was on the Mountain. The Rascal had grown that weak. Nassim and the Ansa dared, occasionally, to move into visual range of Andesqueluz.

The subsidies from Indala let the Ansa spare men to watch. Alizarin kept his lightest falcons deployed, too. Despite the firepowder shortage his crews had permission to fire if they got a good shot. Sometimes a crew moved fast enough. The effects were small but cumulative.

Er-Rashal fought back, ever less effectively.

"What is he eating?" Nassim once wondered. "He was never the sort to garden."

Az replied, "The Ansa say some of their people have disappeared."

"He *ate* them?"

"So the Ansa believe. It's one more reason they've gotten aggressive. They're terrified of what he could become if he resurrects Asher."

Nassim stared across the barren slope. He saw only shades of brown flecked by points of sage gray. Not much lived up there. "What are we doing, Az? Is this really God's work?"

"One must consider the impact on the Faithful of er-Rashal being successful at recalling his devil."

"One should, yes."

"The Ansa fear that he will soon begin capturing sacrifices to finish his ritual."

"Sacrifices? On top of cannibalism?"

"So they say. The missing people were probably sacrifices that he ate afterward."

"Why would they think like that?"

"They have tribal recollections of the old ways." Az shrugged. "They've been setting traps. Some of them are quite clever—and appallingly ugly. They want to borrow a falcon."

Nassim was reluctant to risk his weapons.

Az said, "Give them the four-pounder from Haeti. It's brass. No iron in it. He might not detect it till he's too close."

Er-Selim had it all worked out. That falcon had been installed on an approach to an Ansa encampment already, in a defile where its bite could not be avoided. He found little ways to deflect er-Rashal's supernatural superiority. Most hinged on the sorcerer's natural arrogance.

A *crack!* rolled across the slope. A cloud of smoke rolled up, then began to shred in the air moving up the Mountain. "Oh, my!" Az said. "Look at him go! That old devil is spry for his age."

A man in brown flashed across a clear space several hundred yards away and slightly downhill. He limped. One arm hung lifeless. Still, he put distance between himself and the ambush. He changed course, headed toward the Haunted City. His condition hampered his climb.

Nassim said, "Where are the archers who should be chasing him?"

And Az, "Proof of concept. That ambush hurt him."

"He walked away, though," Nassim objected. "How did the falcon crew do?"

"He got hit, that's for sure. He's really dragging, now."

Nassim harrumphed.

"We can pull the noose tighter. We can get up where we can see the Haunted City all the time." That prospect, set forth, thrilled the Master of Ghosts not at all.

Al-Azer er-Selim had been to Andesqueluz before.

The cost of embarrassing the Rascal became evident quickly.

Three of the falcon crew had suffered convulsions so violent that they had broken their own bones. Two might never walk again.

Az murmured, "It's time the Ansa shouldered more of the burden."

Nassim agreed. The Ansa were not stupid. They would let outsiders do as much of the suffering as they could.

The Mountain said, "Let them keep the falcon. Teach them to use it. Give them four charges and powder for four firings. If they do some good I'll give them more. And what the hell is he doing?"

He pointed downhill. Bone was climbing the Mountain.

Az suggested, "Let's go meet him so he don't kill himself before he can tell us why he's all worked up."

Bone being out here could only be an evil omen. "I'm not sure I want to hear it."

Alizarin's foreboding was sound. Bone had no wind left when Az and Alizarin reached him. The man had to get his breath back. "We have been summoned to Shamramdi."

"We?"

"All of us. Indala is gathering every man who can heft a blade or spear."

"But . . . why?"

"There was a battle with the crusaders who call themselves the Righteous, in the Muterin Valley, near Sailkled."

Nassim did not know those places. If the Righteous were involved, though, those must be in the Antal somewhere, presumably in the Praman principalities. "I can assume the outcome did not favor the Believers?"

"God averted his face. The Qipjaq and Osmen princes lost twenty-two thousand warriors. Fewer than two thousand escaped."

This was ghastly news. The Pramans of the Antal would no longer be able to withstand the predations of the Eastern Empire.

Az muttered, "So Captain Tage *has* lost touch with his roots."

Bone said, "Not the Captain. His lieutenants and some nobles from the Grail Empire."

Nassim grunted. No matter. Else Tage had sent them.

Bone continued, "Sailkled is one hundred thirty miles northeast of Souied ed Dreida." Souied ed Dreida—just Souied to most—was the second city of Lucidia. Or the first, if you asked its own people. It lay fewer than two hundred miles north of Shamramdi. "Souied has no garrison but old men and boys."

That was because Indala did not trust the men of Souied, with reason. He had sent the best to Dreanger last year. Most had not returned. This year's levies had gone east to resist any incursion by the Hu'n-tai At.

The Great Shake had expected the crusaders to come down to the coast of the Holy Lands, never threatening the cities behind the Neret Mountains.

"So. They surprised us by taking an eastern route through the Antal."

"Some did," Bone said. "Two other columns are bound for Shartelle."

Nassim left the Mountain. He made the Ansa understand that he was not doing so by choice. By way of showing his true feelings he left another falcon and ammunition for a dozen firings. He wished them the grace of God and begged them to accept at face nothing involving er-Rashal till they killed him, dismembered him, burned the pieces in widespread fires, then scattered the ashes on the wind.

Nassim was not sure that would be enough. There were folk tales about demons who pulled themselves together after treatment equally harsh.

The Mountain had not yet reached the foot of the Mountain when echoes of falcon fire overtook him.

Az said, "I don't like the sound of that."

"Maybe they're amusing themselves."

The second falcon barked just moments later. Az just muttered, "That can't be good."

34. Creveldia: The Unseen Path

The Ninth Unknown materialized in the square of the former Krulik and Sneigon manufactory in the Eastern Empire. It was high noon on a cool day. The tribal people who saw him thought that he had no shadow. They fled.

A woman materialized a dozen feet from the old man. She cast no shadow, either. Neither did two more women who arrived immediately.

A slim blonde just coming to her full beauty marked the eastern corner of a square aligned with the points of the compass. She sniffed. "They were here, maybe last night. Definitely since the last rain."

Heris occupied the southern corner. Mildly envious, she said, "How can you tell? I spent more time with them. I practically snuggled up with Copper and Korban."

"Bet they loved you running your fingers through their beards," Cloven Februaren cracked.

Vali chided, "Maybe you snuggled so close you got used to the smell."

Heris refused the bait. These days the girls lived to get a rise out her. Vali had a particular knack for implication wrapped in an innocuous observation. It was all in the timing, tone, and inflection.

The girl was a menace.

The old man was amused but threw no oil on the flames. The girls would not spare him.

They were not malicious, really. They were just two young women making sure the world paid for their having to suffer the indignities of puberty. Malicious mischief, really.

They were past the worst. Everyone hoped.

Februaren said, "We ought to take care of business and go before some idiot decides to test us."

Lila responded with a snort. Despite the wonders she had witnessed lately she still considered the Ninth Unknown eighty percent blowhard. The old devil encouraged the underestimation. Someday that would let him teach a valuable lesson.

Vali sniffed. "I smell animals. And filthy people." No surprise there. Heris had predicted that.

The Devedians had built well. The mountain people would have been foolish to let such good shelter go to waste.

Februaren said, "Let's watch ourselves. Let's not get hurt."

His companions stared as though wondering what he meant.

"This way," Lila said. "The scent is stronger from the building with the concrete foundation."

Heris said, "That was where the owners and managers worked and lived." She had come here before.

The girls had, too, and Februaren nearly as often as Heris. Heris growled, "That's where Korban and his thugs took the falcons away." The falcons Piper had left so she would have weapons to use in the Great Sky Fortress. Those falcons were, no doubt, now in the hands of the Aelen Kofer, being radically improved.

Februaren entered the building wondering loudly why the women of the family had to be so determinedly contrary.

Lila said, "They were here." She looked at Heris. "Can you find the gateway?"

"I don't know. They wouldn't let me see how. More the rituals than the way but Iron Eyes was in charge. He has a big lazy streak. He wouldn't have tried hard to hide it. He wouldn't expect anyone to look."

The old man agreed. "Despite being sure that I'm a master villain he would never believe that a middle-worlder was clever enough to open the way if he did stumble onto a gateway."

Vali asked, "Even though you already did it once?"

"A fluke, obviously. Purely accidental. I was just bumbling around. So he would think. If he thought at all."

"He can't be that dumb."

"Aelen Kofer aren't stupid but they aren't thinkers. Not in any abstract sense. They're builders and doers. The Shining Ones worried about consequences. But not much."

Heris said, "We're being watched."

"Of course we are. We're invaders."

Lila opened the door to the office place. She tossed something inside. A flash and bang followed.

Nothing else happened.

Heris observed, "That might not impress this bunch. They saw plenty of smoke and bang when the Deves were here."

"Whatever. There isn't nobody in there." She stepped back out, pointed at curious children watching from forty yards away, laughed maniacally.

"Drama queen." Vali sneered.

"Stick in the mud."

"Girls. Focus," the old man said. "This could get dangerous."

Lila made a face, but said, "Heris, there's an area in there with a really strong Aelen Kofer smell." She headed back inside. The others clumped after her.

There was some chatter somewhere outside, the language unintelligible but the fright plain enough. There was no bellicosity in it.

Februaren muttered, "Why didn't those idiots in Hypraxium put a garrison in here? It couldn't be that hard to figure out how to make their own falcons."

Heris said, "The Emperor believes falcons to be tools of the Adversary. He doesn't want them included in his arsenal. His generals understood the lesson Piper taught at the Shades, though. This was where the bigwigs stayed. And the Empress when she was here. There were partitions in here, back then."

Tribal people still chattered outside, louder but no more intelligible. Heris wondered how they had reacted to the Aelen Kofer, or if they had seen the dwarves at all.

Februaren said, "I got some of that. They won't bother us if we don't threaten them. They already think this building is haunted."

A toddler in a filth-stained rag of a shirt too large for her appeared in the open doorway, fist in mouth. She needed her nose wiped. A frightened woman no older than Lila snatched her up and fled.

"I like this," the old man said. "I don't have to work so hard."

Heris felt bad for the villagers but not badly enough to go away.

"They did use this place till the dwarves scared them off," Heris observed. The grime and rubbish made a clear example of why city folks considered their country cousins subhuman. "Poverty is no excuse for this. I've been poor. I never lived like a pig."

Februaren said, "Never mind. We aren't missionaries. Lila?"

"The other end is where the smell is the strongest."

"Let's open a couple of windows and get some light."

The women moved, Lila leading. Heris wondered, "Did they come through when people were living here?"

Lila said, "They did stuff to scare them off. Can't you smell it?"

"No." Heris had one supernatural talent. She could use the Construct to walk the Night. She was better at that, now, than the Ninth Unknown. She had no capacity whatsoever for smelling magic. Though Lila admitted she did not actually smell anything. That was just the most proximate sensory reference.

Februaren said, "It's there. I can smell it, too. They were definitely here recently. A lot of them."

"Recently we figured."

"Uhm. The strength might be intentional. Maybe they left a little something for us."

Heris, Vali, and the old man formed an arc behind Lila. The blonde focused on what was in front of her.

Heris thought she might be seeing the maturation of the Thirteenth Unknown. Lila might get picked for that before the Twelfth Unknown took over for the Eleventh.

Februaren was as intent as Lila. "Are they aware that we're trying to get into their world?"

"How would they find out?" Then, a thought. "Oh. I see."

"Asgrimmur."

"He might still be in touch. The Bastard thinks he could be. He's for sure always fluttering around in the shadows of the Shining Ones."

Korban Iron Eyes had not been completely truthful when he declared an end to all contact between his and the middle world. There had been numerous dwarfish incursions since, usually technology-related. Heris had yet to catch them, though.

She and Februaren wanted to reach the dwarf world so they could look for a path from there to Eucereme.

The Raneul Hourlr had shown a flattering interest in Heris from the moment she decided to look. He was afraid at the same time. *She* was the Godslayer now.

The Old One was forthright in his interest. He was randy. Secretly, he hoped she could get through to his home world. He wanted her to believe that the Old Ones there could help resolve the Twilight, which could end the middle world.

The Ninth Unknown said he exaggerated. The deity had his personal agenda. But Hourlr would not talk to him. Hourlr could not communicate with anyone male. Nor would Heris allow him near Lila or Vali. She knew that light in his eyes. No more Bastards would drop into the middle world.

As if thought alone could conjure a devil Hourlr stepped out of the doorway vacated by the snot-nosed child without having come in from outside. "Still watching over my shoulder."

"You are endlessly fascinating."

"He said with a straight face." She said with a slight blush.

"We cannot help being interested." Fraught with double meaning.

Heris flashed a nervous smile. Hourlr was a charmer. He made his desires seem so utterly reasonable that you might find yourself making the two-back beast before you realized that he had suggested it.

She told herself she was an old campaigner in a long, tough struggle. She would not succumb. "Of course."

The Old Ones were all charmers. Even sour old Wife could heat it up when she wanted.

Hourlr asked, "Are you sure you really want to get into the world of the dwarves?"

"Yes." And he had been feeding the idea.

"Why?" He wanted to know if she had thought this through.

"You know why."

"Not exactly. No. Unless you have an abiding need to see Khorben Jarneyn again."

"Again said with a straight face."

"I was not teasing, lady."

That left Heris nervous. "What are you hinting at?"

"It's good to be a god."

"I would think so." Had his agenda changed?

"You haven't found a pathway from the middle world to Eucereme."

"We haven't. No." He knew that.

"I'll gift you with knowledge. That is because no such way has existed since the ascendant trapped the rest of us. The free Raneul did not just close the ways, they destroyed them."

"With help from the Aelen Kofer. Of course."

"Of course. The Raneul wouldn't actually do any work themselves."

"Which means I'm on the right road." Heris grinned. "There have to be connections from the world of the dwarves. They wouldn't let it be any other way."

Hourlr nodded. "You might be an Instrumentality yourself, Heris Godslayer." He reeked of charm.

The girls and the Ninth Unknown watched intently, Vali most attentively. A smoldering slow match had appeared in her left hand. Her right clutched a massive handheld falcon, pointed at the floor right now, hidden under a kerchief.

The Instrumentality had begun keeping a wary eye on Vali, unnerved by the fact that his charm had no effect.

Heris said, "We think the rest of the Shining Ones can help us here."

"If you believe that you are deceiving yourself."

Heris was startled. "How so?" That was a change.

"They have no reason. You cannot win commitments from them the way you extorted them from us. The ways to Eucereme are closed for a reason. The Raneul plan to evade the Twilight by sitting it out, an avoidance of destiny by abstention. Which I expect not to work."

The more he said the more she realized that she had considered her choices from no perspective but her own—despite the Ninth Unknown's similar argument when he tried to talk her out of this adventure.

She avoided Februaren's eye. Smug old fart.

"I suppose." It made sense when he said it. "Because I'm me I can't see the doorway, but I know it's here." Hourlr nodded. She added, "I want to see the other world even if we never go there."

Lila sniffed, moved in little shuffles, palms facing outward.

Februaren grunted suddenly. "What the hell? How did that . . . ?"

"Double Great?"

"We're about to solve a mystery. On the other side of this gateway."

"What mystery is that?"

"Open it up. It could be my imagination."

"Any idea how?"

Lila said, "I'll do it." She turned sideways.

Heris squeaked.

A rectangle of reality, shoulder-high and six feet wide, chunked backward two inches, then slid to the left, vanishing behind reality that did not move. Even the Instrumentality seemed awed.

The panel's movement revealed Lila squatting in the mouth of a tunnel with a roof barely high enough to clear a tall dwarf's crown.

The rock appeared to be basalt. Basalt did not underlie this region. The light of the middle world, not bright back with the visitors, penetrated only a few yards into the passageway.

Vali observed, "It's wider than it is tall."

Lila said, "It's really dirty, too." She sneezed. "It would be big-time spider country if it wasn't for regular traffic."

The Instrumentality began to glow. That light all flowed into the tunnel, illuminating it for thirty yards. It ran downhill ten degrees, straight, wide, and low, the floor cluttered with dust and stone chips.

Lila sneezed again.

The Ninth Unknown mused, "It really is," puzzling everyone. He pushed past Lila, bent over briefly, then took a knee and stirred the detritus.

"Aha!" He held up something shiny.

Heris blurted, "Piper's missing pendant! How did that get in here?"

Meantime, the old man picked up what looked like shreds of silk. Like something a woman might once have worn next to her skin. He seemed baffled as he slipped the shreds inside his shirt.

Heris did not miss that.

She did not mention it. It could mean anything.

The old man, moving a foot at a time, produced other bits that must have gotten tracked in by the dwarves.

Hourlr asked, "Shall we see where the tunnel goes?"

Heris suggested, "You light the way."

"Of course."

Lila squeezed aside. The Ninth Unknown did the same. Heris followed the Instrumentality. She told the old man, "Give me that. I'll get it back to Piper."

Februaren surrendered the pendant without comment.

The tunnel ended at a wall of oak planks a hundred yards directly ahead. There were gaps between planks but nothing could be seen on the other side. "It's dark over there," Februaren said.

"Thus spake the Lord of the Obvious," Heris said. "How come there aren't any stars or anything?"

"The sky is overcast," Hourlr said. "Can't you feel the rain?"

Cold, damp air pushed through between planks.

Februaren predicted, "She'll want to go ahead anyway."

Vali said, "If we left the door open the cold air would cool things off up there . . . What?"

Even Lila looked at Vali like she wondered how her mind worked.

Hourlr said, "Leaving it open is not an option."

Heris kicked a plank, hard, by throwing a foot out sideways. Something cracked, evidently not part of her. She kicked again.

Voices came down the tunnel. The Ninth Unknown cocked an ear. "Tribesmen. How long have we been down here?"

"Four minutes," Heris replied. She kicked again. Nails squeaked. The right end of the plank backed off half a foot.

Hourlr said, "For them it has been an hour. They wonder where we have gotten to. A few are working themselves up to come find out."

"You can understand them?" Heris asked.

"Some."

"I thought time matched up between the middle world and the world of the dwarves." She noted that Hourlr had begun to frown fiercely.

The Instrumentality got hold of the plank she had been kicking, pulled it back into place. "This is a trap. That isn't Dwarvenholm. It's the world of the giants. Help me."

His glow revealed that the nails had been driven from the tunnel side. Heris's kicks had broken the plank end.

Dawn began on the other side.

The Ninth Unknown said, "Vali, go scare those people away. Lila, work your way up the tunnel and find the way the dwarves really used. We'll stay here and make sure nothing breaks through."

There was enough light to reveal some of that world—in particular, that world's creatures approaching. They did not conform to Heris's preconception. The nearest pair resembled very large scorpions moving sluggishly in the cold and damp. Farther off, things like giant crabs moved more briskly, headed toward the gateway. The scorpions were a brownish yellow, the crabs pale red.

Hourlr told Heris, "Those are not the giants. Those are their watchdogs. But the giants are coming. We'll need this sealed completely before they get here. Stand back. Let me work."

The giants, Heris recalled, were mortal enemies of those who hailed from the Realm of the Gods. She recalled the giant bones scattered down the cliffs below the Great Sky Fortress.

"Done!" Hourlr muttered. "And just in time. Have a look." Heris squinted through a gap between planks.

A troop of huge beings loomed over a ridgeline half a mile away, barely visible through the drizzle. They advanced with vast, slow strides. The biggest had to be a hundred feet tall. The ground began to tremble.

Heris grumbled, "Why don't they collapse under their own weight?"

Hourlr said, "That's a glamour. They are not actually that big. And they are supernatural. The Night frees them from many constraints of the natural realm."

"Whatever. I find myself moved by an overwhelming disinterest. Let's get out of here."

"Not just another pretty face. She's smart, too."

"Stuff that." Heris headed uphill, toward sounds of agitation that must be Vali's fault.

This time she sensed a change as she neared Lila because she was feeling for it. Lila said, "There's another tunnel here, sealed the same as the entrance up top. We didn't notice because it's on the side and we were in a hurry. Triple Great. Get behind Aunt Heris." She made a simple gesture after he moved.

This door opened as though on hinges, folding out from its downhill edge, to exactly block the tunnel. There was a *click!* when it reached a right angle. Solid stone seemed to close the way. Heris wondered if giants coming up would see a similar wall from the other side.

This side felt like rock to the touch. It was rough and cold and growing damp.

Hourlr entered the new tunnel, which ran level and curved to the right. The Instrumentality moved carefully, assessing his surroundings. Heris suspected that he was embarrassed about having a mere mortal girl find what a god had missed.

She hoped that made Lila less interesting.

After ninety degrees of curvature the side tunnel came to another barrier of planks. It was raining on the other side here, too. Heris snarled, "We're back where we were before."

Lila disagreed. "There aren't any giants."

Hourlr nodded, then slid aside for Cloven Februaren, avoiding contact as though the old man had sprouted cactus spines. He did contrive to brush against Heris, though. She jumped and squeaked. His touch was a sharp shock, not what she expected and not at all exciting.

Februaren peered between planks, grunted twice, once puzzled, once surprised. "This comes out the same place as the gateway in the barge in the Realm of the Gods."

Heris grumbled, "How can that be?"

Hourlr's face collapsed into an expression that defined *frown.* "Aelen Kofer magic," he muttered, withdrawing inward.

The Ninth Unknown kept thumping the planks. "What are you doing?" Heris demanded.

"Trying to break the latch. It's a gate. Latched over there because there isn't anybody on this side who needs to get back."

A plank gave way. The old man shoved a hand through the gap. Heris demanded, "Do you *want* to get their attention?"

"Not a problem. They don't post a guard. You want them underfoot, you have to summon them." He pulled on something. The plank construct swung away. Cool, damp air rushed into the tunnel. "Interesting, though, that different pathways go to the same place."

Lila said, "You don't know that. You know that the two we've found go there."

The old man grumbled but did not argue. She had a point. A scary point, Heris feared.

She had no trouble seeing Iron Eyes make it work that way. The dwarfs had to walk to wherever they wanted to open a gateway home but maybe once they did that they could connect to a central point so no more walking need ever be done.

She asked, "Double Great, can we walk the Construct in and out of there once we've been there?"

"Interesting question. Let's find out. It didn't work for the Realm of the Gods, though." He glanced at Hourlr.

The Shining One had no opinion. He focused on the rainy world. Heris thought he was nervous, maybe even afraid.

Februaren said, "Don't anyone go through before I fix it so we can see the gate from the other side."

Heris recalled him describing how he had done that before. The gateway would have disappeared if he had not left it plainly marked.

"First thing, then, let's jam it open."

Hourlr told Heris, "We should not do this."

"You don't want to get home?"

"They will be aware of us as soon as I step through."

"Then don't do no stepping. Duh!"

The old man had the plank gate open. Heris saw the damp meadow clearly and could just make out standing stones in the distance. She saw drag marks in the grass. The Aelen Kofer had brought something heavy through here.

The Ninth Unknown said, "Lila, loan me your duster thing. It will stand out against the green."

Lila's outerwear fit no category clearly. It was too long to be a shirt, too light to be a jacket, wide like a serape but not hooded like a poncho. She had created it herself, for travel. It was yellow and red. It was not comfortable in the heat of the middle world but it beat the chill down here.

"I don't think so. It'll get all wet."

"I'm open to suggestions."

"Have the devil make a magic beacon."

"That would work," Hourlr admitted. "And, again, it would alert the Aelen Kofer."

Heris asked, "Is there any reason to go out at all?" She cringed as her companions glared.

In a flat, controlled voice Lila reminded, "This expedition was your idea, Auntie."

Her initial reasoning seemed strained. She did want to reach Eucereme and the Instrumentalities there, but . . .

She was no longer sure what she hoped to accomplish. She talked about helping Piper but that would not withstand logical scrutiny. Piper had help.

Piper was at war with the Night only when the Night got in his way. She, though, was at war with the Night directly. She had become the Godslayer. She had exterminated the oldest and hardest generation. Now she would . . . what? End the Tyranny of the Night?

Hourlr shifted uncomfortably.

No. She was not at war with his generation. Not with his kin and kind. Absent Ordnan, Red Hammer, Zyr, and the Trickster, the Old Ones were, generally, rather decent.

Cloven Februaren gave up fingering Lila's cloak thing. "Guess I won't need this if you just stay standing in the doorway." He stepped into the drizzle, which was more a falling mist, now. "They had a watch set after all."

Heris saw squat, wide shapes between her and the standing stones. She recognized Korban Iron Eyes right away.

35. Hypraxium: Interlude

Lord Arnmigal's rush to overtake the Enterprise stuttered when his band reached the heart of the Eastern Empire.

The Emperor, Monestacheus Deleanu, saw in the Enterprise an opportunity to humble old enemies and restore the fortunes of his state. He hoped the westerners would reclaim provinces that al-Prama had nibbled away over the past two centuries. He believed the situation in the Holy Lands would correct itself once his Empire was restored.

Lord Arnmigal had instructions from his Empress. He was to remain polite, agreeable, and, on the surface, amenable. The Enterprise needed Monestacheus Deleanu to maintain its lines of communication.

Lord Arnmigal could not refuse an invitation to visit the Emperor and Hypraxium, nor did he want to miss the wonders of the grandest city in the world. Neither did he want to endure the political weather that such a visit would bring.

He and his senior people were assigned a villa overlooking the westernmost of the Antal Land Bridges. The Phesian Bridge lay on the left hand, facing south. The headwaters harbors of the Agean Reach lay to the right. There were a dozen harbors, large and small, natural and man-made, civilian, commercial, and military, each defended by its own fortifications. The villa was fit for an emperor. It did belong to the Deleanu clan. The comforts included running water, heated baths, and flushable garderobes.

Hecht grumbled, "They mean to seduce us with luxury."

Titus reported, "I've received six more requests for 'a moment' of your time and we're still unloading. How do I refuse without offending anyone?"

Pella suggested, "First, make them come to us. Second, Dad can hold audiences. No private meetings. A lot of them won't say what they really want if there are witnesses."

"Listen to that, Titus. Who are these people, anyway?" Hecht was checking a list.

"Some generals. Some priests. Some nobles. A member of the Imperial family who thinks he should be the next Emperor. Monestacheus hasn't designated a successor. Kalakakian is a merchant from somewhere out east, richer than God Himself. Those two are the factors for the local colonies of Aparion and Dateon. They want to rehash the contracts they made last year. I imagine they think they can twist our arms now that we're here."

"Why?"

"Both senates want a monopoly on access to Shartelle after we take it. Dateon wants to buy it."

"Everybody wants something. Nobody donates anything."

"That's people, Boss."

"I know. It's depressing. Makes me wonder if we ought not to breed it out of them."

That got him an odd, troubled look.

"I think I'll take a long nap, Titus. I'm getting cranky." He had been working his way out of the need for so much sleep. He managed ten hours of work a day, now, and that should keep improving.

Consent nodded. "I'll put out an audience-only alert with a suggestion that you'll consider private visits for anyone who can convince me that their business is worth your time. Even the most self-absorbed understand that you have to go on south. Our lead elements are approaching the northern Crusader States now."

The Shining Ones reported frequent skirmishing. The investment of Shartelle would begin soon. Indala would not be able to save the city because another force would threaten Shamramdi.

Pella was close by most of the time, sulking because he could not be at the tip of the spear with Rhuk or Prosek. "You *have* to be there to coordinate it, Dad. Nobody else can do it." Meaning only Piper Hecht could manage the Shining Ones, whose existence was becoming ever less a secret.

No outsider suspected the whole truth but, clearly, the Commander of the Righteous had resources inside the Night. There could be no other explanation for how he knew so much so fast about events so far away.

The Shining Ones were his best reason for catching up. He needed to be several hundred miles farther along before the Old Ones could reach the nearest Well of Ihrian.

Hecht thought they might suck that dry—and become major Instrumentalities once more. Which would present him with a battery of fresh challenges.

He felt an odd eagerness himself when thinking about the Wells.

He seldom recalled having been Else Tage. Even Piper Hecht had slipped, some. Publicly, he was Lord Arnmigal. He thought of himself as Commander of the Righteous or, occasionally, Empress Helspeth's secret lover.

He did not think of his family often, except for Pella, who was underfoot all the time. The boy made himself almost as useful as Titus. Maybe Titus ought to go back to his field command so Pella could try the staff role.

That would not happen unless Titus asked it himself, though.

THERE WERE FEASTS. THERE WERE A THOUSAND OTHER DISTRACTIONS, including the countless marvels that made Hypraxium a wonder of the world. Lord Arnmigal let himself be shuffled hither and yon while staffers did the real work.

Wherever he went, usually with Pella and a disguised Shining One, he was subjected to introductions and incessant appeals. It felt like the Grail Empire's ambassador to the Golden Gate wanted to keep the Commander of the Righteous entangled.

Hecht mentioned the notion to Hourli.

Hourli was having fun being Lord Arnmigal's mysterious companion.

Hecht preferred the more demure and quietly radiant Eavijne. Pella, naturally, was enamored of Aldi, who was not seen much but who blinded her audiences when she was. She could not help herself.

Hourlr he never saw.

Hourli soon reported, "You were right about Ambassador fon Machen. He wants you kept from moving on. It's ideological."

"How so?"

"He is Katrin's man, committed to Serenity. He has connections inside the Society but is not a member himself."

Hecht grunted. All that was remarkable in these parts.

Hourli continued, "He has blood and marital connections with some of the most vehement, revanchist detractors of Lord Arnmigal and the Righteous."

"Give him credit for his show of being helpful."

"Which was why you became suspicious. Would you like me to do something?"

"Not really. We'll adapt as the situation unfolds."

"His intimates include numerous local villains who hope to become parasitic on the Enterprise."

"No worry. We're having dinner with Monestacheus tonight. We'll drop a few hints."

"Take Aldi or Eavijne. Aldi can turn them into drooling idiots. Eavijne can tempt their sympathy to pathological levels."

"I prefer you. These men are impressed by a woman with a brain as well as a fine . . ."

"Not quite golden-tongued, are you?"

He did avoid observing that he might learn by the time he reached her age.

"You want mature and intellectual, take Wife."

"No. It's you. Or the Choosers."

"That could be entertaining."

"I'd like to save them for another time."

"If you insist, then. I shall be glamour and intellect alike. I shall charm them with my wit. I shall . . . I shall have a good time."

"You do enjoy this, don't you?"

"I do." She sounded surprised.

A NEARLY FULL MOON REFLECTED OFF THE GLITTERING NAVY WATERS of the Agean Reach. Hecht wished the image could be captured for eternity. It was one of the most beautiful he had ever beheld.

He had only to walk fifty steps to his left, round the terrace, to see the fire-lighted smoke above a suburb of hell where convicts and prisoners of war labored to connect the Agean Reach with Lake Antal via a canal across the Phesian Land Bridge.

Canals connecting the Negrine with the White Sea had been a fantasy of the Eastern Emperors for a thousand years. Maybe once a century an Emperor felt secure enough and wealthy enough to take up the grand work. None had lived long enough to complete even one of the three needed links, so far. Competing demands for treasure or manpower always killed the project. It took nature only decades to undo most of the work.

Monestacheus hoped the Enterprise would supply him with thousands more laborers.

"It is beautiful, isn't it?" Hourli had materialized, still in the gown she had worn earlier. She had stunned the ladies of Hypraxium with the intensity of her greens and blues.

"It is. I wouldn't think you would be susceptible."

"Natural beauty isn't apparent only to mortals. Though, admittedly, we Old Ones are more jaded."

He faked a chuckle.

"You're nervous."

"I don't know if this is going to work."

"It will work. You have us to make it work."

"Thank you. I don't know what I'd do without you."

"Manage. You always do. Meantime, I've heard from my brother."

"Really?" He studied her face. Foolish, trying to read anything there.

"He's been traveling with your sister and daughters." She laughed outright. "Look at you! No. He's had no luck at all."

Hecht could not decide if he should feel relieved or foolish. "He had something to report?"

"Sort of. Mainly that you should expect visitors."

"Uhm? They've been up to something, have they?"

"Your sister is always up to something. It's what she is. She has the force of character to drag your daughters and the old man along. And here comes Titus Consent."

Irked, Hecht muttered, "What does he want?"

"He is going to tell you that the preparations are in place. He is going to ask you what you want done now."

Which is what Titus did, while considering Hourli in her glamorous aspect with a muted wonder. She caught his eye and winked. Once he departed, she mused, "I wonder if I ought to have Aldi get after him."

"What? Him? No!" Then, "Why?"

"It feels like he could keep up with her."

"Can we change the subject?" He did not want to think about women. It had been an age.

Laughter. Maybe a touch mocking. "All right." She pointed, made a flipping gesture with her hand. Heris rotated into being facing the harbors. "Oh, Sweet Aaron!" she murmured.

Hourli said, "I'll leave you two alone," in a tone suggesting she expected them to do more than talk.

Hecht was disgusted. But it sparked an old curiosity about what went on between Hourli and Hourlr.

"WHAT WAS THAT?" HERIS ASKED. "WAS THAT HOURLI? HOW COME she was all fancied up?"

"We went to a state dinner with the Emperor."

"She cleans up damned good."

"They all do. They're Instrumentalities. They can be as glamorous as they want. She says you and Hourlr are traveling together these days."

"Piper! No. It's not that. You beast. I'm going to nail Asgrimmur, though, if I can get him to hold still long enough." She laughed at his appalled expression.

"Please don't talk like that."

"All right. But you need to grow up."

The air shimmered. Lila and Vali rotated into existence. Vali was shaking. "That was scary! I thought we weren't going to hit it."

Lila said, "If you'd stop fussing I could cut it easy."

"Girls?"

"Hi, Dad." Chorused. "We just got back from the world of the dwarves." That from Lila. "Triple Great Grandfather was a major pain."

"World of the dwarves?" Hecht looked at Heris.

"We were looking for a way to get to Eucereme."

"By 'we' she means she was looking," Vali said. "The rest of us got dragged along."

"It's important . . ."

Hecht said, "Stop." He did not want to witness another round in an old dispute. "Did you have something to tell me? Or were you just looking for a picturesque place to squabble?"

The girls had discovered the view. They oohed and ahed. Heris said, "Mostly, we wanted to see you. An impulse, really, after we got back. The girls wondered how you were doing."

"I'm fine, right now. But I'll be off to the wars real soon."

"Shartelle." A statement.

"The first serious target."

"It'll be tough to take. It's been fifteen hundred years."

Al-Prama had gotten hold of Shartelle one household and one heart at a time. A quarter of the population was Antast Chaldarean, still, and there were quite a few Devedians. There was a Dainshau neighborhood and a Western quarter. The groups all considered themselves Shartellean first.

"I know. But I have the Shining Ones to help."

"So you'll succeed where so many greats have failed. Piper, don't make Shartelle one of your bloody examples."

"I . . ."

"I know how you think. You'll want to save lives in the long run by being bloodthirsty to start. Make the example somewhere else. Shartelle will resist. They *know* they cannot be conquered. They'll believe that Indala will come to help. But you'll crush them because you have the Shining Ones and the falcons. Be merciful. People there were good to me."

"I understand. I'll do no evil that Shartelle doesn't compel me to do."

Meantime, Vali and Lila leaned on a balustrade, absorbing the view and trading nonsense about how marvelous it would be to live in a place like this. They sounded shallow beyond their years.

Noticing their father paying attention they began speculating about the romantic possibilities.

Heris whispered, "It's all for show. Their suffering in Sonsa . . ."

"They're grown women now, Heris. You all are. I try to remember that. But I can't help being one overly protective son of a bitch."

"I forgive you. I'm sure they do, too."

"So you found a way into the world of the dwarves."

"We wanted to go from there to Eucereme, to contact the Raneul and refugee Old Ones from the Realm of the Gods."

"You failed?"

"Big time. Iron Eyes turned up right away. He ranted and raved. I ranted right back because his gang have been looting that Krulik and Sneigon manufactory." She dipped a hand into a pocket, produced the communication pendant that he had lost.

"Where did you get that? I had no idea what became of it."

Heris explained. "It was tangled up in some silk shreds. The old man thought . . ."

He watched as she decided not to carry on. He chose not to talk about it, either. "Does it still work?"

"The old man refurbished it. Not really likely to be useful since you have the Shining Ones hanging around."

"Always handy to have an extra option. What is he up to? The old man?"

"I don't know. Something with Grandfather, probably to do with the Construct. He's always at that when he's not helping me."

"I thought you were supposed to be helping him. And learning the family trade so you can be the next Unknown."

"I am. But that isn't what I want anymore."

"Oh?"

"I like this life too much."

Hecht frowned, wondering what she meant. The Unknowns could do whatever they wanted. Cloven Februaren wandered more than Heris did. "You didn't reach Eucereme."

"I said."

"Those people have no reason to help us."

"A point Iron Eyes made with considerable vigor, though his opinion was honed by different emotions."

"Uhm?"

"The Aelen Kofer have no love for the Old Ones."

He knew. Still, he suspected that things happened inside Heris's head that she failed to share. "The Old Ones can't survive without Eucereme, right? They *have* to get through so Eavijne can plant a new orchard. We should keep that in mind."

Heris nodded. "Those apples would be good for the Raneul, too."

"They would. So when Iron Eyes is watching you he'd better have somebody else watching for Raneul coming up from behind." He was sure the exiles in Eucereme knew about the trouble with the blessed apples.

Vali and Lila turned from the view, came over. Both hugged him briefly. Vali murmured, "Be careful. We want you back." There were tears under her eyes when she stepped away. She turned to hide them.

What did that mean?

Lila seemed a little choked-up, too.

Heris said, "We'd better go before we're noticed. We just wanted to see how you're doing." Which sounded like a half truth. "To bring you up to date. To say 'love you,' for Anna. And to let you know that Iron Eyes is watching."

"Oh?"

"Take it into account. It might benefit you someday."

Hecht nodded, though he did not understand.

"I'll be watching, too. Especially at Shartelle."

"I'll be good to them if they're good to me."

"Thank you." She hugged him, too, gave him a peck on the cheek, turned sideways.

The girls were gone already.

He stared at the harbors, baffled.

"What was that?" Hourli was back.

"I'm not sure. Is it possible to see the future?"

"Absolutely. Ordnan looked into it and saw that he had to kill you in order to avoid the Twilight. Or something like that. He wasn't always completely logical."

"It's pretty iffy, then."

"Not pretty, just iffy. The ugliest possibilities are the ones that really shine through. Why?"

"I got the impression they don't expect to see me alive again."

"Oh." Startled, she reached out, touched his bare arm lightly. *Crackle!*

"Ouch!" The spark had been so sharp the hair on his arm now smoked. "That hurt."

She started to respond, paused to peer into the darkness inside the villa. "Someone is coming."

PELLA APPEARED. "HEY, DAD. IT'S ROLLING."

Hecht told Hourli, "Time to go."

Ambassador fon Machen awaited Lord Arnmigal, along with a crowd. He was put out and having trouble hiding it.

The Commander of the Righteous said, "Do it, then."

Pella, Titus, and a dozen armed men relieved fon Machen and his companions of their personal arms. No one got hurt. The protests were loud but never violent. Hecht ignored them.

"Move them out," Consent ordered.

Sharp steel encouraged sullen cooperation.

An hour later Hecht's coterie, with the ambassador's people, were aboard an Aparionese trireme named for some dead prince of the republic. The craft was large, lean, sleek, and fully modern. It got under way despite the darkness. Two Shining Ones, pretending to be sorceresses from one of the mystic isles in the White Sea, stood by the helm and ship's master, piloting.

Ghebulli Resteino entered the Reach without incident.

Titus had begun making arrangements the day they reached Hypraxium. Disarming Ambassador fon Machen's venom by taking him along seemed the easiest way of protecting the Enterprise's supply line.

Fair winds and friendly seas followed *Ghebulli Resteino*. The Commander of the Righteous had gods helping, three of whom admitted being prone to seasickness.

The waters off the Antal were far busier than normal according to the ship's master. "That is because of you, sir. Because of the Enterprise. People are coming to take part. Others are running away so they won't get involved. But most of the ships we see are hauling cargo for your campaign."

From the start Hecht had been impressed by the vastness of the undertaking. Coastal traffic only underscored that.

Two days out *Ghebulli Resteino* happened on a cluster of ships, half a dozen small vessels surrounding a fat merchantman wearing Dateon's colors.

Hourli and the ship's master approached Lord Arnmigal from opposite directions. The sailor spoke first. "Those are pirates. Normally I wouldn't concern myself with Dateonese. This year, though, we're pretending to be allies. I would like to assist them."

There would be witnesses other than the pirates and Dateonese. A modest-size merchant showing unfamiliar colors was scooting past to seaward, headed east. Another vessel with sails taken in lay ahead and to landward. Hecht asked, "Would that be the pirate flagship?"

"Possibly. These aren't ordinary pirates. They look like Praman privateers."

"Run up the Righteous banner and my personal ensign." He did not think there would be much fighting. *Ghebulli Resteino* had turned even before her master received permission to attack. The pirates were disengaging already.

Hourli nodded to Hecht. This piracy was what she had come to report. Hecht said, "Help the captain so we don't lose much time."

Hourli smiled. It was a wicked slash, anticipating. "Oh, yes. Let me talk to the girls."

"The girls" had gathered on the foredeck, Fastthal and Sprenghul shimmering black.

Hecht called out, "Pella. Where are you?"

The boy hustled up. "Breaking out some grenados, Dad."

"Good idea. Take them to my friends. Show them how they work."

"Dad?" Disappointment filled the boy's face.

"If we get close enough to throw those ourselves we'll be close enough for them to shoot us back."

Pella muttered but, moments later, he and two staffers were lugging a case of grenados toward the Shining Ones. Below, oarsmen prepared to take *Ghebulli Resteino* from sail to muscle power. The rowers were neither slaves nor criminals, as was the case on most warships. Only free men worked the ships of Aparion.

"Oh, hell," Hecht grumbled halfheartedly. The Chooser sisters had made no effort to hide their nature while flashing toward the pirate flagship. Hourli pounded her own forehead with the heel of her right hand.

Flashes appeared aboard the flagship. It took some time for the noise to arrive. Shouting soon followed. Then the Choosers returned for more explosives.

Now they went after the Dateonese vessel's attackers. Those smaller craft were having limited luck breaking away.

Hecht wondered why the Choosers bothered with the bombs. He went forward to ask.

"Because they like the smoke and bangs," Pella said, before Hourli could answer.

The boy would understand. Hecht asked Hourli, "How do we cover this up? I mean, Fastthal and Sprenghul."

"I'll do what I can. It won't be enough. We can't undo what's been seen. I'll twist it so people who hear about it from people who heard about it from people who might have been here will assume that it's mostly exaggeration."

"Keep the suspicion of deviltry out of it."

"Not possible in the prevailing religious climate."

"Uh?"

"God doesn't manifest. Anything supernatural that does manifest must be an agent of the Adversary. You know that."

Hecht sighed. Of course.

He looked to the masthead. The banners of the Righteous and Commander of the Righteous were up for all to see.

Hourli said, "There is one way to manage the story exactly, one hundred percent."

"Why do I think I'm not going to like this?"

"Because you won't. It's not your way."

"And?"

"Leave no witnesses."

Hecht trembled. He felt weak for a moment. No witnesses. These allies could make that happen. A few score pirates, some Dateonese, whoever was on that wallowing coaster from out west, hustling to get away from the action, the crew of *Ghebulli Resteino,* any Righteous who could not be counted on to keep quiet . . . Maybe seven hundred people? That was manageable.

But Hourli was right. He would not do that.

The ship's master began to close with the pirate flagship.

*   *   *

GHEBULLI RESTEINO ARRIVED OFF ENVI, A SMALL PORT TWENTY-TWO miles up the coast from Shartelle, in company with four pirate vessels taken in prize. The crews had been consigned to the fishes. Freed Chaldarean prisoners were helping work the captured ships. The rescued Dateonese *Consiglieri Reversi Ono* continued on southward, destination Kagure.

Ghebulli Resteino anchored out with her prizes. The sun dropped below the western horizon. Hecht had a boat put over. He went ashore with a dozen men and the Shining Ones, the latter trembling in anticipation.

They would feast at the Well of Peace before morning. Their excitement was contagious. Lord Arnmigal felt the lure himself, some.

The Well of Peace might be feeble and misnamed but it was a well of power and it was within reach.

Campfires burned like shoals of stars across the hills south of Envi. Lord Arnmigal had overtaken his host.

THE MAIN FORTIFICATIONS OF SHARTELLE SURMOUNTED A HEADLAND rising sixty feet above the White Sea. The foundations of the wall, standing thirty feet tall to seaward and as high as one hundred twenty feet to landward, were rooted in the stone of the headland. Entrance was through a massive double barbican behind a dry moat thirty feet deep. The rubble from the moat had been used to fill a curtain wall twenty feet high a hundred yards in advance of the main wall. That lay behind a ditch twelve feet deep. A further wall lay another hundred yards in front of that. All the walls had towers offering enfilading fires.

The harbors that made Shartelle such a prize lay below the headland, to either hand, behind formidable walls of their own. Those stretched out to sea atop breakwaters. There were towers at their ends capable of laying heavy fires on enemy ships. They could hoist chains that would keep ships out of the harbors. Shartelle's own fleet was substantial. It could bring in supplies sufficient to keep the city going indefinitely. A siege centuries earlier had persisted thirteen years with no success.

Lord Arnmigal considered the situation. "Our friends from Dateon and Aparion are too optimistic. We can't take that by storm. Our falcons won't help. They aren't heavy enough to break those walls."

"So we'll use trickery," Titus Consent said.

"Or ferocity."

Hecht glanced at Hourli. He was uncomfortable with her now, and not just because she was so much more potent a presence after having visited the Well of Peace. She was always close by, now. Nearer than the Choosers, usually—and it seemed he needed her to be. He was more confident and decisive when she was.

He suspected that her interest was, in fact, more than personal, serving the cause of the Shining Ones.

He said, "Suppose we go with the historical option and just bypass Shartelle? Keep it closed up on the land side while we deal with easier targets?"

Consent said, "Maybe not the best choice psychologically."

Hourli agreed. "The Commander of the Righteous has a reputation. He shouldn't dodge his first tough challenge."

Hecht grunted. Too true. Events at Shartelle would shape his future in the Holy Lands. Taking the city would guarantee less resistance elsewhere, later.

"There is a problem. I promised Heris not to butcher the population."

Hourli said, "There must be people who didn't treat her right."

"They got theirs already. Grade Drocker was ferocious."

Hourli said, "I'll consult Heris. You study the situation here. You'll find a way, you being you."

"What was that?" Titus asked after Hourli walked away.

"I don't know. She's changed. She acts like I'm one of them instead of the Godslayer."

"You aren't even that, anymore. Heris has taken that. And she wants to keep it."

Titus was right. Heris was at war with the Night.

"Let's walk the ground again. We could overtop that first curtain wall with an old-fashioned ramp." But he was eying the northern harbor. If he could run a causeway to the mole and escalade that wall . . .

Titus said, "We have the Instrumentalities. Like it or not, people think we have supernatural allies. Why not go ahead and use them?"

Hecht grunted. He did not want to rely too much on the Shining Ones. He did not want to remind the world that the Commander of the Righteous was strange. He troubled the world enough already. "Tell me about the tower overlooking the main barbican."

Titus said, "Practically a wonder of the world. Almost two hundred feet tall. Called the Tower of the Bats. Come sundown you can see why. They come out by the thousands. It has collapsed twice during earthquakes. They built it back taller and stronger each time."

"Can we make it fall on the barbican?"

"Maybe with firepowder smuggled in by our supernatural friends."

ANOTHER DAY. HOURLI WAS BACK FROM SEEING HERIS, WHOM SHE had had trouble finding. "I have a better idea who has to be protected, now."

Hecht grunted. He was distracted. His engineers, after interviewing captives who knew the Tower of the Bats, said that it could not be dropped onto the barbican. The stonework would not tilt enough without breaking up first. A wave of rubble might do some damage, though.

"Let's drop it, anyway," Hecht said. "Just to show that we can."

Hourli said, "We'd be more useful picking off key men."

Hecht grunted again. That would cause confusion.

Hourli continued, "I hate to add to your worries. There is another problem developing that will shape every choice you make from the moment I tell you."

"Now what?"

"The Empress Helspeth has decided to join you. She is in Hypraxium. The ascendant and the Bastard are with her. I asked Wife to watch over them."

Hecht gaped. Impossible! But . . . she would. Helspeth would indeed, likely gathering the men she trusted least into her escort. No doubt her deadly uncles would be with her, too, to keep the circus manageable.

The woman was crazy.

He should have seen it coming. It was more in character for her than it had been for Katrin.

Her father would have done it, too. It was in the Ege blood.

"Oh, sigh! I don't like it even a little but there won't be any way to change her mind. I'll have to make the Holy Lands safe before she gets here."

Impossible, of course, even with the enthusiastic assistance of the Shining Ones.

36. Shamramdi, Lucidia: When God Averted His Eye

Nassim Alizarin watched the disguised Ansa leave the Shamramdi house, youthful shoulders slumped. "Bone, I wish we *could* do something. But Indala has tied our hands."

Indala al-Sul Halaladin was distressed and severely depressed by the ease with which the crusaders crushed any who resisted them. Each engagement left the Believers involved defeated in detail. The Righteous seemed to know the very secret intentions of the commanders of the Faithful. Only the rare minor patrol and unknown captain enjoyed any success.

Nassim grumbled, "He doesn't fully see the horrors possible if we allow er-Rashal to indulge his madness."

"Could that be worse than the Arnhander invasion?" Young Az demanded.

Nassim glowered at Mohkam, who said, "He just bulled past me, sir!"

"Those who rise in the shadow cast by a great man sometimes confuse that shadow with their own, thinking it relieves them of the burden of civil behavior." He met the boy's eyes.

Young Az reddened. He opened his mouth twice, probably to apologize. But he did not do so.

"Why am I gifted with this intrusion?" Nassim asked with none of the warmth that he could not help showing the boy normally. Azim did not miss that.

"That strange boy. He had tattoos under his eyes. Who was he?"

There was no reason to dissemble. "One of the Ansa, begging for help. Er-Rashal has started taking children."

Worse news, er-Rashal had discovered a way to make firepowder explode from afar. The discharges Nassim had heard while descending the Mountain had been the sorcerer's test of the new spell formula. That time the madman had not been wise enough to stay well back. That had cost him valuable weeks recuperating.

The Ansa could have gotten him then had not tribal politics interfered. Those who wanted to pretend that er-Rashal was no real threat attained ascendancy till the sorcerer started stealing children.

There was no helping the Ansa now. Perhaps next week, or next month, if Indala discovered a formula for success against the approaching crusaders. They had left a third of their strength to garrison captured cities while fugitives from those cities had joined Indala. Today the Great Shake's army outnumbered the Unbelievers by ten thousand.

Scouts were looking for the perfect place to destroy them.

Nassim was not optimistic. Indala's captains wanted to fight where horsemen could gain glory, ignoring the fact that similar horsemen had been defeated repeatedly already. The captains argued that those fools had chosen constrained battlegrounds where horsemen had inadequate maneuvering room.

Nassim thought that the crusaders would ignore the Believer cavalry—along with the pride of their own equestrian class.

Captain Tage had chosen intimates who could think in whole-force terms and least-cost victories, disdaining individual combats and heroics. Those men compelled their followers to conform. Continuous success had a way of eroding objections.

Young Az suffered the blindness of his class. He would not see. "We will sweep in and tempt them to charge. We will flee. They will pursue. We will keep on till their mounts are exhausted, then we will turn."

The Mountain did not tell the boy that the man who had created the Righteous knew eastern light-horse tactics intimately. He did say, "They will ignore you."

"We'll soon find out, Uncle. I came to warn you that the army moves north tomorrow."

Nassim sighed. "May God be generous."

Old Az agreed. "He has delivered punishments enough, lately."

The morning news from Shartelle said that the crusaders had sailed fireships into the northern harbor. Most friendly shipping had been consumed. The men operating the chain had thought they were welcoming a relief convoy from Dreanger. The ships were Dreangerean but had been captured by the fleets of the Firaldian trading republics. Rumors said those fleets had had supernatural assistance.

Marines captured one of the towers guarding the harbor entrance, too. Shartelle was cut off from the sea, now, too. Heavy firepowder weapons had been installed to discourage relief efforts from that direction.

The Righteous were using stone from the captured tower to create a causeway leading to the low point in the wall facing the harbor.

Mischief was happening inside Shartelle, too, evidently by crusader agents who had infiltrated before the siege began—though none of those agents had yet been identified.

As Indala's host drifted northward, in theory thirty-eight thousand strong, levies and militias tried to relieve Shartelle. Commanded by Indala's cousin Kharsa, they were tasked with investing the crusaders from outside, besieging the besiegers. Their numbers and their fighting skills proved insufficient. Few were motivated, either. The Righteous obliterated them. Prisoners were put to work as siege labor.

The Commander of the Righteous led from the fore, as terrible in the fighting as an angel of death. None withstood him. Kharsa himself, renowned across Qasr al-Zed, fell to the Commander's lightning spear.

Meantime, Indala's host trickled onto the Plain of Tum, which his captains had chosen as the place where the invaders would be humbled. The omens were uniformly excellent.

"This is not good," Mowfik grumbled. The renegade Sha-lug were at the head of the van, Indala being confident that Nassim Alizarin would see more clearly than most.

The Mountain saw despair in the offing. He saw disaster.

The Righteous had arrived already. They were camped on the south bank of a stream beneath low hills marking the northern verge of the plain. They were positioned exactly as Indala had prayed they would be, arrayed to come onto the field as he would have them do.

Nassim did not command the van. Still, he sent word to young Az warning that the Unbeliever appeared to know Indala's thinking and meant to give him what he wanted. Then they would eat him alive.

The message had no effect. Nassim received no reply. Indala commenced the action before his forces all arrived, sending riders forward. They skirmished with light cavalry from the crusader force, mercenaries recruited from the Antal. Most were Pramans. Some appeared to be Hu'n-tai At.

Frightening, that. They would be here not to help the Righteous but to observe their ways while helping weaken Qasr al-Zed.

The skirmishing lasted all day. Casualties were minimal. Young men from both sides wanted to show their courage.

Evening brought a brief round of negotiations. Nassim Alizarin was privileged to observe. Indala did honor his wisdom.

The invaders made no religious demands, which had puzzled the Believers from the beginning. The outsiders never insisted that only their own faith be practiced in lands they ruled. They were not particularly tolerant but were never as harsh as the Believers were once they triumphed over Unbelievers.

The invaders did make demands. They were confident. Many also came in disguise, Nassim believed.

Afterward, Alizarin told Indala, "Those who did the talking were not in charge. They were lords and captains but not decision makers. Those whose wills matter were the younger, leaner men in back."

"That was my impression, as well. They measured us for shrouds while the others blustered."

Nassim said, "Begging pardon, Shake. These old ears heard no bluster, just supreme confidence."

"Why? What cause can they have?"

"The old one, the Admiral, said it. This is not the Well of Days and their commander is not Rogert du Tancret."

"You let them defeat you before you face their swords?"

"Not at all. I just caution you against overconfidence."

At that point young Az paraphrased, "'God's Will shall be seen in the battle's outcome.'" He said it aloud without meaning to do so. His uncle had said the same on more than one occasion. The remark captured the core precept of the Faith. God would decide. God knew the outcome beforehand. There was no evading the Will of God. And so forth, denying cause and effect in the ordinary world.

Indala responded, "God favors those who plan ahead and have the numbers."

THE FAITHFUL LAUNCHED ATTACKS BY HORSEMEN WHO SHOT ARROWS as they swept past the face of the ranked enemy infantry. The infantry remained behind their shields and endured. Light field ballistae flung bolts from behind them, doing little damage but compelling the horsemen to loose their shafts from farther than they preferred. The artillerymen aimed for horses instead of riders. The bigger targets panicked when injured.

When riders approached in too dense a formation a firepowder weapon would belch a storm of iron darts.

Indala told his companions, "They aren't going to counterattack, are they? They're content to let us come to them."

Nassim said, "Yes. And tomorrow will be worse. Tomorrow they will have caltrops and tangle cords out."

Indala silenced him with a hand sign. "I see that. I'd do that myself, with fresh soldiers in the front lines. While I had food and water I'd stand and let the sea break on my rock. So. What is their long-run intent? Besides refusing to play by our preferred rules?"

News of the disaster at Shartelle had yet to arrive. The Believers remained confident of the favor of their God and the wisdom of their Great Shake. The outcome, here, might be difficult but the only final result would be victory.

A distant cousin of Indala said, "The crusaders are protecting their flanks with earthworks instead of cavalry. Their horse aren't numerous and are being held behind the infantry line."

Nassim said, "Their heavy horsemen will fight dismounted the way they did at the battle of the Four Armies."

Indala nodded. "Which means they won't launch one of their massed charges. So. They do hope we'll exhaust ourselves against a fixed position."

Nassim thought they were missing something. Arnhanders were not normally so patient. Their knightly class would not endure inaction. They would demand their chances at glory.

He kept announcing, "We're overlooking something. We need to consider their behavior more closely." But no one wanted to hear him. The situation had to change. Casualties, so far, favored the invaders, who, therefore, had no need to change tactics.

Indala launched three attacks the next day, first to fix the soldiers on the crusaders' line, then to rock each flank. The most massive went in from the east, with the sun behind, three thousand horsemen followed by four thousand of the best infantry.

The other attack was half as strong, its purpose to keep the troops on the western end from reinforcing elsewhere.

The main attack swarmed into the massed fire of a hundred falcons. The cavalry were obliterated. They could not flee. The infantry blocked the way. The falcons fell silent after only three salvos. Righteous horsemen came out to exterminate the stunned survivors.

Falcons decimated the lesser attack as well.

Nassim watched the western knights form for the charge. He said nothing. Indala would fall back, then try to turn in the time-honored fashion. Alizarin anticipated no success. The Unbeliever would be prepared.

At the command level, at least, the Arnhanders were professionals. Those professionals controlled the rest, who had learned to trust them while campaigning through the Antal.

The crusader charge scattered those who tried to resist. That resistance was barely strong enough to let Believers of weaker courage make their escape. The baggage was lost. Many horses were lost. Indala's few falcons were lost, too, most without having been fired. The ambush down the road failed completely. The crusaders knew where it was and waited while light-horse auxiliaries, having advanced by alternate routes, harassed the Believers and kept them from fixing their positions.

No phase of Indala's plan succeeded. Each had been anticipated. In every encounter the casualty ratio favored the invaders, usually dramatically.

Al-Azer er-Selim declared, "The Night itself favors the crusaders."

Indala took the survivors into Shamramdi. Despair haunted the Believers. God had averted His gaze again. The imams searched for the cause of His disfavor.

The Great Shake summoned new levies. He sent to Dreanger for the armies of al-Minphet. And he looked eastward, nervously.

The Hu'n-tai At would take advantage. Tsistimed the Golden would attack once he learned of the despair of Qasr al-Zed.

The Mountain saw the frustration eating at Indala, who was safe enough inside Shamramdi. He could hold on there indefinitely—unable to impose his will anywhere outside.

News from outside arrived regularly. The crusader cordon was porous. That news was never encouraging. Crusaders on the coast had moved on from Shartelle, reducing other Praman towns and cities with no difficulty. The siege of Shartelle proceeded at a leisurely pace, everyone inside and out confident of the outcome. Rumors had the Commander of the Righteous planning to penetrate Peqaa and destroy the holies of al-Prama.

Nassim Alizarin did not believe that but neither did he want to believe that Captain Tage had taken this as far as he had.

When would he reveal his Sha-lug colors?

IMAMS COMPLAINED THAT STRANGE THINGS WERE HAPPENING IN THE holy places. God's presence could no longer be felt. All sense of consecration had faded.

Was God truly turning away, abandoning the Believers completely?

In Shamramdi, as elsewhere where the Believers were besieged, strange evils kept occurring. Few were of great moment but the cumulative effect was debilitating. Key men fell sick. Minarets collapsed. Wells dried up. Vermin got into the granaries. Mortar in the walls washed away in unseasonable showers. A plague hit the horses, killing a third and leaving the rest too weak for battle.

In Shartelle the Tower of the Bats collapsed. Grain rotted. Plague visited briefly. The besiegers found the hidden aqueduct that brought water down from a built-over, camouflaged spring in the hills northeast of the city. Loss of that resource caused severe rationing.

A Dreangerean relief fleet assaulted the blockade at Shartelle. The warships were allowed to break through. The cargo vessels fled or were captured. The warships were then lost while trying to break back out. Slaves aboard several somehow slipped their chains and revolted.

*   *   *

THE MOUNTAIN HUDDLED WITH HIS SURVIVING VETERANS. "THE end of the world is near. What shall we do? How shall we meet it?"

Old Az said, "We'll meet it as we meet everything. Chin to chin."

Bone, on crutches these days, agreed. "This is as it has been Written. We cannot dispute the Will."

More of that fatalism that lay behind everything, Nassim thought.

Bone added, "The Rascal wrote the opening scene. I just hope we can end his tale before ours plays out."

There was no good news from the Idiam. The Ansa felt abandoned, though Indala's indifference was not of his own choosing. Er-Rashal was an apparition of the monster that had been but he forged on, relentless in his determination to raise the dead god and unswerving in his lust for ascension. The Ansa were on the defensive. They would flee the Idiam had they anywhere else to run.

The Mountain said, "Then let us bridle our grand ambitions and beg for that one boon. Perhaps God will grant us that."

Someone muttered, "You would think He'd show more interest in making His enemies weep."

Outside, none too distant, masonry crumbled. People began to cry out. That meant that there had been casualties.

37. The Mother Sea: Pilgrims

Brother Candle argued that he had lived a long, productive life. He had had a positive impact on the world. He had done his share. It was time the world let him go home to the Light. The Good God had prepared him a place.

The Widow and the Vindicated did not agree.

Never had he been so sick for so long.

Kedle, her henchmen, and the Terliagan seamen all promised that he would get over it.

They lied. He was still at the rail, still limp, when *Darter* made port at al-Stikla, on the heel of Firaldia, which was as far east as Terliagans were willing to travel.

There were pirates in the eastern Mother Sea. Also, the Dateonese and Aparionese were lethally jealous of their monopolies. They even fought one another, constantly.

There was a long delay at al-Stikla. Passage east, for groups, was scarce and dear. Countless pious pilgrims and bloodthirsty adventurers wanted to get to the Holy Lands in time to participate in the great event of the age.

At shared prayers Kedle murmured, "You would think that supernatural forces were at work."

The Perfect harrumphed. Solid ground had yet to restore his good temper. "Of course they are! Weren't you paying attention?"

Lady Hope had visited *Darter* several times.

Kedle blushed. The Perfect noticed and was startled. Was there something physical between Hope and the Widow?

Oddities suddenly lined up and made sense, then, though he had trouble getting his mind around the situation. That was plausible only on an intellectual plane. "It doesn't matter."

"You are too liberal, Master." Kedle paused. "It's . . . I can't help myself."

"Let's not talk about it." After his own pause, "She has that effect on *me* and I'm older than stone, nor ever owned strong appetites." Kedle's had been strong from the first. "Just ask the blessing of the Light."

Hope was not the only supernatural visitor. The monster bird with the damaged wing sometimes circled while *Darter* was at sea. Brother Candle thought the ship was being shadowed by something in the water, too. He was too miserable to care much but did mention it to the crew, whereupon the Terliagans grew excited.

There was no such beast native to the Mother Sea.

Kedle observed, "We must be caught inside a bigger story than the one we can see."

Brother Candle agreed. He had no doubts about that.

He did wish that the Good God was the sort who stepped in on behalf of his followers.

Brother Candle did not like being afraid. Being an object of interest to the Night—in particular to those parts of the Night that dogma proclaimed to be unreal—was scary in the extreme.

KEDLE FOUND A FAT DATEONESE TRANSPORT, PURPOSE-BUILT TO CARRY pilgrims, that had room for the Vindicated. Such vessels reaped grand profits by shifting the pious and ambitious.

They did not want to accept the Widow. She was bully enough to get her way. The holy man with the tattoos was terrifying, too. His tattoos looked like they could come to life.

The ship's master finally took them aboard, though, because the approaches to the Holy Lands had become so dangerous. *Consiglieri*

Reversi Ono must pass along shores where she was likely to encounter pirates, privateers, or warships from Lucidia or Dreanger. Even ships from Aparion and the Eastern Empire could be troublesome.

BROTHER CANDLE COULD NOT BELIEVE IT. THE PASSAGE FROM AL-Stikla east was worse than the first leg. *Consiglieri Reversi Ono* left shallow coastal waters for a direct run across those deeps where the big waves stalked. Two days out he begged to be put to death.

Cruel people all, the Vindicated and crew only mocked his misery.

PIRATES CAUGHT *CONSIGLIERI* OFF THE SOUTH COAST OF THE ANTAL, just days from the Holy Lands. A swarm of small ships closed in, under the illusion that the Dateonese could be captured easily. Brother Candle was too sick to wonder. Though the seas were minimal he was preoccupied with his misery.

The pirates soon learned that they had made a lethally bad choice.

They were not accustomed to having to do much real fighting. Kedle and the Vindicated slaughtered them like the amateurs they were.

A pirate no older than fourteen came at the Perfect. Brother Candle thought his death was upon him. He was too sick . . . But his serpents were not. Two came out. The boy went down.

People saw it happen. The fighting slackened. A man who might have been the boy's father wailed, charged, and died of lightning snakebite.

Awed, the pirates began a loud debate.

Then someone aboard one of the pirate craft howled an alarm.

A war galley was headed for the tangle. Its sails were Aparionese. More so even than the Dateonese the Aparionese were merciless toward pirates. They hunted pirates down. They destroyed whole villages suspected of harboring pirates.

There was a particularly dire air about this monster galley.

Brother Candle could only observe, later, that it was a strange old world, and cruel.

The galley broke unfamiliar colors. For the pirates escape was improbable already. That warship lay in the hands of the Night, no doubt about that. Kedle and Brother Candle smelled a smell like Lady Hope, only older, heavier, and darker. Hints of shadow swarmed around the vessel. Another ship, in the distance, noted earlier but paid little heed, began to show flashes of light and puffs of smoke. Thumps came rolling across the water. The vessel caught fire.

Shadows danced round the vessels trying to run from *Consiglieri*.

They brought loud bangs. "Firepowder," Kedle reported. "Top grade and delivered by sorcery. We have found ourselves somebody really, really bad, old man."

"Somebody with a grudge against pirates, perhaps?"

The galley loomed massive. Her falcons grumbled, hurling shot that ripped away pirate sails, rigging, even a mast. The attack continued till the pirate fleet had been reduced to wreckage, corpses, and derelicts.

The Aparionese captain came alongside *Consiglieri,* called a taunting reminder that Dateon owed Aparion a favor.

Brother Candle recognized several of the men at the other ship's rail as a bloody Kedle loudly suggested that the Aparionese kiss her sweet arse. Their interference had been neither necessary nor requested.

The Perfect forgot his stomach. "Girl. Girl child. Dear girl. Kedle. Shut up. You're insulting the Commander of the Righteous himself."

That got through, accentuated by the odor of the Night. "You're kidding."

"No. Those standards belong to the Righteous and the Grand Duchy of Eathered and Arnmigal. The Commander is fourth from the left, grinning like he hears every word I'm saying. I saw him closer than this when he was Captain-General."

"What the hell is he doing out here?" She waved, making a conciliatory gesture that might be taken for belated gratitude. Then, "Crap. You *are* telling it straight." A boy had joined those men. He had been at Mestlé. He had negotiated with Hope.

The Perfect said, "I expect he's headed for the Holy Lands. The Enterprise *is* his show."

Kedle growled. "Where is Hope when I need her?" And was startled. The Instrumentality joined the men at the rail yonder. She smiled and tossed an intimate wink.

The galley began to pull away, moving swiftly under oars.

HOPE VISITED THAT NIGHT. SHE WAS LOW-KEY, PREFERRING TO AT-tract no attention. She crowded into the tiny cabin with Kedle and Brother Candle. The space was too hot and too intimate for the Perfect. She said, "You had a serious encounter today, loves," with scarcely a hint of accent. "You caught the eye of the Commander of the Righteous. He will be watching."

Kedle shrugged, indifferent. Brother Candle, though, caught the resonance of facts unstated beneath Hope's statement. "Meaning?"

"He remembered you, Uncle. Kedle, he worked out who you are

even before his son told him. He explained why you're here. He doesn't know *who* Kedle Richeut is but he certainly knows *what* she is."

Kedle admitted, "I'm confused."

"Understand this, beloved. My whole family is with him, supporting him. They could be here now, in a shadow or in the flame in the lamp, and even I wouldn't know. So from now on, wherever you go and whatever you do, you may be watched by someone more powerful than me. You don't want to disappoint them."

Obliquely, Brother Candle observed, "You seem more substantial, somehow." And, therefore, a greater danger to his soul—though she no longer taunted his worldly side.

The Instrumentality hugged herself, grinned, said, "I made it all the way to the Well of Peace. I'm strong again. I'm young and beautiful. And I talk too much."

She was, for a moment, very much like a stunningly bright and beautiful, mischievous fifteen-year-old. But how was that unlike what she had been that first night in Antieux? Brother Candle could not define it but the difference was there. Perhaps it was a lessened malicious cynicism.

"Oh, my!" For an instant he had pictured her as she had been that night, in alluring mode, but now fully armed with divine power.

Tinkling laughter. "Dear Brother, I love thee too well to destroy thee that way. I have warned ye both. It's time for me to go." She eyed Kedle briefly, yearning plain. A sigh and a shiver, then she just shriveled into a wisp and was gone.

Brother Candle stared, silent. The last he had seen was a conspiratorial wink. Kedle said, "I'm going to sleep, now." Restlessly, no doubt.

The Perfect went up on deck and contemplated the myriad stars. The sky was cloudless, the air crystalline, the darkness complete. The starscape was astounding. He might fall into it if he did not keep his grip on the rail. In just minutes he counted eleven shooting stars.

Suddenly, like taking a body blow, he realized that he had not been seasick since that boy's father tried to kill him.

Thought conjured the demon misery.

He groaned and leaned over the rail.

A dozen porpoises paced *Consiglieri,* trailing bioluminescent wakes. A large darkness lazed along beneath them. The porpoises were not troubled.

THERE WAS AN ENCOUNTER WITH A LUCIDIAN WAR GALLEY AS *Consiglieri* neared Shartelle. The galley came on aggressively, but at six hundred yards sheered off and fled away as though her commander was convinced that he had come within a gnat's whisker of some diabolic Unbeliever ambush.

"What was that?" Kedle wondered.

Brother Candle was too miserable to care. He was obsessed with counting the hours till the torment ended. Forever. Never again would he board a ship. He would die first.

He told the Episcopal captain that, should he have spent his life in error as a Seeker and the Brothen Episcopals had it right, he was bound for heaven anyway. He had done his time in Purgatory.

The Dateonese crew found him endlessly amusing.

THE CONNEC WAS HOT. THE HOLY LANDS WERE HOTTER. BACK HOME the cool of the sea rolled in over the land come evening, making the nights tolerable. At Triamolin the heat of the land rolled out to broil the sea.

Even Kedle was awed. "And it isn't yet fully summer."

There had been ample warning. Connectens of the noble and knightly classes had made pilgrimages to Vantrad and Chaldar before. Some had tarried for years, helping thwart the villainies of those emissaries of darkness, the Pramans. Many of those veterans were willing to share their experiences endlessly.

They had declared that no one ever accepted the truth till they met it head-on for themselves.

Triamolin offered another lesson. The Widow and the Vindicated would not be celebrated in the Holy Lands. They were almost unknown. Those who had heard of them were not impressed. There were hard men everywhere in the Holy Lands. The hard men of Triamolin were of Arnhander extraction, in the main. They had no love for the bandits and rebels who had undone the sainted Anne of Menand. Anne's unwavering favor had sustained their crusader state for a decade.

Brother Candle suspected that disembarking at Kagure or Grove would have been wiser. Those counties had been established by fighters from the Connec.

Kedle told him, "I may have outwitted myself again."

"Again?"

"Again. I do it all the time. I'm just clever about covering it up. Like a cat. I don't let the rest of you know. Come. Let's find a Brotherhood hospice."

They learned that there were three of those, two of which had opened in the past two months. All three were stuffed with armed pilgrims who had arrived with no plans beyond reaching the Holy Lands. None of the three had room to squeeze the Vindicated in, nor could they handle the animals the Vindicated had brought. A soldier older than Brother Candle suggested that they camp in the countryside. The road east led to pastureland eight miles out. Others were camped there already but the water and grazing remained adequate and the locals were not too predatory when marketing victuals. They would be wise to post sentries, though.

"Needs must needs must," Kedle grumbled. She did not like that one miserable choice. Eight miles. Animals took longer to get their land legs than did people. Even that brief journey could decimate those that had survived the passage.

It would take a month for the Vindicated to become an effective fighting force again.

THE CAMPSITE WAS NOT IDEAL. THE BEST GROUND WAS OCCUPIED ALready. Kedle was not prepared to muscle someone and start a feud. She had come to the Holy Lands amply supplied with enemies already.

Her two tagalong gifts from Socia began hauling water immediately, leaving their worshipped mistress, whose wounds still hampered her, to try setting up her tent by herself. Water would remain a constant problem because so much would have to be carried so far.

She fought the canvas and tent poles with help from no one but the old cripple from the siege of Arngrere, known as Grandfather Arcot. She had a bad leg herself. Grandfather Arcot had problems with his arm, facial scars, and lacked three fingers on his right hand. The two of them were not well made for handling common camp chores.

Someone asked, "Could you use some help, then?" in heavily accented Connecten.

Kedle started to snap something in character for Kedle Richeut, nasty or sarcastic or both, but Lady Hope came to mind. Not quite sure why, she held her tongue.

The speaker was the commander of a battalion camped close by. He had watched the Vindicated arrive. It looked like he knew who she was. She thought she ought to know him, too, though she was sure their paths had not crossed before. The feeling waxed as she took his measure.

Grandfather Arcot chirped, "Little help here, please?"

The visitor stepped in as Kedle responded. He got hold of an obstreperous tent pole. "I have three hundred bored soldiers just sitting around. They're gonna start getting into mischief if I don't give them something to do."

Oddly, he seemed disinterested in her as a woman but intrigued by Kedle Richeut, the Widow.

She ignored that, listened to what he said.

In her camps there was always work enough to exhaust everyone by the end of the day. To the Widow all the world was enemy territory. She insisted that the Vindicated take that to be true wherever they were. They had been warned already that trouble might be coming here.

"Why not? I'll use whatever help I can get so long as the helpers don't have sticky fingers."

The visitor put on a dramatic show of being appalled. "Madam! Please! You are speaking to the chief law officer of the Mother City!"

Grandfather Arcot declared, "Not a thunderclap of reassurance to a Connecten, fella." He lost control of the canvas he was wrangling. His eyes had gone hard.

The visitor considered Arcot's face, hand, and arm. "Unhappy encounter with the minions of law and order?"

Kedle said, "With minions of Brothe. At Antieux."

"Ah. Of course. Some of us can't put the bad times behind us."

Still wrestling canvas and poles, Kedle demanded, "Who the hell are you?"

He got no chance to reply. A small man had appeared. "Word just came in, Boss. He's unshipping at Shartelle."

"Hey! Bo! I really hoped he'd give it a skip. Guess he couldn't ignore the challenge of cracking the tough nut first."

"Just Plain Joe will be there. I'm tempted to go see him."

"Not smart in this country. You don't go anywhere on your own. You're a westerner, you're prey." He faced Kedle. "Some crusaders are worse than most Pramans. I'm told."

The smaller man bobbed his head nervously. "Rogert du Tancret."

"And the Queen."

Kedle eyed the smaller man. "I've seen you before."

"I doubt that, ma'am." His nerves worsened, though. He was lying.

She sniffed out the cleverest lies easily, these days. This man was, suddenly, desperate to be away from her.

The other interposed himself smoothly. "I would be Colonel Ghort," he said, while the little man slipped away, studying his surroundings with ferocious care.

"All right. I remember who he is. Or was, maybe." The little fellow had been a Brothen spy in Antieux, pretending to be a Seeker from

Firaldia. He had been bold enough to engage in a doctrinal debate with Brother Candle before vanishing so completely that he might never have existed.

"He's a good man."

She shook her head, unsure that she had her facts right, then focused on Ghort. Pinkus Ghort. Sometimes Colonel Ghort. Lately, Captain-General of the Patriarchal armies Ghort. "I appreciate the offer of assistance. Being Khaurenese I would have no trouble accepting. The Good God knows we could use a hand. But these are the Vindicated, mostly from Antieux. Chances are they would consider you a gift from God."

"Oh, sigh. I had nothing to do with the Antieux massacre."

"You're older than I am, and more experienced. You have to know that you being guilty, or not guilty, means about as much to them as it did to Bronte Doneto, whatever hat he wore whenever."

Ghort managed a grin. "You're probably right. It's an awful old world, chock full of human beings, and human beings are such unreasonable, irrational beasts. Worse than the gods themselves. All right. I tried to forge some solidarity. Now I'll go somewhere where I won't be so much of an object of temptation."

Kedle thought she *felt* the snicker of an invisible, amused entity. Hope? There must be news.

Ghort said, "Come visit me. My guys don't hold any grudges."

More amusement.

Kedle watched the man amble off. "What the hell was that?"

"You vamp." Grandfather Arcot wore a big, scar-distorted grin. "Let's talk about it after we're done here." He was making no headway with the tent.

"Yeah. All right. I'm coming. It's just . . . That was so damned odd. I can't figure what he wanted."

The very air whispered, *Perhaps he noted that you are a woman and recalled that he is a man.* The same air slithered under the edges of the tent and lifted it up.

"There we go!" Grandfather Arcot declared. "That's what I wanted to see. So. You're curious, go on and visit him. You lads! Lend a hand, you don't want to sleep in the rain."

The Arnhander boys from Arngrere put their buckets aside.

The Widow continued to stare after the Captain-General. Hope continued to envelop her in silent amusement. Pinkus Ghort was still officially Captain-General, was he not?

What was his game?

What, for that matter, was he doing in the Holy Lands?

Maybe she *would* go visit, just to unravel that mystery.

BROTHER CANDLE WAKENED FROM THE DEEPEST, MOST SATISFYING, most refreshing sleep he had enjoyed since leaving Antieux. Lady Hope, faintly radiant, was shaking him. She had been in his dreams . . . and was here now in actuality . . .

She grinned wickedly. "What a wicked old devil you are, thinking like that! Too bad. We don't have time. The enemy approaches."

Groggily, he stumbled to Kedle's tent. A dozen Vindicated had crowded in already, few more alert than he was. None paid the Instrumentality any heed.

Kedle was not sleepy. She was excited. Flushed. Breathing fast. "We're all here, now. These are the facts. Pramans have been gathering in the hills to the east. They're mostly regional, modestly armed, but led by professionals from Lucidia. They don't know us. They just see a chance to grab some plunder."

Brother Candle asked, "What about the others camped around here?"

Kedle did not answer the question he thought he had asked. "I sent the boys . . . They're on their own. We'll get hit first, anyhow. We're closest to the hills."

This must be what that old man at the hospice had meant when he said they should post sentries. Local opportunists—not necessarily Praman—considered pilgrims a resource best exploited while still muddled from travel.

"These raiders have done this before. They have the impudence to sell the captured arms in Kagure or Grove." Ominously, "Healthy captives get sold to slavers and sent east. The rest . . ."

She did not have to explain.

"We have been warned." She did not explain that, either. The Vindicated no longer asked. "We have a few hours to prepare. Let's make a statement they'll hear from one end of the Holy Lands to the other. These dogmatic snakes need to know that the Vindicated have come."

Brother Candle shivered at her intensity.

"I want toddlers in Shamramdi, Begshtar, Mezket, Souied ed Dreida, even Jezdad, to wake up screaming at night because they think the Vindicated are coming. I want Indala himself pissing down his leg."

Hope chided, "That's a bit of an overreach, darling."

The men chuckled.

"I want it. I don't expect to get it. We'll start by making the camp look unprepared. Pickets should be drowsing. We'll offer an obvious, safe path to the command tent, where they can lop the head off the dragon before it knows that it's in trouble."

The boys from Arngrere oozed into the tent. The bolder of the two gave a nod and thumbs-up despite all the eyes upon him.

38. The Holy Lands: Reconnaissance by Combat

Piper Hecht opened his eyes after allowing them momentary relief from the sun's brilliance. He sat on a hilltop, behind a cluttered table, overlooking Shartelle and its harbors from the northeast. There were breaches in the mighty wall. Starving defenders strove to fill them before any crusader attack. The Righteous, however, were content to wait.

Hecht's main strength had gone away, to overrun Praman cities along the coast and explore the approaches to Vantrad. He expected to fight at least one major battle getting there. The Pramans dared not fail to try to stop him. Not to fight would constitute acknowledgement that God had chosen to stand with the Enterprise.

The misnamed White Sea was a brilliant azure. Allied warships patrolled beyond Shartelle's harbors. They showed the colors of Aparion, Dateon, and the Eastern Empire. Jackals all, they were eager to feast on the Righteous's kill.

"She always overdoes it, doesn't she?" Lord Arnmigal grumped. Hourli had just brought news from east of Triamolin. "The economic impact will be severe, especially in agriculture. She killed four hundred eighty men with just a handful of followers."

"It was a clever ambush by hardened butchers. And Aldi helped. She could have cleaned up a force five times the size of that one."

Hecht sighed. He did not like having killers out there who were not his to control.

Hourli said, "She wanted to announce her presence."

"Damned if she didn't. Everyone will know the Widow now." He shut his eyes again. The reflection off the sea was not pleasant. "Will it have any strategic impact?"

"Timid souls will stay out of her way. Indala? How would you expect him to react?"

"He'll fuss, but what can he do? He's locked up. And he doesn't let emotion push him into making deadly mistakes."

"Members of his family were among those who organized the

raid. Any survivors will be some of the prisoners the Widow is sending us."

"There were survivors?" That was a surprise, the Widow being so bloodthirsty.

"About a dozen. Three Lucidians, one Dreangerean, the rest local shakes. She wanted to kill them all. One of the other commanders talked her into sending them to us."

"What is that boy doing?"

Pella, halfway down to the nearest siege works, was easy to spot. He favored flamboyant local Chaldarean costume these days. He wanted to be noticed. Hecht hoped he would not regret the conceit.

Wife departed the tent that gave respite from the sun, a pleasure Hecht exploited often. He had forgotten how fierce that orb could be, here.

The Instrumentality murmured to Hourli. Hourli leaned down, told Lord Arnmigal, "Your son has found a city militia captain who will open a gate in exchange for the safety of his family and property."

"Excellent." He was not surprised. Shartelle had been stubborn but most of its people recognized that the end was near. Every relief effort had been crushed. No more would come. Pramans elsewhere were desperate to protect their own homes.

Their God had averted His face.

A traitor, if known, would suffer the hatred of his fellows but his treachery would save lives because Heris had extracted that promise from her brother.

"That's good," Lord Arnmigal said again. "Let him know that I approve. He has full authority to make the arrangements. Suggest that it should happen at night so fewer people get hurt."

EXPLOSIONS HAPPENED IN SUCCESSION IN A BARRACKS, A COMMUNAL kitchen, and during late prayer services. There were casualties by the score and general panic, all far from the sally port the traitor opened. The Righteous poured in unnoticed despite the inevitable confusion and noise.

Few of Shartelle's defenders resisted. Most said their prayers and chose to believe the invaders' promise to spare them. Those who did choose to fight on fled into the big stone box of the citadel. Most of those belonged to the Lucidian garrison Indala had installed before the arrival of the Righteous. They were among the Great Shake's most faithful soldiers.

All Shartelle but the citadel fell before noon. There were problems of indiscipline but those did not persist. The Shining Ones intervened.

Shartelle became a Chaldarean city for the first time in centuries, at less cost than its people had any right to hope.

The Lucidians in the citadel offered to yield their arms and leave the city. The Commander refused. From them he wanted only unconditional surrender. They refused.

Hecht had masons brick up the entrances. The Lucidians could stew in their pride. The Shining Ones kept harm from touching the masons, but, otherwise, stayed out of the light.

"I don't want the whole world thinking they need to get rid of me the way we got rid of those revenants in the Connec," Hecht told Pella when the boy wondered why they did not just turn the Shining Ones loose.

"They would clean up. Of course they would. But no one out there would consider them as anything but devils. The Church wouldn't admit that they exist if the Choosers snatched the Patriarch's robe over his head and spanked his bare ass in front of ten thousand witnesses."

"Getting a little cynical, there, aren't you, Pop?"

"Getting? I've been like this since I was younger than you are." He flashed back on the boyhood of someone named Else Tage, then wrestled identity confusion, trying to understand why he had become the implacable enemy of everything that had meant so much to that boy.

Pella broke the mood. "Spanking the Patriarch would be popular. But the Shining Ones need to do things to make people *want* to believe in them again. Right? That's why they hooked up with us. Helping us helped them get to the Wells of Ihrian, so they could be the kind of gods who actually show up when somebody yells for help, not the kind that are only convoluted intellectual exercises for priests to quarrel over. 'God answers all prayers' is a copout. He doesn't have to exist . . ."

The boy stopped. Such talk was not likely to find favor with the religiously driven.

Hecht stared. What the hell was this? Somewhere, somehow, the kid had gotten his brain engaged. That was scary.

"Pella, you make me nervous when you think about things besides firepowder formulary and falcon deployments."

"Great. I like that. Where is the Empress, now? Getting close?" The answer to that was, much too close.

Lord Arnmigal became an anxious adolescent whenever he considered Helspeth's approach.

He was so eager to see her that he almost danced when he thought about it. His people kept finding him frozen in thought.

That seldom caused comment anymore. It seemed to be another phase, like the massive need for sleep that had gone its way, now, having grown ever less debilitating as the Righteous moved south.

Hecht himself paid little attention. His focus remained on the mundane and daily.

He told Pella, "She'll be here in a few days. Barring disaster." What made him add that?

Determined Pramans had tried to ambush her repeatedly. Sheaf and Wife had become full-time lifeguards, replacing Ferris Renfrow and Asgrimmur Grimmsson, who had then been ordered back to Alten Weinberg to help Algres Drear keep the Imperial peace.

Stupid, stupid tribesmen! Were they blind? Did they not understand that success against the Grail Empress meant disaster would come down like the deluge? Could they not understand that they were *begging* for the extermination of whole tribes?

They could not see that. Of course not. Only Lord Arnmigal did, along with the Instrumentalities who would deliver the genocide.

Much as he anticipated Helspeth's advent, so did Hecht dread it. Having his lover in camp, with no privacy to be had . . . They would do something stupid. It was sure to happen.

He reddened, remembering Katrin. That humiliation returned.

ALMOST THE FIRST THING HELSPETH SAID, FOLLOWING THE CEREMONY attendant on her arrival, was, "I brought that candle you like, Lord Arnmigal."

Hecht's eyes widened. He had forgotten the time candle. Last he had seen it, it had been in his quarters in the Still-Patter house. He recalled several instances when it would have been handy to have.

"Thank you so much, Majesty. That was thoughtful of you."

"And selfish." Lady Hilda had accompanied her empress, clearly without enthusiasm. She wanted nothing to do with this rude end of the world but she was entertained at the moment. "Perhaps you could take that candle along and pray together tonight."

Helspeth gave her friend the darkest possible look.

"Just trying to help," Daedel grumbled. "The old Chaldarean church here, Saint Eules, is famous."

True. The chapel's foundations dated from Aaron's own time. Much early history of the faith involved the site. Lord Arnmigal had been startled by its small size when first he saw it.

Unprepossessing size had saved it from being converted to a Praman place of worship.

Frustration bedeviled the lovers. There were no moments free from the petitions of swarms of natives of local and crusader origin, come to beg peace, to pledge eternal fealty (till the next shift in the wind of war), to wheedle some advantage, or to complain about someone else.

Capture of the invincible city, by a lesser fraction of the Righteous, left an impression. And so did the cruelty of the fall of the citadel.

An opportunity to visit St. Eules did come three evenings after Helspeth's arrival. Lord Arnmigal and the Empress did not go alone. A score of notables escorted them. A hundred other folk crowded into the church. The nearest they came to privacy was in approaching the altar as just they two. Lord Arnmigal whispered, "Probably as well they don't give us time. I'm exhausted. I'm not getting enough sleep."

Mirth edged Helspeth's voice as she murmured, "Nor am I. Much as I yearn for your touch . . . I'd fall asleep, for sure."

"This won't last forever."

A priest of St. Eules blessed them as the new masters of Shartelle. He was Antast Chaldarean but the Brothen Episcopals of the Holy Lands were not caviling about doctrinal trivia. Yet.

That would come. But no one, after hearing what had befallen the garrison of the citadel, wanted to irk the Righteous or their Commander.

Following the blessing the Empress rose and stepped up to light a votive candle. She had brought one of her own. Lord Arnmigal joined her but only for a quick touch and pant and reaffirmation. "Not in this place. Not now," he said. "But soon. I promise."

"Don't disappoint your Empress."

Hecht sensed an oddness. Helspeth had changed, in a small way, while they were apart. It seemed a huge strain for her to be responsible right now, not stealing hours from the world. He watched her light another candle, bow her head, and shiver. He retreated to his place of kneeling. Helspeth extinguished the time candle after just seconds, made it disappear inside her clothing.

She rejoined the Commander of the Righteous, without kneeling.

The priest, puzzled, commenced his final benediction.

Hecht noticed Lady Hilda's smirk. She winked. This time he was sure that Daedel was playing her own game, not Helspeth's.

The Adversary scattered temptations everywhere.

From St. Eules Lord Arnmigal went to make his acquaintance with the full facts of the latest bad news.

* * *

DURING THE FINAL HOURS OF THE SIEGE A BRAVE COURIER FROM Shamramdi, having escaped that city and having survived a passage through crusader lands, had reached the coast of the White Sea. Evading every danger he had come to Shartelle, where he swam the harbor by night, slipped into the city, stole to the citadel, then entered that by scaling its exterior wall. That all added up to an effort worthy of a saga. But . . .

The hero found the garrison all dead, torn up like rats ripped apart by dogs. The stench was overwhelming. Those men had been dead for days. Evil had overtaken them almost as soon as they had locked themselves in.

The massacre left the courier in such despair that he just opened a sally port and surrendered to the first Chaldarean priest he could find.

The Commander of the Righteous knew Fastthal and Sprenghul must be responsible, thinking the effort would please him. Thinking it a nice surprise.

Indala was sure to be outraged. The Praman world would be.

Lord Arnmigal was not pleased. He had to impress upon Hourli the fact that he did not want such actions undertaken without prior approval.

He had to admit, though, that, despite the outrage, the average Praman would understand what the Choosers wanted to make plain. Attempts to thwart the Commander and Righteous would not profit them.

The massacre was sure to raise more questions amongst the Righteous. They and other crusaders would know that their own had not done that slaughter. Some would recall past strange events.

They would suspect that the slayers were Instrumentalities, and cruel Instrumentalities at that. Those who knew some folklore might even guess who those Instrumentalities must be.

"Hourli, darling, I need to see you."

The Shining One appeared in the first instant that she could without being seen doing so. She said, "They have been admonished. They truly believed that they were giving you a precious gift. They are abashed and will not act again without asking."

Hecht was surprised. She was ahead of him. "Assuming they don't forget."

"There is that about them. They do tend to exist in the moment."

Ahead of him. That happened more than left him comfortable.

It was not just the Choosers who were thinking for themselves.

"What?" he asked. She had something on her mind.

"They may not have asked permission but I cannot find fault with their reasoning. Such ferocious destruction will be instructive to everyone inclined to be stubborn. Indala may be offended but Indala is your determined enemy already."

He could not be pleased, despite all.

"You are too fond of your prerogatives, Commander. Even a god cannot manage every detail of every daily event."

He started to protest that the massacre was no tiny detail.

"But it is. To immortals it is no more than overturning an annoying anthill. And it will be trivia to history. One paragraph in the record of the fall of Shartelle, after a dozen lauding the relative bloodlessness of the city's capture. Consider what happened when the first crusaders took Vantrad."

Yes. They had butchered people by the thousand, including Deves, Dainshaus, Chaldareans who failed to cleave to the Episcopal rite, and even some who did but who owned property somebody wanted to claim. The histories did not exaggerate much by saying that the blood ran ankle deep in the streets. It had taken decades for Vantrad's economy to recover.

Hourli said, "With you it's always about control."

He had been told that often, and with some force, for some time, now. "I will concede the point. I may overdo it. But this is a case where . . ."

"I told you. They have been admonished. So. Allow yourself a week before you become more stressed. See what moral impact it really has. Send a message to Indala asking him not to compel you to do that again. He won't listen but you can point to the request forever after and insist that you gave him a chance."

For a moment Hecht wondered how she had been able to deflate his anger so slyly. He was very nearly on the defensive, now.

Hourli said, "That's that. Over and done. I have some news."

"Uhm?"

"There is an army coming up from Dreanger, mercenaries and men who accept Indala's vision for the Holy Lands. Two thousand Sha-lug are with them, having given a truce that will last for the campaign plus forty days. The total force numbers fourteen thousand. They have no idea what they actually face."

"Meaning?" Not focusing completely because, for the first time, he fully understood that he must, before long, make war on his own past.

That had been inevitable, of course. He had seen it intellectually but never truly with his heart.

"They have discounted the lessons of the Shades and the battles in the Antal. Though your weapon was created in Dreanger, they disdain everything to do with er-Rashal. Choose your ground well and you will have no trouble turning them back, perhaps without having to do much real damage."

A place came to mind right away. Any army from the south would come to it before reaching Vantrad or Shartelle. A Dreangerean army had perished in the same place two thousand years ago, in a great clash of chariot forces. He had visited that ground when he was young. He told Hourli about it, told her what he wanted scouted. "And find out who is in command on the other side. That could be critical. A Sha-lug general will take a more flexible, thoughtful, and aggressive approach."

"Iresh abd al-Kadiri."

"Excuse me?"

"Moussa Iresh abd al-Kadiri, husband of a sister of Indala's second wife. Family is the reason he was chosen to command. Though he demonstrated some competence during the conquest of Dreanger, Hourlr thinks he was put in charge so he would become a lightning rod for blame. Bad things were expected to happen. Iresh is not popular."

Hecht grunted. Politics. An army might be sacrificed so Indala's people could shed an unwanted commander.

"Find out who is next after al-Kadiri. Especially the senior Sha-lug." His paranoid side had been triggered. "This Iresh may be in charge only within his own imagination."

"We will examine the facts immediately."

"Wait. You have a wicked notion."

"Excuse me?"

"I am beginning to gain a feel for how you think, dear. You're considering something more than just scouting."

Hourli confessed, "You are getting to know me all over again. Yes. I was musing on what a tragedy it would be if your enemies suffered a plague of dysentery."

His instant response was irritation. Hourli had been thinking without permission or instruction. The reaction disgusted him. Was he becoming a megalomaniac? Maybe not. Those people never questioned it. Could it be a god complex?

For some reason he thought of Osa Stile. Where was that loathsome worm these days? In Salpeno? He ought to drag Osa out here to be his creepy little conscience prod. Osa would not be impressed by Lord Arnmigal's status. Osa had bedded Patriarchs and Princes of the

Church. Osa had known Else Tage as a snot-nosed trainee who could do nothing right. Osa would not hesitate to point out his faults and shortcomings. Osa would make some up if that seemed appropriate.

Hourli said, "You spend too much time daydreaming. You can afford it here but don't take it into the field. You might not make it back."

What did she mean by that? Other than the obvious?

She said, "Ignoring Dreangerean politics, Indala hopes that Iresh will capture Vantrad. He believes Vantrad is vulnerable if Iresh moves decisively. King Beresmond's health is bad. Queen Clothilde is stupid, self-absorbed, and universally loathed. Indala has been in contact with enemies of hers whom he believes will betray Vantrad. He is also convinced that capturing the Holy City will change everything. He thinks that its recapture will obsess you and the Enterprise and that will ease pressure on Shamramdi. He would then be free to break out and begin gathering strength to take the offensive. He is sure that he can smash the Enterprise."

"Why?" Nothing had gone right for Indala so far.

"Because God is on his side. Because there are tens of thousands of Believers who want to be part of a holy war. They just haven't found an effective, unifying leader."

"He thinks he's that guy?"

"He does."

"So he's suffering from a grand and glorious delusion."

"Or he might be right. The warriors are out there. They think something should be done about you but aren't yet ready to uproot themselves. That might leave their tribes vulnerable to predatory neighbors."

"Nor will they abandon hope that a dimwit neighbor might go off with the bulk of his own warriors. Right?"

"The facts of the world are facts."

It was ever thus. The coming of God's Peace to the Believers had not stilled any older enmities.

A FEW DAYS PASSED. THE SCRUTINY OF OTHERS RELAXED. HELSPETH became uninteresting to those unable to gain access. The soldiers got on with God's Enterprise. Men of high station found ways to commit mischief in His Name. So much was happening, in so many directions, with so many towns and cities beleaguered, that the Shining Ones had trouble keeping Lord Arnmigal informed. It began to look like Indala had made a brilliant move. There might be no one left to intercept the army from Dreanger.

In three days that army moved barely ten miles, then stopped altogether while Iresh al-Kadiri awaited anticipated reinforcements. Meantime, news of the army's existence created considerable excitement in Shamramdi. The besiegers grew disheartened because their opponents were so perfectly confident that the Dreangerean host would turn the war around. Capturing Vantrad would reverse Praman fortunes completely.

Other than issue orders to get a reinforced reconnaissance moving Lord Arnmigal seemed uninterested. Seemed to have turned his back on what had looked like a grand opportunity only days earlier.

He had decided that Vantrad needed a good dose of Praman moral salts. Beresmonde and Clothilde were embarrassments, he for his weakness and she for her wickedness. Perhaps Beresmonde could not help himself because of his afflictions. Clothilde had no excuse.

Just since the Enterprise had reached the Holy Lands she had, twice, gone to her cousin Rogert, doing little to disguise the purpose of her visit.

Let Iresh drive the incestuous witch out of Vantrad, to her lover. Madouc of Hoeles would not long suffer her indecency.

Saying that to Hourli and the Shining Ones caused laughter and left him red and digging for excuses. "Katrin isn't a relative!"

"Who?" Sheaf asked.

"Oh, my!" said Wife.

"Helspeth! I meant Helspeth!"

"Whatever," Aldi observed, with paragraphs of sarcasm riding its humped back.

He chose not to dig the hole deeper by defending himself. "That is what I want to happen."

Wife asked, "Why?"

"I want them to occupy Vantrad, to cleanse it of the wickedness that has taken root there. Then I will rescue the city and make it a gift to the Empress." Adding Vantrad to Helspeth's diadem would enhance her place in the Chaldarean world magnificently.

Hourli said, "We don't get paid to understand his motives, ladies. Any ingenious ideas about how to make a difficult wish come true?"

A CHANCE TO BE ALONE WITH HELSPETH sneaked up when she, having lost patience, decided to make it happen. She lighted the time candle, which she had insisted on keeping herself, and walked through Shartelle, the candle hidden in a bucket. She entered the trade exchange center the Righteous had taken for its headquarters, wandered the labyrinthine interior in search of her lover, feeling more foolish by the minute. She found Lord Arnmigal arguing with his son, who wanted to command the falcon battery accompanying the force his father was about to send to shadow Iresh abd al-Kadiri.

Helspeth was unaware of Lord Arnmigal's strategic investment in a Praman success at Vantrad. Nor did Pella know. Helspeth caught only fragments of the argument from inside her time bubble.

Her visit did not go unnoticed. Time also changed for anyone who got too close. It was impossible to remain unseen by someone breathing in your face. Sometimes she had to get close to get past.

Her adventure would birth a fear that the Night was up to something involving a ringer for the Grail Empress.

The Night, the Shining Ones, of course, would have managed without attracting as much attention. They did not have to travel through the space between.

Piper Hecht sensed an unseen presence. So did Pella. The boy thought the quiet visitor might be his aunt or one of his sisters.

Hecht thought one of the more shy Old Ones wanted to talk. For a moment he hoped it would be Aldi. Then he caught a glimpse that Pella, from his angle, did not.

His son would not understand a late-night visit from that woman and was too old to fool with yak about a secret emergency.

Helspeth did not reveal herself otherwise. She recognized the absurdity. She went away feeling sad, frustrated, and foolish.

LORD ARNMIGAL FOUND THE EMPRESS INSIDE ST. EULES, NOT KNEELing before the altar but seated discreetly on a bench in shadow in back. She was crying quietly. "I hoped you'd come here." And, a moment later, "After so long." Another moment. "It's getting harder to give my lifeguards the slip."

She finally lifted her gaze. What light there was glistened off her tears. "I'm sorry. I shouldn't have done that. Did it cause any trouble?"

"There will be questions tomorrow but so many surround me now that they won't bother pressing it."

She scooted over. He settled beside her. She said, "None of the priests are awake. They don't do night prayers here."

"Antasts are more relaxed than we are."

Helspeth slipped her hand into his. "Aaron was more relaxed, too. His Church was more like the Maysalean thing than the Episcopal."

"Uhm. We should light the candle anyway if we're going to be here. There's no guarantee we'll stay alone, otherwise."

"God knows, I hate this. But we can't do anything else. Unless I want to become another Anne of Menand. Or Clothilde, rutting with whom I want, where I want, whenever I want."

Hecht let go her hand while she fired the time candle, then slid the hand across her shoulder. She leaned against him, seeming much smaller than the Empress Helspeth Ege. He said, "We choose to let the world define love for us."

Helspeth sighed.

Hecht was not in the grip of any physical need tonight, nor was she. The moment felt almost exactly right, except for Helspeth suffering those little moments when she trembled as though feeling a chill. Each such moment ended with her trying to burrow closer.

In time, she confessed, "I am with child." She said it in a tiny voice, into his chest, to his heart, but never did he mistake what she said, nor was he completely surprised.

His mind did race. It had to have happened before he left Alten Weinberg. Had to have for her to be so certain now. It would not be long before it began to show. Not long before it became the scandal of the decade. "I'm sorry, beloved. I am so sorry. I have ruined you."

She did not disagree.

He promised, "I will not fail you. I will do whatever needs to be done."

"I know. I know. I've had a long time to worry. A long time to lose a lot of sleep. A long time to dread all the ways you might respond to the news. I imagined some ugly possibilities. But, right now, you sound like I hoped you would."

Hecht sighed. She was not wholly pleased because he accepted the Will of God without demur? "I'm not surprised. It's not something that I expected to happen but I have considered the possibility. There were so many times when we just gave ourselves up to the flame."

"I can still save the Enterprise. I can still make sure that Katrin is remembered for what she bequeathed the world."

"What?"

"I can name Algres Drear as the father."

"You will not."

"The court will accept that. He was always close. They gossiped about him. And he won't deny it."

"That will not happen. I will not have Drear ruined for my sake."

"Piper, I can't play the virgin birth card. That only works when it happens two thousand years ago."

For a moment an exultant Katrin shone in his mind's eye, overjoyed. Wherever her soul resided, it would be jubilant if it was aware. This would be God's judgment . . .

Hecht was startled. People really did put those kinds of black, petty motives into the hearts of their gods. But why would God—or any god—concern Himself, or Herself, with such trivia? There was a universe to be managed. Even gods as small as the Shining Ones cared little about what mortals did to one another in their beds unless they were part of the action.

"Piper, I can't stand it when you just wander off inside yourself like that!" Helspeth's hard voice dragged him back, shaky. "Why would you do that?" she demanded. "You make me feel . . . Stop it. Just stop it!"

It had been a long time. He had been another man with another name, with another woman in a dramatically different culture, where no man was much exposed to his woman while she carried a child, but he did recall that there could be emotional storms, often from no apparent cause. "I don't do it intentionally. I don't know I'm doing it. And I don't know why I do it. It started after that assassination attempt that almost succeeded. The old man who turns up out of nowhere thinks it's because I came so close to dying that I left my body briefly, then never got a firm grip on it again after I came back."

Cloven Februaren had, indeed, so speculated but he did not believe it. Neither did Hecht. There would be another answer.

Helspeth did not want to quarrel. She leaned in again, pressing close. "What are we going to do?"

He had no idea beyond letting the tide of tomorrow come and go, coping as it surged. "There are no challenges we can't handle. You've already shown that you're strong enough to face anything."

"I hope you're right. But it's going to be difficult."

Oh, it would be, on levels both personal and political.

He held Helspeth as tightly as she held him.

HOURLI ASKED, "HAVE YOU FORMED ANY PLANS?"

Hecht was startled. The Shining Ones, even Hourli, seldom just dropped in, especially while he was in bed. "About what?" It sounded like she meant something specific. There were a thousand considerations in search of a plan.

"You know your lover's situation, now. She finally found the courage to tell you."

"You knew?"

"We knew seconds after it quickened. You're never alone. Fastthal and Sprenghul stay on you like those idiot ravens used to stay on Ordnan's shoulders. I wonder what ever became of them?"

"Asgrimmur probably knows." Becoming distracted that easily. "Damn! And damn again. I hope you found us entertaining."

"Only in a somewhat poignant sense. You did show enthusiasm."

He refused to ask what she meant. He had a notion that he would not understand her explanation. "Damn for the third time. Now that will be in the back of my head every time I'm alone with . . ."

"Middle-worlders are never alone. There are watchers always."

He offered a skeptical look in response.

"All right. *Often* may fit better than always. But liaisons remain secret only because the Night doesn't find them worth gossiping about."

"Was there a point to you showing up before I've gotten my feet on the floor?"

"I do want to know if there is a plan."

"Really?"

"Truly. We should know what part you want us to play so we can prepare ourselves."

He began readying himself to face the day, noting, without paying intimate heed, that the morning felt like those times when he was with Helspeth and the time candle was burning.

He had done no thinking. The fatalism ingrained during boyhood had taken over. What would be would be what God Willed. He could only wiggle and whine in a doomed effort to thwart the Almighty.

Startled thought.

He was in the presence of a god. This god shaped his world directly, every day, and did so visibly. He did not have to ascribe anything to her. She talked to him. He did not have to subscribe to the existence of a fathomless Will or Plan.

Hourli observed, "You have had a thought."

"Not a practical one, I expect, but possibly useful."

His apostasy, grown deviously since his betrayal by the Rascal and the Lion, had passed a tipping point. He muttered, "I shall have no other gods before me." Then, puzzled, "Before you?"

Hourli asked, "What?"

"I have lost my connection to the divine."

She burst out laughing. "Oh! Darling! I doubt that very much!"

"Huh?"

"You were thinking in some direction other than what the God of the Pramans and God of the Chaldareans would like. They have pushed you away. You're stuck with leftovers from a time of barbarism, obsoletes without the decency to pack it in and fade away. Not so? You were about to suffer an epiphany."

"Now you mock me," Lord Arnmigal grumbled.

"Sometimes it's fun to mess with you."

He frowned, glared. One hardship of dealing with the Shining Ones was that there was subtext to everything they said. Hourli especially operated on multiple levels. "You're not going to seduce me again?" she said.

"Oh! What? No. Not me." Again? What? The idea never occurred to him. Who was she talking to?

"That was backwards, darling. I'm the bad girl of the tale."

"What are you talking about?" Was he whining? That sounded like whining.

"No worry. When I decide it's time you'll be a dried-out husk before you know you've been asked."

He shuddered. What the hell was she doing? He had more trouble than he could handle already.

Then Hourli laughed. "What a face! Come on. What were you thinking?"

He needed a moment to recall that they had been talking about Helspeth before she decided to rattle him. Helspeth? Helspeth! Who was with child. His child. "I was thinking we should create another Helspeth. One who can be seen not being pregnant while the real Empress stays out of sight."

Hourli considered him intently for some time. "Are you sure?"

"No. I want to save her the . . . But she might not . . . I'd have to find out what she wants to do."

"You do realize that that is begging for cosmic complications?"

For problems he could not imagine right now because worry was crippling his reason? Cosmic? Hyperbole or fact? "I'll manufacture a way for you, me, and Helspeth to discuss this."

"Good. Listen to her when we do. *Hear* what she says. We don't want to repeat mistakes already made before."

What did that mean? She was not talking about Helspeth's situation.

HELSPETH'S NEWS ALMOST COMPLETELY DISTRACTED LORD ARNMIgal. Details slipped past him. He failed to define assignments adequately when the Shining Ones went off to handle shadowy particulars. He did not monitor his captains adequately. The Shining Ones did not come volunteering for work. They basked in whichever Well of Ihrian seemed sweetest, growing supernaturally fat. Captains had to guess at the Commander's intent when acting.

"Where is Pella?" Lord Arnmigal demanded of his lifeguards one morning. He could not find the boy. "I have a job for him."

Titus materialized. "Sorry, Boss. He went off to help deal with the Dreangereans. They've stopped moving again. Sheaf says Iresh is waiting for his siege train, now."

Lord Arnmigal shook his head. "Why? All he had to do was attack while we were busy everywhere else."

"Plenty of strange stuff going on in this war, Boss. Him not wanting to take risks hardly seems odd. Anyway, how could he know that we're all tied up everywhere? He doesn't have our intelligence resources."

"You're right. Send somebody to drag the boy back."

"Sure. What did you want him to do?"

"I was going to put him in charge of the falcons harassing the Dreangereans. But now he'll take an entry-level job in the grave and latrine excavation trade. He needs to learn to take orders."

"Harsh." Titus laughed. "I had a note from the Empress. She wants to see you after midday devotions. She did *not* sound like a woman who is enchanted with Lord Arnmigal."

"Sometimes I don't have sense enough not to say things that people don't want to hear. Plus, I think she thinks she should get more attention than she does. She could have had plenty if she'd just stayed home. Us smelly men down here are too busy with our war."

"Have you had any midnight visitors lately?"

The shift evaded Hecht briefly. His conscience squealed. "You have, then?"

"What are you talking about?"

"I wondered if Heris or your girls had visited. I'm worried about Noë and the boys."

"No. Either they're preoccupied or we're too far away. I worry about Anna, too."

Despite all, that was true. Anna Mozilla did own a firm place in his heart.

Hecht said, "If any of them turn up I'll ask for a report."

39. Shamramdi: The Godstalkers

Young Az came to the house where the Mountain and his men were enjoying the siege of Shamramdi. He was pale and grim. He had lost weight. He had been wounded twice during sorties against an enemy who was always ready.

Nassim Alizarin said, "I hope you feel better than you look, Nephew."

"I doubt that, Uncle."

"Then why are you out of bed?"

"Indala couldn't come. His own health remains poor."

Rumor suggested that the Great Shake was dying, or was suffering from slow poisoning. Or Unbeliever sorcery was sucking his life and soul.

Nassim had not seen Indala for weeks. He suspected that age alone would explain the Great Shake's indisposition.

"Not heartening news, Nephew. But you have darker matters on your mind."

"Complications, certainly. My great-uncle wishes to offer his apologies for not having been more supportive of your effort to crush the Dreangerean sorcerer."

This was odd. "Has a serpent turned in his hand?"

"A courier bringing dispatches from the coast, across the mountains, was held up by the Ansa while they found a tribesman able to read and write Lucidian. They wanted to send you a message."

"And then someone here had to make sure I wasn't getting secret instructions from the crusaders."

"Not entirely. Some people just can't not stick their noses in."

Nassim snorted. The longer he lived the less well he thought of his own kind. "So tell me what it says."

"How? The letter was meant for you."

"You aren't familiar with its contents? Do come on, Nephew."

"As you will." Young Az read, but slowly. Nassim had thought him more literate.

He took the letter. The text was not in the florid style he usually saw. It made no effort to proclaim the author's command of language. The sentences were simple declarative grunts, the words mud bricks only, not an artist's paint. Nor was the calligraphy artful. That alone might explain young Az's trouble reading. Too, the writer did not know his Lucidian as well as he might pretend.

"Damn! This is rough. But I think I get it." Nassim Alizarin certainly had his own difficulties with Lucidian.

"Then explain. If you will be so generous. Because no one who has seen that message understands what it actually means. Most think it's code. If he says camel, you know he means something particular happened . . ."

"He is hard to decipher and harder to follow but he is as literal as a poisoned dagger. When he says camel he means camel. This is a desperate warning. The Dreangerean will resurrect Asher soon. The process may be under way already, after the natural delays suffered in getting this out of the Idiam."

"So. Only my great-uncle truly thought . . ."

"How long, Azim?" The scribe had not dated his missive—which would not have helped had he done so. The Ansa did not date according to Praman custom.

"It's been knocking around court for a week. I only heard about it yesterday, when they wanted to know what I thought it meant. If it is a literal warning . . . Indala will be livid. Several men who think they're smarter than him are about to find themselves reassigned to obscure towns on a border where they can expect to have to face Tsistimed the Golden."

"Indala had sense enough to take it for what it is?"

"The smart men shouted him down."

The Mountain chuckled. "No. The Great Shake might refuse a contest with fools but he wouldn't abandon a conviction. He might have a favorite nephew stand in for him."

"Assisted by the man who knows the evil best."

Nassim smiled. A gap showed in his smile. Another sign of time catching up. Two more teeth had begun to trouble him.

"And what did the Great Shake suggest? Our freedom of action is restricted. Or does he want anything done? If the great evil returns it might fall more heavily on the crusaders than on us."

"Not so, Uncle. Definitely not so." Young Az then revealed the fact that Indala had excellent information sources inside the Episcopal Chaldarean world. "Lord Arnmigal, the Commander of the Righteous, was the Brothen Church's Captain-General before he moved on to the Grail Empire."

"I know that. I saw him close up on Artecipea, when we were employed by Peter of Navaya. He seemed driven, too. But he understood my need to destroy Rudenes Schneidel personally."

Though this had not come up before, young Az betrayed no surprise. He did know the story. "You recall his stated purpose for being there?"

"The siege of Arn Bedu. The destruction of Rudenes Schneidel. Of course. We all had personal motives. The strategic reason, though, was to keep Schneidel from resurrecting Seska, the Endless."

"You destroyed the sorcerer. The Captain-General destroyed the Endless. He exterminated a gaggle of Schneidel's revenants in the End of Connec, too. Some think that he killed another revenant earlier, at al-Khazen, during the Calziran Crusade. You were there, too."

"I was there. I didn't see that. I do recall an explosion and an earthquake said to have been the result."

"There are many frightening questions around Lord Arnmigal—including a suggestion that he is a revenant himself. He has lived a mysteriously charmed life. There is little evidence that he even existed before the Church's first incursion into the End of Connec."

Nassim did not mention the Sha-lug captain, Else Tage. He tried to look alert and interested, a man learning new and interesting things.

"There is a woman named Heris. Rumor suggests that she was once a household slave in Shartelle. She could be Lord Arnmigal's natural sister. How that could be possible is beyond me, given their respective backstories. She has, they say, destroyed five revenant prehistoric gods of incredible power and evil. Gods who were originally put to sleep by later devils like Asher and Ashtoreth, who had to have human worship in order to survive."

This was mostly news to Nassim.

Young Az continued, "Lord Arnmigal and this Heris are known to the Night as the Godslayers. So my great-uncle has been informed by some who supposedly know." Sort of a wink, then, because good Pramans were forbidden congress with the Night. They should not know the thinking of the demonic Instrumentalities. "Both are closely associated with members of the Episcopal Collegium, one being the natural grandson of another. Those two have acknowledged the Heris woman as their true descendant through a man whose name you will recall: Grade Drocker."

Startled, Nassim said, "My old enemy!" Then, "I'm confused." And the more so because he had known Lord Arnmigal as a promising student in the Vibrant Spring School.

"The whole thing is confusing and goes on getting more so. The most powerful man in the west is supposedly a refugee from one of those countries that is now covered by ice. But."

"Does it matter? We have to deal with the man who is here, whatever his background was."

"True enough. But. We should keep in mind the fact that not only has he killed gods, he has begun to show godlike characteristics himself."

"What?" Alizarin fought for breath. His heart pounded.

"He isn't rattling mountains. It isn't an omnipotence thing, it's an all-knowing thing. We can't trick him. We can't mislead him. We can't outwit him. Whatever we try, he's there first, waiting, with dozens of those cursed falcons. He doesn't even have to be in the theater himself . . . Sorry. Self-pity leaking through, there. Because of my wounds. I shouldn't get upset. He isn't why I'm here. My great-uncle believes this message is more important than it looks. He is more worried about er-Rashal."

Azim pointed out that the Faith had been under crushing pressure in Direcia since the disaster at Los Naves de los Fantas. Praman principalities in the Antal and Holy Lands were falling like dominos. The Faithful in the east were being exterminated by Tsistimed the Golden, who was determined to expunge al-Prama from history. The Hu'n-tai At showed Believers no mercy whatsoever, anywhere, at any time. Hu'n-tai At warriors amused themselves in camp by roasting imams alive, then feeding them to their dogs. Their souls would never enter Paradise.

It could have been worse only if the martyrs' corpses were fed to hogs.

"You knew the sorcerer, Uncle. What does he want?"

The Mountain had considered that for years. "He wants to ascend. He wants to become an Instrumentality himself. He wants to turn back time to the age of Dreanger's greatness, before al-Prama, before the golden age of the Chaldareans, before the Old Empire and the Agean Empire. He wants to waken Dreanger from a two-thousand-year slumber. Then he will become Dreanger's god-emperor, the Son of the Sun."

"Ambitious."

"He used to brag about his direct descent from the last native dynasty. He made jokes about being the rightful emperor—and about how harsh he would be once he came into his kingdom. We all played along. But, obviously, he wasn't just having us on."

"If the message is correct, then, he may be about to achieve his dream."

"He'd be settling for third choice, actually. He lost out when Seska went down. He lost out when the Great Shake's campaign forced him to flee Dreanger. Now, again, he has to try to resurrect and manage a god from outside his own pantheon, and for his life, not as a diversion. Still, I'm pleased that Indala finally sees the threat."

Azim simply nodded.

The Mountain's longtime comrades had gathered round, with respect, neither interrupting nor offering comment. Even Old Az, Master of Ghosts, kept his thoughts to himself.

Nassim asked, "So, given this, what does Indala want?"

"Ideas. We no longer have much influence in the rest of the world. Our crusaders are content to keep us closed up while their brethren have their way elsewhere, with Believers who no longer have Indala to inspire them."

"So it would seem. I have an idea. No one will like it."

THE LINES ROUND SHAMRAMDI WERE LOOSE EVERYWHERE AND ESPE-cially sketchy where defenders ought not to be able to offer any serious challenge. The crusaders were content with that. They awaited relief columns that they could exterminate piecemeal. However, even armed with those devastating falcons and intelligence so precise that they had to be wedded to the Adversary, the crusaders could not prevent daring individuals from coming and going. Smugglers smuggled. Couriers mostly managed. City militia patrols stayed informed about enemy dispositions so exfiltration routes could be designed.

The crusaders seldom bothered with individual travelers.

Nassim Alizarin's strategy depended on that.

Unseasonable warmth in a region known for its heat had been melting snow off the peaks of the Anti-Neret. Though there was no flooding, the Bareh-da was running high. That river, flowing through Shamramdi, made it possible for the city to exist and prosper in arid country. Floating out on one-man rafts was how most emigrants departed. Dozens abandoned the city every night.

Getting in was a little more problematic, and much less attractive.

The Mountain, Azim al-Adil ed-Din, al-Azer er-Selim, and Alizarin's oldest companions took the river route, one man at a time over several hours in order to avoid special notice by the Eyes of the Night. Excepting Nassim himself and Indala's great-nephew, all had visited Andesqueluz in the once-upon-a-time. The Mountain had had to reveal that before he could sell the Great Shake on his plan. Too, he had confessed that he knew the Commander of the Righteous better than he had admitted before, though he reserved the heart of the truth. He related only interactions during the campaign on Artecipea.

Wonder of wonders, the Great Shake did grasp how vast a threat er-Rashal al-Dhulquarnen would become, ascended, with an Old God in his arsenal. Indala had the vision to think beyond dogma hammered in since infancy.

Alizarin feared the peril might be beyond his imagining. Asher had not been benign. Should er-Rashal be unable to control it . . . Asher would engineer the resurrection of his spouse, Ashtoreth. The couple would chastise the world . . . which might be an ambition the Rascal shared, but according to his own lights.

NASSIM QUELLED HIS DREAD. POINTLESS, DWELLING. HE HAD OB-sessed too long already, in an endless quarrel with his conscience. Now he was wet and cold and alone on a raft that had begun to come apart. There was no moon. The Bareh-da was not yet entirely free of crocodiles. Lions rumbled beyond both shores. Though nearly hunted out, the survivors were afoot tonight. Then he heard the cough of a leopard. What else might be about, less mundane than fang and claw, he did not care to speculate.

"Entirely imagination," he told himself. "Just imagination. Fear pounded into my ancestors by the Night."

The Night was the true danger. The Night was wickedly clever. The Night was boundlessly cruel—though Instrumentalities seldom showed up in person anymore. Mostly they lurked in scary stories from back before the Revelation.

Nassim Alizarin had seen crocodiles, leopards, and lions, in all their fearsome tooth and claw, and what they could do to people who annoyed Gordimer. He preferred a less grisly fate for himself.

He spotted the wan signal finally, used a rotted board to paddle to the western bank, eventually landing two hundred yards long. Mohkam joined him, armed with a small lantern shuttered so tight it released almost no light at all.

"The others?" the Mountain asked.

"All here. Waiting at the signal, except for the Master of Ghosts."

Al-Azer had left first, on the best raft, his job to pick the landing site and set the signal. "Where did he go?" Then, "My raft came apart. I lost most of my gear."

Mohkam shrugged. "He wanted to check something. You didn't lose your weapons, did you? We can find food and clothes."

They walked while talking. At the assembly point young Az asked, "How long should we wait for the Master of Ghosts, Uncle? We should be under cover before first light."

Nassim said, "Patrols won't be a worry if we don't clump up. They don't bother individuals who aren't obviously smuggling food or weapons."

Young Az remarked, "They are more restrained than they could be."

"Restrained?" Nassim blurted, startled.

"It being a war and all. Of religions. Just saying. Despite the atrocities we hear about, the Righteous have been generous—if the defeated surrender when offered the chance." Azim added, "Compared to the Hu'n-tai At, or Rogert du Tancret, or crusaders and Gisela Frakier who aren't with the Righteous."

It took the Mountain a moment to grasp the implication.

Had Captain Tage survived after all? The Righteous were not systematically exterminating the Believers, unlike the Hu'n-tai At. The Righteous simply disarmed those who served the God Who Is God, with massive destruction and bloodshed occasionally but never to the limits of their capacity.

That deserved reflection, someday when he had leisure time, when the sun was high and no big, hungry things were snuffling about.

Old Az caught up. He did not explain himself, but did report, "We are going to walk a lot. That could be good. On foot and at our ages we won't look so dangerous."

Nassim said, "I begin to entertain doubts about this."

Young Az countered, "It was your idea."

"Time has made me wise enough to admit that I can mess up."

"And have you?"

Nassim grunted a provisional negative. He had grown passionate selling this mission to the Great Shake. Indala had had his doubts but once he made his decision he did not consult advisors or family other than Azim.

Nassim had shielded him from the totality of the scheme.

It would entail a certain level of what might be considered treason.

Treason? Easy for Nassim Alizarin, the professional turncoat. But what of Indala? What of the Great Shake's most favored nephew? Would they be branded forever?

Success or failure would tell.

Old Az asked, "How did Bone take having to stay behind?"

"It wasn't pleasant." Nassim hoped the old warrior was secretly pleased. "He claimed he would rather die out here with his brothers than molder a dozen more years among strangers. I hope that was just for show." The old man had been sure that he would see none of the band again.

Somebody feeling negative muttered, "And ain't there a grand good chance the old goat was right?"

The Mountain felt like his companions were with him mostly because he was doing something, however foredoomed, as opposed to doing nothing in Shamramdi while awaiting the inevitable end.

THE RECEPTION FROM THE ANSA WAS MIXED. SOME BLAMED NASSIM for their troubles since his departure. Others understood that their tribulations were less than a sideshow to the grandees of Qasr al-Zed. Nassim should be honored for having argued his way back into the conflict with the monster of the Dead City. Without him the Ansa had no hope at all.

The Rascal was his weakest yet but he won every skirmish. He had negated the Ansa firepowder weaponry. They could now do him no serious harm. They could not get close enough.

And now the Dreangerean had begun taking outsider victims.

The crusaders had closed the traditional communications routes between the coast and the Lucidian heartland. Today's routes passed through the Neret Mountains. The road that debouched at al-Pinea was most heavily traveled.

Couriers did not always get through, though losses were never so heavy that the route might be abandoned. It had been dangerous in peacetime, the Ansa taking the blame. Usually, they were guilty.

The Rascal was harvesting messengers for raw material. Soon he would resume reanimating his grandfather of devils. He was very close to success.

Neither the Ansa who visited Shamramdi, nor any of the tribe's appeals, mentioned that the Rascal had made himself some helpers by using his ugliest necromancy to resurrect some of Andesqueluz's former residents.

They numbered fewer than a dozen. They were slow. They were vulnerable. They were not much good at carrying out orders but they did ease er-Rashal's life. The terror they caused exceeded that generated by the sorcerer himself.

The terrified Ansa were on the brink of panicky flight despite having nowhere to run.

The Ansa found the situation hard to discuss. It struck to the core of their cultural obsessions. When a few did try to explain, language problems and cultural quirks left the Sha-lug baffled.

Old Az thought about it a lot. Eventually, at the communal fire, he told Nassim, "The Rascal did learn something awful from those mummies he had us steal."

Er-Rashal failed with many more mummy reanimations than he succeeded. Most of the mummies were too damaged. The successes had enslaved the imaginations of the Ansa, though. They would not fight back.

Young Az argued, "It's simple and obvious. You throw flammable liquid and light them up."

"Light them up!" Mohkam barked, laughing.

The Master of Ghosts was more restrained but agreed. "That should work. You'd think they'd try it. They don't because that would amount to outrageous disrespect for their ancestors—who were sorcerers themselves in their time."

Nassim hoped that, as in some old horror stories, er-Rashal would bumble his way into some trap set by the ancients. "Why would they worry about disrespect? They have no ancestors among the dead of Andesqueluz."

True. The Ansa had not occupied the Idiam nearly long enough. They descended from a stiff-necked cult that had fled thither in Brothen imperial times. Nevertheless, they had adopted the older history.

Even the most cooperative Ansa refused to dishonor their presumptive ancestors by defending the living against them.

"We have cultural blind spots, too," Nassim told young Az. "And we're just as unaware. Everybody. Let's don't have any bad talk about Ansa thinking. We want them blind to what we're doing." He stared into the fire. "We'll act. We'll buy time. I have a new plan."

The company moved in around him. He would not want to be overheard. He did not give them much, though, because no truly new idea had occurred. "We won't stand toe-to-toe with er-Rashal. That path can lead only to failure and despair."

The new plan came as a flash of inspiration that was, in fact, not really all that sudden. He decided instantly not to share it till he had no choice.

He began with a diversion. His renegades clumsy-sneakily started building a crude firepower manufactory, claiming to have distilled saltpeter from the waters at al-Pinea. He told the Ansa that he had found a means whereby he could produce weak firepowder impossible to be set afire from a distance. Nassim counted on at least one Ansa having voided his conscience to keep er-Rashal posted.

The process had barely begun, with Ansa youngsters collecting scrub wood to burn into charcoal, when Old Az announced, "Something cold and empty is watching."

"A revenant?"

"Almost certainly."

"The Rascal is being careful."

"We've stung him before."

Nassim chuckled. "He shouldn't attack tonight but be ready anyway, in case he suffers a stroke of bold. Keep the youngsters near the fire. I want the revenants getting hungry."

Events conformed to Nassim's scheme. Er-Rashal took the bait, dreading untouchable firepowder. His revenants moved in next night, intent on destroying renegade Sha-lug and feasting on tender young Ansa. They came in a swarm, anticipating no ready resistance, counting on Nassim to be considerate of Ansa culture and so delay his response too long.

Everyone felt the coldness and emptiness of the revenants waxing. Nassim did not share his intentions with the Ansa.

The revenants attacked. The Sha-lug doused them with oil and chucked them into the fire. The action lasted only seconds. The revenants burned vigorously. Er-Rashal got a dose of oil and fire himself while distracted by rage. Screaming, smoldering, he bounded off toward the Dead City, still remarkably spry.

Old Az opined, "He'll be out of sorts for a while."

Young Az said, "Let's go after him. He'll never be weaker."

Nassim said, "Tactically, we should. But we'd need to have friendly Ansa behind us."

The others were dismembering revenant mummies, making sure no piece of any old sorcerer escaped the flames. The Ansa present, all youngsters, were appalled.

Young Az said, "I see. We should get out of here. They might decide to do something that we'll regret."

Nassim told a son of the tribe's second chief, "We bought you time. It will take the sorcerer months to recover. Keep the living away and he won't recover at all. His evil survives only because of his ability to steal life. Let the elders hate us if they like but tell them not to waste the time we've won. It is a dark gift but the best I can manage. We Sha-lug must now go play another sad role."

The Ansa did nothing till Nassim and his band were long gone.

"THE PLACE IS UGLIER THAN EVER," OLD AZ SAID. GHERIG WAS ILLUminated strangely by a rising sun piercing a massive dust storm to the east.

Young Az said, "The weird light definitely makes it look creepy."

Gherig still wore a skirt of scaffolding. Gaps and cracks still marred its walls. It looked more grimly inhospitable than ever, though hospitality had never been its forte. Hostility, though . . . The boy added, "This would be a good time to attack, had we the numbers." Ignoring his own past failure.

Mohkam muttered continuously, trying to keep his courage elevated, lacking all faith in a white banner's ability to shield those who had irked the crusaders so stubbornly for so long.

Nassim himself had no trouble trusting Madouc of Hoeles. How-

ever, the Master of the Commandery was not alone there. Resenting
his reduced status, Rogert du Tancret might imagine a chance to ag-
grandize himself by aborting any agreement between the Brotherhood
and the renegades from the east.

A needless concern. The Master quietly demonstrated his complete
control over Gherig. Black Rogert's men had come over to him almost
universally. Du Tancret had subsided to a whining nuisance raging
against the unfairness.

Madouc of Hoeles listened closely while the old general stated his
case. He asked perceptive questions. He had paid attention while serving the Captain-General. He grasped the threat shaping in the Idiam.
He knew what er-Rashal al-Dhulquarnen could do. He knew more
about the Ansa and the Idiam than Nassim expected.

Nassim Alizarin hoped his own people would not hate him for, apparently, having turned his coat again.

Young Az was deeply unhappy, certainly, though he insisted that
he understood.

One thing could not be denied: The Believers totally lacked the
knowledge, the power, and the ability to cope if er-Rashal did awaken
his devils. The Crusaders, Lord Arnmigal, and the Godslayer, however,
had shown extreme skill in dealing with powerful and wicked resurrected demons.

40. East of Triamolin: Mischief-Makings

Brother Candle killed a louse, then killed another. Then another,
still, viciously, before announcing, "I begin to understand how
some men become murderous." Lice, people, it was a matter of degree,
and people were the deeper source of aggravation. Killing got the
screaming frustration out, the maddening pressure inside reduced, and
punctuated one source of frustration forever.

Kedle did not quite agree. She winced while shifting to reach for a
peach. Exertions the night of the big ambush had inflamed her old in-
juries. Her leg hurt a lot. But she was Kedle Richeut, the Widow, bloodthirsty avenging spirit of the Vindicated. She could not make herself
stay inactive long enough to manage a full recovery. She told everyone
that she enjoyed the local warmth. Cold weather only made the leg
hurt more. Brother Candle was amazed that anyone could find a bright
side to being baked greaseless.

She asked, "Have we begun to experience regrets, Master?"

"'We' set foot on that trail before *Darter* passed the breakwater at Terliaga."

"So you've done your penance. They'll park your bony arse on the right hand of God, between Him and Aaron." Deliberate sacrilege.

Brother Candle refused the bait. "Just let me mope and feel sorry for myself."

One of the Arnhander youngsters came in to announce, "That General Ghort guy is here again, Lady."

Kedle waved. The boy backed out. Kedle asked, "You heard? I'm a Lady, now."

"He thinks his friend is a lady, too."

That could have sparked a quarrel, Kedle's appreciation for Hope being what it was, but the Captain-General's arrival interrupted. Ghort checked them out while his eyes adjusted to the gloom. "Squabbling again?"

"Still," the Perfect conceded.

Kedle grumbled, "There's nobody else to fight with. The Commander of the Righteous keeps not letting us do what we came here to do."

"I may have some good news, then. May I sit?"

"If the news is what I want to hear you can sit on my lap."

"I shall do my best to polish and spin it prettily, then."

Brother Candle was shocked. Kedle was, too. She had blurted something thoughtlessly to a Captain-General hardly subtle or shy about his interest in the Widow as a woman.

The Perfect thought Kedle found the notion intriguing but confusing. She could not discuss it with him. The only woman she knew was Hope. Hope would, he thought, tell Kedle to grab the chance, being incapable of grasping the concept of monogamy herself. He thought he had a pretty good idea where Hope fit in the old pantheon, now.

The Captain-General said, "I went to Shartelle and spent some time with my old friend. We drank some, swapped some lies about the old days, caught up with friends from back when. Stuff guys do when they haven't seen each other for a while." He sounded disappointed.

Ghort continued, "He's changed. He's always as serious as a thunderhead. He has all his old friends worried. It's like he's made himself the best war leader ever basically by giving up what made him human."

Kedle said, "Rumor says he's been touched by the Night."

"Ain't hardly no doubt about that. And he's attracted a bunch of others almost just like him. Though I got to admit that some of them are yummy. Evie and Aldi, man! Boyhood fantasies come to life."

Brother Candle's tongue betrayed him. "I think we've met Aldi."

"Huh? You have?" Ghort looked baffled.

"Captain-General, you dare flirt with me, then praise other women?"

Brother Candle was surprised. He thought that Kedle had surprised herself, too. But she did have a point.

"You're right." Ghort was wise enough to know that nothing would help, however he said it. "So. I did task my friend about us going to seed, here. He isn't happy with us because he can't control us. That's the big change I saw. He's very controlling, now. He looks at anyone not under his orders like the Perfect looks at his lice. They're pests and parasites."

Kedle grumbled something about how she'd show the jerk a parasite if he ever got close enough.

Grimly, Ghort said, "Don't say stuff like that. He'll hear about it and take it seriously. There have been some ugly attempts to kill him. The assassins did get his sense of humor. Not that he was ever a ha-ha guy."

"So?" Brother Candle wanted Ghort back to his excuse for visiting Kedle.

"He says it's all right if we head east to help hold the gap between Gherig, the Well of Days, and Megaeda, so reinforcements from Lucidia can't come through."

"I thought Indala's gang were trapped in Shamramdi."

"So they are. We're welcome to go play siege there, too, if we want. Under command of the captains on the scene."

Before Kedle complained Brother Candle said, "You left Terliaga knowing you wouldn't have the freedom of action you had in Arnhand."

Ghort laughed. "Hey! No shit! We want *something* left standing when it's all over."

Kedle said, "I'll take that as a compliment. Let's talk, then. The man running Gherig these days. He used to be Lord Arnmigal's bodyguard?"

"The boss lifeguard. He quit because Piper wouldn't listen to him. Which only got him—Hecht, Lord Arnmigal, that is—almost killed a few times because he wouldn't. He's been lucky as hell, so far. Yeah. Madouc of Hoeles. Brotherhood of War. Exactly the kind of guy anybody who goes into that order wants to be when he grows up. I got along with him. Not real flexible, but brilliant. And considerate. Though I figure he's changed out here, too. He'd be more active if he had more manpower. For a long time, though, too, he was up against one of the best damned war fighters that ever was."

"Any chance we might see some action?"

Ghort dared leer and grumble, "Not as good as I'd like, probably. Damn! I said that out loud. Oh, well. You mean opportunities for old-fashioned skull busting. Damn, woman! Weren't you listening? Gherig sits smack on *the* main road, the only route between Lucidia and the Holy Lands with plenty of water. If Indala ever breaks out of Sham-ramdi he'll have to push through there to rescue his cousins over here."

Kedle knew all that. She worked on being the Widow night and day. Brother Candle thought she might be playing dumb girl for Ghort's benefit.

Let him think he was making some headway.

Kedle said, "I imagine Lord Arnmigal just wants his mavericks put where they'll get used up weakening his enemies while staying out of his hair. He does have hair, doesn't he? I'm not big on a man without hair. My husband began going bald before he was twenty."

Ghort ran fingers through his wild mass of brush.

Kedle pretended to miss that. "Well, it's a chance to do something besides go to mold."

"For sure," Ghort said. "For sure," then fell silent and stayed that way, which amazed Brother Candle. The man almost never shut up.

Kedle added, "I *was* considering making a run at Vantrad. Those idiots aren't ready for anything, even with the Dreangereans only two days away."

She had been spying, and not just with Hope's assistance, looking for *something* to do. Her determination irked the Perfect endlessly. It was too damned hot to be banging around!

Her notion of a surprise attack on the Holy City totally deflated Ghort.

Brother Candle had been unaware of her thinking, too. "Kedle!"

"Oh, come on! We could do it! Nobody expects us to try. They figure we'll just loaf around until his holiness, Lord Arnmigal, the Episcopal god of war, grants us permission to inhale."

Brother Candle chewed air like a beached carp. She was capable of such audacity because she was incapable of understanding that she should not be. She was unable to consider possible failure. She would see nothing but a chance to win the Vindicated a place in the histories.

She depended too much on Hope. This was a new war in a new land. That sweet devil must operate under tougher constraints herself. Her demonic cabal had its own secret agenda.

Kedle said, "I'll consider this idea. Let me consult my captains."

Brother Candle indulged a smirk. Kedle would talk *at* the Vindicated, after checking with Hope—if she could lure the Instrumentality.

The Perfect had to admit that he wished Hope were around more. It could be pleasant, being driven by his sinner side, inside the secret society of his mind.

HOPE TOLD KEDLE, "THE IDEA MAKES ME UNCOMFORTABLE, DEAR, though it is better than an attack on Vantrad. Lord Arnmigal is not understanding. He has lost his shadow. If you go after Vantrad, even though he's never said not to, he'll turn on you."

Brother Candle believed her. She was in the moment. Were she human she would be shaky. But he was equally sure that she was holding back something to do with the situation around Gherig.

Hope did not want Kedle headed for the frontier. Why not?

Kedle wondered, too, clearly, and Hope was irked because she had given herself away.

Kedle was not intimidated by Hope. She might not know any intimate details but she did see that Instrumentalities need no longer be dreaded as they had in olden times. She jumped in behind Hope and threw an arm across her throat, playfully. "Give, woman! How come you're all spooked?"

Hope was willing to play, despite the audience, but only briefly. She yielded, talked.

Kedle demanded, "Is that the sorcerer who was behind the resurrections in the Connec?"

"Keep thy fingers to thine own self and open thy ears, beloved. This would be an ally of Rudenes Schneidel. They were after ascendance and supernatural power. Lord Arnmigal wrote Schneidel's last chapter while he was Captain-General. Er-Rashal wants to restore the Dreangerean empire, too, which is a fool's hope, my elders assure me."

Brother Candle sensed a lack of conviction. Hope was not sure of her own tribe.

She added, "This er-Rashal is the cruelest, cleverest, most remorseless of his kind, excepting Tsistimed the Golden. But Tsistimed is an ascendant already." Hope shuddered, obviously disturbed by that. "Fortunately for the middle world, er-Rashal has a knack for creating enemies and suffers from chronic bad luck."

"Which means what?"

"He is so vile that he always has people trying to abort his ambitions."

Kedle mused, "Sounds like a Dreangerean Anne of Menand, absent the redeeming quality of her bedroom skills."

"Perhaps. He's probably a eunuch, but that's irrelevant. The important thing is, he is about to succeed. In only a few months, maybe even only a few weeks, he may manage his breakthrough."

Kedle demanded, "So why hasn't somebody done something?"

"They try, dear. The child's answer is, he won't let them. The unfortunate great obstacle, though, is the belief systems of the peoples in these parts. They won't credit a threat from a sleeping god. They say there is only *one* god, and He *is* God. And a lot of them are willing to commit murder to decide His absolute true identity."

Brother Candle strained to control his breathing and slow his heartbeat. Despite Hope, despite all else, he had trouble getting his mind around the fact that there was so much more to the Night than what he had believed just a few years ago.

That monster in what indigenes called the Idiam should not exist. Not in a truly Chaldarean or Maysalean universe.

Something clicked. It did not coalesce into anything concrete, yet it did add to his disquiet about Hope.

She was being so careful. Carefully careful, hoping not to be noticed being careful, tiptoeing through meadows of information. She did not want middle-worlders to see something to do with the Dreangerean, something not immediately obvious.

Kedle felt it, too. "I'm sure the Vindicated will agree. Any business will be preferable to what we're enduring now."

Hope seemed relieved momentarily, then slightly troubled, caught up in some internal debate. Kedle's ready agreement solved an immediate vexation but stirred a possible new slate of problems.

Hope read his smile, more troubled. She failed to flirt, tempt, or taunt. Nor did she turn her allure upon Kedle.

She said, "I am obligated to report your choice. I suggest you start moving immediately. The weather will turn nasty in a few days. You won't want to travel during the storms." She surprised Kedle with a quick hug and peck on the forehead, strode briskly out of the tent.

Everyone inside saw her leave. No one outside saw her emerge. The guards were bracing for the blustery advent of the Brothen Captain-General, who seemed unable to understand that he was not the stallion of the herd.

The Widow seemed to like Pinkus Ghort, for no evident reason. His presence always complicated the moment.

Inside, Kedle told Brother Candle, "Hope is up to something."

"Dear girl, of course she is. She can't help it. She meant to use us from the start." He rubbed the head of the snake tattooed on his left arm. A lesser serpent stirred, recalling that first encounter.

What had been in the air that night?

Kedle said, "With no more evidence than a gut feeling, I think she's just another piece on the board, now, carrying out instructions sloppily enough that we can tell that her aunts are pushing her into something that doesn't thrill her."

"Your sense of it is finer than mine. Any idea what is really going on?"

Kedle laid a finger to her lips. Brother Candle thought she was concerned about supernatural eavesdroppers till Pinkus Ghort appeared, having talked his way past her guards.

Kedle growled, exasperated but not actually unhappy.

The Perfect suspected that the Captain-General had been touched by the Night himself. He had more substance than his reputation suggested.

Brother Candle's tattoos moved. Responding to Ghort? Was he a danger? The snakes had not stirred since the Praman raid, when their poison had added several stains to the Perfect's soul.

41. The Holy Lands: Ad Hoc Scrambles and Royal Mischief

Hecht was moments from descent into a deep sleep. That need was back. He hated it. It cost too much time. He dreamed dreams that were far too disturbing. He could not afford to waste the time and stress.

Something had changed. Something had shifted after Helspeth's arrival.

The air stirred as someone materialized. So much for his drift toward slumber. Uncharitably, he hoped that it was not Helspeth with the time candle.

Uncharitable, yes, but he felt the same toward his sister and daughters though he had seen none of them since Hypraxium.

When rested and working he did miss them and Anna. He was starved for family closeness.

Strange. He was a split beast for sure, ever less at home inside himself, liking Piper Hecht less and less as he morphed more concretely into Lord Arnmigal, master of the Enterprise of Peace and Faith.

Hourli said, "I know you aren't sleeping. You snore villainously."

Hecht offered the universe a put-upon sigh, unwound, rolled to face the goddess. She glowed, putting the shine in Shining One.

"It can't wait?" He felt ferociously cranky yet actually was pleased. He always started to feel better when Hourli came around. Much better if she stayed a while.

Was some destructive fragment of self, buried too deep to recognize, driving him toward another ill-advised liaison? He hoped not. He felt none of the obsession that had begun with his first glimpse of Helspeth, nor the comfortable correctness he had always known with Anna. Nor did he feel coerced, as with Katrin. Hourli was more like a lifelong friend whose presence eased his aches and cares.

The old friend was not above an occasional oblique suggestion that she would not mind amusing herself with a dalliance.

He shuddered.

That would not happen. He had female complications enough, and more.

Silence stretched. It did not become uncomfortable. He felt better by the moment.

This improvement in energy and mood and recession in weariness occurred with all of the Shining Ones, to a lesser extent, excepting Eavijne. Eavijne could be more refreshing than Hourli when she wanted.

Evie offered a suite of temptations, and was pliable enough . . .

Again, no!

But Evie smelled so good, like apples, pines, cherry blossoms . . .

He shuddered, bore down. "To what do I owe the pleasure, then?"

Hourli smirked. She produced a locally baked sweet seed cake, heavy with raisins and honey. He took it, knowing he would feel better for having gotten it down. She said, "You needed that. And I thought you might be intrigued by interesting things happening elsewhere."

"Do they affect us?"

"Of course they do. Sooner or later. Maybe both. A grandson of Tsistimed the Golden has been given leave to raid Qasr al-Zed, to test its defenses."

"There are Hu'n-tai At mercenaries with the Righteous at Shamramdi. No doubt they report to Tsistimed."

"Would you like them to stop? It is a long, dangerous journey from Shamramdi to Ghargarlicea."

"One of your better ideas. What else?"

"Pella handed Iresh abd al-Kadiri a serious rebuke today."

"Oh?" He debated himself daily about the wisdom of having re-
lented and let Pella command the falcon force harassing the Dreangereans. The boy should be safe if he did not decide to show off.

Evidently, he had suffered that lapse.

"Is he all right?" Anna would never forgive him if the boy got
killed.

"He bombarded their camp. Their casualties were nasty."

"That's the nature of falcon fires."

"Pella hoped to provoke them into attacking. The Sha-lug convinced Iresh not to let his men be massacred."

"Too bad."

"Iresh's indecision hasn't buoyed morale. After the bombardment,
once night fell, hundreds deserted. Another demonstration could scatter all but the Sha-lug. Nobody wants to die just sitting around camp."

While on short rations and squabbling over water.

Iresh's indecision would consume him. The Sha-lug would stay but
would turn on Iresh when the armistice ended.

Lord Arnmigal was not pleased. The gods themselves seemed determined to save Vantrad from the scourging it needed.

He chuckled suddenly, surprising himself.

"What?"

"Just something about that situation." He was the boss of the gods
in these parts. Well, he was the boss of those a mortal could see and
touch and engage in a canoodle or conversation.

Hourli wondered, "Are you having problems again?"

"I'm sure you know the answer to that."

"So I do. I know the cure, too, but I doubt that I can get you to let
it work."

Tired of being tired, and at sleep's mercy, he demanded, "Tell me!"

"A little intense there. It's easy. Surrender. Come with me to the
nearest Well of Power, lie down in the hot waters, and just surrender.
Go to sleep and stay asleep till you don't need to sleep anymore. This
war will simmer right along without your nose in every little pot, everywhere, micromanaging, and making everyone who works for you
angry about the excess supervision."

Her remarks irked him more than was reasonable. He recognized
that. And Hourli recognized both his response and his recognition of
its injustice. She did not back off.

The Shining Ones showed him no special dread, Godslayer or no.

They did defer in accordance with their contract but Hourli had grown less deferential lately.

He snapped, "You aren't here to check on my health or start an argument."

"Oh, yes I am. But the fun stuff doesn't top my list. I wanted you to know about Pella and Iresh. Then I wanted you to know that we've successfully pulled together all the mystic tools salvaged from the Great Sky Fortress."

"What?" Had he missed something?

"Heartsplitter. Red Hammer's hammer. Geistrier, the rope that is always long enough and strong enough. Bottomless, the pail that always holds enough but is never too heavy. The necklace, the Brising Stones—though we don't have that one in hand yet. That scatterbrain Aldi lost it in Antieux when she was out there trying to manufacture a way around the requirements of destiny. She's never gotten a handle on the fact that the Twilight, the way it used to be foreseen, is as dead as Kharoulke the Windwalker. There *could* be a Twilight. There probably *will* be a Twilight. But it won't be the Twilight we expected before Ordnan screwed up." Softly, she added, "The old fool might have traded the wrong eye."

"And the search for Grinling?"

"You're so clever. Sneaking that in so casually."

"Your answer?"

"The search is over. Grinling's story has been discovered. In reality, the Aelen Kofer found it a long time ago. King Gjore hoped to use it to break the dwarves' bonds."

"So that's why they became so bold and devious."

"Bold and devious they always were, as well as overconfident but inattentive. The ring was stolen and taken to Eucereme by a clutch of half-breed girl-children who had Lucke for a father."

"Oh." Lord Arnmigal felt the ground sink. "That's not good. Can they can use it to resurrect . . . ?"

"Not even if they owned his soul egg. They could only revive a fraction of him using the combined magic of all the surviving worlds. Too much of Lucke expired with the Realm of the Gods. Which doesn't mean that those nasty little bastards won't try to fill their father's shoes—though they'd probably end up fighting amongst themselves more than against the rest of us."

"Still not good."

"They can't cause trouble here while they're cut off in Eucereme."

"But we have to open the way to Eucereme so Eavijne can start her new orchard."

"That's not a concern for tonight. We're here, Grinling and the daughters of Lucke are there, and Korban Iron Eyes is sitting in the middle. The dwarves aren't famous for their mercy."

"Uhm." As Hecht understood the mythological imperatives the Raneul and Shining Ones both were doomed if the middle world could not connect with Eucereme. Neither the Raneul nor Shining Ones could sustain their immortality without the golden apples.

Now potentially vengeful children of chaos might be amongst the threats the Shining Ones faced.

Hourli said, "The children of Lucke were always involved with the Twilight. Aldi and her brother Tug would handle them. The daughters of Lucke are ferocious but they lack their father's cleverness and cunning."

"If they were *really* cunning they would foster the illusion of being dim."

"Don't borrow trouble. The search for a way to Eucereme goes poorly, though Heris and Hourlr keep trying."

Hecht growled.

"Act your age. Heris is a grown woman. She can make rational choices." With a hint that Heris might be better equipped for that than was her brother. Heris had no foolish dalliances hanging over her. "She and your daughters are immune to Hourlr, which he finds cosmically frustrating."

"I suffer from prejudices impressed too deeply at an early age. I can't be comfortable with the lax western morality."

"You always were a tight-ass."

"Excuse me?"

"Never mind. The tools have been gathered. We can keep them together if we concentrate. We should keep the kids on that. They remember better."

"The young have their own distractions."

"Ha! You noticed! Even Aldi and Eavijne are only human when it comes to their boom-boom—though Evie gets embarrassed when you ask about hers."

Like Grinling, other mystical artifacts crafted by the Aelen Kofer had a knack for disappearing. Hecht was sure that was inbuilt. The dwarves had produced to order but made sure the toys they created were useless most of the time because they could not be found.

Hecht was in no mood to banter. However, he did feel better. He did not wonder why, nor did he see that, as he accumulated more responsibilities, he became less engaged with everything immediate. "Is that all?"

"Pretty much. I do wonder if you've had any inspiration on how to handle the Empress's situation. Her women have begun to wonder. Most aren't smart enough to figure out how it happened, but Lady Hilda *knows*."

He slumped. "An induced miscarriage would be easiest, ugliest, and least morally acceptable. Hiding her till afterward seems more sensible. The child could be attributed to one of her court women." Lady Hilda might volunteer, for a dear price.

"We could have Aldi or Eavijne assume her aspect and cover for her while we put the real her away on Mount Athos."

Hourli laughed. "Either would be happy to play Empress. But they might want *all* of the Grail Empress's roles. Evie especially." Her full meaning evaded him. "Or I could do it. I've regained enough strength to make myself look young enough. And I wouldn't be as demanding as the girls."

That might work. Hourli doing it.

Her hint about Eavijne finally sank in. Disgusted with his thoughts, he said, "I'll discuss it with the Empress. Substitution might be the only way to save her the Grail Throne. The least potential for complication would be for you to do it."

"You couldn't behave with those two?"

"Considering my record? Why take the chance?"

"Really? They'd giggle like children if they heard that. Well, self-denial was never in our nature. And even Evie would consider it a challenge if you turned her down more than once."

Evie was shy but, like the life she was aspected to, she was stubborn.

"You'd be safer if we could get Hourlr to do it. But he couldn't play it in your presence."

"He wouldn't keep his hands off Lady Hilda, either, and that would complicate things even more." He shuddered. Hourlr in the Helspeth role was a creepy idea.

"You're right. He can't help it. Better idea. Wife. She'd keep her skirts down and her hands to herself."

Hecht shivered again. Having Wife play Helspeth was almost as uncomfortable as having Hourlr do it, yet she might be the real best choice. She was around Helspeth a lot without making the Empress aware of the protection.

Lord Arnmigal asked, "May I get some sleep, now?"

Hourli faked an internal struggle, then shrugged and nodded. "You were right, really. There isn't anything so critical that it can't wait till morning."

Somehow, Hecht suspected, her real opinion differed. Not for the first or even one hundredth time did he wonder if his peerless help-meets were not pursuing an agenda entirely their own.

But what? They were open about feeding on the Wells and want-ing to kick down the gates of Eucereme. What else could they want or need?

Believers?

But . . .

This reach of the middle world was too isolated from those parts that had known the Shining Ones. They were here for the Wells, feeble as those might be. They left only scraps and dregs for the lesser de-mons, djinn, and ifrits plaguing the region. Believers in the God Who Is God might soon be right when they denied the existence of those Instrumentalities.

Believers in the Shining Ones were next to nonexistent. Conver-sions seemed unlikely.

TITUS CONSENT SAID, "WOULD YOU BELIEVE I GOT AN ACTUAL PHYSI-cal letter from Noë? A courier brought it from Ghort's camp. She got a City Regiment messenger to bring it out."

Lord Arnmigal grunted, having trouble wakening.

"She's pregnant again."

"I am astonished."

"Aren't we all. There was no message from Anna. Noë says she's fine but depressed. Never leaves home. Everybody has to go see her. She did give Addam Hauf a letter. He is supposed to relay it through Madouc."

"Why not have Heris or the girls bring it?"

"I don't know. Maybe they can't reach us because we're too far away." Titus knew a lot about the Unknowns now. There was not much that he did not know.

He did remain ignorant of Helspeth's condition. But how secret could that be from the Night?

Lord Arnmigal and the Empress might become hostage to the whim of the Night.

A rumor or two, not satisfactorily refuted, could leave them facing disapprobation worse than any showered on Queen Clothilde and Black Rogert. More virtue was expected of the Grail Empress. She and the Commander of the Righteous were mistress and master of God's most holy Enterprise of Peace and Faith, abjuring wickedness and the temp-tations of the world.

More or less.

"Boss?"

"Sorry. I was treating myself to a reverie filled with high drama."

"If you say so. There's something." Consent dropped to a whisper, as though that would help should the Shining Ones be determined to eavesdrop. "You ever make up your mind if we can trust our Old Ones?"

"The only answer is that we can trust them one hundred percent to be what they are and have always been."

"That doesn't help much, going forward."

"No. It doesn't."

"Uh . . ."

"As long as it suits their perceived needs—like being able to stay alive and healthy till Heris finds a way to connect with Eucereme—we can count on them to be helpful. They'll keep their word to the letter but the spirit will be malleable. They'll leap through a loophole if they see one that looks good."

"Exactly what I'm thinking. And more so each time I talk to Eavijne or Aldi. They're quite open about it."

Hecht gave Consent a quick, sharp look. No! Titus would never respond to Eavijne. Likely, he was even immune to Aldi. He could see no one but Noë in that light. "You have a reason for asking?"

"Something is going on that they don't want to discuss. It takes a paranoid ear to hear it but it's there under the conversation, now."

"Some aren't as clever as they think. Any idea what it is?"

"No. But you asking Pinkus and the Widow to go help Madouc makes them uncomfortable."

"Why? Sorry. Rhetorical. That makes no sense. Why should they care what happens at Gherig? They should be glad those two are out from under foot. What's out there besides Gherig?"

"Been thinking about that. Their reports from that area aren't as crystalline as most. Ghort and the Widow are difficult people but they still ought to be able to work with Madouc's gang. Madouc, though, is supported by some top men from the Special Office. That may be what makes the Shining Ones uncomfortable."

"Really? There must be something more. We just haven't recognized it. And it won't be the Faithful. The most dangerous Believers are sealed up in Shamramdi." Could a new Praman host be gathering in Lucidia, unnoticed? Not likely. The Shining Ones would not hide that. Just the opposite, in fact.

Titus mused, "What else? How about er-Rashal al-Dhulquarnen?"

Lord Arnmigal stiffened. "Er-Rashal?"

"A sorcerer. Sometimes called the Rascal. Used to be the court wizard for Gordimer the Lion. They called him something else because Believers can't consort with necromancers, sorcerers, or diviners. He ran for it after Indala's victory. He headed up the Shirne toward tomb country. They cut him off, so he turned back north. Nobody noticed till he attacked a Lucidian watchtower near Gherig, where he got his ass handed to him. He lost his henchmen and animals and ended up injured himself. He scuttled into the Neret Mountains. Some renegade Sha-lug went after him."

Titus knew more than he realized. "Into the Idiam," Lord Arnmigal breathed. "Into the land of ghosts. To the Dead City."

There had been hints before, of course. Soldiers loved their rumors. He had paid no attention because neither the Rascal nor Andesqueluz ever got mentioned directly. Nothing suggested that the rumors were based on anything real.

The Shining Ones had reported nothing.

That was suggestive itself.

"Into the Idiam." In mildly wondrous dread.

Titus said, "To a ruined city remembered in sacred texts as Andesqueluz, home of one of the uglier Instrumentalities of the god times."

"To Asher. The Mountain. And Ashtoreth, which means Bride of the Mountain. I've heard that much."

"Then you paid closer attention than I thought."

"Maybe. I like to know about those things."

"I have no concrete evidence but—based on rumors and the circumstances of this er-Rashal's association with Rudenes Schneidel—he may be trying to resurrect Asher."

"Plausible. And our divine associates have neglected to tell us."

"I would assume they're not hiding anything, they're just failing to point fingers."

"Oh, those clever devils."

"Could they possibly want Asher back?"

"No. They wouldn't want to share what little magic is left while they're finding a way into Eucereme. It must be something else."

"Any suggestions?"

"No. Keep your ears open. There are facts missing. The Shining Ones may have them. If so, they must be inconvenient somehow."

"Shall I sneak out there myself?"

"You'd never get away with it. Go to the horse pasture east of al-Sar. Find Just Plain Joe. Tell him what we need."

Consent saw his thinking. "I'm on my way."

Hecht wondered if it was worth the bother, trying to keep a low profile, hoping the Shining Ones would not consult the Choosers of the Slain, who were always with him.

They were abidingly disdainful of Fastthal and Sprenghul, who seldom gave anyone an excuse to see them in a better light.

It might be worthwhile to create some diversions.

There was always something diverting him from pursuing the triumph of the Enterprise. Oft times it was difficult not to believe that a malignant Night was meddling.

He had seen Gordimer the Lion succumb to that kind of thinking, abetted by the Rascal's whispers. In his more rational moments Lord Arnmigal saw himself starting to externalize blame the way Gordimer had.

He was in the first stage of creating his own demons.

And was that not one way tadpole Instrumentalities came into the world?

Hecht started.

Titus was long gone. Hourli had come in. She had just snapped her fingers under his nose, a gesture outright disrespectful. "What?" he barked.

"You always were broody. It's part of your manly charm, though I don't find it particularly endearing. Put your mind's house in order, quickly. We have no time to waste."

Lord Arnmigal was confused. "What?"

"The Empress."

"Oh. Got you. I'll ask for an audience."

Helspeth ordered everyone out.

Hecht said, "Lady Hilda needs to stay."

"I'm not that concerned about my reputation, Lord Arnmigal. I'm already considered a freak for being here. I understand that the locals call me the Iron Virgin."

Lady Hilda made a face, and leered.

"Chaperonage isn't why she's needed. She knows our troubles. She was involved from the start. We can't get by without her now."

Seconds passed. "Oh? You're probably right. Stay, then, Hilda." Helspeth's sudden desperation begged Hecht to be sure.

"There is no getting around it."

"You have some fresh ideas?"

"Some. Let's not discuss them here. Too easy to eavesdrop."

"There are no quiet rooms handy."

"There's another option. It won't thwart Instrumentalities but it will keep the mortal sneaks off."

"The candle?"

"Exactly."

Helspeth needed less than a minute to locate and light the time candle. That did not have the elusive nature of many artifacts associated with the Shining Ones. It had not been made by the Aelen Kofer.

The candle blazed up. Blushing, Helspeth talked to her friend. Hilda said, "I thought it might be that, though I prayed that I was wrong." She hugged Helspeth, for the moment no more than an empathetic friend.

Helspeth said, "You must be sure of your suggestions, my lord, or you wouldn't have insisted we meet."

"I have an idea loosely based on something Hourli suggested."

"She knows?"

"She's known since the quickening. She is what she is. I don't like it, either. It gives her leverage. But that's the way it is with the Instrumentalities of the Night."

Helspeth blew out a chest full of exasperation. "Of course. Sure. All right. We know how to deal with that, don't we? Go on."

Hecht hoped none of the Shining Ones heard that but feared that any hope for an absence of eavesdroppers would be a vain one.

"I'm going after Vantrad. If I surprise them and take over I'll lock Beresmond up and run Clothilde off to Gherig. I'll install the Grail Empress as Queen. Shining Ones will surround you. They'll become you whenever you have to be seen. Lady Hilda will be your shadow. If Helspeth is forced to be in the presence of an outsider the Shining Ones will disguise you. Hourli says they can fix it so you won't even smell like you." He nearly suggested that, with practice, she might even be able to fool those who knew her well.

Better not give her any dangerous ideas.

She was the daughter of the Ferocious Little Hans and nothing would keep her from hitting the streets in disguise if the notion took her.

Despite all she had seen lately, she might not believe that a hostile Night might take advantage of self-inflicted exposure.

"There you go, drifting off again."

"I apologize. I don't know why it happens. It's not just with you. I do it with everyone."

"Instead of saying you're sorry all the time, why not *do* something about it?"

Lady Hilda observed, "I'm sure your Night friends could scrounge around in your soul and figure out why your head don't work right when you're awake." Swinging a well-honed double-edged blade, there. "They might even find out why you fall asleep in the middle of something crucial, like a future-changing discussion with your lover."

Daedel was in a harsh mood. *And* she knew things she had no business knowing.

He turned a hard eye on Helspeth.

The Ege blood shone through then. The Empress was not intimidated, nor did she offer explanations. She had thought that Daedel needed to know.

"What is, is," Hecht muttered, like a calming mantra. "It is, and cannot be changed. I will focus. I will take Vantrad. We will proceed from there. Moves are underway already." Pella was pressing Iresh abd al-Kadiri in hopes of attracting regional attention to himself. A limited Righteous move along the Vantrad road should be interpreted as a flanking effort.

The Shining Ones would know the truth. He could imagine no reason they would betray him, yet still did not trust them fully.

A consequence of status gained? Was that what had turned Gordimer weird? Might the Lion's paranoia have been due to more than dark prophecies and the Rascal's evil whispers?

"And there he goes again," Lady Hilda cracked, voice edged with irritation and possible contempt. "Despite the pretty promises. A man's man indeed. And here I be in the oven of hell's kitchen, being rendered down for jerky and people grease, for the sakes of ingrates, when I could be basking in the coolth of Alten Weinberg, having my way with some starry-eyed boy."

She flashed a wicked smile at Hecht's appalled response.

"I'll get that Hourli creature to curse you. You know those sparky shocks you get during the winter? This curse will let me smack you with a big one any time your eyes glaze over. It will be like teaching a pig to dance."

Hecht did not understand that but did grasp her general meaning. It might even work if he got stung enough.

He had earned himself a shock already.

PELLA LAUNCHED NUISANCE ATTACKS AGAINST THE DREANGEREANS. De-spite strong cautionary advice from the Sha-lug, Iresh gave in to rage, perhaps seduced by the murmur of unseen powers. He launched two counterattacks directly into the face of falcon fires from prepared positions. Casualties were terrible. Desertions trebled. The Sha-lug refused to execute further unreasonable orders.

The Grail Empress and Commander of the Righteous, traveling with the battle group apparently flanking the Dreangereans on the Vantrad road, decided to tour the Holy City while they were close by.

They entered Vantrad with entourages but no large companies or heavy weapons. The locals relaxed. The Commander of the Righteous never made an aggressive move without his falcons.

Western pilgrims had visited in large numbers since the arrival of the Enterprise. Some of the most recent visitors had served with Lord Arnmigal for years.

The Choosers of the Slain, prepped with detailed instructions, isolated King Beresmond and Queen Clothilde while Righteous pilgrims secured key points of the city.

The Shining Ones added illusion and misdirection. There were few casualties and no fatalities, unlike the last time crusaders captured Vantrad.

Thirty-two hours after entering Vantrad, Lord Arnmigal set his seal to a document wherein Beresmond abdicated in favor of the Grail Empress. Local prelates added their own seals and pretended to be thrilled.

Temblors of change radiated quickly. Princes great and small, of every religious odor, quavered on dangerously shifting footing. Beresmond had been a spook, doing little but what Clothilde demanded. She was a shallow vessel. The Grail Empress and her warlord were sure to be harsher weather.

Clothilde resisted, though she controlled her tongue admirably. Those strange and wicked women with the Commander of the Righteous admonished her privately, revealing a detailed knowledge of her undercover transgressions. She was cunning and clever, if shallow and caring for no one but herself. She grasped the fact that hope depended entirely on abiding the favorable day.

She had friends. Allies, really. Among those were a few minor Instrumentalities, though none like the monsters guarding Lord Arnmigal. She would persevere. She would come back.

She was not wise enough to be afraid.

Hourli warned Lord Arnmigal: it was dangerously kind not to save the future from possible pretenders to Vantrad's throne.

Lord Arnmigal was preoccupied with the Grail Empress. He cared little what people thought, though he did concern himself about their perceptions of her. He intended doing nothing to stain her reputation more than he had.

He failed completely to notice the Shining Ones sketching a fog around his all-too-revelatory behavior.

He and she settled in comfortably, against inconsequential resistance, which the Shining Ones handled easily. Wife began to appear with Lord Arnmigal as a more glamorous and warmer Grail Empress. Her audiences thought that must be because she had added the Holy City to the Imperial diadem.

Lady Hilda enjoyed the change, at the real Helspeth's expense.

The Praman community fell into anguished despair. The Believers were being battered and decimated everywhere, with the Hu'n-tai At now gnawing at the Realm of Peace in the east.

The Dreangerean host southwest of Vantrad evaporated. Even its Sha-lug components fled in despair.

Pella strutted like a gamecock when he reported. He had learned from masters and had learned quite well. He had lost only a handful of men.

VANTRAD'S CITADEL BOASTED A QUIET ROOM WORTHY OF THE PARA-noia of Queen Clothilde. It was perfectly maintained and one of the stoutest ever built. Its walls were three feet thick. It had been reengineered and improved by senior brethren of the Special Office. Titus Consent met Lord Arnmigal there following some sleight of hand meant to divert invisible watchers. Hecht asked, "What's with the sneakery and shadow dancing?"

"Just Plain Joe is back from visiting his pal, Bo Biogna, out by Gherig."

Lord Arnmigal probed his Else Tage memories for the lie of that land.

Gherig loomed on high ground to the south. The land in front fell away to a plain, then gradually rose again to the north. Those highlands became the Neret Mountains and haunted Idiam. The Well of Days, site of Indala al-Sul's signature triumph, lay not far north and east.

Lord Arnmigal opined, "I hope Joe enjoyed himself. He comes nearer being a true good man than anyone I know. He deserves more joy of life."

"I would argue that we all do. God won't give it to us."

"He got back quick. Did he find out something important?"

"In a nutshell. Nobody out there is making a big deal, maybe because they haven't seen the implications. I think our demonic allies *have* and are hoping we won't." Titus raised a hand, forestalling Hecht's impatience. "The Dreangerean villain, er-Rashal, has created a spell that makes firepowder explode at a distance or at least fizzle and clog the falcon."

Lord Arnmigal gulped some air and chewed.

"The spell reaches beyond the reliable killing range of most falcons. Falconeers who can fire don't have much hope of actually hitting anything."

"And the Shining Ones know."

"They do. And want to keep it quiet."

"So they think they see a way to be safe from the mortal instruments of a would-be Godslayer."

"If they can get hold of er-Rashal's secret."

"They don't have it?"

"They do not. Only the Dreangerean has the spell, and that only inside his head. Spying on him won't do any good."

"Unless they catch him in the process."

"Maybe. But they have to be careful not to show their interest. Also, the sorcerer has put up some formidable supernatural barriers. I doubt they can get close enough to watch him work." Consent went on with other news from the frontier, adding some speculation. "Madouc hasn't seen all the possibilities but he's definitely worried about Asher. The Special Office types at Gherig are pressuring him. Too, Joe says some Pramans have joined Madouc. Indala's men, supposedly there to help handle er-Rashal."

Hecht grunted. That was puzzling. Indala helping Madouc with the Rascal? With the Special Office, Black Rogert, the Shining Ones, and who knew what all else there to see?

Er-Rashal had somebody really worried. Something major must be about to break.

The old Norns came to mind, silently spinning, lamplight painting their silhouettes on the paper screen that was the wall between them and the universe, a boundary neither man nor god dared violate.

He spurned the image. Illusion! Wicked imagination! Only the God Who Is God could write one's destiny . . .

He suppressed a burst of hysterical laughter.

"Boss?"

"We have a world of people playing their own games, me included. Suppose I just jumped in like a bear into a gaggle of puppies?"

Titus considered. "That might be too risky."

"Good. Then that's what we'll do. Nobody will expect it."

"Boss . . ."

What else to do now? Vantrad was in hand. Iresh abd al-Kadiri had been chased off. The Enterprise had achieved most of its goals against almost feeble resistance. All of the Holy Lands cities had submitted to the Grail Empress. The natives were not happy. If they behaved, however, changes at the royal level would mean little to farmers, herders, shopkeepers, and artisans. They would face the same old challenges and complain the same old complaints. They would lie to the tax collectors with fabulous imagination. They would bully neighbors who failed to demonstrate an adequately enlightened attitude toward the divine. Life would go on much as it always had.

The Commander of the Righteous, however, would have to make new choices soon. Once Shamramdi fell the Enterprise would have to find an expanded mission or begin to come apart. King Stain might get no chance to assemble his reinforcing wave.

Dreanger would be recovered for the Chaldarean faith. Lucidia, too, with the capture of Shamramdi. But that would set the Enterprise face-to-face with the sons of Tsistimed the Golden and the Hu'n-tai At.

There was the du Tancret option, of course. The dearly held dream of the most fanatic Chaldareans would be to capture and destroy Jezdad and the holiest holies of al-Prama.

"Boss? You still in there?"

"Eh? What?"

"Are you serious? What you suggested? Us heading out to Gherig?"

"Sure. To deal with er-Rashal. It doesn't take a lot of thought to see that he's the biggest threat at the moment. Once he goes down we can impose whatever realignment we want in this region."

He had no desire to obliterate al-Prama. The Faith had been a part of him. Never had he entertained the notion of that religion's annihilation. He would have been outraged had the suggestion been offered.

"Boss?"

"Yes?" Irritated now. Titus ought to be off to get things started.

"What does it mean when the Shining Ones say, 'He lost his shadow somewhere'?"

That startled Lord Arnmigal. He knew that must have meaning but could recall none. "I'm not sure. It sounds portentous, though. Why?"

"Wife and Hourli say it about you. It bothers me."

Hecht had overheard the phrase himself recently without paying heed or realizing that he was its object. "'Lost his way,' wouldn't quite fit, would it? I'll ask Hourli. She'll turn up fast once she hears that we're headed east."

An air-clearing session with Hourli might be especially useful before the cloudy side developed deeper shadows. Once the Adversary began threading lies into things . . .

42. Gherig:
Congruence, Conjunction, and Union

Nassim Alizarin stood alongside the crusader Madouc of Hoeles. He could not have imagined that possibility two months earlier. They shared the parapet of a Gherig watchtower. Several others, equally ill at ease, were observing traffic below Gherig with them. Nassim felt ensnared in a surreal fantasy. The Master of the Commandery had accepted his story and offer of alliance. Madouc of Hoeles was seriously practical and pragmatic in spite of his religious convictions. Madouc grasped the magnitude of the threat developing in the Idiam. He had seen other resurrections. He had been warned by his own Special Office: this could be the ugliest resurrection yet. He would employ *any* tool or weapon to abort the menace. Nassim's renegades might be a godsend.

No one knew the devil er-Rashal better. No one hated him more.

Rogert du Tancret, on crutches, radiated ill-concealed spite. Nassim Alizarin had been a curse on his existence. Nassim Alizarin had come within a toad's whisker of annihilating Gherig, and Rogert du Tancret with it. Nassim Alizarin had made it necessary for him to go round on these sticks. Black Rogert was biding his time. He would have his revenge.

Black Rogert might be black but he never considered achieving his revenge by allying with the Dreangerean evil.

The dark-haired, dark-eyed, wide little bully laid looks on Madouc that were no more friendly. Madouc could expect his own day of reckoning.

Rogert du Tancret had chosen to play against character, biding his time though he was not known for his patience or subtlety. Cunning had him smile exactly when the converted and motivated ought to show enthusiasm.

Nassim and Madouc were observing a wild swirl and swarm of newcomers sent out by the Commander of the Righteous as they put up a canvas and trash-wood city surrounded by a ditch and a freestone wall. Villagers disgruntled by the loss of pasture had been complaining since the first new crusader appeared. Nassim wished he could help. Those people had supported him well.

They would not resist. The newcomers had slaughtered scores of Believers who had tried to raid their camp near Triamolin. Their woman commander was an abomination made flesh. She devoured Praman souls.

Since that massacre the Widow's story had become widespread, growing madly in the retelling. Publicly, Madouc of Hoeles credited every wicked accusation. He hinted that more and darker remained to be seen.

Madouc had the Special Office mumbling in his ear.

He observed, "Those people seem professional but you can tell the Brothens from the Connectens by each group's casual style."

Nassim did not see that. He saw Arnhander mobs caught up in efficient chaos. Setting a semipermanent camp was not something new to them. He saw very little real wasted motion. "Ah. And now they've started building a conduit to bring water from the spring."

Young Az eased up beside Nassim, on the side away from Madouc. Nassim had been careful to conceal the youth's identity. Possession of Indala's favorite grandnephew might be a temptation too potent for bleak, brooding Black Rogert.

The Master of the Commandery knew Azim was no Sha-lug. Age alone did not give that away. What made one Sha-lug was difficult to verbalize but plain to the veteran eye.

Nassim turned toward Azim slightly. The boy had gone out among the Believers with Old Az, tasting their unhappiness, trying to show the elders why the Mountain would ally himself with the oppressor.

Only Ansa, foreigners, and strangers had suffered because of the Dreangerean. That did not make him an instrument of the Adversary. Such people were barely human.

"It didn't go well," Nassim guessed. "Too tough a sell."

"True, but there will be no bad behavior. They will remain toads in their holes. They are terrified of the Widow, who is more real and far nearer than any fabulous Dreangerean."

"Indeed. They might be less rattled if the Adversary himself turned up dancing." The Adversary seldom took the form of a fighting woman.

One of Black Rogert's few remaining loyalists eased up to his lord and whispered. Du Tancret blanched. He gasped. He slammed both hands to his chest. His eyes rolled up. He shook like he was going into a seizure.

Everyone gaped.

Du Tancret suppressed the shakes, visibly reclaiming control. He engaged in obvious internal debate momentarily. Then, "My lords. My lord of Hoeles. A courier from Vantrad brings word that the Grail Empress and Commander of the Righteous have compelled Beresmond and Clothilde to abdicate in favor of Helspeth Ege."

His audience boggled, to a man. Impossible! The Master of the Commandery declared, "The Commander of the Righteous would not arrogate a crown!"

Du Tancret bobbed his head. "I did not mean to suggest that. You're right. He didn't seize the throne himself. He made the Grail Empress Vantrad's Queen." Muttering, he added, "Surely he'll be rewarded royally."

Madouc faced Nassim, one eyebrow raised. What would the Praman side think?

Nassim could do nothing but shrug.

He was not supposed to know the Commander of the Righteous. Nor did he, anymore. His recollections of Else Tage amounted to little more than nostalgia. He knew nothing about the man behind the layers of identity and character he had acquired since being sent out to die in exile.

A Madouc henchman made the obvious concrete. "This could mark a sea change for the Crusader States."

Yes. It could.

This could be the first temblor of a vast cultural shift. The Grail Empire was not Arnhand. Arnhand was not going under the ice. Parts of the Grail Empire were. The displaced had to go somewhere.

All the Crusader States, large or small, were ruled by families rooted in the nobilities of Arnhand or the Connec. Knights and pilgrims hailed from every Brothen Episcopal principality but mostly Arnhanders and Connectens stayed to colonize the land of their God's birth. Several generations later, now, the eastern branches of the families were almost as foreign as the peoples they ruled.

Vantrad the kingdom was now a fragment of the Grail Empire, where traditions were alien and the ruling class was actively hostile toward the Brothen Episcopal Patriarchy despite a deep connection to the Brothen Episcopal faith. Paradoxically, the Patriarchy might gain influence, now. Its lip-service-only Crusader States supporters, heavily dependent on moral, financial, and manpower support from Arnhand and the Connec, might be overthrown for a more honest regime.

The founders of the Crusader States had been as much land-going pirates as warriors of a holy cause. Today's Black Rogert was, simply, an extreme exemplar.

The exemplar added, "The Queen evaded capture. She is headed here with such people as she was able to save."

Nassim took that to mean that Clothilde's companions were people who had been able to keep up.

His estimate of Clothilde had formed based on her popular reputation.

Garnering little response from the Brotherhood, Black Rogert reminded everyone, "Whatever the military situation imposes on me, Gherig still belongs to the du Tancrets."

Not strictly true and easily rendered moot but neither the Master of the Commandery nor his companions cared to debate. Madouc simply nodded. "Of course."

Could he be thinking that Clothilde might be better wrangled here than elsewhere? Wherever she was she would spin wild, irrational plots and contrive insane conspiracies.

Black Rogert was at a loss. He had been stripped of place and power. Now his last anchor was dragging.

Nassim entertained himself with an idea so wicked it was fit to have sprung from the mind of a villain like Clothilde or Black Rogert.

He could suggest that they flee to Shamramdi.

Indala would welcome them. Of course he would. It would be no sin, promising protection to draw them into his power. The God Who Is God had no problem with the Faithful deceiving Unbelievers. And Indala owed Black Rogert so much.

Du Tancret would never amble into that. His nose for danger should be itching already, simply because the Mountain had had the thought.

Du Tancret, frowning, did turn Nassim's way, as though he *had* caught a whiff of malice.

Madouc of Hoeles stared into infinity briefly, then told du Tancret, "Begin preparations to receive the Queen. Right now Gherig boasts no suitable quarters."

Black Rogert started, at first amazed that Madouc would receive Clothilde, then realizing that Madouc had stated a bald truth. Reconstruction was focused on Gherig's defenses. Even Madouc and du Tancret lived as rough as their soldiers and workmen.

News of Nassim's latest defection should have reached Indala by now. Hopefully, the Great Shake was clever enough to reason his way to the truth.

Nassim thought that Indala did have the intelligence, in both senses, to understand. Young Az swore that Indala knew his grandnephew would never defect in fact, but only in appearance, for tactical reasons.

Madouc of Hoeles said, "That man is out of the way. We can speak freely, now." Du Tancret was gone.

"Yes?"

White flashed, Madouc smiling behind his artfully sculpted beard. "You are a cautious man, General."

"More a man so nervous that, you should note, he has successfully shied off deadly shadows for ages, in a chancy trade."

"I do keep that in mind. Also, the fact that you're so clever they should have called you the Fennec instead of the Mountain."

Nassim flashed his own smile. Another tooth had gone missing. He thought the desert fox was more elusive than crafty but would accept the compliment. "That may be, but I have managed about as long a run of luck as a man can carry. Whatever the outcome this time, this will be my last skirmish with the Night."

"We will triumph," Madouc predicted. "God stands with us." He gauged the proximity of his Special Office brethren. "As do you, the Widow of Khaurene, the Captain-General of the Brothen Church, and, possibly, Indala al-Sul Halaladin. And ever lurking in the shadows ready to pounce in a wolf-strike, the Righteous with all the hooligan Instrumentalities the Commander of the Righteous has recruited."

Nassim said nothing. Young Az did the same, preferring to remain unnoticed by Madouc. Then Nassim did ask, "You actually credit those theories?"

Could anyone be as successful as the Commander of the Righteous had, absent help from Heaven or Hell?

Hell always seemed most likely to the envious.

Human nature assumes that anyone successful must be a liar, cheat, and deadly backstabber.

Sometimes that was true. Gordimer the Lion, for example. In the case of the exiled Sha-lug Else Tage, the condemned man appeared to be an orphan beloved of the Night.

Stories of the sort were uncommon but existed. Witness Aaron of Chaldar or the Founding Family of al-Prama. Or, more recently, Tsistimed the Golden, a demigod ascendant not known to have sought the power deliberately. Not in er-Rashal's willful way.

Nassim shuddered, awash with dread. He might actually know someone who would ascend to Instrumentality status.

"General? Are you unwell?"

"My apologies. A curse of age. I have reached a stage where staying anchored and focused is difficult."

The Master of the Commandery, as he often did, put any questions aside. "Should we invite the Widow and Captain-General up to discuss combining our knowledge and strengths?"

"The Widow has a reputation for not working well with others."

"There are ways to work around personalities. I want to confer and have something decided before the Queen gets here to complicate our lives." He paused but, before Nassim could respond, told young Az, "You will join us, of course." Saying so much while saying nothing specific.

So. Madouc knew who Azim was. Nassim would speak for the Sha-lug and old enemies who knew the Rascal best. Azim al-Adil ed-Din would be the eyes, ears, and mouth of the Great Shake of Lucidia and Qasr al-Zed.

Azim inclined his head, an equal deferring to a more qualified equal. "As you wish, Master."

Nassim felt pride. The boy had handled that well. He might indeed be the future of Qasr el-Zed—if he could shed the emotional encumbrance of his early failures.

The boy would face fierce challenges. God Himself might not surmount the circumstances of the times, with the Righteous triumphant everywhere and the Hu'n-tai At stirring, despite all their suffering of late.

The situation could only get worse. There would be another wave of western adventurers next summer but no Believers to replace the Faithful already fallen.

The Adversary should be dancing in his black palace, all was going so well for the children of darkness.

Nassim said, "We can but do what we must, and quickly would be best."

43. The Vindicated: A Tempest Gathering

Brother Candle bestrode a ragged donkey, a mangy beast, if mange was what made the creature look so pathetic. It was the simplest and gentlest conveyance available yet the Perfect feared losing his concentration for even a moment. Did he, he would fall for sure, despite everything.

This was no venue for slapstick.

The overawing mass of Gherig reared above. He could not tilt his head back far enough to view its battlements. The awe extended beyond mass and scale to the widespread evidence of firepowder damage that had yet to be repaired.

He did not want to ride. Kedle had ignored his every protest to install him aboard this gargantuan hoofed rat. Hope had smirked and patted his cheek and applied a spell to help reduce his chances of falling. That did not stop him from tipping way too far, to one side or the other.

He could not have survived the climb to Gherig on foot. He was too feeble. But Kedle would not make the visit without him.

The child did very little without his attendance anymore.

She and the Captain-General led from out front, her only lifeguards the nervous boys from Arnhand. Pinkus Ghort flaunted his supposed confidence, too, having brought just one shifty-eyed little devil that the Perfect was sure he knew from somewhere. Ghort called him Bo. The runt insisted that Brother Candle must have him confused with someone else. Bo seemed to know his way around.

Kedle made Bo nervous. He stayed clear of her.

Hope, in a restrained guise but plenty recognizable as a woman of allure, led Brother Candle's charger, playing with her role as a nun from some obscure Holy Lands order. But . . .

She was Hope. Dawn. She riveted the attention of every man they passed, leaving each troubled and confused and breathing hard.

Seven souls made up the deputation. Kedle thought fewer would be more in the eyes of Gherig's masters. Hope and the Captain-General agreed. Brother Candle was inclined to trust Hope's judgment. She had scouted ahead.

Pinkus Ghort's agreement rested on his past association with Madouc of Hoeles. He knew nothing about Hope's talents, nor did he fully fathom the Perfect's lethal capacity, though he had caught a glimpse at Triamolin.

Brother Candle thought Ghort's assessment of the Master of the Commandery could be excessively optimistic. And he believed that Hope thought too highly of the advantages owned by the Vindicated and their allies.

This Madouc of Hoeles, this Master of the Commandery, would be the lifeguard of the former Captain-General that Ghort remembered no longer. The runt Bo had argued as much during preparations for this visit. Unfortunately, Ghort had enjoyed some wine beforehand. Once he had a taste of the grape he became disinclined to hear statements of fact that disagreed with what he wanted to be true.

The Master of the Commandery and other hard men awaited them just outside Gherig's innermost sub-fortress, nearly half a mile beyond and uphill of the barbican gate. They were surrounded by rubble. Scaffolding and engines used to hoist materials skirted the keep. Even here the damage remained intimidating.

Hope pointed out the Pramans, though they would have been no less obvious had they been standing on their heads—though they did seem to consider themselves disguised. Brother Candle rehearsed the names that Dawn had reported. Important men, but not Gisela Frakier.

Smirking and flirty, Hope stayed beside the donkey's neck, holding the beast. She assisted in Brother Candle's inelegant dismount. Briefly, he failed to recall that he was *supposed* to look inept. Those men were supposed to underestimate the Vindicated.

He was expected to carry the weight of the conversation.

Why? These people were supposed to be allies.

He doubted that anyone would be fooled.

Only . . . Those *were* Pramans. One of them belonged to Indala's own family.

Hope helped him walk, alternately radiating an implication that she was a favored concubine or a favorite granddaughter. She distracted the receivers completely—excepting Madouc of Hoeles. Her efforts went right past the Master of the Commandery. Brother Candle whispered cautions he might have given a sulky fourteen-year-old.

"I know! I know! I can handle it!" she whispered back, too loudly for his comfort. "But I don't have to like it!"

The Master made introductions as they moved into the keep, if such a monster could be so called. Entire castles in Arnhand and the Connec were smaller than this forlorn hope. Brother Candle offered introductions in turn. He did not introduce Hope after Madouc failed to introduce Azim al-Adil.

The Master of the Commandery went straight to a huge quiet room that Hope had not known existed. Rogert du Tancret waited there, in a chair rigged to support his bad leg. He was pleased by their surprise at his secret room. "This is new. Our enemies were way too familiar with our thinking before." He glowered at the elder Praman. "Master Madouc and the Special Office were quick to see my point when I raised the matter."

Brother Candle read that as du Tancret actually complaining.

"This will be the first use of the room for its intended purpose," Madouc said, ignoring du Tancret. "Tests finished up yesterday. It's sound. Once the door shuts you can speak without fear of eavesdroppers."

Brother Candle kept a straight face. Kedle did the same. The Instrumentality already in the room gave nothing away, either, though the room's integrity would be compromised already.

Brother Candle said, "We came to listen. We've seen revenants before. The circumstances in the Idiam are extremely dangerous. We want to support you—if we can accept your overall intent."

He hoped that sounded good. Hope and her aunts believed that getting involved was a fine idea—though he thought they were not entirely, fully forthcoming. He was sure that he was not the only one clever enough to work out why, either.

The good host, Madouc of Hoeles offered places around a table large enough to seat two dozen. The boys, Bo, and Hope, though, he left against the wall by the door. Brother Candle beckoned Hope to come sit with him. The locals were not pleased. Bad enough, one woman being involved, but two, one a total mystery?

But no one objected—though the old Praman looked like he had run into his mother walking the street naked.

He must not be used to women.

Brother Candle rested a hand on Dawn's once she settled. He said nothing but she understood that he wanted her to go easy on the old warrior. She nodded but, even so, she practically sparked off an intent to commit mischief.

She spoke without permission or recognition. "This confab is premature. The Commander of the Righteous and Grail Empress have also decided that the sorcerer is a huge danger in need of being crushed. They have decided to deal with him themselves. They are headed here now."

That was news to Brother Candle—and everyone else as well. None were pleased, Hope herself the least.

Roger du Tancret broke the ensuing silence with an unpleasant, belittling commentary.

The Master of the Commandery told him coldly, "Stop it." Du Tancret stopped as though smacked.

Brother Candle said, "That was uncalled for, my lord. Lady Hope is never wrong." He feared that du Tancret would waken her anger. She refused to be taken lightly.

Kedle said, "Be calm, Dawn. We knew the man was a jerk before we came here." She spoke plain Connecten in a conversational tone, which Madouc understood. Black Rogert must not have, or he managed an uncharacteristic moment of self-control.

The Master of the Commandery said, "My lord of Gherig doesn't handle the novel well. I don't ask your forgiveness, just that you suffer in patience. He is a vicious little pervert with an irredeemably foul soul but he's still one of us. We face a villain of considerably more substance who isn't. This lesser villain will mind his manners." He spoke stiff, stilted, accented Connecten while meeting each eye around the room.

Brother Candle saw du Tancret following the conversation after all. A wicked ugly something stirred behind his empty expression. The man had more command of his awful self than was generally supposed but a dark pressure *had* to be building inside. He would explode eventually.

The Master of the Commandery had taken complete control, however, with no more pretense.

A clash avoided, Madouc shifted to Arnhander. "The lady is correct in suggesting that the coming of the Righteous be considered. However, none of us belong to that chain of command. Even did we, we would be remiss by not preparing for conflict, and should do so sooner than later. The enemy will only get stronger while we dither." He waved to the Arnhand boys, proving that little escaped him. He used their regional dialect to say, "Bring that roll from the corner to the table."

They jumped to it, groaned and strained, were too feeble to shift the thing. It was a foot and a half in diameter and eight feet tall. The younger Praman joined them, showed astonishment when he discovered how much heft that roll really had.

Madouc pointed out where he wanted it placed. He then unrolled it personally, nudging bodies aside.

The insides of the hides sewn together to create the roll boasted a colorful map. Gherig lay represented at the heart of the finest detail.

Madouc confessed, "I have trouble sleeping. I fill the time working on this." He would have personal experience of much of the territory shown.

The map portrayed a strip far longer than it was wide, consisting mainly of the valley that Gherig overlooked. It might, perhaps, be of limited value in the north and south directions. But then the Perfect noted that there were really four distinct charts. The largest was that most accurate strip portraying Gherig and environs he had noted immediately. The smaller adjacent frames were less well realized. Even so, Brother Candle recognized landmarks well north and south of Gherig.

The last small frame was the weakest. It wanted to portray the Idiam. Characters from the alphabet used in the Eastern Empire arced over a symbol for a mountain, forming the syllables *An-de-ska.*

Bold as ever, Hope said, "Pretty good for guesswork but foreshortened in the north-south direction."

"You know that country?" Madouc asked. His tone remained carefully neutral. He would not prejudge even the most absurd remarks.

"I've never been. This is my first time east of the Well of Days. Others of my family have explored there, though. They are deeply interested."

Brother Candle shook his head. Kedle did the same.

Hope was volunteering too much.

The Perfect wanted to bark, "Tell me you have a plan, girl!"

At times it was hard to remember that Hope belonged to the Night and was not the empty head she pretended.

She said no more. Madouc surveyed them all, looking for something more. He got a head shake from Brother Candle.

Only Hope knew what Hope was doing. She did not share her thinking because she was seldom really sure where she was headed herself. Today's iron plan could fall into ruin by next week—though every plan had to do with the Twilight and the new age to follow. Change mainly touched the day's choice of route.

Brother Candle felt small when he considered the Twilight. Hope was painting on a large canvas and dared no conservative brushwork. She did not mind flashing some gaudy color once in a while, either.

He did not think that she was careful enough about hiding her true nature.

He should remind her that few mortals were flexible enough to accept a supposedly impossible Instrumentality. And these men knew that gods could be murdered.

Kedle's blank face failed to mask her own similar thinking. Then Hope's flirtatious wink told the old man that she knew his mind. She was being deliberately provocative. Probing for something to do with the Special Office brothers?

Madouc offered a probe of his own. "My lady, if your family knows the Idiam around the Dead City I would be interested in engaging in a conversation."

"How familiar they are I can't say. They don't confide in me. They think I talk too much."

Brother Candle stifled a smile. She had used the truth to tell a lie.

The more he knew about her tribe—learning in snippets—the more the true lie seemed a family convention.

Hope said, "I recommend patience. Wait till the Righteous arrive. You will receive informed answers then." She tipped a hand toward the Pramans. "Those gentlemen know more than I do. They have seen the Dead City, and the devil er-Rashal as well."

Again Brother Candle was troubled. Hope went right on being too open. She was demanding trouble.

Why?

He did not think he could work that out by observation and reason alone.

Madouc said, "Suppose we stop posturing and speculating and review what we do know, collectively. It's almost certain that we have more tools than we think." He made a two-handed gesture toward his map.

Brother Candle said, "My lord Master is correct, Hope." She flashed him a look that caused serpents to stir.

44. Gherig, the Idiam, and the Lord of the Dead City

It was evening. The sun had settled to the horizon, behind the rearguard. The light got mixed weirdly in as-yet unsettled dust from an earlier windstorm, then painted Gherig an unflattering orange. Ugly when Lord Arnmigal had seen it as Else Tage, the fortress shone uglier still in that light. Lord Arnmigal scowled. Despite having suffered vast damage, still being repaired, Gherig looked even more formidable than it had back then.

Titus Consent rode on Lord Arnmigal's right. Bold as death, Empress Helspeth rode to his left, with an ease and style that recalled her elder sister. Wife played a more mature, reserved, and dignified Helspeth than did Hourli but her Empress lacked the sly, warm good humor of Eavijne's. Lord Arnmigal sometimes tried to pick his players to suit the moment.

The differences were fine but Titus had noticed. He had wondered aloud why the Empress had become so mercurial.

He remained uninformed of Helspeth's condition. God willing, gods willing, he would never know.

Lord Arnmigal did not normally ride with the van. He did so now because he wanted to see Gherig while there was yet light enough and, further, wanted to escape the constant complaining of Queen Clothilde, whose battered company his scouts had taken captive that morning.

Only a few people remained with Clothilde. Most had deserted because she was so unpleasant. The few sterner folk had been depleted further while fighting off Gisela Frakier in the pay of a crusader noble with a grudge.

Lord Arnmigal cared nothing about that. That was past. Clothilde was inside his shadow, now. Future foul behavior would be punished.

Never had he encountered anyone with a greater sense of entitlement than Clothilde. She would fit well with the most self-absorbed pre-Revelation devil-gods. He asked Wife: "Is there a formula for dealing with her sort?"

Clothilde refused to recognize that she was at the mercy of her captors.

The Helspeth avatar smiled as though at a private joke. "Are you hinting that something be done? Murder works."

"Now you've planted an ugly idea."

"Ah. You're too much of a gentleman."

"Not an accusation often directed my way."

She nodded. "Perhaps not by the true Empress. But she is mad, in her special way. I suppose something *should* be done just to rivet the Queen's attention."

"She's no queen, now. Don't let it be anything fatal, really."

"Still the surest cure."

"There would be repercussions."

"Then fix the possibility in her mind. You don't want her to become even more unbearable."

Something did happen. Something actually rather small.

Clothilde lost her voice during a fuming rant at a hapless servant. The more she strove to rage and roar the more constricted her throat became, to the point where she could no longer breathe.

She collapsed. She never got another word out but kept right on trying. Three collapses were required to make her understand. She would smother herself if she insisted on being herself. She could end the attacks whenever she was ready.

So Clothilde did begin to hold her tongue—and swiftly became terrified. Insidious reality gnawed furiously at the roots of her universe.

It dawned at last. No one cared. She was at the mercy of this gang who had taken her everything. Many clearly would not be loath to make sure she became no threat in the future. The Commander of the Righteous had but to nod.

Clothilde was servility personified by the time the Righteous reached

Gherig, but she did not deceive Lord Arnmigal's strange women. They recognized every malevolent impulse as it spawned. The Commander of the Righteous restrained the malice of the Shining Ones but allowed them to make it crystal that Clothilde would own no power or significance other than that of a prisoner.

Empress Helspeth told her directly, "Discard any hope you have because your cousin awaits you. His situation mimics your own, though he tells himself that it is otherwise. He will be a hostage to your behavior. You will be a hostage to his. The Brotherhood of War could win great favor with Indala by delivering Rogert du Tancret."

Indala's attitude toward Black Rogert was secret from no one but Rogert himself. Du Tancret was willfully blind and cared nothing for the opinions of others.

Wife told Lord Arnmigal, "The woman has grasped the enormity of her situation at last."

"And still you have a caveat?"

"A wolf never stops being a wolf. A wolf will remain a wolf even when it should become a lapdog in order to survive."

"Meaning she won't be able to control herself?"

"She will not. She is what she is. Point out any of her sort who ever changed their nature."

He knew of no one, of course. "Then smart money wouldn't bet on changes for the meeker."

Wife chuckled. "Oh, naturally not. However, if *you* put your ducats down it wouldn't be the first long shot you ever bet. But this one wouldn't come up a winner. I still say smart money ought to consider a surprise viper bite or fatal accident."

Easily arranged with allies such as her.

"Maybe someday. But not yet."

The question she did not ask hung in the air.

"That's too much going the easy way. That's the kind of thing that gives us men like Gordimer and er-Rashal."

Wife stared with eyes gone entirely blank.

"All right." He confessed, "You are correct. I have made some easy choices myself." The transition might be an inalterable consequence of changes that came with the advance up the ladder of command. "Whatever, that isn't our problem now. The Rascal is our problem. He is our *only* problem. The coming few days could shape the Holy Lands forevermore. They might shape the fate of the Shining Ones, too. Do we know what's going on at Gherig?"

"They have no secrets. Aldi is there. The Master of the Commandery has gathered the Captain-General, the Widow, and a few renegade Lucidians more interested in smashing the sorcerer than in fighting westerners."

"Who would they be? Pramans seldom look beyond today's sunset. They've heard from birth that whatever happens will unfold the way God wills it."

"There is an old Sha-lug general named Nassim Alizarin. Accompanying him are several longtime comrades and a grandnephew of Indala, one Azim al-Adil. He is young enough to have noticed Aldi."

"That just means he's still alive. Right?" Having suffered Aldi's effect himself. "Do you all thrive on tempting mortals?"

"Yes. Yes we do. A goddess needs her fun. You know those names?"

"Nassim, I do. Our paths cross occasionally." Though it would be effort wasted trying to hide from the Night, he offered nothing more.

Could this become another thread of complication?

Wife asked, "Rather than obsess, suppose we just see what unfolds?"

He sensed an implied suggestion that the direst threats could be resolved in a heartbeat. Or in the stopping of one.

He bobbed his head once, sharply.

IT WAS A RARE MOMENT.

"Pinkus. You've found a local source for spoiled grape squeezings." Then, "Bo. I heard you signed on with Hell's Legion."

"They threw me out, Boss. Too dirty for them. I'm just another rat in the shadows nowadays. Did Joe come with?" Biogna exchanged hand clasps with Titus Consent. They were never close but had known one another for years. Each held a grudging respect for the other.

Hourli, in Grail Empress guise, observed without expression, as did Ghort's companions. Lord Arnmigal recognized Aldi despite physical changes and Holy Lands apparel. She winked, then wilted under a glower from Hourli.

Hourli's irritation did not get past the old Seeker, nor the leathery hardcase Lord Arnmigal took to be the Widow. She stank of lethal power in a supernatural direction, as though she was halfway to ascendance via sheer violent inertia.

His gaze met hers.

The world stopped. His vision went tunnel. For a moment there was nothing but her eyes, fathomless darknesses. Then she reeled away.

Contact broken, Lord Arnmigal felt as though he had looked into some dark mystic mirror from the arsenal of the Old Ones. Or as if he had peered into the deeps of his own blighted soul.

The Widow was more shaken than he. She collapsed. The old Maysalean caught her, tried to sustain her dignity.

Lord Arnmigal thought the man seemed vaguely familiar. Where? When? But . . . there stood Nassim Alizarin. Madouc of Hoeles observed from farther back. People reentered his life, some again and again.

The stage of the world might be large but those pulled by similar threads of fate would inevitably collide when warp met woof as the blind sisters spun the thread and wove the tapestry of destiny.

Such heresy!

He looked down, turned slowly.

He did have a shadow today.

Needlessly, not apropos of the conversation, he said, "Keep an eye on those two." Meaning Rogert du Tancret and Clothilde, who had left moments earlier, du Tancret supposedly intent on showing his cousin the quarters he had had prepared. Really, they hardly pretended that they did not mean to begin conniving immediately.

Head shakes all round, his people, Gherig's, the Firaldians and the Connectens. He would win no friends trying to micromanage people here. These folks did not recognize his right to give orders in the first place.

Hourli said, "Suppose we focus on the matter that brought us together? On the lion roaring beyond the light of the campfire."

Lord Arnmigal agreed. "You do the talking, Your Grace." Unlike Helspeth, Hourli did not mind the honorific.

She bobbed her head in irritation recognized all round. She was the Empress. She needed neither permission nor instruction from any general.

The goddess stand-ins were touchier than the woman they played.

Having Helspeth do the talking was the plan. Lord Arnmigal did not want to be seen as bulling in to take over. Nurture of allied egos was as important as maintaining your weapons when at war.

So far he sensed real resentment only from Nassim Alizarin and, more strongly, from Nassim's Lucidian mentee.

Young Azim did not want the old man's thunder taken. Nassim, meanwhile, did not like the changes he saw in a one-time Sha-lug hero who had, somehow, reforged himself as a prince of the Unbelievers.

The others were more inclined to defer to the man with the loudest weapons and nastiest resources. Lord Arnmigal suspected that Aldi had not offered them any real appreciation of the magnitude of the latter.

The gallery included Special Office brethren of stony mien. They would suffer this congress with the Night only until the horror in the Idiam was extinct.

Those humorless men had no true apprehension of what was spawning out there. Why should they take the word of Nassim Alizarin? The man was an Unbeliever, for Aaron's sake!

Yet they were convinced that something dreadfully big was shaping.

Hourli said, "The Righteous have brought several mystic tools that will help." She neither enumerated nor described those tools. The Special Office gentlemen were distressed enough. The Church insisted that those were imaginary toys associated only with rustic fantasies like the Shining Ones. Total fairy-tale stuff, they. "Most noteworthy is a new formula of firepowder. The sorcerer will find it uncongenial. It is much harder to set off from a distance."

Lord Arnmigal caught a whiff of steaming unhappiness floating around that remark.

"The new firepowder won't be proof against the sorcerer's spells, just more resistant. Our falcons will be able to get close enough to gift him with some truly unpleasant weather." She did not report that only limited quantities of the new formulation existed. What her audience did not hear, er-Rashal was unlikely to learn. Once the falcons started firing the sorcerer should be too busy dodging to find time to create inconvenient new spells. "He won't get the leisure to look for ways around his new problem."

Lord Arnmigal puffed up with pride. Pella, assisted by his artillery mentors, had reformulated the firepowder. His idea had been stunningly simple, if not obvious, but, alas, was also stunningly expensive. They added a minuscule amount of silver dust to make the firepowder spell-resistant. Less expensive, but of weaker effect and so necessary in greater volume, copper and tin also worked. Even lead might help.

The metals certainly caused colorful muzzle blasts.

Pella and his accomplices had not yet gotten close enough to the Rascal to test the new powder under combat conditions.

These people would understand that. Still, new powder would buoy morale, heading into the Idiam.

Lord Arnmigal also had a notion that it would be handy to head into unfriendly country with a clearer picture of what waited there.

The Shining Ones scouted reluctantly. They were disinclined to alert er-Rashal to the magnitude of what was coming.

Lord Arnmigal wondered if there was more to the story. He did not fully credit anything anyone told him these days. Sometimes he even doubted Titus's reports, again having misgivings about Consent's religious conversion. Pella he did not trust, either, though in the boy's case because the kid was determined to do things denied him only because his mother would never forgive his father if something went wrong.

"General Alizarin, they say you know er-Rashal best. As Her Grace reported, the Righteous have some unusual resources. I'd like to hear your thoughts on how those might be used."

He and the Shining Ones meant to use the Great Sky Fortress relics to bump the Rascal through the gates of Hell.

The allies would be encouraged to believe they were in charge but the real power would reside with the Shining Ones. The rest would serve to keep the villain from running away. He would stroke their egos, though.

He did not hide his thinking that well. The others began to suspect. They grew increasingly uncomfortable. The Righteous staff and the Shining Ones became least comfortable of all.

He strove hard against the quickening megalomania—seemingly with lessening success.

In his secret heart, stirring ugly, lay the dread that he had begun to walk the road already taken by Gordimer the Lion. Might he be unable to turn back even while aware of how he was changing? Could it be that the spite of the old women hidden in the shallows of Night made them weave inescapable evil destinies?

No sisters of fate at all, they, but sisters of malice instead?

THE TALK WAS DONE. ARGUMENT WAS AT AN END. ACCORDS HAD BEEN accorded, every participant with secret reservations. Negotiations with the Ansa, heavy on the "gifts," had been finalized. A loose picket line slowly became a siege line as the encirclement of Andesqueluz shrank. A city's noose, Titus declared it.

Skirmishes with er-Rashal's resurrected sorcerer-defenders took place, brief encounters of pain dealt exclusively to the Rascal's minions. Anxious rage inside the ruins grew steadily. Though the darkness inside Andesqueluz was supernatural rather than quotidian, those drawing the noose tighter swore that a black glow waxed and waned there, like the beat of a great slow heart.

The Shining Ones guarded against demonic outbursts while soldiers of the Righteous, the Brotherhood, the Vindicated, and Pinkus Ghort's Firaldian volunteers, with the Ansa and even Black Rogert, labored unto dehydrated exhaustion hauling water and supplies, and dragging falcons to positions Pella chose. The boy picked his sites based on scouting done by the Shining Ones. His choices favored the finest lines of fire.

Pella proved the worth of his new firepowder right away.

THE BROODING MALICE IN ANDESQUELUZ GREW BLACKER BY THE HOUR. His dead operatives lost, er-Rashal came out himself. Cockily, he anticipated inflicting misery on the Righteous by exploding their firepowder inconveniently.

Once more he enjoyed the improbable good fortune of the truly wicked. He survived a hail of poisoned metal and limped to his lair feeling sorry for himself. He resumed his desperate effort to resurrect Asher.

He was very close.

But his new wounds further sapped his strength and hindered his work. He lapsed into sleep when sleep was too much a luxury. If an attack came during a nap, he was lost.

Any attack *would* come then, absolutely. Unseen eyes, of Instrumentalities great and small, heard his every breath and counted his every heartbeat. But they were goats to his tiger! Once he dispelled the last misty chains binding Asher . . . He would need just a handful more souls.

Those were out there in those people so eager to still his own soul. A grand ironic jest it would be, his most dedicated enemies offering up the final installment on the price of his dreams!

Only, those villains were truly, thoroughly, stubbornly committed to putting period to his tale first.

Er-Rashal's present entourage was minuscule. It included three damaged resurrected sorcerer-lords of ancient Andesqueluz and three reanimated corpses that had been Ansa warriors. Then there were two live Ansa children, brother and sister, twins, seven, so deeply terrified they might never recover. They had escaped sacrifice so far because they were useful for physical labor. Lastly, and of least worth, were several dozen terrified and abused trivial Instrumentalities, none with more power than a hummingbird's shadow.

Still, the Rascal's servants might manage an inept guerrilla campaign still sufficient to tip the scale by collecting the remaining hearts, souls, and flesh their master's triumph required.

Such was er-Rashal's hope.

Too weak and too much in pain to leave the filthy pallet that had become his home, the sorcerer husked, "The night comes." A statement, not a metaphor. "Our hour bestrides it."

An ugly, deep chuckle erupted from the female twin, far too ancient and evil for a child. Her eyes glowed a baleful green. "The hour of the Night doth come, indeed."

The glow faded. The child collapsed. Her brother stared in consternation. What was that?

The air quavered with a sense that some dreadful visitant had just departed. A musty, moldy earthen smell, and a chill, marked its passing.

Then the enemy's falcons began to belch out songs of cosmic indigestion.

Stone shot rattled against tumbled walls and fallen roofs. A jagged flint bounded off a building block, took a reanimated sorcerer squarely on the side of the head. That exploded in a cloud of bone splinters and dust.

Desperately, fighting his own recalcitrant flesh, er-Rashal began his last forlorn hope of an invocation, leeching power from the lives of his enemies to turn against their physical forms.

Lord Arnmigal, with Hourli as Helspeth, slouched in shadow atop a short bluff overlooking what once was the temple district of Andesqueluz. Another dozen onlookers lurked nearby. Some thought the Empress and her number-one soldier were entirely too cozy. Close by, falcons and traditional artillery engines worked leisurely. Fires burned in the ruins, ignited by fireballs thrown by counterweight engines. The falcons barked just often enough to remind the world that they were there. Their propellant *was* immune to the seductions of the Rascal. They would sing in unison if the choirmaster required it.

Those with the Commander of the Righteous included leaders from most of the factions determined to thwart er-Rashal. Even Black Rogert had brought himself to the engagement. The price in pain of his journey through the Idiam and up the Mountain had won grudging respect from everyone.

Captain-General Pinkus Ghort quietly nursed a wineskin. Nassim Alizarin knelt beside Ghort. Alizarin had yet to show any sign of remembering Piper Hecht from Artecipea, let alone some scoundrel who might once have gone by the name Else Tage. Two Ansa chieftains known to Nassim muttered with the Sha-lug, less comfortable with so many foreigners than with the evil in the ruins. The Widow lurked by

Pinkus Ghort, too, accompanied by the woman she called Hope and the feeble old man she kept handy with an invisible iron emotional tether.

Lord Arnmigal feared all tonight's physical effort might be the undoing of that old one.

Madouc of Hoeles was not present. Having consulted the Ansa, Alizarin's renegades, and his own Special Office thugs, he had created his own mission. He and his team were in ambush along the one flight route available to the Rascal if things went bad. Madouc was sure that er-Rashal would survive the worst and try to run with crucial relics that would let him commence fresh villainies wherever he went to ground next.

The Shining Ones thought he might flee to the Hu'n-tai At, hoping he could hornswoggle Tsistimed into thinking he might be useful.

Azim al-Adil was absent, too. Nassim had sent him to Shamramdi to bring Indala up to date—hopefully before that city fell. Rumor had it on the lip of the precipice, with no relief expected. Lord Arnmigal thought, and hoped, that al-Adil would broach the peace notion he had tried to fix in Nassim's mind, in such ways that the Great Shake would see it as his own fabrication. Quiet nudges from the Shining Ones should help bring him to the right frame of mind.

The Old Ones were able to reach Shamramdi now. They got up to divine mischief there all the time. It was they who reported the city so desperate that resistance could collapse given one seriously fierce thump.

"Time to hit it," Hourli whispered. "And let's be careful." She gave Lord Arnmigal's arm a nervous, possessive squeeze missed by no one but him.

Only Aldi understood that Hourli was not Helspeth. And she was not pleased by Hourli's familiarity.

Lord Arnmigal rose. He seemed to stand taller, wider, more starkly than usual. His shadow, prancing in firelight from below, stretched deeper and longer than any other. An illusion? A trick of the light?

His shadow was missing a hand.

Lord Arnmigal slung a coil of rope down the precipitous slope. The stub of an old stone post anchored its near end. The rest floated out and down, uncoiling slowly.

Lord Arnmigal hefted a weird hammer left-handed, rigged its handle into the same harness that held a long sword across his back. The hammer moaned eagerly. He used both hands to loop the rope around himself before he began a quick, sometimes rappelling, descent from the height.

His weight was on the rope, which thrummed and shook, but the Empress picked it up and looped it around herself, then followed. She carried a light backpack. She used only one hand on the rope. She hefted a spear with the other.

The gallery gawked. What they saw could happen only through the intercession of the Night.

THE WIDOW SAID, "DAWN, YOU'RE NEXT." WORDS WASTED. HOPE WAS gone. No one had seen her vanish.

The old man peered eastward. "Of course."

"What?" Kedle asked.

"A full moon rising. It wasn't up before but it had to be."

"I give up. Why?"

"Asher is the Mountain. He comes with Ashtoreth, Bride of the Mountain. She was a moon goddess. So I'm told."

"Oh." The Widow made a raspberry sound. Who feared dead gods?

The old man would never say that the only real fear Kedle actually knew was of normal human relations—though she did seem to be tempted, perhaps unconsciously, to start making an exception for the Captain-General.

Moon shadows danced with those from fires started by the artillery. The former had no power. The Shining Ones were all over the Mountain. No other side of the Night would interfere.

The Widow elbowed past Pinkus Ghort, snatched up the rope. It seemed as lively as a snake. It lacked any tension because of the weight of the people on it. She looped it around herself easily. A pulse in the cable encouraged her to move.

This was sorcery, indeed.

The old man, muttering prayers to the Good God, started down behind her, eyes squeezed shut.

Pinkus Ghort lined up for his turn.

LORD ARNMIGAL WATCHED HOURLI DISENGAGE FROM THE ROPE. SHE joined him in a clot of darkness. He secured a fat candle from her pack. She said, "Light it before any witnesses show up." The rope's end lashed like an injured snake.

He willed the candle to life.

Nothing happened.

Hourli snarled. The candlewick burst into flame. Time slowed. She grumbled, "Stay close. We'll end up sorry if I stumble outside the light." He would carry the candle in the hand that had no shadow.

She did not suggest that he might suffer a lethal trip himself.

What a cosmic anticlimax that would be, clumsily breaking his neck moments before er-Rashal could be conducted to his doom.

"Through there." Hourli indicated a gap between memorial stelae. Those leaned against one another like drunken comrades. Flickering firelight splashed their inner faces creamy yellow and occasional orange. "Careful. He could smell us out even like we are now."

The earth trembled underfoot—despite the candle.

The leaning stelae shifted slightly. Detritus fell from where they met. Lord Arnmigal watched a small chunk, guessed that it would take a minute to reach the ground. Time was moving slowly but it *was* passing.

"He does feel us coming," Hourli grumbled. The Commander of the Righteous heard nothing. She swore. "Damn! The big devil is stirring." The falling chunk, behind them now, was halfway to the ground. "We walked into a trap. Not us. Not you and me. The company. He doesn't know about the candle. Oh. And he isn't expecting us two, after all. He just feels the threat from those behind us. He is vampirizing them somehow. The middle-worlders. Not us. But he is weakened by the presence of the Shining Ones, some. He wasn't watching the right way. We got close. He should have noticed. But we weren't part of his calculations. Even so, his human trap is working. We could end up sorry if we don't distract him quick."

She kept moving as she chattered, as briskly as she thought they dared. Her speech seemed awfully slow.

Time constantly moved a little faster as they neared their goal.

Lord Arnmigal was so focused on being wary of supernatural pitfalls that he was not ready for more mundane dangers. Blessed be, he had the candle in hand rather than a blade when he stepped past a drunkenly leaning column and collided with an equally startled, bug-eyed little boy. A girl of the same age, size, and mien slammed into the boy's back.

Hourli hissed a warning, too late. It would have been too late ten seconds earlier. Those children were in full charge mode, headed out to lay an ambush, unaware that invisible invaders were closer already than those they had been sent to murder.

Disarming them took but seconds. The children abandoned bellicosity instantly. They became completely pliable. The Widow caught up just then, and was amazed by the effect of the candle—which lost most of its impact once five souls crowded the space it warped. Lord Arnmigal was surprised by the gentle sympathy she showed the children, then recalled that she had her own she probably felt guilty about having deserted.

He felt guilty himself—and his children were growing into their adult lives.

The Widow said, "I have them. Go ahead on."

KEDLE'S *IN LOCO* LASTED ONLY AS LONG AS IT TOOK HER TO FIND Brother Candle. She passed the twins along. The Perfect got no chance to refuse. He got the children and the Widow got back to sniffing after fresh blood.

HOURLI EASED PAST LORD ARNMIGAL, SPEAR POISED. "STAY CLOSE. And don't step on my heels." She was a hound on track. The cock of her head said she heard directions to which everyone else was deaf.

The Widow caught up somehow. The candle's field had degraded seriously. Lord Arnmigal put down an urge to shove her out and run.

She had worth. She was receiving intelligence from elsewhere, too, he presumed from Aldi.

They pushed ahead. He failed to notice the move but the hammer was in his hand when they met the waiting dead. It flicked. The heads of dead sorcerers exploded, becoming dust and bone chips adrift in the moonlight. Heartsplitter glittered in Hourli's hands. Once-fallen Ansa braves went down once again and returned to their rest. The spear groaned softly, like a woman trying to keep the kids from over-hearing evidence of her culminating intimate moment. Witnesses outside the candle's glow would have missed the destruction. It happened too fast.

Even inside the candlelight it happened blindingly quick.

Meanwhile, the ground indulged in slow rolls with an orchestral accompaniment of lesser vibrations, like something vast was drawing a long first breath.

Time to move a little faster.

Lord Arnmigal's foot did not want to come off the ground. Suddenly, he was slogging through what acted like deep muck. Moments earlier the footing had been barren, slightly tilted stone.

He was ankle deep in dust deliberately clinging like mud, clumping on his calves and ankles.

Bone chips sparkled within that dust, reflecting moonlight.

The dead Ansa, at least, had lain down, abandoning the fight forever.

"Keep moving, you." Hourli sliced the dust with Heartsplitter's edge, weakening its power to clump dramatically.

Someone or something not far off definitely was not pleased.

The earth shuddered more vigorously.

Hourli positioned herself on Lord Arnmigal's right, caught his elbow, slowed him slightly. Heartsplitter darted into and sliced an unnatural clot of darkness. Lord Arnmigal hoisted the hammer. It did not feel unnatural to use his left hand.

The darkness parted. He looked into a room he had visited years ago. Old Az had stood where Hourli did now. Bone had been on his left with a ready crossbow. The room had been home to fox families that had lived and squabbled there for ages, filling the place with an eye-watering stench. The Sha-lug had surprised them there in the holy of holies of Asher's cult.

There were no foxes now. The fetor was gone. There had been one time-gnawed altar back then. Another had been added recently, crudely built from piled stone. A dried-up husk of an old man half sprawled, half sat amidst masses of rags once worn by people whose bones now lay scattered all round. Gnawed bones.

Carrion stench had replaced that of fox.

The shard of time the candle shaped was small. Time within was moving faster now but still dragged enough to let Lord Arnmigal see everything and fix it in mind before darkness slammed down again. He flung the hammer Bonecrusher. It groaned, produced a dry *thunk*, then a *thud!* of collision with stone, and, finally, a stinging *thwack!* as its haft slapped back into his open hand.

Hourli used Heartsplitter during Bonecrusher's flight. The spear reached and reached, extending in a violet shimmer providing just enough light to show the Dreangerean being lucky again. He dodged the hammer well enough to suffer only a passing blow to his right clavicle, not fatal but enough to stifle that one arm. He also twisted so that Heartsplitter only scored his ribs instead of living up to its name.

He howled in pain and rage.

The violet light went away, but then the darkness flickered and went out as er-Rashal lost the ability to quell the light.

Lord Arnmigal prepared to throw again. Hourli shifted Heartsplitter for an overhand strike in the classic fashion.

Despite tonight's abuse and his previous debility er-Rashal al-Dhulquarnen rose halfway up, climbing an old serpent staff he had brought out of Dreanger. His face was ghastly pale, twisted in disbelief. He could not fathom how this had come upon him—till he acknowledged the hand of the Night, and no faction of that which aspired to delight er-Rashal al-Dhulquarnen.

A snake-dagger appeared in his left hand, blade its body and head its pommel. Its eyes burned, one lemon, the other a deep lilac rose. He extended that pommel toward his uninvited guests. Those eyes waxed brighter.

Bonecrusher flew. Heartsplitter thrust. Blinding light burst from those demon eyes.

But Death chose to avert its gaze from everyone.

The earth heaved ferociously at the critical instant.

The Dead City shook to a grandfather of an earthquake. Everything standing began to come apart. Brother Candle, minutes after having taken custody of the Ansa twins, went down hard. The youngsters helped him up, showing reverence as they did so.

He began a prayer to the Good God on their behalf. There was no point trying to flee the epic disaster about to come.

Kedle hustled, determined to rejoin Lord Arnmigal. Her leg did not hurt. The pain dwindled when she was sufficiently engaged. Then Hope was beside her, pleasantly warm despite the heat of the Idiam. She hissed, "Get thee down and cling to the ground, dear one. Now!"

The earth began to stir.

Pellapront Versulius. Pella wondered how he had come to have the same name as a fictional character. He wondered what had become of the blood sister he had not seen since he ran into the man he now called father. Would his life echo Piper Hecht's when his own lost older sister resurfaced several decades down the road?

His past seldom occupied him. Mostly he did not care. Other than Alma, whose comforting arms he did recall fondly, there were few good memories. There were plenty from the years with Piper and Anna and the girls. But sometimes, when the waiting stretched, he could not help sliding off into bouts of wondering.

He did that while leaning on a ready falcon, trying to stay awake. That was a struggle common to the company. A plague of drowsiness had set in.

Then the ground heaved. Parts of the bluff slid down. Left of where he had been told to expect it a huge head began to emerge, shedding stone and adobe. It was a black of a sort that devoured light. It leaned back to consider the moon.

The falconeers did not stand around with their thumbs in, gawking. Weapons not charged with godshot fired immediately, whatever direction they were laid. Those properly charged quickly shifted and ranged—and the first to declare spoke fewer than forty seconds after the Mountain opened its womb.

Godshot hit the revenant at the nape of the neck. Two balls passed through what in a human would have been the brain stem. They exited through a piggish right nostril. The rest rattled around inside the devil.

It continued to emerge from the earth, ever more spastic, while trying to face the roaring that presaged its pain. Moonlight splashed an ugly, apish face drawn in both amazement and agony.

Gods were beyond challenge. Gods were the *source* of pain, not its object. That was the supernatural order. That was the Tyranny of the Night.

Crews stricken shaky by the magnitude of the demon nevertheless adjusted their aim. Another falcon bellowed. Shot hit the rising form with a wet, resounding *splat!* The demon swayed, groaned louder than any falcon's shout. It freed a seven-clawed hand, reached for one of the nasty mortal engines. The soil around the devil, though hard to see in the moonlight, shivered, danced, boiled.

Every falcon with a clear sight line fired during the next twenty seconds. The Asher revenant was too close to miss. One blast tore the reaching hand off between wrist and elbow.

NASSIM WAS ASHAMED. HE SUFFERED FROM A TERROR SO DEEP THAT he clung to Old Az in a ferocious, moments-from-death hug. His faith had been murdered. The demon shrieked like a mortally wounded war elephant. It leaned toward its attackers, head lolling as though it was about to come loose altogether. The severed hand hit the ground with the impact of a man-size tombstone. The demon bellowed again, then grew a new hand equipped with even more daddy-longlegs fingers. It snatched up a falcon, pulled it in for examination.

Pella's falcon spoke again. Silver-plated grapeshot hit the monster in the face. The meaty *splat!* was plain even to ears that had been near a falcon. Gangrenous pocks spotted that face. Parts melted, dripped away. The monster began to subside. The falcon it had meant to study dropped from its hand. A brace of unfortunate gunners fell with it.

Then the great face resumed rising and regaining its ugly original form.

Falcon doctrine was set. It was fixed, established, and acknowledged by the men who served the weapons. They pursued doctrine ruthlessly, now. Every weapon able to bear fired as briskly as it could. Those without a clear sight line moved to find one. Once godshot charges ran out crews used what they had. No Instrumentality had yet shown itself fully immune to physical law.

Every hit weakened the monster. That was the design. But it kept pulling itself together. Its enemies grew weaker each time it did.

Several invaders collapsed, too weak to go on. Rates of fire declined. The falconeers worked slower and slower.

A timely salvo melted more godstuff. The emerging Instrumentality stopped moving.

And the night filled with shrieks.

In Asher's salad days the Choosers of the Slain would have been hornets to his tiger. Asher revenant was a shadow of the horror that had been. Its strange flesh sagged under the weight of the godshot it had absorbed. The poison of all that never stopped poisoning.

The flow of stolen life energy ceased.

And the Choosers, fattened in the Wells of Ihrian, went for the devil's eyes. Other Shining Ones, equally well fed, followed on, wielding weapons gleaned from the Great Sky Fortress. They hammered, stabbed, slashed, and strangled. Seldom before had Instrumentalities ever joined in so malevolent, deliberate a plan to destroy another major Instrumentality for all time and ever, in all the worlds.

Lord Arnmigal and Hourli each lost their footing twice because the earth would not lie quiet. Both were down, facing a Rascal trying to get to his feet, when Hope and the Widow arrived. The latter tripped. She fell forward onto Hourli's back. Hope had no trouble staying upright. She charged the bug-eyed sorcerer, who recognized her as a serious Instrumentality targeting him for some extremely special attention.

Er-Rashal squealed the first word of some prayer, invocation, or spell. Hope blurred. Her hands clamped on his throat.

The gale generated by Hope's sudden movement extinguished Lord Arnmigal's time candle. Almost anticlimactically, from his point of view, er-Rashal's head popped off.

What?

The pretty girl had a grip that savage?

A man might ought to keep that in mind and not get on her bad side.

Reality wavered. Lord Arnmigal heard the roar of falcons. He had not, before. Their bellowing lasted a short while, then was replaced by the shrieks of Fastthal and Sprenghul. Other Shining Ones added their own ferocious commentary.

*   *   *

THE CONFRONTATION BETWEEN INSTRUMENTALITIES ENDED BEFORE
Lord Arnmigal and the Widow climbed back high enough to see the
slag heap that had wanted to become Asher renewed. Aldi and Hourli
had gone ahead, joining the assault by skipping the space between.

The Instrumentality carcass resembled newly excreted magma.
Heat boiled off. Scarlet winked through cracks in its crispy black crust.
Nearly invisible little Instrumentalities cavorted around the heap, jubi-
lant. The monster would never claim dominion.

Lord Arnmigal settled on a broken block as close as the heat would
allow, ignored the celebrating demons. He tapped the earth with the
end of a broken Ansa spear, lost in thought.

Hourli, still in Helspeth guise, settled beside him, nearer than what
was appropriate for the Empress's reputation. "She knows I'm not her."
Meaning the Widow had seen more than she should.

He shrugged. Aldi would handle it. An errant bit of curiosity: how
come nobody ever asked why Lady Hilda stayed in Vantrad instead of
sticking with her Empress?

"That was some all-time weird shit," Pinkus Ghort mused, from
behind Lord Arnmigal. He took a long pull off a fresh wineskin.

Before Lord Arnmigal could reply, Pella said, "Totally weird." He
stepped out of shadow into the moonlight, which had grown thin.
"The weirdest." Then, "Dad, the girls are here. As usual, after all the
heavy lifting is over. They claim they need to see you."

Startled, Lord Arnmigal turned, stared past Pinkus and his liquid
companion. Vali and Lila looked embarrassed, put out with their
brother, more grown-up than he remembered, and worried. Heris stood
behind them. She eyed Hourli grimly. He figured that none of those
three, schooled by the Ninth Unknown, would be deceived.

Heris looked like she had survived some hard times recently.

He sighed. Likely sooner than later he would pay for his latest poor
choice involving an Ege sister—though it was not a choice he would
unmake even if the magic candle had the power to turn back time.

He might show more care about avoiding the natural consequences,
however.

"What is it, ladies?" Resigned and ignoring the baffled, fearful looks
of people who *knew* those three could not possibly be out here, half a
world away from home.

Lila and Vali glowered at Hourli. Heris talked about Hourlr, Asgrimmur Grimmsson, the Ninth Unknown, Korban Iron Eyes, the road
to Eucereme, spicing all of it with targeted snippets from the life of
Anna Mozilla, waiting quietly in Brothe.

Humming a Connecten rondelet celebrating romantic love, Aldi seated herself beside Lord Arnmigal, to his left, opposite Hourli, and leaned against him. She showed no consciousness whatsoever of the ferocious disapproval steaming darkly off every woman in sight, Hourli preeminent. She held er-Rashal al-Dhulquarnen's head in her lap, stroking its hairless scalp as though petting a cat. Song sung, she whispered to the dead sorcerer, issuing prophecies for a journey into Twilight. She finished with, "He'll find his shadow again. I will make that happen."